The Critics on Henry Roth's **Mercy of a Rude Stream** *sequence*

'Our curiosity at Roth's remarkable reappearance in print should now be replaced by admiration for his continuing and powerful account of a lost world' *Times Literary Supplement*

'An intensely moving and inspiring human achievement'
The Times

'Roth has once again skilfully re-created the drama of immigrant life in early-twentieth century America'
Sunday Times

'Utterly absorbing' *Times Literary Supplement*

'At last, a genuine publishing event . . . alive with the hubbub and smells of his New York childhood . . . something brand new, wholly without cliché' *Literary Review*

'Richly evocative of its time and place'
New York Review of Books

'Dynamic and moving . . . a stirring portrait of a vanished culture . . . a poignant chapter in the life-drama of a unique American writer' *Newsweek*

In 1994 Henry Roth broke his sixty-year literary silence following his classic novel *Call It Sleep* with the publication of volume one of *Mercy of a Rude Stream*, called *A Star Shines Over Mt. Morris Park*. The second volume in this six-part sequence, *A Diving Rock on the Hudson* was published in 1995. The series is being hailed by critics as 'unsurpassable' in the annals of twentieth-century American literature. Henry Roth died, aged 89, in Albuquerque, New Mexico, in October 1995.

From Bondage

Volume III
Mercy of a Rude Stream

HENRY ROTH

PHŒNIX

A PHŒNIX PAPERBACK

First published in Great Britain
by Weidenfeld & Nicolson in 1996
This paperback edition published in 1997
by Phoenix, a division of Orion Books Ltd,
Orion House, 5 Upper St Martin's Lane,
London WC2H 9EA

A CIP catalogue record for this book is available
from the British Library.

ISBN: 0 75380 004 7

Printed and bound in Great Britain by
The Guernsey Press Co. Ltd, Guernsey,
Channel Islands

To the memory of Leah,
my mother.

THE FAMILY OF IRA STIGMAN

Ira's Mother's Family Tree

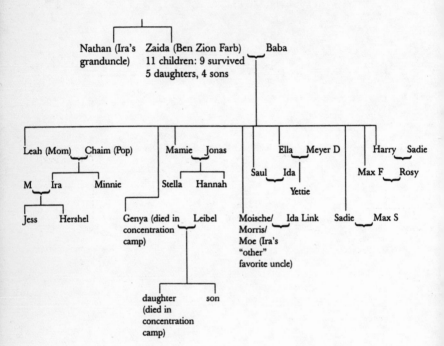

⌣ Married

┬ Children

THE FAMILY OF IRA STIGMAN

Ira's Father's Family Tree

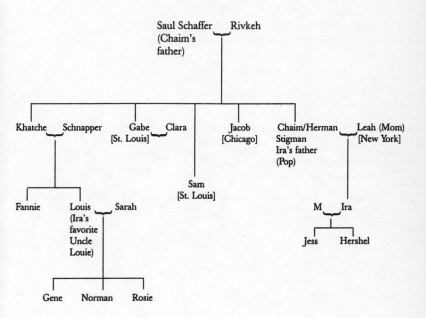

Saul Schaffer (Chaim's father) — Rivkeh

Khatche — Schnapper Gabe [St. Louis] — Clara Jacob [Chicago] Chaim/Herman Stigman Ira's father (Pop) — Leah (Mom) [New York]

Sam [St. Louis]

Fannie Louis (Ira's favorite Uncle Louie) — Sarah

M — Ira

Jess Hershel

Gene Norman Rosie

⌣ Married

┬ Children

I acknowledge the sustaining help of my agent,
Roslyn Targ, my editor, Robert Weil,
my assistant, Felicia Jean Steele,
and my attorney, Larry Fox.

CONTENTS

I pass, like night, from land to land;
I have strange power of speech;
The minute that his face I see
I know the man that must hear me,
To him my tale I teach.

—Samuel Taylor Coleridge,
   The Rime of the Ancient Mariner

PROLOGUE

He was a widower, one in whom his bereavement for his lost wife never vanished. Even five years after Ira Stigman had lost her, grief over his loss sometimes assailed him unbearably, shook him with strange, dry sobs. . . . He was eighty-nine years old now—on the verge of becoming a nonagenarian. Much that had once greatly exercised his attention, his partisanship, national and international strife, Israel, even things literary, the field of his own calling, these things interested him only marginally now, remotely—something to be expected of a man nearing ninety. What did he have left? At best? A year or two more of life. A year or two of feebleness, of dependence on others for almost everything, even locomotion, a year or two in which he might suffer the humiliation of incontinence—in short, a year or two left of life he didn't want, would be quite ready to dispense with. And he would, if he could find some easy means of doing so.

The only thing that still interested him, that meant anything, helped pass the burdensome time, was his word processor. It not only helped tide him over to the awaited end, but made possible his earning the income necessary to supply him with the sustenance, the human assistance, and the creature comfort that served to mitigate this last onerous lap of the journey. Modern technology, that ambiguous genie, might prove in the end an enormous bane or an enormous boon for mankind, but at the moment, it enabled him to transmute this otherwise worthless, pain-ridden time known as old age into something of value. The computer provided him with a modern analogy of the legendary philosopher's stone, dream of the alchemists for transmuting the base into the noble. In this case it transmuted the pain-racked into the pleasurable, or at least into a kind of anodyne, a respite from his woes. He owed modern technology a debt of gratitude.

With those thoughts in mind, he sat nervelessly eyeing the small puddle of urine on the floor where he had missed the urinal. Like that puddle, he was probably all wet, as usual, befuddled and illogical. But if he had come anywhere near the truth, then he had accomplished something of immense benefit to himself, almost a beatitude. He had already reconciled himself with himself. And now, he had freed himself from the necessity of that reconciliation. To have suffered so much over so long a span of time over nothing. Liberated. Liberated at last in the year 1995 from bondage imposed on himself more than seventy years ago, from bondage whose depiction he had begun, and would now endeavor to continue.

PART ONE

I

Sunburned by hours of trudging on the highway, and with the unruly air of the vagabond about them, Ira Stigman and Larry Gordon were scarcely an ornament to the Spring Valley Retreat. But even the dusty mess they were, Ira never expected the cold, scant reception that Aunt Sarah gave them. A dark-haired, dark-complexioned woman, conscious of her American-born superiority, her manner toward Ira's family had always been condescending. She was visibly taken aback by the two young wayfarers; she could barely muster a minimum of tolerance, let alone cordiality, in greeting Ira and his best friend. Even more disappointing, though, was Uncle Louis's distant, preoccupied, and impersonal manner. Ira's long-idolized uncle was like a different person. Gone was the wide, golden smile Ira had so glowingly described to Larry on the way over, the smile that appeared on Uncle Louis's face when he heard the whoop of joy his nephew uttered the moment he caught sight of his uncle's postman's uniform. Where was his lean, magnanimous uncle, who never left without thrusting a handful of small change into his adoring nephew's palm?

Ira had told Larry all about Uncle Louis as the two hiked along thumbing rides: about Uncle Louis the soldier, the teller of wonderful tales about the Far West, about Indians and forbidding landscapes and buffalo, while the entranced young Ira sat on the fire-escape windowsill listening to stories about the Rocky Mountains and the torrents of Yellowstone. Uncle Louis, the real American, ever ready to unroll the Socialist *Call* on the kitchen table, described the future world of Socialist equality, the fraternity of Jew and gentile. In his fervor, he swept away Pop's vacillations, and spun hopes out of doubts: the *mujik* would never again be the same *mujik* under socialism; pogroms were forever ended with the execution of Czar Nicholas, the *Kolki*, the bullet; the epithet *jhit*, Yid, was finally outlawed in the new Russia, as were all manifestations of race hatred. A new world had miraculously come into being in the year of 1917, and it would breed a new order of mankind. Uncle Louis had even made Ira want to be a Socialist himself.

Four years later, the glow had receded. Poor health—poor lungs, Mom grimaced significantly—had compelled Uncle Louis to apply for a medical retirement at half pay from the post office. As soon as it was granted, he and his wife, Sarah—and their three children—moved from the Socialist colony in Stelton, New Jersey, to a large farmhouse in Spring Valley, New York. At first, to eke out Uncle Louis's decreased salary, and at the initiative of Sarah, they took in a small number of boarders for the summer. Apparently, the venture exceeded expectations. The next year they were at capacity all season. Thanks to their successful catering to their Jewish clientele, and because of their proximity to the metropolis, and because their rates were reasonable, the place by this year of 1925 had become quite, quite well known. With the help of a partner, who provided the finances, they had built an entirely new summer hotel. It was a high-class one, according to Pop, who had been out there and furnished the details, a large summer hotel with private rooms, private bathrooms, equipped with a swimming pool, a tennis court, and a resplendent dining hall.

With all that he had heard about the spaciousness of the new hotel, Ira was sure Uncle Louis would have room enough to put up his devoted nephew, who was, in fact, Louis's first cousin, but enough younger to be considered a nephew, and his nephew's friend for the night. Although both had left their probable itinerary with their parents, Larry telephoned his mother long distance to let her know in what fine fettle they were, and to keep her posted on their whereabouts and destination. They might be home a day later than planned, if they liked the place they were heading for, and please not to worry. Their eagerness had been sharpened by inviting billboards on both sides of the highway setting forth the desirable features of the retreat.

It would happen so often in later life, that dim bewilderment at the change that had taken place in another, as if he—or she—had sloughed off an accretion of attitudes, like a skin, like a sheath. Conversation with Uncle Louis was perfunctory. The two youths were obviously in the way. They were fed an early supper on the oilcloth-covered table by a serving woman in the former farmhouse kitchen—scrambled eggs, bread and butter, and coffee and jam. And then with Uncle Louis's older son, Gene, in the van, they were shown a well-worn army field tent some distance from the hotel, and furnished with a couple of canvas cots and blankets. That was to be their lodging for the night. Gene hung the kerosene lantern on a tent pole, and bidding them an embarrassed good night, left them to their own devices.

It was a humiliating reception, after so much anticipation, not in the slightest approaching the welcome Ira felt he had led his chum to expect. Crestfallen, he tried to explain how much his uncle had changed; he stressed his own mystification, his inability to account for the change. Was it because of Mom's rejection of Uncle Louis's passionate appeal? But how could that be? That was years ago. Ira apologized for misleading his friend, expressed his confusion at the change that had taken place in his uncle.

"Jesus, he's miles away from the man I knew as a kid, the mail carrier in his blue uniform, so fond of me, so liberal with his small change. I don't know what happened. I'm sorry."

"Quit apologizing. His wife fed us some supper. We've got a place to sleep." Larry made light of it all. "They may not have room in the hotel. Beside, look at us. What we'd look like to his guests: a couple of tramps. What we'd do to the towels, the sheets."

"Yeah, but his attitude. Jesus, I wish I—we hadn't come. I'd remember him the way he was. The American. My idol."

"Well, he's busy. You could tell the man's tired."

"You don't mind?"

"Mind? This is a relief to me. You have no idea how bad things are at home since Dad died. This is a real adventure."

* * *

Ira could not believe it had already been three weeks since Larry had stood in the light of the kitchen window, the kitchen window next to the iron sink, Larry in the Stigman kitchen, his handsome face framed together with the backyard fixtures of washpole and washlines, against the background of the rear of Jake's dreary pile of a tenement. There he had stood, prosperous Larry, his cherished friend!

It was the first time he had ever visited that lowly flat on 119th Street. The homely kitchen became luminous with his presence. Ira could have embraced him out of pure joy at seeing him, but whooped delightedly instead, and the two shook hands. What was he doing here? Why had he come back to New York? He had written Ira in his most recent letter that he intended to work until Labor Day.

Larry snuffed sharply at Ira's joyous inquiry. He snuffed sharply, as he always did when he was deeply moved, and he blinked, and with an effort held his eyelids wide open. His father had suffered a heart attack, and died before help reached the house. He had breathed his last by the time the ambulance arrived. The young intern who had accompanied the vehicle pronounced him dead.

There was nothing Ira could say at this abrupt shearing of his glee by mourning, nothing other than an earnestly attempted expression of condolence. "Gee, I'm sorry, Larry."

And Mom, attuned to sorrow as she was, despite the narrow range of her smattering of English, readily grasped the gist of Larry's message. If not his words, his sad mien and the tone of voice were sufficient signs of his bereavement. She stroked his arm. "*Mein orrim kindt.* Sit down. Sit down, pleese." And when he seated himself, his eyes stricken, lips pinched with grief, "*Alles* mus' go sleep, *mein kindt, tsi* rich, *tsi* poor," she said. "So is it *shoyn millt alle fon* us, vee *menshen.* You should excuse me mine English."

"It's all right, Mrs. Stigman. I understand. Thanks."

"Come, sit closer by the table," Mom invited, indicating with a movement of heavy arm toward the green oilcloth-covered round table. "A cup of coffee? A *keekhle.* I have fresh *keekhle.*"

"It's a kind of cake, Larry," Ira translated. "It's dry. It's good for dunkin'," he diffused his embarrassment.

"No, thanks, Mrs. Stigman." Larry smiled up at Mom. "I had all kinds of things to eat before I came here."

"A little bit, no? And coffee? Something like this should make the heart a little heppier. No?" She shook her head in sympathy with Larry's polite, mute refusal. *"Azoy shein und azoy troyrick,"* she said.

"Talk English, Mom," Ira rebuked, and for Larry's benefit: "She says you look sad." And to Mom again, *"Noo, vus den?"*

"I don't mind your mother speaking Yiddish," Larry assured Ira earnestly. "You seem to think I do. I really don't. I can't tell you why."

"It's atavistic," Ira quipped uneasily.

"No, there's something warm about it. Honestly. Please don't stop her. Don't be embarrassed, Ira. Some of it I think I can understand. Your mother is very eloquent, do you know? She's really comforting. I mean it."

"Yeah? I'm glad." Ira still begrudged. "I don't like it, that's the trouble. I become kind of—I don't know. I'm afraid she'll get sentimental."

"Sentlemental." Mom had heard Ira accuse her of being that so many times, she recognized the word. "Then I'm sentlemental. What better way to ease an orphan's grief?" She ignored his ban on her speaking Yiddish. "A great deal you would have sorrowed for your father. How loudly you would have lamented."

"As loudly as you would," Ira retorted in kind.

Larry looked from one to the other in candid wonderment.

"Just mother and son," Ira explained, and added resentfully, "I'm glad you don't mind."

"I don't mind, not at all. What I do regret is that I don't understand."

"Oh. It's about as far from the way you and your—your family get along as I don't know what. You can see."

"Is that it? You know there isn't much harmony between myself and my folks right now, and you know why. Besides, it isn't as if we always got along. We don't, of course."

"I feel almost outta kilter. You come here to tell me about losing your father, and we're all sidetracked onto something else. What about going for a walk?"

"Oh, no. This is doing me a lot of good. Don't rush, Ira. Please."

"Anything you say."

"He died, your father, in the house?" Mom persisted in asking.

"Yes. He was still eating lunch. He said he didn't feel well. He wanted to lie down."

"Aha. On the bed he died?"

"Yes. My mother had no idea he was having a heart attack."

"*Sie hut nisht gevissen?*" Mom addressed Ira.

"Yes, *sie hut nisht gevissen,*" he corroborated sullenly.

"So venn she know?"

"My mother went into the bedroom when Papa didn't come back. He was just resting, she thought. But when she spoke to him, and he didn't answer—" Larry relied on gesture. "You know what I mean?"

"*Ikh farshtey, ikh farshtey. Mein* son he don't believe I *farshtey. Auf eibig* he laying there."

"*Ewig?*" Larry caught the word. "That's right. *Auf ewig.* You say *eibig?*"

"*Tockin. Aza gitteh kup. Aza gitteh kharacter,*" she commended Larry to her son. "You a goot kharacter," she repeated for Larry's benefit.

"Thanks, Mrs. Stigman."

"*Noo,* he had a good life, no?" She clasped thick fingers.

"I think so. He was always—busy. Busy in his dry-goods store—it was in Yorkville, Ira may have told you. Downtown, in the eighties. We lived there, too. He liked trading, buying and selling, bargaining."

"Aha. Business."

"Yes."

"*Noo, a yeet* oon business," she addressed a scowling Ira. "Only *mein sohn,*" she informed Larry. "And a quviet man he vas too? In the house vit his vife and children?"

"Oh, yes. He was mostly quiet. He was happiest with the family. He liked being with the family. He was happy with all the kids around him, his grandchildren especially. He liked buying them presents."

"Okay," Ira interjected. "What d'ye say we go, Larry?"

"*Loift shoyn,*" Mom chided. "I tell you, Lerry, you name? How he die is a bless to him. *Auf mir g'sukt.* How old he was?"

"Seventy-one."

"All right!" Ira raised his voice.

"Lusst nisht ausredden a vort."

"You've already said more than a *vort*. Mom can jabber all day, and call it a word."

"I don't mind, Ira. I think she's wonderful. I think I understand practically all she's saying. She's so kind. It comes right through."

He gazed at Mom in steady admiration. "I was telling Ira what a wonderful mother he has."

"He biliffs you? *Hairst vus er sugt? Gleibst?*" she asked of Ira.

"Yeah, I *gleibst*," Ira said mockingly, stood up. "What d'ye say, Larry? Let's go."

"If you say so—but you know, I'm getting a lot of pleasure talking to your mom."

"I know."

"What about my coming here again."

"Sehr gut."

"No, I mean it, Ira."

"Okay. We'll swap places."

Larry got to his feet. "I'm glad I met you, Mrs. Stigman, even under these circumstances. It's been a real pleasure to be talking with you."

"If he would leave talk longer. But you must know already *mein sohn*. I'm only sorry you didn't eat a little from something. A coffee—"

"That's all right, Mrs. Stigman." Larry suddenly sighed, smiled at Mom in frank, gentle affection, and said, tilting his head, "I don't need the coffee. I feel so much better than when I came in, just talking to you. You have no idea."

"Yeh? I'm gled. *Noo, gey gezunt, mein oormeh.* How you say?" Mom hesitated. "I don't know." She turned to Ira. *"Oona tateh?"*

"Orphan. For Christ's sake, don't get sentimental."

"Noo, bin ikh sentlemental," Mom retorted defiantly. *"Gey gezunt, meine oormeh,* my orphan."

"Thanks, Mrs. Stigman."

"You should come back soon. *Mein* Minneleh, his sister, *oy,* ven she hears you was in the house." Mom rocked head and shoulders in disappointment. *"Und* she didn't see you. Ay, yi, yi!"

"You tell her all about it," Ira suggested with provocative drawl.

"Ai bist die a hint, mein ziendle."

"Okay." Ira turned the doorknob. "Thanks again, Mrs. Stigman."

"You *fulkomen* velcome. *Gey gezunt.*"

Larry sat down on the canvas cot. "Ah!" He stretched out. "This feels great. Ah." His face shone with pleasure in the lantern light shed above him. "Come on. Forget it. Stretch out on the cot."

Ira could scarcely believe that Larry's mourning had been so brief, that it was only three weeks ago that he had stuck his head in the Stigmans' window. But following Larry's lead, he lay down on the bedding. "Boy, it does feel good." And after a few seconds' pause, "Honest, I wouldn't mind the tent or the cots or anything. It's the change that's taken place in my uncle. Boy." He paused again. "If you knew what he was once like. He carried the *Call* rolled up like a baton. Well, you saw our kitchen table, he'd unroll it, and give us a lecture on that beautiful world to come. Even though I was a kid, and understood less than half of what he was saying, preaching, still, boy, it made a Socialist out of me. That's what I wanted to be."

Larry chuckled upward at the sloping khaki ceiling. "Relax. That's what I'm doing. I am. I'm just dying to see Edith after everything that has happened. I imagine we'll both have a lot to tell each other. I'll bet she'll have plenty to say about French cooking when she returns from Paris. Maybe more than about the museums she visited." He chuckled again. "Say, this isn't bad, the tent, the cot. We have privacy at least."

Ira listened in relief. Larry made it all seem part of the adventure: sleeping under an army tent, with the packed dirt for a floor, on a canvas cot, under a scratchy army blanket for cover. Larry was right. What a rare, what a jolly occasion, what a lark, almost like an escapade. And with so little attention paid them, with so little sense of obligation to the onetime affection between himself and Uncle Louis that Ira had expected, and had led Larry to expect, that suddenly he felt guiltily blithe and carefree. Attachment had vanished, adoration had vanished. Like a couple of droll intruders, tired and elaborately at ease, they lay on their army cots, joking, chaffering, slapping at the all-too-frequent mosquitoes that got through the torn netting.

And to beguile his friend away from the last undercurrent of chagrin Ira felt, as the long summer twilight leaked away, he began reminiscing in the darkness: his very earliest memories in the new land to which he had been brought, an immigrant. Of contemplating the majestic russet rooster with the arching tail feathers in the backyard, when Ira's parents lived in the same house with Uncle Louis and his family, the one on the "first" floor, the other on the "second" floor of a frame house in a place full of open fields and telegraph poles and billy goats in East New York. Maybe he was doing more than merely contemplating the rooster, Ira admitted, maybe he was chasing it, because Aunt Sarah leaned out of the second floor, her home, and scolded him. "I guess she's still the same," Ira added wryly, and laughed. "So am I." He and Rosie, Uncle Louis's only daughter, just a little older than Ira, and away in St. Louis at the moment, visiting Pop's side of the family, had vowed to marry each other when they grew up. She and Ira, at Ira's suggestion, had sat side by side on the floor examining each other's sexual parts. "That ruby-red slash she had instead of the peg I had is still vivid in my mind when I think of it," Ira confided. "However, when my Uncle Louis made the mistake of inviting me out to their Stelton farmhouse, was I ever a scamp. Did I ever pester the hell out of my prospective fiancée."

Larry's teeth gleamed in smile in the shadow. "The engagement was broken off at that point, I assume?"

"I guess I broke its back," Ira rejoined. "It's too bad she's not around for me to see what she looks like, and how she feels about me. And about *you* especially. We might have gotten a better reception in that case."

"It doesn't matter," Larry answered across the dark space between cots. He had taken his shoes off (both had done so), and he wriggled and spread the toes in his socks. His indulgence in the matter made his words seem peculiarly malleable. "It doesn't make the least bit of difference. I told you, not in the least. I'd rather stay right here."

"You sure make me feel better."

"And I'm grateful to have my mind taken off my father. That's one thing. The other thing is . . . it takes my mind off waiting for Edith to come back from Europe. A little anyway." In the interval of a pause, his sigh was less audible than inferred.

"Now it's all going to be new. Strange. My father dies. It seems to put a period on things. You know, even if you're sure it would have gone that way, no matter what you did, you can't help feeling a little guilty. My switching to CCNY. Did it have any effect on him? My giving up dentistry. My falling in love with Edith. I don't know." His brow was troubled, and he held his big hands in front of him. "One thing, though, I don't have that feeling of solidity I once had—you know what I mean?" He let his hands fall quite heavily on his thighs. "It's something I can't explain. Until I went to NYU, I lived in one world, the same kind of world my folks live in. That's what I mean by saying that my life seemed solid. Now it's a—it all revolves around Edith. I should say centers around her, maybe. Yes. Centers. That's what I really mean." He paused. "Not that I want things to be different. I love Edith. You know that. But what I'm worried about is the writing, my writing. Will it come out of me still. It will have to. I feel as if it's tied up with my love of her. M-m-maybe more true the other way: her love for me. It depends on it. My being creative. She puts so much store in it. It's very strange."

Ira had nothing to offer. He sensed the gist of Larry's statement, but no more than that. His words made intermittent contact with Ira's fantasizing, but like his own fantasizing still lacked the substance of everyday reality.

In spite of Edith's departure for France, the summer had begun auspiciously for Larry. He had gotten the job he applied for early in the spring, a singing waiter who also collaborated with the recreational director of the Camp Copake summer hotel in the Catskills.

Larry's good fortune, however, had left Ira with no one to turn to in any meaningful way, which brought on an increasing sense of isolation, anomie, and futility. There were always the few Jewish working youth on the block, or in the group whose nucleus was on 119th Street. But he cared little for their company, Jake, the airbrush commercial artist, included: they shared neither his interests nor aspirations, fuzzy as Ira's were. More and more self-engrossed, self-enclosed, swamped by quandary, all but immured often by appetite, appetite always morticed to fear and self-reproach, he ignored *their* strivings, excluded their commonplace temperament and mundane activities from his range of curiosity—something he was to regret deeply later on, when, as a writer, he sought to give distinctive nature and substance to characters such as these, characters drawn from the past, Jewish youth deprived of formal education.

No matter how enervating the summer became, Ira could not go to Rockaway Beach more than once a week: he might arouse his Aunt Mamie's suspicion. Besides, she gave him a dollar each time he appeared, and there was a limit to his ostensible *shnorring*. Only one thing provided relief from himself, from the slur of his existence that summer, from his bored, disdainful participations with the other youth of the neighborhood, his idleness, lethargies, feral, panicky escapades at Rockaway, despondency and guilty worry. It was Edith's letters to him, not only to her young lover, Larry, from abroad.

She had booked passage to Europe in May, and was away in Europe that summer . . . and Ira, more than half aware of his propensity for the wish-fulfilling and the farfetched, continually fantasized, continually dabbled with the fancy—or the hope—that somewhere in the matrix of Edith's decision to go to Europe was also the hope that during her separation from Larry, he would find a young woman to his liking, and thus bring their affair to an innocuous and conventional close. He was wrong, as usual, as far as Larry's finding someone in the summer resort that would divert his affection from Edith. For when Larry returned abortedly to New York, he expressed his disgust in no uncertain terms about his encounters with the young female guests at the resort, because some went so far in their aggressive amorousness to make a grab for his fly.

"I don't like that, do you?" he asked Ira, who felt, as he shook his head vehemently like some kind of mechanical toy, wound-up double springs of intense envy and disappointment. "No, I don't either." Goddamn crumb he was, reduced to smutty, futile, and vindictive importunings, who couldn't get—Christ, he could hardly say it even to himself out of shame and self-loathing—out to the beach to screw his cousin often enough. "No, I don't either," he who had to risk everything to get at a pudgy, simpering fifteen-year-old. Or sixteen, as if another year would palliate—

Edith was traveling through Europe, through Italy and France mainly, and almost every week Ira received a letter from her. She had taken her small portable typewriter with her, the portable in its rigid black carrying case, and her letters were typewritten in a style Ira quickly came to recognize, even the darkness and spacing of the type. What surprised him at first, all but astonished him, was her style. It was peculiar to all of her correspondence: hasty, disjointed, discursive, unrevised, and with words occasionally misspelled. She poured out her impressions of places visited, food consumed, the state of her "innards," sundry reflections, with no attempt to sort things out, no attempt at order whatever. But how he treasured those letters! How he gloried in them! How often he reread them! They were the first he had ever received from a college instructor, a college English instructor, soon undoubtedly to be elevated to an assistant professor! A professor! And she deigned to write to him, nay, wrote to him as informally and vernacularly as if he were on an equal footing with her, one near to her, one whom she could trust to be discreet about her chatty confidences about her roommate Iola, about the university, the head of the department, even about Larry, her lover. Ira was relieved Larry was away when he received the letters, however much he missed him otherwise; he didn't have to share Edith's letters with him—for Larry would certainly have asked Ira whether he had received news from Edith, and it was easier to write a few words in general in answer to Larry's letters from the summer resort than to speak to him in person about them. They were her messages to him, Ira felt, her bond to him alone, an augury, so he yearned, of the realization of the only future open to him. In it he could make some sort of restitution—what else call it?—redress— find some, no the only, outlet for the discontented, the sorry mess he felt he had become. Ah, to find redress in print, in words, as his piece in *The Lavender* foreshadowed. They called it *métier*, they called it *forte*, oh, Jesus: call it the shape of release on the pages of something he had written. Oh, in time perhaps, in time, a whole book!

For him, the dented, tarnished brass letter box in the much-trodden vestibule of the tenement took on a sudden glory, became transmogrified, when he descried through the curlicues the black type on an envelope that could only be Edith's. Or already brought upstairs by Mom, a letter from Edith lying in wait for him on the kitchen table. To cherish, to read with pulsating spirit: words that sprang up before his eager eyes like a plume. Her letters praised his exceptional sense of humor, his descriptive powers, his latent abilities as a writer, his unusual maturity for his years, his astonishing gravity, for all his humor. Her words filled him with a glow of worth, discernible even to Mom.

"She writes you nice things, the Professora?"

"Yeah."

Filling him with buoyancy, with aspiration, her letters inspired him with an eagerness to reply, and in replying, confirm the model of himself that she held up before him. And in that very reply also—adumbrated first on a scratch pad, and then carefully afterward elaborated on lined paper—certainties infused him that he was, that he could be, what she said he was, that he could rise to what she said, certainties sinking to uncertainties, and then suddenly waxing to elation, reflecting from the enthusiastic words he had committed to the page—and a moment later dampened by doubt again.

He sent his letters to her forwarding addresses—and received in return others that boosted his spirit skyward. His letters were so full of colorful detail and interesting observation, she wrote. He made her feel she was at the very place he was describing, experiencing his sensations. His letters were so direct and unaffected. She looked forward to them. She wished Larry could learn a little of that knack. He tended to poeticize his prose too much, and that was too bad, because it made his letters too studied. Followed immediately by remarks that although traveling was interesting, and she had met interesting people, traveling in general didn't agree with her. French cooking especially. It was too rich, was always served under cover of rich sauces. It was constipating. She had to take frequent enemas. Ira could feel himself duck in embarrassment at her frankness, and yet at the same time feel a stirring of pride that she trusted him to the extent of imparting such confidences. She missed the absence of plain American cooked vegetables. She might have to curtail her trip by a week or two because of her constant "indigishchin," she deliberately misspelled.

*   *   *

Silence separated the dark space between them, a solemn silence. As they lay there on their cots, Larry began again. "Only one thing matters," Larry said, trying to convince himself more than Ira. "Edith. She's the only person in the world that really matters to me. . . . Ah, to be able to solve that problem." His words, so full of gravity, distributed themselves throughout the semigloom of the tent. "We're back again to the crux of the problem—whether I should leave my family and marry Edith. I know that's what you're saying to yourself, Ira, that I should not care what anyone else thinks."

"Oh, no, go ahead, go ahead."

"Leave home now, with my father gone? It seems less possible—I seem less able to do it now than ever. It becomes more cruel. Really cruel. I'm at a crossroad. Up till, up till Papa died, I thought, if necessary, I had the—the necessary heartlessness. I thought I'd mustered up the courage while I was at Copake to carry out my resolution. The more some of these, you know, sex-hungry ones threw themselves at me, the more resolved I became. But Papa's death was a cruel blow. More than the loss of a father. I mean, it shakes up everything I've made up my mind about."

The time for bantering, for flightiness, was indeed over, at least for a while. Ira couldn't fathom Larry's world, that was all, he couldn't fathom it. What the hell was he doing here with Larry in the first place? With Larry and his proper, decent problems. Problems of love, of solicitude about his mother, and still influenced by family judgment. Scruples, yeah. And he, Ira—talk of love, talk of family! No, all he could hope for, speculate about, was his slim chances of a quick screw with Stella in Mamie's front room. Jesus. Yes, Larry's solemnity affected him, but by the very incongruity of it all. As if the two were like clouds in the obscurity of the tent. What a place. What an interlocutor—

"All right, I know you don't get along well with your father. The situation is—or I should say was—" Larry's big hand moved in a pale arc through the shadow. "Was. Say you're in my shoes. You've got no father. You've lost him, right?"

"Yeah?"

"Your mother is a widow. Oh, you've got family—but if she ever needs you, it's now. Your sister is soon going to be married. You're the last child. I've asked you something like this before. But now the question has really become sharp, intense."

Two pale hands plowed the gloom. "Would you, if you could, go off and leave your mother? Get a room somewhere, a part-time job somewhere? Whatever. I know you're attached to your mother—as I am to mine, maybe more. Would you leave her—to herself? Remember, your sister is gone. We're going to sell the house, move to an apartment in Manhattan."

"Oh, yeah?"

"Would you?"

"Leave Mom?" Ira asked.

"Yes."

"Where am I going?"

"I told you. Some one-room place in the Village maybe. Leave your mother and go to a rooming house. I don't know. You get some kind of a job, part-time. Nights. You can't afford an apartment."

"What's the aim?" Ira temporized.

"You know the aim. The same as it's been. Break all the ties that I, you, have."

"*I* don't have any, any like yours."

"But that's not relevant. Break all the deep, close family ties. Change your whole outlook. What's dear to you. What you value, enjoy. You've got to undo what you were. All right? I've said all this before. I'm repeating myself, I know. Become a bohemian, toss out ambition, career, profession, live any old way," Larry suddenly stressed. "Live just to write poetry, live to be a writer. Live I don't know how." He paused. "Well?"

Was the guy looking for a way out? The thought drilled through Ira's mind. Nah. "Listen, pal, you're practically asking me to decide your life."

"In a way, yes." Larry spoke as grimly as Ira had ever heard him. "Decide my life now."

"Wow!"

Silence again in the space between the two cots. *Decide my life now,* Ira heard repeated in his own mind. Literally. It could be that. Then what did he want? *Decide my life now.* If he told Larry what he would do, if he told Larry the truth, about his own willfulness, callousness,

self-centeredness, stemming from what he had become, yes, stemming from his own contemptible gratifications, his corroded character—in which the once resonant Lower East Side world, holistic,
Jewish, with its *cheder*, reverence, fear of God, and all the rest, were all
lost in the fog of himself, all turned to pulverized, floating sensations, impressions in a self devoid of integrity—hell, he had gone
astray—in more ways than one.

Silence, presumably deliberative, meditative. Larry was waiting.
Start again. If he told Larry the truth, the course of action he would
have blindly pursued, blindly, instinctively, *his* course of action—he
would have said: sure. He would leave Mom. With somebody like
Edith the goal, the prize, that kind of future, or whatever to call it,
option—and for himself, he knew damned well there was no other,
no other avenue open to him. But hell, for Larry, a hundred avenues
were open. A hundred twats too. Nah. Then he would have to lie.
And if Larry took him seriously, if his answer counted seriously in
forming Larry's course of action, he was bending Larry's destiny, he
was consigning Larry to his fate. Unless he, Ira, was willing to play a
subordinate role to Larry indefinitely, as he had told himself before,
feed Larry with all his own wild imaginings, his agonies and capers,
he was advancing his own future at Larry's expense. It was like an envisaged sacrifice of Larry to his *own* aims. Ira imagined he could see
his own face in the lamplit canvas overhead, see eyeglasses and all,
leering at himself in knowing mockery at his imminent betrayal.
Jesus, it wasn't right. He tried to stall. One last opportunity to ward
off perfidy: "'Decide my life now,'" Ira finally said. "You mean if I
were in your place?"

"No! You make the decision in *your* place. Not for me. For yourself." Larry's voice filled the tent with vehemence. "*Your* mother."

"My mother?" He was nailed to an answer—no, he was nailing
Larry with his answer: "I guess I wouldn't."

"Wouldn't what?"

"Leave Mom—all alone."

"You wouldn't?"

"Well, with me it's different. I don't have that kind of family you
have. We don't have any of that kind of—well, affluence—"

"We're not really all that affluent."

"Compared to me, for Christ's sake. And different life, background. Years in Bermuda. Culture. All right? So you don't have to do as I say, as I advise. If I didn't have a sister, I wouldn't leave Mom alone, that's all."

"It makes my leaving home all the more difficult, judging from what you say." A note of irritation at Ira's manifest lack of logical coherence crept into Larry's voice. "According to you, I have so many advantages; in other words, I have a dozen times more reason to stay at home with my mother than you have, and yet what I'm trying to tell you is those are the reasons I ought to leave."

"Well, you asked me what I would do in *my* case," Ira said forcibly. "It's hard." The argument made him feel less like a traitor. "I can't do both, you know. Be poor as we are, and be well off as you are."

"Would you stay home if you were well off? I mean, you lacked for nothing. All right? You're making it seem that you would stay home because you don't have anything. That's not an issue."

"But now you're asking me to be as *you* are."

"We're not considering money." Larry transmitted his insistence across the dim interval. "Would you leave your mother at this point? Yes or no?"

"No." He had committed it, the ultimate in transgression, betrayal.

"That's what I want to know. . . . Why?"

"In your case, or my case?"

"In my case."

"You told me yourself why."

"Does it seem like a good reason to you?"

"No."

"Oh, for God's sake!"

"I can't help it. It's just too tough for me." Ira raised his voice. "Christ's sake!" He swatted at the thin fine sting of proboscis penetration. "Bastard. I think I got him. But I'd have to get out in the light to see if there's any smear of blood. But—aw, nuts, if I got out into the light, they'd eat me alive. I'm sorry I dragged you into this place, adventure or no adventure. We could have hitchhiked right home."

"It's all right. I told you I have no complaint," Larry insisted strongly. "As a matter of fact, it's paid off better than hitchhiking home. I mean, talking to you clarifies a few things in myself. I can't leave my mother. I'll have to work this thing out some other way. If I could just talk to Edith, and get her opinion. But then again, I know what she'd say. Stay home. Get my degree. Do the sensible thing. All that. But we're both in the same situation. She's uncertain too. I would have to do the thing that would make her certain. Do you follow me? It would depend on my action. Am *I* certain? Am I ruthless for her sake? And so I go right around in a circle again."

Silence once more. Something else to talk about, to distract. It was too taxing, all they had been discussing; it was too fateful. Jesus, he was caging himself into a future as well as Larry, a possible future. If he was instrumental in excluding Larry from occupying the space, there it was. That didn't mean it was automatically his, of course, but maybe a step closer. Oh, hell, what was he thinking of? He couldn't stand anything so strict as behaving the way Edith expected. He wasn't built that way, no matter what kind of insidious perceptions pricked his mind. Aw, bull.

"I was telling you we lived in the same house as Uncle Louis in Brownsville," Ira said to change the subject. "We shared a flock of chickens. Mom told me that all the chickens were stolen one night. Including the marvelous rooster. Disappeared."

Larry seemed not to have heard, not to be listening.

His attempt at diversion scarcely glanced off the brooding Larry. Ira pondered. How the hell was he going to get the guy off the subject of their destinies? He had to get off it. Jesus. Get off it, and away from his sense of guilt. "Mom told me that the reason we moved away—to the East Side—and how different everything would have been if we hadn't—was that Pop, as usual, got into one helluva row with Uncle Louis, his nephew. They called each other all kinds of terrible names, cursed each other. *Ze vun sikch balt geshlugen tsim toit.*" And expecting as always Larry's "What does that mean?" he prefaced translation with remarks about the Yiddish tendency toward horrendous invective. "'Drop dead' is the mildest of them," Ira tried to humor his friend. "'Be burned to death, be slaughtered.' 'Be drawn and quartered.' Hey, I'm rhyming," he added comically.

No acknowledgment came from the outstretched, discernible figure on the cot on the other side of the tent.

"I think maybe it's what Jews may have seen or suffered over the centuries." Ira spoke more slowly. He was becoming discouraged, as though he had no audience. Surely, Larry's silence wasn't owing to Ira's counsel, which Larry perhaps perceived as false, as treacherous. Nah. "I have a hunch that's it," he continued, paused, received no confirmation of being heard. "Funny thing is they never swear by genitals. Know what I mean? Wops'll say 'yer mudder's ass,' or 'yer fodder's hairy balls . . .'" His voice trailed off. No use. The best thing to do was to turn over on the cot, forget the whole damn thing, wait, sleep if he could, till morning. Jesus, Larry was in a bad way. Larry was in a bad way, or he himself was *in bad*. Boy. Ira bent forward to reach for the rough blanket at the end of the cot. "My father had better hoss blankets than this," he grumbled, barely audibly.

"You know, I've never asked you," Larry said, almost abruptly. "Have you ever been in love?"

The ground had shifted. In the ambiguous gloom under the sloping walls of an army tent, a bell tower reared up from the summit cf Mt. Morris Park hill. "Well, I told you about Rosie, my uncle's daughter," Ira stalled.

"Oh, no, that's just kids investigating. Have you ever—well—it's personal. Do you mind?"

"Oh, no. God, after you telling me all your—all the private things about yourself."

"All right, I've told you. Have *you* ever been with a woman? Or a girl? I realize I've volunteered information. But asking is different. So—"

"Oh, no."

Larry let a few seconds of silence go by. "I have a reason for asking. I'm not just prying."

"Okay. Shoot."

"Have you ever gotten so excited you came too fast? You got a premature orgasm?"

"Oh, is that it?" Ira debated, foresaw consequences—in every answer, save one: profession of complete ignorance. What was the next best choice to outright lying? "Oh, maybe once or twice." Ira still felt secure behind seeming casual curiosity. The locus of concern was within Larry's province.

"Once or twice. But not usually?" He rolled about to face Ira. "I seem to have run into some sort of trouble that way. It really bothers me. I don't know how to get over it."

"Yeah? Maybe you ought to see a doctor."

"I may have to. I'm sure there are any number of men who've run into the same thing. You didn't do anything special about it?"

"Me! Oh, no." It was gratifying how little truth it took to deflect, to stopper up the genie within the vase.

"Then I can be frank about the whole business. I didn't think you'd had any experience. You never mentioned it."

"Mentioned what?"

"Sexual intercourse."

"Oh." The scrawny colored woman who had replaced the comely Pearl of the ladies' rest room atop Yankee Stadium? Scrawny Theodora, apparition in the doorway opening on a stuffy ground floor, *shmatta*-draped room. Jesus, you couldn't mention that. "Well," Ira began, had to clear his throat to dispel reluctance. "Nothing to be proud of."

"Oh, sure. I wasn't interested in romantic adventure. I was just interested in whether it was usual, that's all. You said once or twice. I guess that answers it."

A boxer hung on the ropes in Madison Square Garden. Strands in his own brain shuttled back and forth, twisting to a cable of last refuge: I used to lay my sister. Try and say that. All right, make Stella older: I lay my cousin a lot. I still lay my cousin every chance I get. Jesus, he'd been afraid of that, afraid at the very moment when Larry proposed the trip. Lucky it wasn't a whole week, as Larry had suggested, a suggestion he had shrunk from in advance, within his own mind. Lucky. The urge to unburden, to claw at the toils of the net holding the pent-up self. Boy, if he ever got started, there was no telling where he'd end. Older cousin, older than what, than he was, than she was? "I . . ." he began. "It isn't very nice. But you know, sometimes the damn thing runs away with you."

"Sometimes?" Larry echoed mirthlessly. "That's the understatement for today. Runs away with you is right. If I wasn't keeping faith with Edith, listen, I'm no prude, you know? I made up my mind."

"You sometimes get started early. By surprise. Well, nearly by surprise," Ira corrected himself. There it was: he stood on the threshold of the moment of transfer. Transfer of what? Energy. The potential trapped within himself. Motive force. Power. Explosive memory. The anguish and folly that supplied the sole, the unique surge that drove him toward his chaotic visions.

II

How did his day begin? He sat there not so much trying to recollect as marveling at the amazing diversity of reflections and revelations that could occur, that the mind could generate in the course of a couple of hours—between arising from bed and sitting down before the word processor. So much more, yes, so much more interesting, valuable, than the snarled skein of yarn he spun. In the first place, in the time when M was still alive, the day began drearily, cold, with a fine snow falling. He hadn't arisen from bed yet. M had come to his rescue, as she did more than once in their last few years together, slipped her hand under his neck, and helped him sit up. Then she stood beside the bed, making sure he was steady enough to be safely left alone. He had a whistle, a small plastic whistle, that M had equipped him with, attached by a string to his pajama buttonhole, a child's police-type whistle, which trilled when he blew it, and which he blew when he was ready to get up, or needed help.

On such mornings, M had gotten out of bed a half hour or so before him, had turned the furnace up, set in motion coffee-making procedures, and begun the arduous diurnal chore of pulling on her heavy elastic stockings—not mere support hose, but the heavy anti-varicose-vein stockings she wore, and had worn for many years. So strongly elastic was the fabric she had to exert herself to the utmost to draw the stockings up, a task made all the more difficult because of the reinforcing pads she also had to keep in place at the same time, powder-puff pads against her ankles, where she had to contend with dormant ulcers. He groaned when she hoisted him to a sitting position, and then sat on the edge of the bed after she left. He sat with eyes squeezed shut against the atrocious pain.

Every joint in his body ached, from finger to elbow, to shoulder, to neck—worst offenders of all were the neck joints, where they connected with the left side of the head—the pain they caused often kept him from sleeping, *and* from getting up. That was the way consciousness returned in the morning, giving vent to its advent in a scarcely suppressed howl: "Ow-o-oh!"

So to his study, shuffling along in the moccasins he wore in bed (to keep the winter bedding from chafing the skin off his big and middle toes).

—What a recital, my friend, organ recital, as they say.

I know, Ecclesias.

To his study, because he had provided it with its own wall heater, and it was next to the bathroom, and because he kept his shorts and trousers there, and could get them on by himself after his shower. (M had to help him with his upper garments.) Next, he sat in the swivel chair beside his computer, which had a white hood over it, which came to a peak, like that worn by the KKK, an amended trash-can liner, improvised into a dust cover. There he sat, groaning while he toilsomely removed pajamas and white socks. Then to the bathroom, into the tub, turning on the water of the shower, and adjusting its temperature as hot as he could stand it.

Where, empty-headed, he often sang "La donna è mobile," and all the songs he still remembered, and he still remembered them all, songs that Miss Berger, that hatchet-faced crone, had taught him. He knew and loved almost all.

> *A tinker I am.*
> *My name's natty Dan.*
> *From morn till night I trudge it . . .*

Or:

> *Out on the sea when the sun is low,*
> *and the fisherman homeward turns . . .*

Or:

> *Men of Harlech, in the hollow,*
> *do ye hear like rushing billow . . .*

The other juveniles, his fellow classmates, snickered and sang:

> *A stinker I am.*
> *My name's snotty Dan.*

They sang, "Men of Harlem, in the hollow . . ." But she singled him out to bring Mom to school. He should have gone straight to Mr. O'Reilly, poor, damn fool, timid Jewish oaf he was, straight to the principal with the twitch on his cheek, who understood him, and said, "I didn't do anything, Mr. O'Reilly. I didn't do anything bad. I just grinned. I forgot what you told me." Oh, appeal to the dust. Where was Mr. O'Reilly? Where were seventy years? More than seventy. My God, it was now nearer eighty than seventy.

Meanderings, reflections in the hot shower that limbered grateful joints and sinews, limbered, eased their rheumatic ache. And as the pain abated, allowed him to think, after a fashion, and with nothing else importuning for attention, he would invariably address a group of his peers with his favorite, nay, his perennial thesis: the reason for our failure, yours and mine, to go beyond that first book or two, or trilogy, whether we were black or white, we practitioners in black in white, in print, Jew or gentile. The reason for our failure was the discontinuity we suffered during our development, or having reached the peak of our development. There was the central reason. The first few years of our lives, the psyche laid down the basis, the foundation on which we expected, consciously or otherwise, to build upon all the rest of our lives. What did he mean by that? Perhaps he had made these foundations seem too static; they were not; they were dynamic; they were processes. Those first few years built an interpretational system within each human being—Christ, why didn't he write it all out, and deliver it as the content of a lecture? Which he had been invited to give so many times, and declined: because he knew himself to be the world's worst lecturer, a sheer flop on a podium, a stranded jellyfish.

—As you are now.

Sí, sí, amigo Ecclesias. Verily. As I am now.

---

*　　*　　*

Write the goddamn thing out, and read it. Memorize it after a while. Jesus, the dough they offered him: all expenses paid, and a fat honorarium to boot. He could have been affluent, he and his beloved spouse.

Lecture like crazy (well said): a grave discontinuity was what he suffered from, a grave and disabling discontinuity. The child expected that those things implanted into his psyche would flourish as he developed: the landscape, the field or farm or village or barrio, would also comprise his larger world as he grew up. And the language: how important a factor that was: Yiddish, in his case. He witnessed its drying up, his mother tongue shriveling in a single lifetime. For the Italian, the few who wrote, DiDonato, the same, or the Chicano, Anaya, or even the Southern black. And the people, the kind of people that composed his ambience, the same thing could be said of them, the way they spoke, what they did, the way they did it, their mannerisms, parochialisms, whether of region, of enclave, all were built into the nascent personality, all were expected to continue: the folkways, the people, their pursuits. And they didn't. That's the whole point. They didn't. They were truncated—

Ira's lecture increased in fervor as physical distress was relieved: sometimes more drastically, sometimes less, he declaimed in silence, the *cosmopolitan* world displaced the *parochial* one. And simultaneously much of the parochial world also disappeared, also was absorbed in the cosmopolitan one, at times dramatically as with the Jewish East Side, at times more slowly, as with rustic existence in America. The hick town ceased being so, the barrio as well. Fortunate the author who could return to what was left, or was still undergoing change, and draw on the remainder, the vernacular and the folkway. Because otherwise, he found that he would have to start again with a new landscape, a new ambience, a new set of conditions and characters, customs and behavior, functions that didn't match the foundations already laid down, the interpretations settled upon for maturity, didn't jibe with the pristine norms. The two were incommensurable. Yes.

And much of it, nay, most of the motive force driving the transformation was economic. Economics, the drive to get out of the precincts of impoverishment, the drive to escape the restrictions imposed by the parochial milieu, restrictions closely associated with poverty, restrictions that were part and parcel of penury.

The mind, informed now with awareness of the greater opportunities of the cosmopolitan world, chafed in revolt against prohibitions, prohibitions that only yesterday were *nurturing traditions,* but now newly perceived as constraints. Thus, when the revolt against the parochial world succeeded, and the individual, say a writer, cast off the restrictions that were part and parcel of his formative milieu, *he simultaneously abandoned his richest, most plangent creative source: his folk, their folkways,* his earliest, most vivid impressions, *the very elements of his formation.* Hence the price of success in his best work was to condemn him to discontinuity, if he was to continue. What a paradox! Condemned him to draw on shallower, lately acquired sources different in kind, in nature, from those that imbued his best work. Hence he was condemned to repetition, to academia, to Hollywood, to booze, to immobilization, singly or in combination. Q.E.D.

Ira shut off the shower, and bent over the faucets to turn the small handle between them that deflected water from shower to tub, and also allowed the residual water in the shower pipe to trickle into the tub. Then, holding on to a variety of handgrips he had attached long ago, to prevent M from slipping on the tub bottom—and now, what irony: it was *he* who needed them, not M—he trod carefully on the antiskid toadstool shapes M had stuck to the bathtub bottom. At the other end of the tub, he reached around past the shower curtain to the yellow bath towel hanging on the clothes hook affixed to the narrow door of the small utility closet close by.

Yes. Therein lay the contradiction. He might have returned to his source, he might have continued to write about a dwindling, a crumbling away of life, once lusty and flourishing, and—how unbelievably soon!—disintegrating. But who could do so with any validity and conviction—after he had rejected that life, after he had been infected by association with the cosmopolitan, the larger world in which he now functioned and moved freely? Others had managed to do it, return to a stagnant or depleted source. He too might have done so, and continually extruded a different model of it, the same sausage in a different casing, a different version of a world no longer extant, or no longer viable. . . . He could have echoed and reechoed himself, rung variations indefinitely . . . sold hundreds of thousands of copies of each new edition . . . lived in luxury off the royalties . . .

Head and neck, neck eased by hot water, he could towel off without too much trouble; it was armpits he couldn't reach, couldn't stretch stiff, unyielding sinews that far. With his back he had difficulty too, in drying it;

still, if results weren't wholly satisfactory, the effort was tonic. No use striving to dry his legs below the knees. No use and dangerous too. He might topple over—so. Sold hundreds of thousands of copies.

But that was a minor, minor point, though how nice to have all kinds of dough, but that was a minor point. He began folding the bath towel. Dropped to the floor just below: to raise the makeshift elevator he had devised for getting out of the tub: oddity of oddities, oh, everything about him was oddity. It was a pretty piece of wood, supported underneath by the wooden drawer knobs, which added height, knobs of drawers; but a pretty platform the pretty piece of wood made. It had been the cover of the outhouse toilet of Ira's home in Augusta, Maine, when he and M had first bought the place. He stepped out of the tub safely onto the platform—no, the important question was: why were those first novels so often the best ones? No, that was obvious. He had already answered that. The earliest were the freshest. But still, other first writing, fresh though it might be, might also suffer from ineptitude, the crudity of the novice. No, no. The question was: why did those first (and sometimes only) novels frequently have such wide appeal? They were often best-sellers, if not at the outset, then, like his own, and others as well, eventually. Why? The answer was that it was not only the writer, the literary artist, who suffered from disabling discontinuity; it was the multitude, the populace, the reading public who were troubled by the selfsame thing as well. He was certain of it—

His moccasins on, he padded back to his study, where his shorts lay on the open pages of the unabridged Webster on its improvised stand, a flimsy TV serving table on wheels—certain of it as hell. That was what his fable had been all about without his knowing it; unwittingly he had struck the universal chord of what had affected millions of people. In the U.S., in foreign countries via more than a half-dozen translations. Why the hell should a dope like him, who could write nothing of any consequence thereafter, have established an international reputation of sorts? Imagine: on that teeming East Side, who would have dreamed, who would have wagered a dollar to a kopeck, among all those millions of immigrants, that the Stigman brat, who lived in the corner house on 9th Street and Avenue D, would distinguish himself in any way except maybe becoming a rabbi . . . well, maybe one guy might have surmised: the boarder in their fifth-story aerie, before Uncle Morris came to America, Feldman by name, who prophesied to Mom, with extraordinary clairvoyance, even if a bit wide of the mark, "There grows another Maxim Gorky." Who else would have dreamed that the little gamin whom the poor harassed rabbi, or *malamut*, was preparing to translate *Lushin Koydish* into *Mama Lushin* would one day see his English step-*Mama Lushin* translated into modern *Lushin Koydish*.

But really—Ira chided himself—the thought was a bagatelle, a bauble, a one-liner. The genuinely significant idea, which one Israeli reviewer writing in *Haaretz* delivered, was: "Childhood is not a step of the way, but the whole way." The man was uncanny! Without knowing more about the author than the book itself, he had unerringly probed to the truth. The source of the novel's strength lay in the novelist's weakness; the adult may have accreted literary techniques and virtuosity; the creator was still the child, precocious perhaps with respect to letters, but still a child.

Well—after trunks, pants, after shorts, trousers, take your choice. Standing up, following even a brief period of sitting down, was a consideration these days, with knees what they were, capable of a single poor and painful thrust. He tried to "rationalize" the business, spare himself superfluous movements: put shorts on partway, then draw his pants up to his knees, before getting up, so that he had to stand up only once, not twice: pull his shorts up to the waist, then his trousers while still standing; keep his trousers from falling down by tightening the belt so that the garment stayed above his knees. Oh, there were tricks in every trade, more than one way to skin a cat, or outwit rheumatoid arthritis—chief point was that in his novel, he had stumbled on a fable that addressed a universal experience, a universal disquiet, more prevalent in this age, undoubtedly, than ever before in human history: the sense of discontinuity.

He didn't have to be a supreme literary genius—Ira walked barefoot through the hall toward the kitchen. M had already transferred there, as she always did, his socks, his wristwatch, his sneakers and upper garments—it was John Synge, Ira reflected, who had already discovered the foregoing. John Synge, whom Ira admired as man and writer, who had taught Ira so much, from whom he had never grown estranged, whom he had never grown to detest, as he did Joyce, but admired to this day. It was Synge who had observed, to paraphrase him, that talent wasn't enough. The writer had to strike a chord reverberating in harmony with something deep within his time. That was why a dub like himself could write a classic of its genre, as it was called. A real fluke.

He entered the kitchen, where M had everything ready to finish dressing him. She waited for him, ever kind, ever forbearing, in pink skirt, brown sweater, her long, elliptical, Anglo-Saxon countenance wrinkled and beautiful, her hair gray and ivory, and she uttered consoling, cheerful words as he came in. He sat down in the big armchair bought especially for him, because its high back provided support for his neck. On the table, already collected in a Chinese enameled spoon, were his vitamins and minerals, capsules and pills, about six of them, and there was fruit juice to get them down with, and near at hand the little kit with swab and tub of anti-athlete's foot cream which M dabbed between his toes after drying them. Within reach was the small square wooden platter that bore utensils, salt and pepper-grinder—and the vial containing the Imuran tablets, of which he took one, and the other vial containing the prednisone five-milligram tablets, his cortisone, of which he took two. Meanwhile M at the stove spooned out the whole-grain porridge she had cooked this morning. . . .

III

A faint light came through the mosquito netting at the entrance of the tent, and lifting his head, Ira saw someone light a lantern on the back porch of the farmhouse. They had been given their supper there. Probably the help ate there; it seemed to have become a satellite to the hotel. And now light gleamed on the eyeglasses of the figure bearing the lantern down the porch steps—and toward them. . . . It was Uncle Louis. Ira felt a resumption of affection, a renewal of boyhood gratitude. Uncle Louis had considerately taken a little spare time to come over and talk to them. Away from the hotel and his cares, perhaps he would indulge in a round of friendly conversation, display a token of his former heartening sympathy that had so endeared him to his nephew in years gone by. Now perhaps Larry could see for himself that Ira's praise of his uncle was at least partly justified.

"My uncle is coming over." Ira sat up, swiveled about on the cot, then stood up . . . waited until the approaching figure was within earshot.

"Uncle Louis. Gee, I'm glad to see you, Uncle. Come in away from the bugs." Ira held open the mosquito netting. "Come in and sit down."

"No. I didn't come to talk."

"No?" Ira was at a loss. "I'm sorry, Uncle. I thought maybe you would." His regret was intermingled with appeal. "I was telling my friend here, on the way"—he indicated Larry, who had lifted his head and soberly regarded Uncle Louis—"how much you knew about socialism, how much you influenced me in wanting to be a Socialist."

Uncle Louis was never other than lean, but now he looked gaunt. As he hung his lantern on a second hook on the tent pole, the cords of his skinny neck crossed above the open collar of his striped shirt. The second lantern's light seemed to dredge creases in his careworn, leathery features. Uncle Louis shook his head.

"I can see you're tired, Uncle," Ira said forgivingly.

Curtly, his eyes behind rimless eyeglasses glinting disapproval, Uncle Louis turned away from the lantern. Gone was all indulgence, the gentleness that had disabused Ira when at fourteen he announced he wanted to go to West Point, and Uncle Louis said, "They don't like Jews in West Point," a different voice, but the same person, now said: "It's a waste of time."

"What is? You mean socialism, Uncle?"

"Yes, socialism. Don't waste your time on it."

Ira was too confounded to say anything more, to do anything more than gaze. Uncle Louis's disillusion, like the light of the lantern he had hung upon the center pole, drove away everything of an entirely different personal nature that had instilled the semidark with a different strain and crisis only a minute ago.

"It's nothing. It's worse than nothing." Uncle Louis scarcely raised his voice, as if the subject had long ago become a matter of indifference to him, had died. "It didn't turn out to be anything like we thought. No idealism, no principles, no brotherhood. What is there in Russia? Socialism? They murder Socialists. The Communists are greater tyrants than the czar ever was. They oppress the common people more than ever, the honest, hardworking farmers. What kind of socialism is that? Freedom, we thought, freedom. They tell you what to do, where to go, what you should think. Nobody is safe. You can't open your mouth, you can't disagree. The bureaucrats'll take your head off. It's total subjection. You know what subjection is?"

"Of course, Uncle." Ira could hear the plaintiveness in his own reply.

"That's what they have in Russia. It's subjection, it's not socialism. And Jews? Ah! *Jhit* is on every Russian's lips. The same as it was before. Worse than it was before. Stalin is a murderer, he'll be worse than anyone thinks. You talk about anti-Semites. He's an anti-Semite of anti-Semites. Every Jew is trying to slip out of Russia, even Socialist Jews. Lenin's friends Stalin sends to the firing squads. A murderer. And this is what we waited and prayed for, the Socialist revolution. What a Socialist revolution." Uncle Louis stood in gaunt immobility a few seconds, hopeless. *"Noo."* He dismissed the subject with a wave of the yellow slip of paper in his long bony hand. "Take my advice, don't waste your time on it. You'll only be disappointed in the end."

"You really think so, Uncle?"

"I guarantee it. It's only a question of time."

So once again, Uncle Louis quenched the illusion he had kindled within his nephew's mind. Only now that Ira was older, and able, at least fleetingly, to perceive motives that he had scarcely been responsive to before, hardly ever taken the pains to probe, he wondered whether the things Uncle Louis was saying in disparagement of socialism and the Soviet Union were true. Or whether it was because he now owned a summer hotel, or had just naturally become disenchanted because he was growing old, or both. How strange that so much could happen within the space of time in which less than a decade of disillusion was compressed. Compressed into a small bail, yeah, bale: Ira felt that Uncle Louis's withdrawal from the ranks of idealism meant his withdrawal from life. He had given up, and it was now Ira's task to carry forward the bold ideas his uncle had abandoned. It seemed almost inevitable that he would have to be that youth who bore a new banner when shades of night were falling fast. That was how it always went: that stupid "Excelsior" of Longfellow that anybody with the least modern attitudes, with the least taste, just plain gagged at for its sappy sentiment. "Excelsior." No wonder the kids snickered: wood shavings. You packed shipments with it. But it was more than the ideals of onward and upward, justice to the down-

trodden—and tolerance of Jews—that had moved Ira toward socialism, that made him so ready to absorb Uncle Louis's fervor, and
transform it into something personal, into an answer to a deep
need—with scarcely the ability to put the need into words. It was
what he felt he had become, was ever more becoming, a thing he despised. Socialism addressed his self-contempt; socialism fluoresced
against the pall over him. He could never be Larry sitting there, almost immobilized with indecision, in love, in love with a mature, cultivated woman, Larry harrowed by conflicts between decent, coherent
choices. But maybe *he,* Ira, could stop being himself, through socialism. Within the space of a minute, the unexpected became the preordained. He would have to pick up where his uncle left off. Without
benefit of words, inner colloquy signaled assent and difference like
patches of color.

"Thanks for the lantern, Uncle," Ira said. It wasn't surprising that
his uncle's visit would mean so much to him, and so little to Larry,
still sitting motionless on the cot, his incurious gaze directed upward
at Uncle Louis. "Don't you want to sit down even for a minute,
Uncle?" Ira motioned to his cot. "Funny, I was sure you brought the
lantern to talk."

"No, no. I just came for a minute." Uncle Louis warded off the invitation with curt flap of the yellow slip in his hand. He bent toward
Larry on his cot. "Are you Larry Gordon?"

Through all sorts of turbid perspectives, as through a spectral
shimmer and shadow, the yellow slip in Uncle Louis's bony, veined
hand materialized into the slick surface of a Western Union telegram
envelope.

"Yes, I am." Larry's apathy gave way to attentiveness, his bent posture straightened in concern. "Is that for me, Mr. Sanger?"

"Here you are." Uncle Louis tendered the yellow envelope. "I
knew we didn't have any guests by that name."

"Thanks. This can't be—" Larry stood up. "I lost my father the
same way. A telegram." His voice and hands trembled. Every bit of
light in the tent seemed to focus on him as he tore open the thin yellow envelope, scanned—

"Ohh!" He threw his head back in prolonged cry. He slapped
hands and yellow paper together. His features were transfigured, his

countenance beatified, his impassioned gladness cast new light in the tent itself. "She's back!" he cried. "Edith is back! Edith is back! She's back in New York! Oh, thanks, thanks, Mr. Sanger! Sorry I'm so excited. I couldn't get better news than this! It's wonderful!" His words tumbled out in rapturous disorder. "Oh, great! Oh, marvelous!"

Ira grinned in embarrassment at his friend's ecstasy, in embarrassment looked from Larry to Uncle Louis in the hope he would understand, make allowances. He and Larry were about the same height, standing close together in lantern light under the ridge of the sloping canvas walls, their faces level, the one young, handsome, exalted with joy, the other drained, wasted, creased.

"I see you've got some good news," Uncle Louis, unbeguiled, wearily sanctioned.

"Oh, have I, Mr. Sanger. I don't think I'll get news as good as this if I live to be a hundred years old! I can't tell you how happy I am. I mean—" Larry's head tossed shadows on the tent walls. "It's just impossible. It's fantastic, it's so good."

"I'm glad for you. Glad you got it. The Western Union boy left it at the desk. I just barely happened to think it might be you." Uncle Louis stretched a lank arm for the lantern. "You won't need this. It only draws more mosquitoes."

"Mr. Sanger, I wonder if—if I dare—please—beg a favor of you— on top of all your kindness," Larry entreated. "May I make a long-distance call? Collect, of course. May I use the phone? Would you mind? Right now? To New York." Winning, breathless, Larry importuned.

"No reason you can't. Go ahead. You can use the phone in the kitchen." Uncle Louis brought the lantern down, beckoned with it. "Just follow me. It's the same way you came." Dour and exhausted, his suppressed groan trailed after him. "Be sure to tell the operator to reverse charges."

"Oh, certainly. I know. I know. Certainly, Mr. Sanger! Thanks." Larry quickly made shift to hold the mosquito netting open to follow his guide. He turned to Ira as Uncle Louis moved away from the tent. "Coming?"

"No. I'll stay here." Ira remained standing—and called, "Good night, Uncle. Goodbye."

"Goodbye, goodbye," came from the laconic voice in the dark above the departing lantern. "Give my regards to your father and mother."

Larry paused, beckoned for Ira to follow, his pale hand fervent in obscurity.

Ira signaled him to go on.

IV

And leaves the world to darkness and to me, Ira thought as he sat waiting, glum, confused, perturbed—"Anh," he heard himself flout himself. Too much, too conflicting, too contradictory. And boy! Agitated, yeah. Amid Larry's hopes, problems, hopes, elations, and joy! Contrasting with Uncle Louis's weary disenchantment, as if his main concern was to survive amid the ruin of his hopes and ideals. Jesus, pathetic, what a sight! And he, Ira? Seeing both, seeing both together, in his own goofy way, through his own twisted cravings, and nearly giving way, betraying himself to Larry. "Anh." Go there, go back to the kitchen with him, listen to his rapturous outpouring? Sure as hell he was calling Edith. Love, dove, love, shove. My darling, darling, and all the hotel help there too maybe, listening, while Ira tried not to shrink. And Uncle Louis there also. Jesus, wasted away, wasn't he? Like his ideals of socialism. And strict, exacting, patronizing Aunt Sarah, making sure the call was collect. . . . So Edith was back. Yeah, tender words, sighs, endearments, verbal caresses—by Larry, gushing with rapture. And himself bystander, lamely attending, for everybody to see, hanger-on. But what the hell was that about premature orgasm? Ira had to tear it off in a hurry because, because, Christ, anybody knew why. Larry had all the time in the world. Jesus, life was full of jokes. Contrarieties. How much he had once wanted Uncle Louis for a father. Once wanted him to lay Mom. *Lyupka.* Sarah should know. Uncle Louis should know he made his nephew dream a stiff peg against Mom's rump, and she laughed. Pop should

know. All that socialism was a waste of time, said Uncle Louis. Oh,
nuts.

Edith had called up Larry's home first, Larry informed him when
he returned to the tent. She had been told where he was, where he
probably was—by Larry's sister, after some hesitation. And so the
telegram . . . delivered to the tent in the dark, and by lantern
light . . . by lank and changed and spent Uncle Louis . . . delivered to
Larry brooding on his cot, brooding about his predicament.

Ira had never asked him, in the years afterward, during the decades that
went by, Do you remember that time? Has anything happened to you
more exciting than that? He had never asked. Strange that he hadn't—
well, not so strange. That was his own, imperfect, egotistical nature—or, to
give him the benefit of a little charity, his tactfulness, sensitivity: why drag
that up, the illusions, the infatuations, the hopeless emotional entanglements of youth? What could you say to Larry about an eventual loss, an
eventual defeat—at *your* hands? Wasn't that a thrill, Larry? Something
banal as that. Boy, wasn't that something? The tent, the dark, the dirt floor,
the mosquitoes—real New Jersey mosquitoes in New York you could throw
a saddle over. And Uncle Louis coming in with the lantern and the
telegram. Maybe you could, after many, many years, hark back, when it
hardly mattered any longer, muse on it, share it, add a jot to the patter . . .
No. For obvious reasons.

Sit with hand in pocket awhile, head hanging. It was the summer of
1925, again. And the mind stands still or seems to, but of course it doesn't.
Silly business, the whole thing, like existence itself. That he, Ira, to reiterate,
should be with a well-bred, tenderly reared youth like Larry, should have
had designs on the guy already, wavered, shaken off loyalty in the nick of
time, compulsively determined to make of him, his friend, a vehicle for a
future with only the vaguest definition, haziest outline. How do you do it?
It wasn't done consciously, that was the odd part of it; it was done by an
act of involuntary imagination. Nobody else could have been that
crazy. . . . How the hell did you ever dream you could do it? Well, he had
told himself before how he had done it, a dozen times, or tried to. Think of
that dreary cold-water flat on 119th Street, think of Larry's comfortable,

well-furnished, roomy apartment in the Bronx, an apartment occupying the entire floor, and Larry with a room of his own. Oh, fare thee well, friend, friend and stepping-stone. Larry accused Ira of using him just for that—much later, when recriminations were in order—Larry told Ira what he was. And he was right. But what the hell can you do? *Nada.* The guy had to make life fit fiction.

So, as a consequence of all these circumstances, coincidences, connivings, conscious and unconscious, he, Ira, managed to write a novel that eventually won wide acclaim. Whether the acclaim was merited or not, it would take a few more generations to decide, just as it would take a few more generations for a firm appraisal of Joyce to be made: whether Joyce deserved to be ranked with a Milton or a Shakespeare, deserved to be enshrined among the supreme in literature. Even if the acclaim for his own novel remained firm, say as firm as the deserved esteem accorded to an Oliver Goldsmith, or somebody a lot less worthy, a Jack London, a Nathanael West, a Mike Gold, maybe Lowry, Wright, Ellison, Abe Cahn, the question Ira directed at himself was: was the achievement worth it in terms of the personal suffering, and the suffering of others, Larry's, Edith's? Was the achievement worth it at the expense of the man too? His integrity, his character? Foolish question, futile question, it would seem at first cry. And yet the whole thing involved a moral element that could not be denied or rejected. Who could say that the impaired moral element, the moral canker inherent in the achievement, did not exercise a subtle retaliation when again he came to assay the next stage of the creative process, this second novel—whether it was not that same moral canker, metastasizing within him, that disabled him? The thought had come to him in the midst of what seemed an easy disposal of the question. *That was the way it happened, the way it went* was already on the monitor, when the new insight intervened—succeeded by the words *Foolish question, futile question.* And yet, was it? Deterioration of character was the price of a serious moral flaw, deterioration of character or of identity, and when the next stage came, when both character and unified identity were required, mature and sound, he was found woefully wanting. Over just such moral questions, Ira surmised, did old man Ezra Pound rue the day he ever set pen to paper. And what did he think of Joyce afterward, of *Finnegans Wake*? Something about writing a gospel? Or Scripture? Was that it? Something disapproving.

Well, of what use were these lucubrations, even if true? And what of value could he, Ira, any more than Pound, transmit to his fellow humans, to posterity, what glimmer of enlightenment could he impart, that would help others avoid the pitfalls he had been prone to, help others, in a substantial way, to live lives more befitting human beings, with dignity, with decency, with a sense of probity—and some sense of fulfillment? Probably not much more than any preacher. Salvation, such as it was, moral improvement, character change for the better, very rarely derived from homily or from sermon. And for each one improved, changed for the better, social conditions, the environment, probably bred a hundred in need of redemption—or rehabilitation. The great changes, the mass changes for the better, required mass action, the concerted activity of the mass in converting the society to one more favorable to the promotion of decency, *their* decency; and that meant, in the first place, improvement in the material conditions of life, the quality of life, and in the second place, tangible incentives to improve their lot, convictions that would translate into action. And much more. One thing was a fairly safe bet: anybody, damn near, could behave virtuously in his dotage without too much difficulty.

It was predawn dark when Ira was awakened—by Larry insistently calling him from across the tent. Larry was already sitting on his cot, lacing up his shoes. Predawn darkness for the predent. Jesus, what a time to get up. Ira groaned in protest, yawned long and uncouthly, clawed at mosquito bites, hissed and swore, sat up, and dug his feet into his shoes.

"How the hell'd you wake up?"

"I've been lying here awake for I don't know how long. I wanted to make sure it was near morning."

Predawn. There it was, faintly marbling the sky on the other side of the netting. Neither knew the time. Cool, bleary, Ira got up from the cot, slipped around the tent, urinated against the nocturnal damp, huffed, puffed, broke wind, rejoined Larry in the tent. Larry had his jacket on, ready to go. Lights were on in the kitchen windows of the farmhouse. Uncle Louis was probably up. Maybe if they went in to bid goodbye, they could get a cup of coffee. But Larry urged they skip it, skip the coffee, and get out on the highway to New York.

The earliest hours offered the best chances of getting a lift, he reminded Ira, who agreed, but reminded him in turn they only had a short way to go: they were close to the city, about forty or fifty miles. What was the sense—he tried making his grumpiness sound amusing—of hitchhiking by starlight. "We'll need the Big Dipper to know which way."

Larry's urging prevailed. Striding along the narrow ribbon of pavement to the main highway was invigorating—and reviving. Dawn pried the night open, like an entering wedge, making room for sunrise. They reached the three-lane concrete Route 1, and both tramping New Yorkward, Larry wheeled and thumbed, aggressively wheeled and thumbed.

Soon, the countryside took on form and green, and houses along the road variety and shape; the concrete road began to glare. Larry thumbed for rides, back-walking tirelessly toward destination, exuberantly imploring the motorists. Within a half hour after sunrise, a truck slowed down, stopped on the shoulder of the road. The two sped after it for dear life. The driver was a Jewish poultry-and-egg farmer, Manhattan-bound with crates of eggs for the wholesale market. In a glorious moment, full of breathless laughter and exclamations of gratitude, they boarded the vehicle, slid into place beside the ruddy, middle-aged, thickset man at the wheel.

Identities were confirmed. Larry entertained their benefactor at once with his enthusiasm, his large gestures, and his non-Jewish appearance and Jewish charisma—and with snatches of song and story, recent acquisitions from his weeks as singing waiter at Copake. The harassing dilemmas of last night quickly disappeared. Buoyancy and self-confidence were restored. He was Larry again, receptive and congenial, as if both indecision and mourning were a thing of the past. Those few hours in the tent between the arrival of the telegram and the first light of dawn must have been spent coming to some kind of resolution. Although he said nothing about it to Ira, it was evident he still found the resolution valid, even exhilarating, in the full light of day. His alacrity this morning, the springiness of his step as they hurried to reach the main highway, his cheeriness, assurance, all seemed to indicate that a crisis within himself had passed, and a happy faith in himself had taken the place of misgiving.

Ira wondered, as the truck bowled along, with new tires alternately whining and thumping, in transit from concrete slab to slab, like a train over the gaps in rails, whether the intense discussion he and Larry had had last night had determined anything in his decisions, whether Ira's own compulsive self-serving—was it the creating of reality, or was it self-creating?—had misled his friend. At the moment he hoped not; it weighed on his conscience. Let Larry determine his own future. It already sounded to Ira as if, from *his* point of view, Larry had decided to do exactly the thing Ira could secretly exult about: Larry had decided to do the wrong thing—for Larry, for his hopes as a writer, for that future that imperceptibly (to Larry) the two had begun to vie with each other.

Oh, it was crazy, it was crazy. But there it was. What was his gaiety and gladness all about? Just because he would soon see Edith, be with her? Certainly. But Larry himself had said that Edith wanted him to stay home, live at home, get his degree, and he was acting in accordance with her advice. And yet at the same time, last night he had said that it was up to him to lead the way, lead the way by doing the opposite of what she advised, convince her by an act of the depth of his sincerity, take the crucial step, the drastic step, even if it wasn't the wisest one, that marriage to him would be feasible, that he was ready to break all other ties to marry Edith. His behavior didn't seem to indicate that kind of indomitable resolution—if intuition had anything to say about it. Larry had somehow reconciled his love for Edith with his affection for family, with his ties to his family. At least in his own mind, and he was happy with his compromise. Again, dumb hunch prevailed: Larry could avoid disruption and pain and strife that way—postpone it. Well . . .

Thoughts unreeled against the passing countryside, trailed past buses and meadows, slipped over houses, floated against the clouds beyond the trees at the margins of hayfields.

As if he were eavesdropping, Ira remained silent, trying to assess the implications of his friend's merriment—and the implications they would have for himself—for potentialities, the advantages. Meanwhile, Larry entertained the Jewish poultryman. And he— Asher was his name—never lost his smile of contentment. He beamed as he drove. Even as they approached the city, and traffic began to hem them in, he steered through it with a smile, with the look of a man getting the better of a bargain, the bargain of Larry's anecdotes, Larry's mirthful borscht-circuit tidbits, acted out with infectious enthusiasm, with all the vigor of a seasoned showman. If the resolution of last night's conflict with himself had liberated Larry from dilemma, his release showed itself in something Ira had only seen traces of before, never seen exhibited with such verve and aplomb as Larry demonstrated, seated beside the beguiled poultry-man in the cab of the rolling truck: it was Larry as the performer, Larry enjoying his role as performer.

They entered the city, reached the last station on the elevated subway line. When the two offered to alight, Asher told them to sit still, and then he generously drove them all the way through the Bronx. At length he drew up to the curb under the platform of the station after which he would have to branch off from the subway line, stopped, extended his hand, invited them to drop in at his farm not far from Spring Valley. "Asher's Shady Brook, everybody knows it. You wanna see good farmerettes, like they called them when the war was on? My four girls. And they're all pictures too."

Assuring him they would try to avail themselves of his hospitality, the two set off, with much laughter. Ira, too, felt himself suddenly possessed by a vivacity he could scarcely recognize, that didn't belong to him. And indeed, there was something inebriate about it all, blithe, the spell of Larry's release. No, he was all wrong—Ira felt a fleeting giddiness, as though he were displaced from himself. This was the way to be. Stop scheming, stop calculating, furtively nourishing fancies he ought never spawn. Larry's choice was the right one. Who the hell was *he* to think he had any part in the matter, could conceivably benefit one way or the other, no matter what Larry decided? Who the hell was *he*? Nobody. He was a *shlemiel*. So get back to being one.

They dashed up the stairs at the rumble of an approaching train, jabbed coins in the slot of the turnstile, and charged into the train, cheating the closing doors . . . panted, grinned in private frolic, hung on to straps and stood, although there were empty seats interspersed among sitting passengers.

After a two-station ride, they separated; Larry got off the train. "Call me in a couple of days. Call up. Day after tomorrow! I'll be home." Moving along the platform, Larry shouted through the partly open window, loud enough for the whole car to hear, and Ira, secure in his induced excitement, felt no embarrassment, but shouted in return:

"Right!"

The train went on, it left Larry behind, but for a second, the window through which Ira last saw him seemed to trail after it the lover's face, blissful, radiant with happiness and anticipation.

What a splendid, exciting span of time, of existence, so heady, so vicarious, spent in another's enamored, ardent state, vicarious and ephemeral. It had been great. Like the difference between a completed drawbridge and a single cantilever, open, himself. yeah, what he was. . . . Let's see. He could sketch a little strategy while he rode, serve up a pretty little core within the racket the train made traveling, traveling over the rails downtown. Do a little planning on the banging din, Gunga Din, let's see, as he swayed, train-*davening* toward the 96th Street and Broadway exchange that would take him back uptown to Lenox Avenue and Harlem. Then let's see how lucky he was: if he was lucky, no explanations were needed. Catch Stella in a favorable moment, home now from a month at the beach. Easy as pie. Oh, maybe bestow on her, and Mamie, and Hannah, if they were home, a few bits about his trip with Larry, like sprinkles on a cake, to improve the tedium of temporizing while he waited his chance. Oh, he was cunning, he congratulated himself, versatile and devious. In that department, nobody could beat him; he knew the most ingenious moves. But if he wasn't lucky, if he wasn't lucky. It happened often—he suppressed a shrug—if he wasn't lucky, then tough luck, tough luck. He couldn't fall back on Minnie on Sunday mornings any longer. Jesus, that *goy* with the car, he got his licks in these days on Saturday night, after work. He laid her first, humped her in the back of the car, sure as hell. Dished him out of his whack on Sunday morning, the way the Irish kids said, dished him out of his turn at bat. It was over. She spurned him, that was all. He'd be wheedling; they'd be arguing, till Mom got back from shopping. Stella was his only bet.

He cast his gaze down from knees across the aisle to shoes on the cement subway floor. He reduced exposure of prurient maunderings that way, with his head down, as if examining trampled tabloid headlines beneath his own feet: SCOPES TRIAL BATTLE LOST BUT NOT WAR: DARROW; FRANCE DEMANDS DEMILITARIZED RHINELAND. Only trouble was, it made him drowsy when he tried to read the smaller type. And drowsy he might well be, after last night's wakeful excitement, Larry sputtering away, like a fuse, wasn't he? And e-e-e, the whine of mosquitoes, and then suddenly, boom, the telegram: looky, looky, looky, here comes nooky. And Uncle Louis, what a pathetic wreck, what a difference between him and the lean sinewy guy in prestigious postman's blue who tried to lay Mom—only about seven or eight years ago. She should have let him.

What the hell are you gonna do? Suddenly surly with himself, he rebuffed his internal thoughts, his self-esteem, with its hated sneer. Who the hell was he to tell *him*? Did *he* get a fancy, dainty Ph.D. to lay, like Larry? No. So quit yapping, goddamn you. Get a job after school, spend two bucks for a lay, like other guys. Yeah—his demurral dripped with skepticism: lazy bastard. Broke. Get a dose maybe. Excuses: he was shy, he was timid. Hell, why could Larry go to a nice, clean, white apartment in a house on St. Mark's Place, with that pretty view outside the window in the late, late afternoon, when all four came back from that excursion up the Hudson River to Bear Mountain? And back of the house, what a pretty yard down below, the sculpture on the lawn, the trees, the shrubs. Like a landscape framed in the window. All the time in the world to enjoy each other, stroke each other smooth, and *shmooze* and smooch and smooch and *shmooze*. Minnie wouldn't even let him kiss her anymore, and Stella half the time exhaled onions, canned salmon and onions. And never a word to say, just cover-up gab. But with Larry and Edith, they mingled kisses with talk about Beauty, Beauty, Beauty, like Edna Millay, talking about Euclid alone. While he? Yeah. At Mamie's, he knew all too well, he would—with the dance band blaring—drive it into her with a front-room straddle of an evening by the Stromberg Carlson Superheterodyne radio.

They were passing the 110th Street station . . . just passed . . . 103rd next. Next 96th. And he, he got a couple o' crumbs out of it, out of Larry's romance. Like the *khoomitz* Pop used to brush up with a feather the morning before the first Passover night, crumbs of unleavened bread. Went into a wooden spoon. Tied up with a rag. And burned in the street—Ira snorted silently, sourly, joke. Who bothered today? You could really make it funny on 119th Street: hey Mickey, hey Feeney, hey Maloney, you know what this is? It's *khoomitz*, a few dry bread crumbs. So they'll say, Yeah? Waddaye do wit' it? And you'll say, Burn it in the street. And they'll say, Go ahead, we'll piss on it. You Jews are nuts. . . .

103rd Street. Passover. Pesach. Matzohs. When Moses led the Hebrews out of bondage. When the landlord, the Irisher, did Mom a favor and painted the kitchen. And painted the toilet, and painted the big tin bathtub in its wooden casket of matchboards, cheap green house paint that stuck to your ass in hot water. But, boy, was the bathtub big. . . .

96th Street was next, he'd better stand up. . . .

So big you could float in it. Passover, 1918, when he was twelve. When the World War was still on. Talk about bondage. Boy, he could yell, Nates, nates, nates! He knew the fancy name, as he did so many others. Natey, nickname for a Jewboy. But to be understood, he'd have to yell like a wop. Boy, was it smooth and slick: levitation, levitation, right out of the tepid water. And that was before Passover. Moses—or was it God?—parted the Red Sea with a titanic—nah, cosmic command. How the hell could one little Israelite guy with one little staff split a whole sea asunder, cause such a cataclysm?

Ah, the hell with it. Here came 96th. Try your luck, you never lose. The train slowed, stopped. He eyed the gray rubber pads between doors, waiting for them to part . . . smirked. Anh. Maybe Larry was at this minute just getting ready to go to Edith's.

Nonetheless, Ira wasn't lucky at all. Having gone home first, he didn't try Mamie's right away, and when he did, Stella was out. So Minnie was at home. She had, she said, stopped "dating" her gentile boyfriend, the gentile "buyer" of the firm in which both worked, Rodney, "the *goy* with the car," as Ira jibed. He wanted to come to the house, her last week at the job, and why not? He liked her a lot. He wanted to meet her parents. His folks lived in Schenectady, otherwise he'd already have taken her to meet them. He was serious about her. He wanted to go steady with her; she was nice, he said, she was sharp and shrewd, and feisty too. But mostly, she was faithful. He was sure of it. She was the kind of woman he wanted for a wife; she would never two-time him. And how was he going to meet her other than in her home, if he was serious about her? On a street corner? That wasn't right. He had a good job, and Minnie had one year more to go in high school. She could say yes or no to an engagement, right then and there. He was sure she would say yes; they hit it off so well together. After they were married, and had a place of their own, she could go right on to Hunter as she planned. That was okay with him if she wanted to teach for a few years.

"Oh, no, listen," Minnie confided to Ira, informing him of developments, "I could never marry him, he's a goy. I'm breaking it off. I shouldn't have started in the first place."

And to leave no doubt about her intentions, she announced that she would be home for supper this Saturday. "And don't ask why. Never mind. I'm going back to Julia Richmond. I don't need him. I want to be a schoolteacher."

"Ah!" Mom said resignedly. "*Noo,* I won't ask."

"We never even saw him once." Pop's mien bespoke his sympathy.

Minnie prefaced rejoinder with a flap of her hand. "Who wants him to see this place?"

"Well, let's move, let's go in search of new rooms." Pop was generous where Minnie was concerned.

"Let's move to the Bronx," Mom suggested. "There are fine rooms in the Bronx, and it's becoming very Yiddish—more and more." She began to enumerate neighbors and acquaintances who had recently moved there. "And kosher butchers, and live fish stores, for Friday. And delicatessens and bakeries too. You'll show me two or three times how I should travel to Mamie to see Zaida. Then I'll be able to go there alone."

"Never mind moving to the Bronx! I told you. After I'm finished with Richmond, then I'll talk about steady boyfriends. At least I'll have a high school diploma. Right now I don't want to talk about it anymore. So do me a favor."

Ira knew why, and gloated. She had to ditch her *goyish* goldfish. If she brought him to the house—not that Mom would mind. Maybe not even Pop. But *oy, oy, oy*, Zaida, the relatives—*oy, yoy*, a *goy!* She was a good kid, though, Minnie, to give him up, chase him off. Jesus, *he* wouldn't have, if he liked him—or her, Ira bridled at the idea—to hell with Zaida and everybody else. But she liked the guy—a lot. Rod looked as if he were going to cry when she told him she wouldn't go out with him on Saturday-night dates anymore. Minnie sniffed in the telling, and before she was done, she also shed an honest tear or two. And how Ira sympathized with her, in true crocodile fashion, with "Ah, tsk, tsk, tsk," and "Gee, I'm so sorry, he sounds like such a nice guy," and he stroked her bare arm in her nightgown. "You'll find somebody else, Minnie, somebody Jewish. Don't worry. You're a real grown-up, and good-looking. Sure, if *he* thought you were smart, and if he thought you were good-looking, what're you worrying about?"

"Mostly I thought, if you wanna know the truth—maybe he would *shmott*—you know he's circumcised? They did it in the hospital."

"Yeah."

"But I gotta get that Hunter diploma. I can't take any chances. If we got married. Something came up. I got pregnant. Or—" Minnie nervously pushed back a lock of auburn hair from before mobile features creased in frown. "Something else comes up. I already heard about trouble with mothers-in-law. She's gentile, I'm not. If I had a baby, the baby would *have* to be Jewish. Suppose he didn't want to, or she didn't. I better end it while there's a chance. I'm going back to get my high school diploma."

"That's smart," Ira commended, with the approving pat of an older brother on her bare shoulder. "Lucky too, because it's a natural break."

"You know, I was really beginning to love him."

"Tsk, tsk." Ira sedulously wrung each precious minute of Mom's absence. "You poor kid."

Tears welled up in her eyes. "My dear brother. I got nobody else."

"Oh, you will have. You'll see. Right now you got Julia Richmond High School to keep your mind off him." God, why was he built that way; why did he have to *know* he was built that way? Conscious of a dual conscience: like Mercury's caduceus in the doctor's office, medical caduceus, with the two snakes twining up the single staff, twin sine curves intersecting at nodes: sin curves abbreviated in trig, sin curve was right, in frig . . .

He felt sorry for her, at these moments, he really did. He could let her grieve, be a brother, a real *mensh* of a brother, for once.

V

He could summon up the tableau at will, many years later: Edith standing in the open door of the weather-stained day coach of the railroad train. In a light sage summer dress, figured with pale vines, petite, olive-skinned, she stood framed within the gunmetal sides of the railroad car that appeared to have slid apart to make room for the slight figure between. It was Edith Welles herself, her large, heavy-lidded brown eyes searching, seeking for a familiar face among the few people awaiting the train. The station had no platform, only stout planks between tracks. And while the gold-spectacled conductor in his blue uniform, with his immemorial brass plate on his visored cap, and his heavy gold chain across his vest, stooped paternally to set the snub pair of wooden steps to supplement the iron ones on the train, she continued to survey the scene before her. Her chin was tilted, which gave her whole mien an aspect of defiance, proud defiance and determination. And yet, about the large brown eyes, and the brow under its black cloche, something contrary hovered, something akin to doubt, to concern. Within a bland, September-sunlit doorway of a day coach, a small figure, her countenance selfdenigrative, but still brave, she peered into the light drenching the primitive station that was Woodstock.

At the hail of her joyful young lover, she smiled, tenderly, ruefully, resignedly, as if accepting her foolhardiness and folly, as if claiming her prerogative of enjoyment at her own deliberate act of imprudence. Pleased and unbeguiled, she descended the iron steps of the day coach to the wooden ones below, steadied in descent by the conductor, who solicitously relieved her of the suitcase she was carrying—in the one hand—and set it down on the planks below, while she held on to her black portable typewriter case in the other. And in the dusty train windows, faces of passengers, contemplative and discreet witnesses of a glowing reunion of a handsome youth bounding with a cry of unrestrained rapture to greet the new arrival, a woman of indeterminate age, not girlish, though girlish in figure, girlishly diverted by the brimming ardor of the youth who took her portable typewriter, her suitcase, and guided her to the single taxi already engaged and waiting. . . .

Eyed by the departing passengers in the train windows, the two would be left behind forever, it seemed to Ira, who trailed, conscious of his inveterate, twofold role of being part spectacle, part spectator—the two would be left behind in unresolved attitude, while the passengers themselves would be borne away to their obscure destinations.

A wave of the conductor's arm. He stepped aboard the train, in his hand the stumpy auxiliary stairs. To the accompaniment of gleaming wheel and chuffing locomotive, the mystery of arrival and departure was accomplished.

The three got into the taxi. Not venturing to embrace, Larry and Edith sat hand in hand, gazing at each other. What transport of love Larry exuded, while Edith, indulgent recipient, patted his large hand with her tiny free one. And Ira, conscious of self as always, slum youth from a shabby tenement in East Harlem, privileged to assist at this wondrous, romantic encounter: so beautiful, beautiful, yes—and beyond him, as someone in limbo, or on the other side of a diaphanous, intangible partition of blissful, acceptable amorousness, of love, love, the state he was barred from. He had forfeited empathy, or ruined it. Yes, once again, who would understand? He had ruined it by knowing the end before knowing the beginning: knowing the shattering consummations, but torn out of the context of tenderness, the sanctity of tenderness and affection he witnessed here—that was it. By craving, or cravenness, stealth, or collusion, coupling having once united him with Minnie, now Stella, only to bar him from all else that love meant. "Don't kiss me," his sister had said. And Stella, except that once, who wanted to kiss *her*? Watching you come in her astride, her shallow, wide-open blue eyes glazing in orgasm. So where was love? Love, shmuv, shove.

They had come there to spend the two weeks just before college opened, to tryst in the mellow old stone cottage on the outskirts of the town of Woodstock. Enchanting to Ira, unbelievable the freedom within unity, of its random, stony façade that seemed to draw its enduring strength from the rambling white veins of lacy mortar that bound rock to haphazard rock. The house gave him a sense of nestling in continual shade, whether of vines clinging to the walls, or the large trees overshadowing the front lawn, or the sunken front entrance in a corner, a sense of shade—and seclusion. Even the mowed backyard, a retreat rather than a yard, though open to the sky, was walled about with a high and stately, yet rustic wall. Green lawn, late flowers, flagstones embedded in turf, shaded by hemlocks above. Natural beauty everywhere floated on the surface of sensation—anchored unseen below by sights and scenes of East Harlem.

The house had been made available to them by John Vernon, Edith's colleague in the English department. "My fairy godfather," Larry quipped. Not that John owned the place. It belonged to his sister, who planned to join her husband, a corporation executive, at present in Scotland. With great aplomb, with worldly urbanity, Larry met the very finical, well-nigh askance scrutiny of the proper mistress of the estate, and won her over with a convincing display of responsibility, maturity, and appreciation of the antique charm of the appointments and decor. They conferred about kitchenware and facilities, the care of the grounds, the gardener, who would come in at least once during their stay, and his wife, who was the cleaning woman. Debonair, yet deferential, Larry listened with close attention to all the lady's instructions. In the end, obviously satisfied the place would be well cared for, she named, as she said, a nominal sum, little more than would cover the utilities. Larry made out a check, a blank check, which Edith had already signed, and handed it over to the lady—who, after a glance at it through her lorgnette, stood for the briefest interval, contemplating Larry. Never had he looked so expressive, handsome, and worldly-wise. . . . All this while, to one side, scarcely taken note of, stood Ira, like a mute in a play, hat in hand, hearkening intently, feeling his face flicker with the wonderment within, but too bewildered with novelty to grasp more than the merest snatches of what went on.

They were alone that night, Ira and Larry, after Larry telephoned Edith to confirm that he had successfully obtained occupancy, and the place was beautiful. She called him the next morning to tell him what train she was taking, and when it would arrive. It would reach Woodstock by late afternoon, and though Larry chafed with impatience, Ira secretly welcomed the interlude. It gave him time, time to orient himself, accustom himself to utterly new surroundings, isolate their elements, hedge them within memory. He was grateful for a chance to admire, humbly and slowly to appraise simple elegance, and to try and judge what made it elegant. Again and again he felt like shaking his head: he shouldn't be there; he was learning too much, and hardly understanding what he learned, just feeling it. Yes, he wanted to learn. But he was too susceptible, impressionable, or something; he was being—he was being spoiled. That was funny. He didn't really mean spoiled; he was being moved away, further away than ever before, from his customary round of existence, his established base, like being moved away from his center of gravity—and once moved, he couldn't return. Elegance didn't just grow, didn't sprout out of having a lot of possessions, a lot of money, being wealthy, a *pooritz*, as Mom would say in Yiddish, a magnate. None of that by itself made for simple elegance. It went beyond that. How should he say it to himself? That's what was spoiling him: taste. He could feel it right away—like that feeling he got inside the brownstone house into which he mistakenly delivered his first Park & Tilford steamer basket when he was twelve. He was vulnerable to it. It made his mouth water like something delectable: good taste. The rough gray flagstones before the sunken entrance to the cottage, the thick rich ivy draping the fieldstone walls. And the flowers and shrubs, he didn't know what, between cottage and road. The spruce tree sentinels before the house. And inside, in the big living room, the fireplace wrought out of boulders, under the mottled marble mantelpiece, and the brass andirons, so appealing, Hessians in Revolutionary-time uniforms, in tall, imposing hats. And on the wall, paintings of early Americans, in the colorful vests and knee breeches, against a background of light blue, and women in high white bonnets. You could really study them, portraits of once living people, maybe the owner's own ancestors, in their wrought-gilt frames posing so tranquilly in the azure atmosphere of another age. And those opulent and *plain* wooden chests, and the sideboards with deep mirrors, and those spindly high-backed rocking chairs, and settees and divans with striped cloth. And that lustrous piano—and even the round, rotating piano stool with wood that was warm and dense and rich.

He went outdoors again, to the lawn in the backyard: leafy-covered walls surrounded it, walls conferring delicious privacy, communion with sky and cloud. On the grass stood filigreed iron garden furniture, so white, so heavy—how lovely to eat out there. So informal, so lovely and pleasant everything. Elegance. What else should you call it? And now all of a sudden, go back in your mind to East 119th Street, near Park Avenue and the Grand Central overpass, the stoop with the kids sitting on it above the cellarway, the dark hallway after the battered letter boxes, the dingy stairs, climb them, enter the scrubbed kitchen, clean and bleak, Jesus, and after it, through the railroad flat with the vile air shaft on the way. It wasn't fair: Mom and Pop arguing about how much allowance was still coming to Mom for the week. Arguing about the relatives, about money, about who ought to pay for the new washline. Upbraidings and beratings, and Jesus Christ, his own machinations and designs, having devised secret snares for Minnie right in the house, while Pop and Mom argued, right there, around the kitchen table, figuring out enticing webs, disarming wiles. Like a crook casing a joint for the best entrance. Best entrance was right. Wasn't that funny? Now that she had dismissed her Rod, her "*goyish* feller," Minnie tried to steer clear of her brother, steer clear of Ira, suspicious of him still.

But, boy, was he a coaxer, when he wanted to be, what was the word? What a wheedler, wheedler, yeedler. Cajoler, cadger. Well, what could you do? He wanted it, and having seen when he was eight that rusty pervert pull off, his scum dripping from the tree, he just fought it; he wasn't going to do it. Nearly every time he did, he felt like cutting his prick off afterward, as if he'd sunk to something worse than he already was: like "Joe," that pederast in a porkpie hat. Anh, kill yourself, you bastard. No. Better to assume his well-practiced fake negligence, say he would walk to Mamie's, show his duty to Zaida, pay his respects to the old hypochondriac. Sure his grandson was a louse. But to whom wasn't it fair? Were they doing him a favor? Right away his head turned into a mulligatawny, the word he read in a book, a farrago. Why couldn't things be straightforward within his mind, the way they were within Larry's mind, clean, unlittered, instead of always crisscrossed with shunts and with crazy Moebius detours, like those Dr. Sorel showed the math class? Why?

And he had to be careful, on guard. It was just at these times of baffling rumination that Edith would regard Ira with her large, solemn eyes, trying to fathom him, and he would hang his head slightly, and grin. Step up and call me crazy Moebius the Dopius, he should have said to her, and maybe made her laugh. But then she would have asked him to explain. And hoo-hoo, that crawling, infested mire he had inside him; his hideosities, he called it, admiring his triple portmanteau. Even to hint of it, even as close as he had come with Larry, was unthinkable. But what the hell, enough of that.

He tried to think, those two days while he and Larry were awaiting Edith—and after she arrived. He tried to think of matters outside himself—in this sumptuous house he was living in, in this all but bizarre situation. He tried to think, to conjecture, to grope toward motives: perhaps Edith was deliberately coming to test the feasibility of marrying her young swain, as he had continually implored her to do. Perhaps not. The idyll at Woodstock might be a defiant assertion of her right to a private life as a woman in a male-dominated world, as she so often emphasized. Defiant. But necessarily cautious, because it *was* a male-dominated world, and her livelihood, her position at the university, could be jeopardized. Her own and the welfare of those dependent on her, her mother, father, sister, all of whom she was supporting in part, the younger brother she was helping through college;

their welfare was in jeopardy, if her highly unconventional behavior was discovered—highly unconventional at best, turpitude at worst.

Foggy as Ira felt himself to be about all kinds of sophisticated matters like these, he couldn't escape awareness of how dangerous this adventure was for Edith, altogether different from his sordid ones, but just as clandestine. So alike in that respect, it made him all the more keenly mindful of the trust placed in him, all the more determined to deserve it, to protect Edith. She was violating accepted mores; she had to be circumspect, very much on the lookout for friends and acquaintances who might recognize them, and especially recognize Edith. What a scandal, what a commotion, that would whip up at the university! Certainly there would be much ado in the English department, that was certain. Confronted by it, Professor Watt, respectable and decorous head of the English department, for all his flirting with the unconventional in the hiring of his teaching staff, would undoubtedly protect himself by dismissing Edith. She could expect to be fired. A love affair with a freshman, an eighteen-year-old freshman. Bad enough with a graduate student.

So Edith was tense, on edge. The more so because Iola, who had agreed to join them in their rendezvous, and had all but decided to go when Edith did, reneged at the last minute, leaving Edith to bear the whole burden of exposure herself. An illicit ménage, Iola had blandly avoided it, disloyally too, shirking the debt she owed Edith, who had helped get her the position in the NYU English department. Edith was piqued, Ira disappointed. Edith attributed Iola's refusal to join them to the imminent return of Richard Smithfield, to whom she was as good as betrothed—if he opted in favor of heterosexuality, and not, as John Vernon hoped, homosexuality. Some such picture as that, Ira fuzzily gathered: Iola didn't want to offend her quasi-fiancé who would soon be returning to America on completion of his Rhodes Scholarship at Oxford. But Richard had been "raped" by a sodomist, or someone like that, in a taxicab in Paris, and the shock had unnerved him to the extent that he had become ambivalent about his own sexuality, uncertain in his relation to Iola. She was no longer sure of him.

But Ira had his own surmise to account for Iola's last-minute defection from the symmetry her presence would have conferred on the group: how the hell could a grown man get raped in a taxicab, Parisian or otherwise? A man, not a woman, get raped, without consenting? Christ, stop the cab, even if he didn't know French, and Richard, scholar that he was, must surely have known the language. And how would a man get raped? Open his fly, get at his cock, suck him off, pull him off, or what? Without compliance? Jesus Christ. Nah, the guy must have had half a mind to submit to the experience. No wonder Iola was beset by doubts, and Vernon was licking his chops in anticipation.

Iola would have taken a chance and joined Edith, made it a foursome. There was plenty of room, and bedrooms and bathrooms, in the fine two-storied abode. No, he himself was the reason Iola declined to accompany Edith: it was his irresolute, his tenuous appeal, his wavering sex appeal. The supposition refused to be lulled or staved off: it was his timidity, his shyness, his accursed flimsiness of libido because of what he had become, or had made of himself, with his never ending steeping of himself in incurable guile and guilt, stealth, fear, degradation, and worst of all, in an ambience of violated taboo. No, he had wrenched normalcy apart forever, for aye and for good, that terrible afternoon, when only a few problems in plane geometry leashed frenzy from committing murder. Leashed madness, yes, but gnarled something in the mind too far, irrevocably. That was how it felt.

That was how it was. That was why Iola didn't join them. What would Richard have known about it if she had? John Vernon wouldn't have told him. He might be a homosexual, but he was honorable: look what he was doing for Edith, like a good sport who had lost: securing this wonderful place in Woodstock for her and her young lover. No. It was he himself who was to blame. Iola could sense his vitiated manhood, suppressing virility, his shrinking from adult encounter. No. Ruined for the rest of his life his—his—ability to rise to the occasion. Yeah, some joke. That time she took the rolled-up papers out of his hand—rolled-up prospectus of CCNY courses of study, or something like that, after his "Impressions of a Plumber" appeared in *The Lavender*: "You've written another piece? For me?" She reached out her hand and took hold of it, her blue Scandinavian eyes sinking into his as she reached for the scroll. God, you get the cuckooest ideas, you know: phallic, her holding it, veiled incitement in her gaze. But no, he didn't have a manuscript for her. No. Goddamn it. How arch she was, that afternoon, that matinee, when they had all met on the upper balcony of the Theater Guild to see Shaw's *Arms and the Man.*

A dark fearful anguish once more assailed him in a way it hadn't for a long time, and he smiled drearily at Iola's teasing. Christ, yes, no doubt about it: he had telegraphed once again his botched virility. So why the hell should she come here and join them, if he had nothing to offer? Not Richard she was concerned about, but Ira, his perceived lack of phallic response. He saw in her droll, Scandinavian-thin features that she could be wanton. She could flirt, and did. But what did he have to offer her? Nothing but his rolled-up CCNY course summary. Epitomized it: braided-haired blond woman provocative in green dress, coquettish before curtain call to *Arms and the Man. Arms and the Man!* Jesus, everything scrambled around in horny symbols, and you, paralyzed long ago by the illicit—you, riven by shameful false alarms—flinched away from the overture. But hell, months ago you could have asked her to stroll through the woods of Bear Mountain, if you could have screwed your courage, as Bill Shakespeare said, to the sticking point. But you couldn't. So goodbye. You stripped your threads, or most of 'em. . . .

They settled down in their elegant quarters, each in a different study by day. At night, Larry and Edith shared the same bedroom, the master suite at the other end of the house. Ira had a smaller one off the hall near a separate bathroom. Mornings were fresh and crisp—the three breakfasted in the kitchen. By noon, the day had warmed enough to have lunch outdoors on the white-painted iron furniture on the lawn enclosed by the high stone walls. Larry usually prepared breakfast, though sometimes Edith did, with Larry—or Ira—squeezing the oranges on the latest leverage orange-squeezer. Luncheon consisted of soft-boiled eggs and asparagus, or chicken à la king out of a can, and boiled fresh peas and carrots. She needed bulk, but had to avoid too much roughage, she said, because she had colitis. Ira ate ravenously as usual, barely able to keep from wolfing his food, at each meal consuming twice as many slices of bread or toast as both Larry and Edith. Talk about roughage: nothing was better than bread, good loaves of Russian rye or heavy pumpernickel, not fluffy slices in packages. Boy, if it were up to him, he'd have eggs, he'd have lox, he'd have chopped tomato-herring and onions for breakfast. But he had to try and behave, to avoid *chompken,* as Pop chided him for doing: masticating out loud. "When the *fress* falls on him, he's like one possessed," said Pop. And even Larry called him aside and said gently, "I don't mind, but you ought not smack your lips after every mouthful."

Ira was surprised—and embarrassed. "Gee, I do?"

"Yes. It's very noticeable."

Ira was penitent, silent.

"You don't mind my telling you?"

"Oh, no. I'll try to stop. Anything else I do wrong?"

"It isn't wrong exactly. It's just a habit."

"I know. But you might as well tell me," Ira urged. "You know how it is: you know what it is."

"Do you realize you keep saying 'gee' all the time?"

"I do?" Ira suddenly realized he did. "Boy!"

"And 'boy,' too," said Larry.

"Oh, boy."

Larry chuckled.

"Gee, I'll try. Boy, I'll try. I mean it."

Edith's portable chattered away a good part of the day. She had two reviews of books of poetry to do, one for the Sunday *New York Times,* and one for *The Nation.* She didn't think much of the verse in either book, she said, and neither did she get paid very much for the reviews, but she was especially pleased to have made a contribution in the *New York Times*: small as the notice was, it was her first. Larry read the book, read her review afterward. They discussed it. Ira was given the book of poems to read, and scratched his earlobe apologetically: "I don't know. I read it, and I don't understand it."

"Oh, you do too!" Edith refused to believe. "Anyone as sensitive as you are."

"I mean, I know the words. And I get the similes too. But I don't get the—" He gesticulated. "I don't get the jumps from one thing to another."

She and Larry laughed.

She wrote letters, many of them, dashed them off, like those he had received from her when she was traveling in Europe. The typewriter clacked without pause. She was rewriting some of her lectures too, those on modern English and American poets. Glancing at the thin books strewn on her table, Ira secretly marveled. She had brought them along in her suitcase: books of poetry, by Wallace Stevens, by Elinor Wylie, by Archibald MacLeish, by Edith Sitwell. How could she extract meaning from all that disparate, oblique wording? It was beyond him. How could she perceive so much, type so much about what she read? It mystified him, when he leafed through the pages; the poems were either too opaque to penetrate, or they were like a wide-open grid through which he fell, missing gist to grab on to, missing enlightenment. He was ashamed to admit it. He looked at a poem that was given him to read, nodded appreciatively, or tried to show his appreciation by illuminating his features with pleasure, like a glowworm. Why didn't they say what they meant? They didn't have to say something simpleminded, like Longfellow's "Village Blacksmith." But why couldn't they say what the particular figure of speech meant? Say it was this or say it was that. Or come close enough to the meaning so that he could comprehend it, and maybe even be moved by it, the way he was by Robert Frost in the Untermeyer anthology: "The woods are lovely, dark and deep, but I have promises to keep." Anybody could guess what that meant. Or the poem by Baudelaire, "L'Albatros," that Iz Rabinowitz, who was going to major in French, showed him: *"Le poète est semblable au prince des nuées . . . ses ailes de géant l'empêchent de marcher."* Gee, that was good. He felt like that himself sometimes: a prince in fantasy, and a dub in practice.

Maybe he *was* both.

The first two days after they moved in, while Edith in the master bedroom industriously plied her portable typewriter, Larry sat in the library, reading the book Edith had brought from France. When not reading, he devoted himself to writing poetry, "lyrics" as he called them, which he returned to in the evening, when he felt the poetic mood more strongly. Ira took naps, and brought back staples and groceries. Or, still hopeful that his interest in biology would revive, he sat in the sunny, enclosed yard, studying the biology text that he had brought with him. It was an outmoded Biology 1 text, which he had gotten from a sophomore for nothing, because it was being supplanted next term by a later edition, and the college bookstore refused to buy the outmoded one back. "The bastards don't want it," said the sophomore. "Here. You can have it." So Ira conned pages of mostly familiar material, alternated reading by catching grasshoppers, and with his jackknife crudely dissecting them. Oh, he knew every part of a grasshopper—its name and function, the spiracles and the mandibles, the ovipositor and the tarsi. He could draw a diagrammatic sketch of a grasshopper's anatomy from memory. Maybe next term, not that he didn't have to compete with sophomores or with droves of bright, incoming freshmen eager to get started on their medical careers, Biology 1 would be open, and he could get started on his own career. He could test his own interest again, awaken his forte maybe. For Edith's and Larry's edification, Ira discoursed learnedly about the grasshopper, its anatomical features and exoskeleton, the insect's species, genus, phylum. "You know, the funny thing is," he observed, "I think they're kosher. I think Jews can eat them. I'm not sure why, but I think that was because they spent forty years in the desert, and maybe that's all they could find to eat sometimes. Gee, I'd like to find out what the rabbis think the ravens fed Elijah, whether it was grasshoppers or what? I must remember to ask my grandfather when we get back. He lives in Harlem now with my aunt Mamie."

Edith would just sit with her tiny hands in her lap and gaze at him with her large, brown eyes fixed on him unwaveringly, the expression on her face sober, yet, to Ira, inscrutable. What was she trying to plumb? Larry seemed to welcome the disquisitions; he encouraged them. Still, he really didn't seem to listen—that was the peculiar part of it. He sat receptively with big hands locked, but it was clear his mind was elsewhere—about what? a poem? And yet Ira got the feeling it wasn't that, something else was disquieting Larry, and Ira's lectures about biology filled a kind of troubled interlude in his friend's mind. Where the hell Larry got his ideas for poems anyway, Ira didn't have the slightest notion, but he seemed more and more receptive of late to Ira's impromptu lectures. A little puzzling, wasn't it? But if that was what Larry wanted—

"They're called Orthoptera, because they have straight wings,"

Ira discoursed. "You know, insects are cousins to crustaceans, like the lobster. But just the same, Jews can't eat lobster. Isn't that funny? My father once when he waited at a fancy banquet ate so much lobster that was left over on the plates he got sick and threw up."

Edith laughed. Larry smiled—absently.

"My Uncle Moe loves lobster too. But not clams. He can't eat a clam."

"Why not? They're seafood," Edith said. "Is that the kosher thing again?"

"Oh, no, they're neither of them kosher." Ira hesitated, grinned apologetically. "Boy, have I got myself into it. It isn't very nice. It's because of what people commonly call them. Common people call them."

"What do they call them?"

"It isn't nice. I said I'd get myself in trouble."

"Heavens, Ira. I'm not that squeamish. Do I seem to be?"

"No."

"Then why not tell me?"

"Another time. I know, I'll tell Larry. I'll leave it up to him."

Edith smiled, unenlightened, but indulgent.

There came a day, the third or fourth day after Edith had joined them, on which one of those not entirely casual episodes occurred, not entirely casual because it seemed fraught with remote rumor, or stirred by a hint of challenge. It would only be later, when all that remained of the environs of the incident was the spacious, quiet living room in which the incident had taken place, later condensed into a workaday patch of daylight, with a woman standing in it. The woman was Edith, and with simple generosity, she proffered a book, a fairly thick volume, proffered it to Larry. It would only be some time later that Ira came to realize the import of what took place in that elegant living room in that small fraction of time. And yet, the very fact that the event left behind, however small, an irreducible knot within memory would forever mark in Ira's mind the momentous instant of transition when the past departed from its old aim, its previously envisaged future, to a new one, the instant when sensibility redirected its commitment from an old to a new function.

The book that Edith held out to Larry was one she had brought with her from France. She had smuggled it through customs, a blue paper-bound book, an untitled copy of James Joyce's *Ulysses*. And that was something else to mark, to note about her—the errant insight fluttered through Ira's mind—that behind her steady, gentle gaze, deception could lurk, duplicity within the friendly dimple of her smile. Yes, she had broken the law deliberately, she explained, and she took pride in doing so, and was jubilant that she had succeeded. "It tickles me no end that I slipped the book through the barrier they've built around it," she said. "Of all the silly prudishness. As if a book that demanded so much from the reader could possibly impair anyone's morals. Only Mr. Sumner or other prigs like him in the Watch and Ward Society who hunted for the four-letter words might think a reader would take all that trouble for so little titillation. But anyone with ordinary common sense would know better."

She not only saw no reason to abide by the puritanical standards of the Watch and Ward Society, which she characterized as nothing more than a lot of inhibited prudes, but she was also genuinely curious about the book, which had won so much critical acclaim, on which so many encomiums were bestowed—by Eliot, by Pound, by other leading critics of English literature, critics who appeared in *The Hound and Horn* and *The Dial*. She wanted at least to become acquainted with it. Above all, she was eager to have Larry read it. She hoped that its daring literary innovations might provide impetus to his own writing, might steer his imagination into uncharted regions. "It may give you some new ideas, darling," she said, when she tendered him the blue-covered volume. "I'd love to hear your reactions. It's made such a clean break with convention. And of course it's so daring in its treatment of sex."

"You're so sweet to do it." Larry kissed her. He took the book from her, leafed through it, glowed with pleasure. "I don't know how else I'd have gotten to see it. And speaking of taking a chance." He shook his head in admiration. "I've gone through customs coming through Bermuda. Even with nothing really valuable to declare, I shook in my shoes. I don't know if I'd have had the nerve to look those customs officials in the eye with this in my suitcase."

"Oh, poof. The worst that could have happened was confiscation of the book. They would have relieved me of it—if they had recognized that it was banned from the country, and that's dubious. And of course, I would have played innocent. I didn't know it was banned. I just hope it does something for you, dear, encourages you to experiment."

"And so do I." Larry opened to the first page, read: "'Stately, plump Buck Mulligan . . . *Introibo ad altare Dei* . . .' My Latin can certainly handle that. Well, there's no time like the present. Thank you, darling. This is just the right required reading for Woodstock." He kissed her again.

Edith fondly watched him depart for the library, and when he settled into an upholstered leather library chair, she went to her portable typewriter among the scattered papers, folders, and carbon sheets in her master bedroom study, leaving Ira to wander out to a seat in a white filigreed chair in the enclosed lawn and absently mull over the incident, while he studied the grass to catch sight of some unusual insect.

He had heard about the book. He had heard it spoken of with bated breath by the literary elite among his classmates, the vanguard aesthetes in the '28 alcove in the basement of the college. One of them, goateed Seymour K, though older than the average freshman, was already on the editorial staff of the CCNY *Lavender.* And it was Seymour who sought out Ira, in order to make his acquaintance: "Oh, you're the one who wrote that piece about the plumber?" he asked Ira. Seymour had a twitchy tic that affected one of his cheeks above his goatee, and when he heard Ira's diffident admission of authorship, his tic registered with great positiveness. Neither he, he told Ira bluntly, nor any of the upperclassmen editors had thought the thing ought to be published in a college magazine. It wasn't only an amateurish piece of writing, "it could really have been written by a plumber's helper." He laughed at his jest. It was only at the insistence of Mr. Dickson, the faculty adviser for the magazine, that the piece was considered at all, and eventually published.

Anyway, the CCNY literati were all conversant with *Ulysses,* the imposing literati like Leon S and Yarmolinsky and Lester H, upperclassmen and for the most part only names to Ira, but all reputedly bursting with modern trends in writing, who knew all about something called the New Humanism, who read *The Hound and Horn* and

The Dial, could descant on Gerard Manley Hopkins and sprung verse, and poets named Pound and Eliot and Wallace Stevens, and—they made Ira feel like a maundering dub without an opinion to his name. James Joyce's *Ulysses*—it was like a fetish to them, to the highbrows in the alcoves. The rare one who had read the book seemed invested with a veritable luster; he was like one inducted into an esoteric sodality, an ultramodern one. Even to demonstrate familiarity with the book warranted pretensions to the intellectual vanguard.

So here was Larry, not only a poet and writer, but one privileged to read the fabulous book of the decade, perhaps it would prove to be of the whole century. And after college opened, to meet, to mingle with the initiates on equal footing, mingle with the cognoscenti, the avant-garde of the class of '29, condescending even about the faculty of the English department, none of whose professors, they were sure, was privy to this supernova that illumined the literary firmament, in all likelihood had never heard of the *Ulysses*. But—

Two days after he received the volume from Edith's hands, Larry returned it. He had spent most of the last forty-eight hours perusing the book; then, frustrated, skimming here and there seeking a window of interest; in the end, irked, yawning with boredom, he gave up further investigation, and called it quits. "Thanks, my love," he said to Edith.

"Have you read it?" Edith asked.

"No, and I doubt if I ever will. I'm afraid I can't."

"I'm sorry. Is it too packed?" Edith sympathized. "As I said before, it's not light reading by any means."

"No. I didn't expect it would be. But oh—" Larry rolled his eyes up in comic bewilderment. "Oh, no. It just takes altogether too much work to find out how little happens in pages and pages of print. I'd much rather spend our next week together here doing something else—if you don't mind. I feel time's too precious to waste on something I'm not getting anything out of. Time with you, especially, darling."

"You do what you like," Edith urged tenderly. "That's more important than the book. Please, lad, don't feel you have to read it."

"I don't."

"You shouldn't, if it doesn't contribute anything to your literary development. I'm sure the book isn't for everyone, and might even be harmful to the lyric, romantic state you're going through. I should have thought of that, before I burdened you with it. I'm so sorry." Fondness and contrition mingled on her face as she held the volume in her hands. "I didn't mean to impose it on you."

"Oh, well, it hasn't done me any harm." Larry put his arm around Edith's waist. "It's satisfied my curiosity. I just wish you'd gone to all that trouble, taken those risks for—a little better—return." He smiled down at her.

"My beautiful lad." She looked up at him, her slightly protuberant eyes shining with adoration. "You do what you please. Just be the sweet, sensitive lad you are. You'll get there your own way, I'm sure."

Boyoboy—Ira tried to feign inattention, play the stock figure, the stock presence, which he thought was his role. But just look at the way they loved—the way fine, tender, sound people loved. Look at them: so unsullied their affection, their love, they didn't have to hide it, except for gossip that might endanger her college position, things like that, concessions to prudence—but otherwise, so pure, elevated, yeah. Boyoboy. As if your—Jesus, he hated to say it even to himself— your cock were a mile away, had nothing to do with your balls in this kind of seraphic love. Boyoboy. So what the hell *did* they do at night?

VI

The opportunity to read the novel devolved upon Ira. He was aware of a ripple of craftiness coming over him when Edith turned to him, saying, "Would you like to look at it, Ira?" and offered him the blue paper-bound book. He felt as if he were about to steal a march on Larry, good, kind, generous Larry. And yet there was no help for it. If Larry couldn't or wouldn't subject himself to this shibboleth of modern novels, he had to accept the consequences of his refusal. Yet Ira felt ruthless, nonetheless. He couldn't help it: he needed to enter any gateway of esteem far more than Larry did, any gateway of esteem, of prestige. Ha! Why had he clung so to Farley? And been deflected into the shameful disaster of Stuyvesant High? What an insight that was, yeah. Gone to Stuyvesant instead of Clinton for the same reason: because with Farley he entered a gateway of esteem. Why did he need to? On account of what he himself had become, had done to himself, damage inflicted on himself, that had never scathed Larry. Maybe Larry was right, for all Ira knew. The book wasn't worth all that tedious, unrewarding conning of all kinds of literary stunts, as Larry called them, just for the sake of the fancy panaches the vanguard of supercilious CCNY aesthetes who had read the *Ulysses* prided themselves as deserving to wear. The outcome was something Ira couldn't tell; he could glimpse things, all kinds of things, notions that had come to him unbidden when he saw his Composition 1 sketch printed in *The Lavender*—and also when Edith complimented him on his letters to her in Europe. Notions, farfetched fancies for one who wanted to be a zoologist—or a biology teacher. But you never could tell. One thing was sure: he would butt his way through the book, cost what it might, the *Ulysses* that Larry had just rejected. Still, maybe it was more than that, maybe it was the way one had to go. Fainthearted and shirker though he knew himself to be, he had a dullard's plodding tenacity within himself, an unsparing resignation to drudgery. The grind, they sometimes called it: the scholastic grind. And yet, he wasn't a grind. Discipline wasn't the right word either. He wasn't disciplined: he was a slouch, a *folentser,* as Mom so often railed at him, a sloven. Anybody could tell that. But he had—it wasn't a sense of destiny—goddamn it, that was too fancy a way of stating it anyway. A hunch? No, not even that. It came back to the same thing, some kind of spasmodic, dumb determination he was going to find a way out of *himself,* out of what he had gotten himself into, cost what it might. Larry didn't have to pay that kind of price. He didn't need to. Neither did most everybody else, classmates Ira had begun to hobnob with: Aaron, Ivan, Iz, Sol. They didn't need to either. Ira did. He needed to, and he was willing to pay the price. That was the only way he could put it into words for himself. What other way was there? What other gateway?

* * *

How does one treat all this—Ira thought—while the computer growled, and requisite amber primed the monitor into legibility—how does one treat of a literary antimony, attraction, repulsion, still eddying ecumenically in the same breast? Say you're treating the tender inception of a love affair, and at the same time completely cognizant of its rancorous termination? Oh, well, a minute's reflection would reveal that most of life was that way: the furious flouting of the once warmly espoused, the eviction of enchantment from the bosom, and its preemption by disenchantment—or worse: hatred. Any grown-up was familiar with the dyad, and any writer worthy of the name had dealt with it at some time in his life. He needn't have raised the question at all, Ira told himself, except that he was intellectually slower than most.

His disaffection with Joyce had been slow indeed, for at first he had regarded this book brought by Edith rapturously, his irritation growing at first imperceptibly, yet over sixty years later to reach this crescendo of loathing. Such was his disavowal of the greatest seminal work of English literature of the twentieth century. *Ulysses* had become to him an evasion of history; its author *resolved* to perceive nothing of the continuing evolution of Ireland, refusing to discover anything latent within the seeming inane of a day in 1904. History may have been a nightmare, but the ones who could have awakened him were the very ones he eschewed: his folk.

The man loathed, the man quailed before change—that was the crux of Ira's present aversion to his quondam idol. The book was the work of a man who sought to fossilize his country, its land, its people, to rob them of their future, arrest their ebullient, coursing life, their traditions and aspirations. Within the compass of a single day, he would embalm their élan in intricate irrelevancies, and mummify them in the cerecloth of correspondences. (What horrible analogies came to Ira: of the corpse and the ghoul, the corpse and the necrophile!) In short, even as evolution developed the predator from among its own kind, here was one in whom the wretchedness and degradation of his people had instilled such appetite, it amounted to a vested interest, to societal cannibalism. He opposed alteration of the wretchedness and famine of their lives. The sordidness these inevitably spawned became his stock in trade, his literary storehouse. For him to have transformed his contempt for "the sow that ate her young" into sympathy for the desperate strivings of his people to free themselves from abysmal want, from their proverbial *tha shane ukrosh* under British economic and social domination, would have required a complete overhaul of the haughty psyche that derided the very source of its identity, the Irish folk; would have demanded a complete humbling of that psyche, indeed its abnegation, its reversal, which alone could have effected the regeneration of that psyche. There was no other way.

—You know what that entails, do you?

Oh, I have some notion, Ecclesias. I too used my folk as mere counters in nugatory design. Far worse than the humiliation of nonentity, or the morose disorientation of lost identity, is the despairing contest between aging and a new beginning—

Oh, there was much more he could say—Ira felt himself flag—much more that had occurred to him in the heat of his antagonism to Joyce. What had changed Ira's view of Joyce so radically these last few years—Ira drew pent breath at the intensity of his introspection—what was it that had changed his view so radically? Ira's views of Joyce had changed, not suddenly, but irresistibly, the result of small dissents, cumulative contentions, that at length reached a critical point: the point of outright repudiation. Again the process was dialectical in character; his increasing discontent with his great master culminated by changing quantity into quality. The illustrious author, greatest prose writer of the twentieth century, from whom, wittingly or unwittingly, Ira had drawn method and guidance, to whom he turned as to a touchstone of tacit approval, to whom he paid boundless homage, the supreme author had renounced his people, renounced their trials, their yearning and their suffering. Even as Ira had renounced his, without slogan or fanfare, but to the same degree, as if Joyce were the very paradigm of the kind of severance it was incumbent on every genuine artist to do whose goal was greatness. But severance from folk had provided no exchange, certainly not the exchange Ira had expected, from a specific people to a universal one, from the parochial to the cosmopolitan. There was no universal transfer inherent in the severance, no pending renovation. Severance from a people meant just that: to be cut off from them. To be liberated from them, yes, but at the same time to renounce belonging to them, to remove himself from the opportunity to tap their inexhaustible diversity, their vitality and invention. The reaction, to borrow from the language of chemistry, went to an end: to an irreversible precipitation: a novel, yes, out of one's folk, out of solution, out of ionic interchange, precipitated into estranged immobilized sediment. And as had happened to Joyce, so, on a humble scale, to Ira. Oh, the analogy proceeded ineluctably (a word Joyce favored), proceeded clumsily, but ineluctably. Sequestered by his own monstrous ego, isolated from access to the dynamic vitality of his folk, Joyce crystallized the sterile precipitant of his art into pyrites of portmanteaux, the ultimate in antic medium, the ultimate in imposing stasis in human interaction. Unlike his great mentor, Ira couldn't go that far, neither did he care to try. He came to terms with his dearth, became resigned to sterility.

But now—and for some time—Ira's direction had changed, and changed to diametrically opposite to his original one, the one that had supplied the initial guide to his only novel. His new direction was diametrically opposite to that of Joyce. It was a direction *toward* a reunion with his people, growing with the passage of years ever stronger, more purposeful, more partisan, more informed, more steadfast. Even though at times it seemed to him that his reunion might be a reunion with a lost cause, that history and social change might overwhelm the small nation to which his spirit had fused in hope and pride, nevertheless, he clung all the more loyally to the midwife of his rebirth: *Israel.*

His people were Israel. Not the Diaspora, the mercantile, the professional, the urban, the business Diaspora, a people of the past, as far as he was concerned, who might well disappear in another century, and might do well to disappear—and from whom his estrangement had been very little reduced—but Israel! A people of the future, a people redeemed, redeeming their land, his people were Israel. Not some idealized country, but all of it, ranging from the slattern in the chain store to the snide male bus driver waggling insulting hand under his chin passing his female counterpart, who was driving her bus in the opposite direction; from the proverbially rude clerks and civil servants, from the exacting little despots presiding over desks in the post office, to the myriad of harassed, intelligent, and cordial folk, bearded or clean-shaven, observant or indifferent, the researchers at the universities, the keepers of fish ponds, drivers of tractors, cultivators of cotton fields under Mount Gilboa, harvesters of the avocado groves near the Jordan River. Kibbutz and *moshav* and posh hotel and run-down Tel Aviv seafront: Israel. It was Israel that had rescued him from Joyce, had rescued him from alienation, modified him even to tolerating the Diaspora. It was late in happening, true, but it *had* happened, and it succeeded in altering the orientation of the once withdrawn individual. Ah, for the gift to express the changes that had taken place within him, since the end of that withdrawal—the accession of judiciousness along with partisanship, of steadfastness along with deep concern. To Israel he owed a new staunchness of affirmation, a sympathy with people, a unity within and without, a regeneration, that by contrast made Joyce recede into the distance like a black hole, pathologic and pathetic, a black hole of English letters, beyond whose event horizon change become stultified, illumination became trapped, trapped and retarded as in *Finnegans Wake*. . . .

That was how he felt about Joyce *now*. Not when Edith tendered him the *Ulysses* to read. Not how he felt *then*. It was those two things, two strophes, toward and away from the altar, he had to bear in the same breast. Nothing uncommon, he told himself. It happened all the time. And yet, he knew very well, it didn't happen all the time. Would that the time spent in reverie on why it happened, why and when and where it did and didn't happen, would repay for itself with an answer, one that his limited analytical powers could set forth.

Still, two things had come out of his rendering of his cogitations, the one trivial, the other too late, though of immense importance in contributing to his understanding of himself. The trivial one he named an aphorism for an aphid, a wisecrack of dubious quality: *Sure, Bloom is some sort of hybrid; he's a Hybrew.* And the other was that in "analyzing" Joyce, in attempting to probe Joyce's character, Ira had stumbled on his own fatal, or near-fatal, weakness. It was one that he shared with Joyce, and probably was the reason for the intense initial affinity with the other: both sought escape from milieu, from environ of folk, and eventually succeeded—but in doing so, both arrested maturity. Oh, it would take time, it would take time to ponder *that* one anywhere close to its depth.

It was like a letter that one left unfinished, and returned to the next day. Ira had "saved" his day's writing, and switched off the device. And then he had ruminated further on his last statement, whether it truly reflected the actual state of things, that both Joyce and he had sought escape from milieu, from environ, and in so doing had arrested personal maturity. The realization came to him that the statement was not a true reflection of actuality. Rather, it was a surface observation. The truth was that during those first few years, when both identified with their folk, when both belonged to their people, perception was a window on the world around them, perception and its accepted setting of opinion and inference and practice. But more and more, as time passed, each driven by his own compulsions, each employed the activity of mind, of mentation, as a *baffle* against perception, against its accepted setting of opinion and inference and practice. Ira had sat well-nigh stunned by the realization, stunned and appalled: so this was what he had spent a lifetime doing? Not transforming his perception of reality into art, but transforming *mind* into art as a way of buffering, of screening out, reality. And now near ninety, he finally understood: he had continually, increasingly—until the act had become inveterate and automatic—responded to the buffer, to the screen, not to life-derived actuality, but from the resonance of the very thing that occluded actuality. . . . Too awful to think about, too awful to think that the revelation had come at the end of life. Crushing was the only way to put it. All those years of not perceiving, but responding only to the resonance transmitted by the protective sheath against perception. It was not something Kantian that he was discovering about himself (and Joyce), a *ding an sich*. It was the common response to ordinary perception shared by all mankind, but which *he* had learned to alter, to create by muffling the data of existence.

The first chapter of the *Ulysses* seemed delightfully narrative, pungent, wry, precisely focused. Above all, the writing flowed freely, as a sparkling stream of disenchanted realism. The light and air in the round tower was clear and crystalline; the seascape was glorious; stately Buck Mulligan bearing in his shaving articles was delectably sacrilegious. Ira wondered how Larry could have found impediment obstructing his enjoyment of the book: certainly not by Buck Milligan and his spoofing, his blasphemous intonings over his shaving mug, certainly not the arrival of the old milk-woman, and the badinage of the three youths in the tower. To him, the atmosphere of the narrative at first felt transparent, the movement and posture sharp, the tone engaging and natural. The chapters were brilliant—and

completely accessible. Ira was delighted, delighted and triumphant:
Ira understood it: the great, the redoubtable *Ulysses* of James Joyce,
all its nuances seemed open to him.

As the clandestine love affair circulated about him in the ivy-
covered stone cottage at Woodstock, the pages, even for Ira, began to
grow opaque, the story to grow labyrinthian, loopholes within a massive masonry. He could see what Larry had objected to, why he had
put the book down: it became a labor to read, an arduous, unrewarding groping, a groping often beset with perplexity, often in the
dark. All too often, he felt as if he were besieging a citadel of narrative bristling with devices to protect, to fend off comprehension. He
stumbled through long, esoteric passages that humiliated him by his
inability to understand. Never once did it occur to him to make any
association between the episodes in the narrative and the title; never
once did he descry parallels between characters and situations in
the novel and their Homeric prototypes, satiric parallels, ironic parallels, parallels of any kind. Sheer drudgery to endure, most trying
of all to contend with, was that the story went nowhere, with inter-
ludes, Bloom and the Citizen, Bloom's grief for his dead son,
Bloom's stagy *shmertz* at the hour of his cuckolding, Bloom consuming his "feety" cheese sandwich (Go know his fellow diners, gobbling,
gnawing, chomping, were Lestrygonians. Poor guys. How else do
working commoners eat?). As long as the pub was full of Lestrygonians, that's what counted: *Lestrygonians* (as later parsed by the Gilbert-
ian synoptic chart), *the Lunch, 1PM, Esophagus, Architecture, Constables,
Peristaltic* . . . Now, *there* was something to engross the consummate
artist, the construction of a learned three-dimensional crossword
puzzle.

Oh, despite that, there were many peepholes, there were a multitude of apertures through which one beheld facets of Irish urban
life, matchlessly depicted, his throbbing catalogs of locale and landmark. And yes, yes, not to forget, of especial poignance to Ira, that
rift in the dense texture of prose when the disapproving priest spied
the two young lovers emerging guiltily from the bosky seclusion of
their fornication. How like the two young Irish lovers who had saved
Ira from that rusty pederast in Fort Tryon Park, the one lover trailing
the other down the path, the flushed, glowing domestic, the depre-

cating, muscular swain, husky caretaker or freight-handler. How Irish that seemed to Ira, having spent so many years among the Irish, on an Irish-dominated street.

Yes, it was more than these now mundane observations that had enthralled him as a young man. Despite the carping of the dour, refractory old codger who, because he had himself reunited with Judaism in the form of Israel (and thereby had sharpened his once dull consciousness of being a Jew), had become the adversary of his renowned preceptor, and kept injecting his present bias, his revisions and reservations, into the impressions of the youthful reader that was once himself, the *Ulysses* was more than that. It was an immensely liberating experience for the as yet preembryonic literary man, the amorphous, larval novelist. Oh, it was not merely because of the trail it blazed, the conventions broken, the daring situational and verbal precedents it set, Bloom sitting on the crapper, Molly's monologue while menstruating.

They were of immeasurable importance in breaking down conventional barriers in literary representation. But more important than anything else, of supreme importance to Ira: the *Ulysses* demonstrated to him not only that it was possible to commute the dross of the mundane and the sordid into literary treasure, but *how* it was done. It showed him how to address whole slag heaps of squalor, and make them available for exploitation in art. Equally important was Joyce's tutelage in the sorcery of language, how it could be made to fluoresce, to electrify the mood and rarify the printed word. No more awesome master of every phase of syntax, no more authoritative mentor—nay, taskmaster!—of subtlest effects, subtlest distinctions of word or phrase, had Ira in his desultory way ever encountered than Joyce. Wryly, Ira remembered the old saying about the Chicago packing houses: that they used every part of the pig except the squeal. Joyce elucidated ways to use even the squeal: lingo as well as language, the double entendre, the pun, the homely squib, the spoonerism, the palindrome, pig Latin and pig Sanscrit.

*   *   *

So Ira read on, toiling doggedly through hundreds of close-knit pages, wrenching his brow in perplexed concentration, seeking denouement—going unrewarded, save for Bloom's escape from near-altercation with an Irish jingo, save for Stephen's smashing the gaslight in a whorehouse, and being punched in the jaw by a vociferous British soldier. Ira sought a meaning that was absent, without ever realizing *that* was the meaning. But as the days passed, and he read and wrestled, read and floundered, the strange conviction took firmer and firmer hold of him, that within himself was graven a crude analogue of the Joycean model, just as he felt within himself a humble affinity for the Joycean temperament, a diffident aptitude for the Joycean method. Opaque though many and many a passage might be, Ira sensed that he was a *mehvin* of that same kind of world of which Joyce was an incomparable connoisseur: of that same kind of pocked and pitted reality. There were keys that evoked that world, *signatures* by which they were recognized, and he was ever receptive to them—why, he couldn't say. He could summon up words that connoted those signatures, signatures that were keys to their quotidian.

What was there in that stodgy variety of Dublin city through which Bloom and Dedalus went to and fro that was so very different from the stodgy variety of Harlem's environs, the environs Ira knew so well—and the East Side environments that memory retained like a reserve of impressions? If a one-eyed Irish jingo heaved a box after the ignominiously fleeing Bloom, Ira had just as cravenly allowed a couple of micks to spit on his blue record card while he waited in line to enroll in P.S. 24. If Bloom knew the hour when his wife cuckolded him, what did that compare to Ira's knowing the equatorial hour on Sunday morning when Mom and Pop were gone? And worse, worse than anything Bloom ever suffered: that agonizing afternoon when murder flapped bat wings over his plane geometry text, because Minnie hadn't menstruated. And talk about the nastiness of the diurnal—talk about the absolute vertigo of furore of a chance weekday break, what was looking up a statue's buttocks compared to that . . . or the colossal jape of compassionate Mamie's sentimentally "forcing" a greenback on him, a buck, right after he had hoisted her drippy kid daughter, Stella, on his petard. Hell, of nastiness, of sordidness, perversity, and squalor—compared to anyone in the *Ulysses*, he had loads, he had droves, he had troves. But it was language, language, that could magically transmogrify the baseness of his days and ways into precious literature—into the highly touted *Ulysses* itself. It could free him from this depraved exile, from this immutable bondage. Sensibility and need, given language, could beat silence, exile, cunning anytime, especially if sensibility and need, given language, was a past master at silence, exile, cunning.

The forlorn backyards of tenements, the dreary, Felsnaphtha-mopped hallways, enlivened sometimes by homely emanations of cabbage (it could have been the spicy aroma of stuffed cabbage, the *hullupchehs* that Mom was cooking). Oh, the round iron coal-scuttle cover in the sidewalk, and the roar of coal down the chute, and the coal-streaked visage of the Irish toiler—the ex–hod carrier he might have been—down in the cellar, at the other end of the chute, lugging his basket of anthracite to the tenant's storage bin. It was in the cellar too where the one-eyed Jewish painter, the Cyclops of 119th Street, stored his paints and brushes and turpentine. Speak of the worn lip of the stoop stairs, the battered brass letter boxes in the foyer, the dilapidated flight of linoleum-covered steps past the window at the turn of the landing, and up to the "first floor." And oh, into the gloomy, narrow corridor, between the toilets of opposing flats, to the door under the paint-spotted transom light, the door that meant home.

Weren't fourteen years of school, from kindergarten to college, the raw material of literature? Didn't it qualify for alchemical transformation, like those chunks and hunks of iron the avaricious Puritans brought to the faker in the Ben Jonson play? If that was latent wealth in the domain of letters, why, he was rich beyond compare: his whole world was a junkyard. All those myriad, myriad squalid impressions he took for granted, all were convertible from base to precious, from pig iron to gold ingot. The kids rolling dice under the shadow of the railroad trestle on Park Avenue—ah, the very job of painting the trestle itself every four or five years! First, after the chipping, the undercoat of red, then the finishing coat of gray. Tell them, Ira thought, tell them what a simpleton you were: how you fancied they painted the trestle red first, not to provide it with a tough undercoat, but so they could see how far they reached with the second coat of gray. Such was the level of your boyhood inferences. You fancied that the huge stone ramp which brought the trains up from underground to the trestle at 103rd Street housed within it pirates and buccaneers. You could hear them wrangling over their booty, could hear the clash of steel from their cutlasses. . . .

Petey Lamb, the janitor's son, humping Helen under the stairs. The housewives setting out to shop in the Park Avenue pushcart market in the morning, summer morning, the immense, moted sunlight glistening on their black oilcloth shopping bags. And you watched Mom from the front-room window on a Sunday morning to make sure, shamefully, miscreant, craftily sure, traced Mom's steps around Jake's squat brown pile of a tenement, and disappearance around the corner. Ponderous Mr. Clancy, the street-repair foreman, mounting the creaking stairs at the close of the day: they actually creaked under his weight. Flora Baer, Davey's sister, whom you tried to get to play bad down in the cellar, but couldn't. The foam on top of the simmering pot of thin soup you sopped up with a crust of bread, and ate with relish: *Greasy Joan doth keel the pot,* a delicacy of destitution. Meanwhile Flora's scabby infant brother in his bleary high chair clutched a cockroach he had just grabbed in his little fist and offered to throw it into doting, ne'er-do-well cardsharp Papa's cup of tea; and dark with penury, the meager mother looked on.

No, you didn't have to go cruising o'er the billows to the South Sea Isles on a sailing vessel crowded with canvas, or fist a t'gallant, like a character in *The Sea Wolf,* or prospect for gold in the faraway Klondike, or float down the Mississippi in a raft with Huck Finn, or fight Indians in the young Wild West nickel magazines. You didn't have to be an escaped criminal like Jean Valjean or the Count of Monte Cristo in glamorous France, or a corsair with a cutlass clenched between his teeth climbing a hemp boarding ladder or a treasure hunter with a pegleg, or a swashbuckling swordsman like D'Artagnan. You didn't need Scottish moors or desert islands, and you didn't need tiger-infested African velds or the jungles of remote India. You didn't need to go anywhere, anywhere at all. It was all here, right here, in Harlem, on Manhattan Island, *anywhere from Harlem to the Jersey City Pier*: from the feisty Irish urchins who patronized the old Jewish couple's candy store, saying sidemouthed, "Gimme two o' deze, an' t'ree o' dem, and one o' doze," to the bigger guys who bought two Sweet Caporal cigarettes for a cent. "Oim as dhroy as a loyme-kiln." The sewer cleaner handed his helper the tin beer bucket. "Will yez rush the growler, me b'y." Garish though the contents of the great glass amphorae in Biolov's drugstore show window seemed during the day, how vividly ruby and emerald they glowed at night, suffused with incandescence. Language was the conjurer, indeed the philosopher's stone, language was a form of alchemy. It was language that elevated meanness to the heights of art. Like the irritating particle that bred the nacre of the pearl, language ameliorated the gnawing irritant of existence; it interceded between the wound and the dream.

What a discovery that was! He, Ira Stigman, was a *mehvin* of misery, of the dismal, of the pathetic, the deprived. Everywhere he looked, whole treasuries were exposed, repositories of priceless potential ignored, and hence they were his. It brought back to mind what he had just vaguely ruminated about when he had the impulse—an impulse he had suppressed—of sharing this unique world, this bonanza of penury, with Larry. It was *his* world—again he could feel the base, proprietary thrust of his niggardliness vindicate him: he had suffered for all this, earned it by years of indenture to the foul and the pitiful: to wraithlike old Mr. Malloy, seated in the sunshine before the wrought-iron cellar barrier of the tenement, sucking on his stubby, blackened clay pipe, with a rubber baby-bottle nipple at the end of the stem to protect his toothless gums. That vignette, that gem, was his, Ira's. Yonnie True on bare-ass beach between the freight tracks and the Hudson, standing on the diving rock, to which Ira in his anguish had once returned, sporting a Bull Durham sack on his dink, because, said Weasel reverently, Yonnie had a dose of clap— and Yonnie had just wriggled into Fat's tights, and who was Fat but Ira! It was indecent, but it was literary, and Ira had paid his fee in full for the right to use it. The repulsive and the graceful stood opposed; only language could bridge the gap. Ah, how to say it?

At Larry's suggestion, from the first day of their stay in Woodstock, he and Ira let their beards grow. Whether Larry's aim in their doing so was to foil casual recognition with a hirsute mask or to mediate the contrast between their callow youthfulness and Edith's maturity, Ira wasn't sure. Nor whether their droll disguise accomplished anything. His own beard flourished with surprising vigor, curly and black. For diversion, and again to lessen the risk of recognition, the three avoided town; instead they took long walks in the country, explored lonely dirt roads and lanes. With Larry and Ira on either side of her, Edith did most of the talking as they strolled along, edifying her young escorts about life in general, and her own in particular. When she dwelt on her own past, and she often did, she invariably adopted a matter-of-fact tone of voice, underplaying her role in the enduring of the many outrageous and tragic circumstances in her life.

Dispassionately minimizing, she conveyed the impression—which Ira could only feel, feel, but not define—of long-suffering innocence, of quiet, self-sacrificing fortitude. Listening to her talk about incidents in her past, Ira felt at times as if he were recalling passages of the few long-forgotten ephemeral romances he had read: of wistful heroines caught in the fell toils of villainy or baleful misfortune. Though most of the specifics had eroded, the contours remained and were still recognizable: *Edith was the heroine of her own drama.* She wasn't the kind of central character who struggled against the various impulses in himself, good or evil, and triumphed or surrendered: a Jane Eyre, a Dr. Jekyll, a Dorian Gray. No, no. She was a heroine in the tried-and-true tradition: kind, benign, brave, and unselfish. Ira recalled a line in one of her later poems: *My generous gesture gone astray.* She could have been right. Why not? Her gestures might always have been generous, and as often gone astray. But her life, when he came to know her, didn't present itself to him that way. Well, perhaps he was biased in his attitude toward her.

Ira mused on the sad, olive-skinned face that once was Edith's, the solicitous reproach in her protrusive brown eyes. He could have been wrong, he could be wrong now. Who was to say? *My generous gesture gone astray.* . . . On the other hand, M, his wife of more than fifty years, had never said anything of the sort, or implied anything of the sort, though she was to him the finest among women, the finest person he had ever known. But she was human, fallible, sensible and amused, acknowledging her needs, wants, appetites, foibles. Nevertheless, she was peerless among women. And an artist too, a musician, composer of growing note in her old age: Mother M, as Ira teased her. Well . . .

Edith spoke often of her unhappy childhood in Silver City, New Mexico, spoke as they strolled along the country road. Her tales of her inebriated father, her mother's refusal to have sexual intercourse with Edith's dad, a former—and fallen—legislator, her mother's favoring of her younger, inept sister, Lenora, were all familiar to him from earlier in the year. Larry had confided these secrets to his best friend during their evenings alone the previous winter and spring, and Ira had absorbed every word with the greatest of interest. Yet when Edith repeated these tales of personal travail, albeit with a new slant, Ira feigned astonishment and wonderment and thoroughly enjoyed hearing them from Edith in person, as if for the first time.

But many of the stories that Edith told them about literature, especially poetry, were new. And to these passions, she joined the study of anthropology. She long ago in New Mexico had become acquainted with the Navajo Indians. In the company of schoolmates, under the guidance of teachers, she had often ridden out to the Navajo reservation on horseback, and camped out in the desert. She admired the innate dignity of native Indians; she respected their oneness with nature, their reverence for nature. And as she did with all the oppressed, she felt a great sympathy with them, because of their mistreatment at the hands of the white usurpers of their lands, the ignorant and heartless desecrators of Navajo religious traditions and culture, in whose place they left a ruinous legacy of epidemic, depravity, and alcohol. Feeling as she did, it was natural that she would turn to their literature, learn their lore and language and their tribal and ceremonial chants. Later, when she embarked on her doctorate, she combined the two disciplines in a single study of Navajo poetry, its religious content, its rhythms, its structure and forms.

VII

Two or three times during their sojourn in the stone cottage, as the cooler evening skies presaged the imminence of fall, they ventured to walk the long, dusty, though pleasant distance upward to a fine restaurant, almost circular in shape, at the very summit of a hill. The dining room, large and shaded, was sparsely patronized, perhaps because of the lateness of the season, and this lulled their fears of recognition. Edith felt secure when they dined there, so secure that instead of choosing a table in an alcove or next to a wall, she chose one next to a window, because of the lovely view. Every window had its own panorama of mountains. The nearer ranges were solid with conifers, thick as the nap of a carpet, the farther ones less and less shaggy in appearance, until the last ridges seemed to lose opacity and become almost translucent. It was all so new to Ira, gazing out, half enchanted, at mountains, mountains in ridges like motionless waves, waves at the very last ready to blend into sky.

Larry took pleasure in his friend's rapture. "Enjoy it," he prompted. "That's why we're up here."

"Gee, do I!"

"You've never seen a mountain before?" Edith asked with that sympathy so inseparably a part of her. "Really?"

"In the Carpathians maybe, where I was born. But I don't remember them. In America," Ira tried being facetious, "I only know Mt. Morris Park."

"Where is that?"

"I'm just joking."

"It's near where he lives in Harlem," Larry explained. "It has a wooden bell tower on it. Quite a picturesque place. Without intending to be, you know."

"Really? I didn't think there were any mountains in New York. Even hills of any size."

"That's the biggest one I knew when I was little," Ira said, soberly remembering. "You know how it is to be a kid. The top once looked a mile high. But I've also seen Bear Mountain."

"I once intended to write a short story about the bell tower on top. It was a kind of alarm bell, mostly in case of fire," Larry said.

"Did you?"

"No. It wasn't so much because I lost interest. I realized I had a wrong view of Ira—and his neighborhood too. Quite different from what I thought."

"Why didn't you become acquainted with it? You had Ira here to ask."

"I know. But—something strange." Larry looked off through the window at the distant mountains. "That's something I can't answer." He drew in his round lips reflectively, then laughed shortly. "I realized that I really didn't know a thing about Ira. Or almost. All the things he told me about—say, the ball games where he used to hustle soda—he's told you about it too."

"Yes."

"They're different."

"Well, it's the same way when I went to your brother's dress-manufacturing loft there on 119th Street. You just take it naturally when you go in there. I get stiff self-conscious."

"You do? You never said anything."

"Well." Ira shrugged deprecatingly. "I'm not used to it." And a moment later added with uncommon quickness, "Like you, but opposite."

Edith looked from one to the other, appraisingly. "Larry is so much more worldly. I suppose that's the chief difference." And after a few seconds of silence, "Would you like another one of these French rolls?"

"I'll say. So crisp." Ira grinned apologetically. "I can't let this gravy go to waste. My mother says it's a sin."

"Does she?" Edith smiled.

"I'll order it." Larry raised his arm. "Oh, miss." And addressing Ira, "We can't let you do that."

"What?"

"Sin."

"Oh."

Larry and Edith laughed.

"I wonder what either of you would say to a real mountain out West?" Edith said. "To the Rockies, for example."

Ira noted with satisfaction that more than one roll arrived in the napkin-lined basket. "You mean because they're so high?"

"Oh, yes, the plain is a mile or more high. The mountains are two or more in some cases."

"Two miles up!"

"And not in the least friendly, the way these mountains out here are. We'd call them hills out West. People have become lost for days in the mountains near Silver City. In the Gila Wilderness, in the Mogollon, as it's called. People have actually died before they were found."

"Well, I—" Ira caught himself. "I almost died in Mt. Morris Park." They laughed.

"Are you serious?" Edith asked. It was typical of her to inquire into morbid details. "Did you fall?"

"Oh, no. I just slipped."

I just slipped, Ira thought. His eyes strayed from the amber monitor of his word processor to the east window of his study—at no great distance loomed the Sandias, two miles high at their crest, exactly the kind of mountains Edith spoke of in a dining room on the summit of a hill in Woodstock seventy years ago. Seventy years ago. Now he resided in the state of New Mexico, the very same part of the country in which she was born and once lived, in which almost certainly his life would come to an end where hers began. Elegiac, wasn't it? But elegies had nowhere to go. Best gobble a half-tablet of Percocet, like drinking at an oasis, and get back to the desert. . . .

One of his most salient recollections of their dining in the summit restaurant was his recurring qualm of embarrassment, to which he could scarcely refrain from giving utterance: he had no money, not even for the tip to the frilly-aproned young woman who waited on them and brought him repeated servings of rolls. And at Edith's and

Larry's assurances that it was all right, they'd take care of it, "I'm especially conscious about tips," he confessed.

"You are? Why?" Edith asked. "I honestly just make a practice of
giving them ten percent of the bill."

To which Larry added, "That's what everyone does. What makes
you so sensitive about tipping?"

"You forget? My father's a waiter."

"Oh, is that it?" Edith smiled at him sympathetically. "I suppose
it's bound to change your thinking about them."

Larry burst into a laugh. "I was a singing waiter. I told you about
Copake. It was only a few weeks, but I have to feel self-conscious
about it. I've been initiated."

"That's right. I forgot."

"Don't worry about it, Ira. You're our guest," Edith reassured
him.

"Thanks."

And they went riding on saddle horses. It was the first time in Ira's
life that he had been astride a horse. How politely bemused was the
look on the face of the attendant at the riding stable at the sight of
this curious trio: a petite, mature woman in riding breeches and
boots, completely at home in the saddle, easily managing her mount,
accompanied by two fuzzy-bearded youths, the one, self-confident
and handsome, who had evidently acquired a little experience as a
horseman, the other, who obviously had none.

Ira trailed Edith and Larry, who were walking their mounts, undoubtedly out of consideration for his inexperience. Conscious of
the ludicrous figure he cut on a horse, Ira was glad to get out of sight
of the stableman. Only the equally ludicrous overlap of memory: of
the kid who was himself behind Pop's favorite horse, Billy, riding in
Pop's milk wagon; or sitting in the driver's seat alone while Pop entered a small workshop with a few pint bottles of milk in his steel tray.
America, America: a step at a time, a phase at a time. Here he was,
from riding in his father's milk wagon through a cobblestoned city
street, to mounted on a saddle horse riding over a country lane. And

how pristine, how rare with hue, with shape and silhouette, with spareness, with contentment of being, the rural landscape poised toward assuming the crispness of autumn, audible in the crackle of a few fallen leaves under the stamping hooves of the living beast he rode. Assuming autumn both audibly and visible. For overhead, the branches of trees wore a garb that had become mottled now, a fabric of variegated green and brown. Grown dry and sparse, boughs yielded supremacy to sky, retreating in solitary leaves drifting down. And the rail fences, rustic and weather-beaten, crooked, gray staves, split and knotty, rail fences parted the dirt road from the stubbled field on the other side. How daintily Edith cantered ahead, wheeled her mount, and cantered back, so modest and unassuming, almost apologetic of her equestrian mastery, petite, sober-eyed woman, against autumnal azure in a primordial landscape.

The cat—

A few times, a very few times, Edith and Ira walked to the outskirts of the town, where she purchased an item or two from the general store there. Or again, they walked on a wooden path, Ira duly and respectfully keeping his distance, except when he felt he ought to take her arm a moment in token support over some obstacle. Once or twice she patted his hand in thanks. And the difference in the coolness of her hand and the heat of his own startled him: as if he were betraying what he thought, and what he thought was so tightly sealed within him, fantasies immured so tightly, no faintest trace could be detected. Still, incorrigible intimations kept cropping up in his mind, intimations that had no business being there. He was faithful, he was faithful to his friend. He strove to adhere, as impeccably as he could, a veritable stickler, to his notions of the role he was expected to play according to the tacit provisions of the covenant of his friend's romance with his English instructor. He strove to behave in such a way as to be a credit to the code of boon companionship, a credit to his own integrity, to his sense of appropriate behavior in such a situation. The least he could do to repay Edith and Larry for the trust they vested in him—and for all the privileges that went with it—was to comport himself with rigorous loyalty, conform to every tenet of uprightness—to behave with honor.

Yes, honor, that was the word that clung to purity of thought, in spite of self and the flicker of perverse promptings. He was determined to shield Edith from the brunt of *his* nasty world, and yet at the same time, he wished to draw Edith *inside* his world, a peculiarly complex world dominated by complex numbers, imaginary numbers, where ordinary rules often applied with extraordinary results, where he could think of Edith with chivalry and knightly probity, where both could abide by the rules of fairytales. While he wished to shield her from his own unimaginable bondage, he believed he hankered for her to recognize what he was, was endowed with; was destined one day to win her consent, her passionate consent, because he sensed it was *that* more than anything else which appealed to her, that kind of depth, of range, of imagination, abominable, desperate, reckless, but boundless. Hadn't he done those things? Wasn't he that way? He had breached the margins of fantasy; he could reach out and collate all manner of loony tag ends of the world. He could do all that, and at the same time do his utmost to act, to try to think and feel as he was expected to—as he thought he was expected to: be preoccupied with grasshoppers and with Joyce's *Ulysses*; seem phlegmatic toward sex, seem inoculated against romance, seem oblivious. And he thought he succeeded. He prided himself that he had—oh, that was no trick for him, that kind of dissembling—*except* how to dissemble completely, how to dissipate the remnant of that familiar and impermissible incitement that caused a recalcitrant shifting from his vile and predatory practices into the chaste world of Edith and Larry's love affair.

He was sure that was it, that it was his vileness that spawned those despicable, immoral notions when he was alone with her, that he needed only to take her hand in his, that she wanted him to take her hand in his, transfer the heat of it to her coolness, impress his desire upon her, not by a token, not by a tentative touch, but by forceful possession. And she was prepared to answer in kind. If he took the initiative to carry matters further, she was poised to reward betrayal of friend with betrayal of lover. What nuttiness! Jesus! He was projecting his own shameful proclivities. That was all it was, nothing more. Make a pass, like a mug from his East Harlem street. Make a pass, as if she were—not Stella—he didn't make passes at her; he got right down to business first chance, wasted not a second. Nor as if she were some floozy on 119th Street, Helen, receptive in the hallway, as Petey Lamb had prompted. Jesus, he didn't know how to make a pass at someone refined. What would he do? What a fool he'd make of himself, worse than a fool, reveal who was really behind that artless, that pretend-abstracted, callow dreamer he strove so earnestly to appear. Disastrous. Wow! What would happen to her opinion of him, to his reputation? And if she told Larry—boyoboy! His contempt. No, no. Never mind the impulse in him that she aroused by her intangible tension, the meaningful momentary gravity of her features, that emanation of aloneness, like something sealing the two together. Nothing doing. It was a figment of his own construing. Lucky he had sense enough, a last iota of self-control—shyness enough, thank God—to interpret things right, keep himself in check, avert exposure, fiasco. Boy! Lucky he didn't get a hard-on just then—

It would have been a snap had he been someone else. And he knew he was right. He knew. Of course. Poor woman. Oh, to have been a mannerly roughneck! Some stud off 119th Street: *he don't know no better, see?* But then, he wouldn't have been there, in Woodstock, playing the role of the wool-gathering patsy.

Ivan, you remember my friend Ivan?

—Are you speaking to me?

Yes, Ecclesias. Edith invited him to dinner in her apartment, dinner she had cooked herself, when we were both still CCNY undergraduates. Strong-thewed Ivan, crack hurdler once, and promising physicist, with a score of 168 on the Binet IQ test. And he said, oh, many years later, as we sipped the twelve-year-old bourbon he had presented me with, said, as we sat outdoors in the shade of the mobile home before supper, that on the evening on which Edith had invited him, he had shaved as closely and dressed as neatly as he knew how. He was in a swivet to appear at his most presentable. And they had dinner, he and Edith, and they talked. And after a decent interval, after a proper visit, he thanked her for the delicious meal she had prepared, and took his leave. Here Ivan began to perspire. Even in the reminiscing, he mopped his brow, mopped it repeatedly. And regret, never more palpably—never more palpably did regret wring a man's features.

"I thought that was all I was invited for," Ivan said. "To have dinner in her apartment. The things you don't know when you're young." Never more wan did a man look, contemplating his past, nor more slowly, lugubriously, shake his head.

I chortled, Ecclesias, I chortled cruelly at the spectacle of my friend's rue. "I thought I was the only one imprisoned in my regret," I said. "Incarcerated in crestfallen repinings, you might say."

But he wasn't diverted by my glee, Ecclesias, nor shared it in the least. His was the intelligent face of a man studying the irrecoverable—for the *n*th time—not to recover a lost sensation, but to alter the course of his life: "Too bad," he said. "I might have got over those damned inhibitions a lot sooner, inhibitions that were killing me. I could have gone on and got my doctoral at Columbia, instead of an ulcer that cut it short."

"And swelled Edith's undergraduate trio to a quartet," I twitted. "Too bad is right. We could have had something else in common, you and I." I could just see Edith, after her young guest left, daintily shrugging off mild disappointment before the mirror, while her little hands bunched about an earlobe, removing an earring. . . .

And Ira cackled again . . . as wickedly as he had then . . . and thought awhile. No, there was more to it than that. Reverie held inestimable reserves. What if he had said to her—what if he had confessed the truth, as he eventually did, *though many months later.* While on one of those walks, what if *he* had done the talking—implored, thrown himself on her mercy, then blurted out, "Edith, there's my sister, she continually preys on my mind, continually overpowers me. These are the circumstances, this is how it happened. There's my kid cousin, Stella. My aunt Mamie thinks I come there for the dollar she gives me, her nephew, the indigent collegian. Listen, I know all about sex, sex that's wrong, horribly wrong. I'm driven wild by it. . . ."

Then what? No. Impossible. Impossible for him to confess. Confess against or through the rigidity of the disguise he wore, the mask he lived behind? But how remorseless was the frenzy to wreck time, to demolish the past, the way—so it was said—professional house-wreckers were sometimes so carried away in their excitement to raze an old structure that they actually endangered their own lives. As there was rapture of the depths of the sea that overcame scuba divers, so there was rapture of demolition, demolition of buildings, demolition of the past. And she couldn't have resisted, could she? This exposure of who he was. She'd have made shift to rescue him. No? Of course she would. The strongest instinct in her was to rescue, to pacify, to allay another's need. The very thing he *was* was all the lure he needed. He needed nothing else. Jesus, wouldn't that have been a tricky situation, had it happened? A love-trust double-cross in that timeless stone cottage in Woodstock? Because in another time, in other surroundings, happen it did—

Assume he laid her in some bosky dell, Ecclesias, as once in fact he did, in some bosky dell by the side of the road, betrayed poor, gentle Larry. Hey, does this latter generation, from which I'm as distant as they will be from me by 2070 A.D., does the word "betrayed," in the sense I mean it, Ecclesias, have any significance or utility in *their* vocabulary any longer?

—I doubt it.

Ditto.

Well, anyway, there was a cat.

The cat pawed partway down the rough mortar joints in the stone wall, the way felines do, seeking the lowest elevation before having to drop, and then leaped clear—to the lawn below. It happened that the three inhabitants of the stone cottage were having luncheon in the delightful privacy of the enclosed backyard at the time. They were seated on the white iron lawn chairs around the white filigreed table, and enjoying the fine air and sky as they ate: savory grilled cheddar cheese sandwiches and bacon, tossed salad, fresh-brewed coffee, a repast prepared by Larry, who enjoyed exercising his culinary flair.

Ira followed the animal's movements: the cat was a calico tabby. They had seen her before. A friendly pussycat. They had spoken about her, and Ira had even learned something new about cats. Calicoes were always females, Edith had informed him, and Larry had added something about the possibility of becoming rich developing a new breed: "You're going into biology. There's your chance, Ira," he spoofed. "Breed a calico male, and your fortune is made. Because then you can produce a stable line of calico cats, a distinct breed. They will be known as the Stigman Calicoes."

And Ira, facetiously in character, recalling a speech from Ibsen's *Hedda Gabler*, replied, "Fancy that, Hedda."

Motley orange, the feline landed on the grass; then leisurely, tranquilly, traversed the turf between wall and table, and in mélange of pigments approached. The question stirred within Ira's mind whether he should apprise Edith of the animal's presence; had she noticed it? Would mention of it be superfluous? Or did he refrain from doing so—as it would seem to him later—deliberately, out of a subliminal curiosity to ascertain how Edith would react, when the cat was close by? Would the cat surprise her, and if so, what would she do? And yet, why should he want to learn how Edith would react? In what obscure way was that connected to the aberrant, refractory, sullied promptings that had reached such a pitch those few times he walked with her alone?

He saw the animal disappear under the table. A second or two passed, a calm interval, almost long enough to dispel, to dissipate Ira's negligible suspense. And then—

She screamed! She screamed hysterically, piercingly, at the very extremity of terror, her entire visage concentric to the wide-open screaming mouth. Ira knew why. But not Larry. Poor fellow, he jumped to his feet, he rushed to her side. The color had drained from his fine young face, and frightened, bewildered, with outstretched hands, he sought to protect Edith—from what? From no visible danger, but as if she had a seizure.

The startled cat sprang out from under the table, scooted across the grass for the wall—

"It's just a cat," said Ira, knowing full well that his warning, his advisory, came too late.

She had thought it was a skunk, she explained, seconds later, after she regained her composure. A hydrophobic skunk, she added, implausibly. "We were all deathly afraid of hydrophobic skunks out West."

So that's how overwrought she was, hysterically, morbidly over-wrought, Ira thought. Why? Was it because of the strain she was under, the strain resulting from her defiance of conventions: risking her position at the university for the sake of some feminist principle about her rights to an affair with a younger man, a freshman student? No. The intensity, the abandonment of that scream, went way beyond that. It was shattering, it was corporeal. And once again crowded into Ira's consciousness misshapen conjectures, spontaneous and insurgent and yet so overweening they made him wonder at their very peremptoriness. They usurped every other surmise, so insistent were they, though embodied out of nothing, out of lascivious intimations, as sure of themselves as if he were dealing with something definite, a textbook problem, and no other answer was acceptable, only one: she wasn't deriving the kind of reward she had risked coming here for. She wasn't getting the comfort, the release, the easement, her lover should have been able to give her: the assuagement of anxiety, relaxation, remission of tension—maybe just the assurance that this being together meant they would stay together. That scream! So rending, what else could it mean? All right, he was a dope, Ira conceded, he always got snagged on the one thing, always on the same thing. But what else could it mean? If something wasn't wrong with him, with his intuition of what was wrong with her, then what the hell was wrong with Larry? Jesus, that was a funny one—

It was a funny one, all right. Ira removed his hands from the keyboard, thrust them halfway into his trouser pockets: that was the worst of being a novelist, especially an autobiographical novelist. You knew what the actual answer was. You knew what she had expected from her lover. And then you found yourself in a dilemma. Protect the memory of the guy you once loved? Your friend, your benefactor in so many ways, that gentle, sweet, generous guy who was Larry. Or reveal the truth? Dilemma horn number one. Dilemma horn number two: should you resolve the mystery right here and now, and deprive the narrative of its suspense? Strange. He had ventured into territory that as far as he knew, few if anyone had ventured into before. You met your past, vis-à-vis an amber monitor.

Strange, Ecclesias, you know I was right? Guided by sensibility alone.

—You mean right in part.

Very well, right in part. It was Jake B, an engineer-turned-editor, a hard-boiled sort, who told me, Jake B, another of Edith's transient lovers, whom I met years and years later, at the old Chelsea Hotel, that landmark of a posh past on West 23rd Street. Jake stretched out his hand, his countenance glowing with pleasure in every aged seam: "Ah, Ira, the same youth, but now a man!" It was in him Edith confided the fact, the story of the young lover's premature release, and it was he who told it to me.

—It happens that I know all about it.

Oh, you do? In that case I'm very grateful to you. How do you manage to arrive at such intimate knowledge?

Something was wrong with Larry. That's all that sifted through. Ira could bet on it. In the very midst of reading *Ulysses*, the film of unappeasement on Edith's face, when he took that last walk with her, would make the closely printed lines on the page ripple afterward, ripple through Bloom's words in a flattened sine curve: "A nation is the same people living in the same place." That sad-eyed appeal could give him a hard-on, like the predator hard-on Stella gave him, or maybe the opportunistic, windfall hard-on at the prospect of seclusion here in the isolating expectancy of clumps of roadside trees, instead of blistered kitchen walls. No, no. What was Bloom saying, "A nation is the—" Don't walk with her, Ira ordered himself. You hear what I said, Stigman? You got bats in your belfry. Finish this goddamn book you're reading—while you've got a chance. . . .

Came the end of their stay in the cottage, time to pack, to separate and depart. They left as discreetly as they had come. Edith, via a taxi from the cottage, took an earlier train back to the city. Larry and Ira took a later one, after a hike to the station. Hilarious, as though they were intoxicated with release from the strain *they* had been under the past two weeks, Larry from the constraint of an enforced maturity, Ira from the constraint of his model behavior—their mirth mounted with every passing mile aboard the train. At the train terminal on the New Jersey side of the Hudson River, they were howling like seventeen-year-olds in Dr. Rickets's elocution class, with laughter—over everything and nothing.

They crossed on the ferry to Manhattan at dusk—convulsed by each and every silly remark. Youthful again, all but juvenile, young companions free of all responsibility, they sat briefly in the weakly lit, stale-tobacco-laden, bulging midships of the ferry, object of curiosity of fellow passengers. Then, overcome by new fits of hilarity, they left, left for the inner, vehicular area. There they skulked in the deepest shadow, where they could double up with laughter, merely catching glimpses of each other's fortnight's growth of beard—or when some startled motorist still behind the steering wheel of his car chanced to spy them through the windshield.

It was not until they walked from the ferry slip to the escalator of the high dark 9th Avenue El, scaling overhead like a sable sash about the evening, that their laughing jag, as Larry called it, subsided. With merry so-longs and the jolly "Abyssinias" of high school days, they parted, Larry for the train that would take him to the near Bronx—and to a house of mourning, he suddenly recalled—and Ira for the crosstown trolley that would take him to East Harlem.

On the corner where Ira waited, alone again, for the trolley, an unreal soberness began to enfold everything about him, and through which everything, passing cars and pedestrians, moved. He had laughed too much, and now he was paying for it, paying for it with almost painful assessment of the past two weeks. Yes, with constraints removed, they had both snapped back, reverted to the ones they really were. But it didn't matter as far as Ira was concerned—or did it? He was just a witness, a spectator—as yet. Something in him had changed; he was sure of it. But where Larry was concerned it *did* matter, or it ought to matter, a lot. Wasn't that the whole purpose of the tryst that Edith had arranged for them to have at Woodstock? That Larry would grow closer to her level, bind their intimacy more tightly together? Something like that. Was he all wrong? Larry hadn't grown, Larry hadn't developed. All that guffawing and all that squealing with laughter at every word when homeward bound, it was as if Larry had shared an escapade with his boon companion, shared a unique adventure, and not grown at all in the serious outlook, serious intimacy Edith hoped they would share. So she had failed, she had failed, Edith had failed.

If anything, it was Ira who felt himself genuinely and *permanently* changed, drawn closer to Edith's level, to understanding even better the gravity that imbued her. Was it the walking with Edith alone through woodland paths that somehow diffused her personality through him? And despite all his shameful flaws and his slum Jewish rearing, his intellectual backwardness, his arrested masculinity, despite all that, compatibility of minds kept growing between them. While Larry, left behind in the stone cottage, was trying to write a poem—and tearing it up in frustration—Ira's sense of consonance with Edith kept increasing, empathy kept growing. He could feel himself gain in insight when with her, grow toward equality, psychologically. What was it that kept nourishing his sense of confidence? Was it the detecting of that film of discontent on her face? Was it watching the two lovers together? Or was it his moiling through a book, the *Ulysses*, that made him feel grown in comprehension? Or the cat, the cat! Edith's shattering scream. Jesus, if that wasn't a trick of destiny, *La Forza del Destino*, as Caruso and Gigli sang on the record, that things should turn out that way. Pivot in Woodstock, yes. Christ, try and figure things out.

Before the crosstown trolley came—fix that clearly in mind, see if you couldn't keep it defined: the way luck worked, bringing you a step nearer to the blurry, intangible goal you aspired to, but never really expected to reach. Quick, just as you got your jitney out to have the fare ready, you never thought so much about what things like that could bode for you, never pondered the augury of Larry's sitting before two candles at night, striving to write a poem, so visibly, so raptly hushed, and finally so dissatisfied: "I can't seem to sustain the mood." Why was that desolate voice, those handsome features, invaded by something akin to despair? Why did the large white hand in the instant of crumpling the paper impinge on the conglomerate night of the bustling 125th Street corner? What was the significance for you of the words of defeat sounding above the din of traffic and overhead subway train? "I can't seem to sustain the mood."

Ira climbed aboard the trolley, dropped his nickel in the coin hopper, barely aware of the prolonged look on the face of the conductor cranking the coins down into the little till. He went inside, chose a straw-covered seat to his liking. Oblivious of the lighted, monotonous, miscellaneous ranks of store windows that passed with the trolley's eastward course toward Park Avenue, passed like a tawdry curtain on which beautiful scenes of the last two weeks were projected, he sighed. And with his old square valise resting on the floor between his ankles, he girded himself for a resumption of all that life in East Harlem had come to mean, life in East Harlem approaching resumption crosstown block by crosstown block.

He had turned aside to scan his journal, feeling guilty about interrupting his narrative (he would have to sooner or later, so much had happened). He could hardly believe that it had been over five years since M had died. He recalled the February day, a week after his birthday, just a few years before she died, when it had snowed continually, phenomenally, for about three days consecutively, piling masses of snow on roof and canopy of the mobile home, the trailer as it was commonly called. Across the court, poor epileptic Diana's canopy had collapsed under the weight of frozen snow—what a sad sight: a sheet of painted aluminum leaning against her doorway. Snowed, melted, snow froze. The day before yesterday, ice had evidently formed under or between the seams of the sheet-metal covering on the roof of his mobile home, with the result that for the first time since he owned the place, drops of water pattered down from the ceiling onto the shelf where the black box of the transformer between the power source and the IBM PC*jr* rested. That necessitated setting a pail underneath the trickle to contain it, which Ira had just finished doing when the rapturous warbling of geese or cranes overhead reached his ears. So early in the year, so soon in the winter, the warbling of the wildfowl heading south! Geese or cranes: *E come i gru van* (his italian was negligible) *cantando lor lai, facendo in aer di se lunga riga* . . . Ah, how beautiful! *Cantando lor lai* . . . He simply had to go outdoors to look at them. He went out on the back porch. Nor was it an easy matter to locate them, so near the sun they flew, and so high, barely visible, a troupe—how could he resist the alliteration?—a troupe of transported troubadours. They seemed to the earthbound wight either disoriented, for they flew round and round warbling, or so delighted within the scope of sunlight that they warbled almost giddily in an azure zone with the bare branches of the young locust tree in the backyard. *E come i gru van cantando lor lai* . . . as the cranes fly singing their lay. Six, seven hundred years ago Dante wrote it, died, and left his legacy to lesser mortals to use, to fuse his words with the sight and sound of wildfowl returning. *E come i gru van cantando lor lai* . . . as the cranes fly singing their lay.

Oh, there was so much he had to write, so much had accumulated during this snail's pace of his setting down of the narrative, so much that had occurred during the real time of the narrator. His supply of new, highest-quality floppy disks were formatting erratically. What did that mean? Were the disks imperfect, or would he have to disconnect the system, and impose on his ever-obliging wife to drive him *and* the system to the supplier's?

Glowering, he looked up at the ceiling: small blessings! Respite. The dripping had stopped.

VIII

Ira gave Mom and Pop quite a start when he walked into the kitchen. A Sunday evening, Minnie was away on a date, and there was always the chance Pop too might be away on an "extra" at an evening banquet, rather than the usual communion or fraternity breakfast.

Instead, both his parents were home, sitting at the round table, not covered with the usual green oilcloth, but with a white linen tablecloth. He could see part of a pan of strudel on the table beside the half-empty teacups. Mom baked strudel only on festive occasions, high holidays.

"Here I am," he announced in Yiddish. "What's up? What's today?"

They stared at him in astonishment. The door he had just entered open inward, between him and them, and he hadn't knocked. They stared at him questioningly, a full second or two, until he put his satchel down, before they recognized him. And then Pop exclaimed in rare commendation, as though surprise had stripped away for a moment his usual cursory or tacit salutation, "Now you look like a man! Strong. As a man should look. *Azoy*. Look, Leah, no? With a man's front, a man's will."

"Yeah? Thanks, Pop. Gee, I forgot about it. Even on the trolley car. No wonder they"—Ira pressed down the shallow, curly mat on his cheeks—"they kept staring at me."

"Such a comely beard." Mom reveled at the sight. "Who would believe it could have grown in so short a time—ach! Black, thick. *A ganzeh yeet*." She got up from her chair. "He speaks nonsense." She turned to Ira. "Are you hungry? I have a fine barley and mushroom soup, a piece of fricasseed chicken left over."

"Fine. Left over from what? What day is this?"

"It's the end of the New Year's. The end of Rosh Hashanah. You didn't know?"

"No. How should I—where *I* was? Rosh Hashanah? Say."

"You're growing to be a total *goy*," Pop said indulgently.

"*Noo, a gutn yuntiff.* A happy New Year," Mom invoked. "May it be with good fortune."

"You too," Ira rejoined shortly. "Boy, my *mazel* sounds pretty good right now. I'm ready for that barley and mushroom soup. Ah, no wonder I thought I smelled Polish mushrooms when I came in."

"That you didn't have there."

"I'll say."

"Well, you haven't given me a kiss yet, my handsome bearded son. A kiss before I serve you."

"How can you tell I'm handsome? You can't see me behind all this pelt." Ira kissed her soft cheek, and grinned. "I'll have to get rid of it soon."

"So glossy. Like a young *khassid*, a yeshiva student. At least let Minnie see you," Mom adjured.

"Oh, sure. Where is she?"

"Indeed, as your father says, you have a man's lineaments, a man's bearing."

"Oh, we just—just had some fun. We grew whiskers."

"And handsome ones. His, too, your friend's?"

"I think so. Mine were thicker maybe."

"Like a full-grown man. *Noo,* you enjoyed yourself?"

"Oh, sure. I even rode a horse. We all did."

They both laughed. *"A ferd noch!"*

"A horse!" Pop echoed. "What kind of horse?"

"A regular horse, what do you think? With a saddle on him and with stirrups, they call it in English—you put your feet into them."

"With her, the Professora?" Mom asked incredulously.

"Of course! You should see her ride a horse. A little woman like that. Better than we could."

"Azoy. A professora on a horse."

"A professora on a horse!" Pop mimicked. "What else? She's from the West, no? You see them in the moving pictures in the West. Men and women ride horses."

"To many moving pictures you took me, my generous spouse, that I should behold." And to Ira, "You ate well?"

"Oh, yeah. Plenty. Larry's a good cook. He did a lot of it."

"What did you eat?"

"Oh, bacon and eggs for breakfast, soup, sandwiches for lunch—"

"Treife. Naturally. Your grandfather should know."

"Yeah," Ira grinned. "I worried about him a lot. We sometimes had pork chops for supper. Broiled outdoors. Boy, they're good."

"Indeed. And lived?"

"In a wonderful house. Made of old stone. You should see it. Clinging vines around it, you know." Ira gesticulated in spirals. "And outside a beautiful yard. A gardener came twice while we were there. He mowed the lawn, trimmed the bushes—with long scissors."

"Azoy? Noo. People have money. Why shouldn't it be beautiful?"

"You wouldn't live in the country anyway," said Pop.

"Such country as you would have chosen, indeed not," Mom retorted. "Live in another Galitzianer Veljish. In a hovel. Without water. Dung in the dark. The mongrel on the road is news—"

"Here she goes again, the mongrel on the road is news."

"Go. With you there's no talking."

"All right. All right," Ira arbitrated. "We're not in Galitzia."

"You may say that again. And praise the Lord we're not."

"The second night Minnie celebrated the *yuntiff* with her high school friend, Bessie. She ate there. We ate here. She stayed there overnight."

"Oh, yeah?" Second night of Rosh Hashanah. Saturday night, last night. Pop would have been home most of today. Might have gone to *shul* for a couple of hours. Mom wouldn't have shopped today. No pushcarts anyway until tonight, the way Jewish holidays ended. Oh, well . . . "I'm not going to shave it off till tomorrow. She can see it in the morning." Again he rubbed his beard. "I got a bush, haven't I?"

"A what?"

"A bush, a bush," he said in Yiddish, gesticulating. "Don't you know? It grows on the ground."

"You know what? Come with me tomorrow," Mom urged eagerly. "Tomorrow morning I'll have to go shopping. Let Zaida, Mamie, see I have a son with a beard."

"What? Tomorrow? In daylight?"

"But you rode home already in a trolley car."

"Yeah, but I didn't know about it."

"Timid. Shrinking," Mom chided. "What difference?"

"Why do you have to wait until tomorrow? Let him go now," Pop urged. "Go now!" he enjoined Ira. "It's dark, it's night. Who'll see you?"

"The very truth!" Mom agreed enthusiastically. "I beg you, Ira. Go show yourself to Zaida. How the old man will rejoice! It's Sunday night. The whole family will be there. My brothers—"

"Indeed, the whole tribe," Pop added.

"Nah. You want me to go all the way to 112th Street?" Ira demurred. "Just to show my whiskers."

"I beg you," Mom implored. "Be a good child. This once, for my sake. Is it a hardship for young legs like yours to stride a mere six blocks—"

"It's eight blocks. Not six blocks. And crosstown all the way to Fifth Avenue. I'm hungry as hell."

"Let it be eight blocks. How long will it take you to stride there and back? Say *a gutn yuntiff* and be gone? I'll have supper on the table waiting for you the minute you step through the door."

"Let the old man see you," Pop seconded in rare concurrence. "It won't harm you. Compel him to admit, 'Well, Chaim sent me a grain of comfort for a change.' The old shit. *Noo?* The others will be there too: my purblind sister-in-law, my well-disposed brothers-in-law—"

"I beseech you!" said Mom.

"Okay, okay," Ira acquiesced. "Lucky it's dark. *A yeet mit a boort* on 119th Street."

"My beloved son! I'll take out—I'll wash everything in the satchel. Right away."

"Never mind." Ira raised his voice. "I'm gone, I'm gone. Jeez, to tear myself away from that mushroom and barley. I want you to know I'm doing you a favor."

"My precious child. Go, go."

And go he did. He left the kitchen, skipped down the flight of tenement stairs to the hallway, and from hallway to stoop to street. The three or four familiar faces he had passed when he turned the corner of Park Avenue into 119th Street on the way home from the trolley hadn't recognized him. Even Irish Mrs. Grady, the Little Tusk, as Mom called her in Yiddish, because she had only the one front tooth, didn't recognize him, though she had seen him close by many times. The poor, thin, angular woman, who always flushed animatedly when she talked to Mom, didn't recognize him, though they passed each other in the light of Biolov's drugstore window.

At a quick pace, he wheeled downtown around the corner of 119th and Park Avenue, hurried in the dark of the railroad trestle, through the familiar, frowsy neighborhood that became more Jewish with every block south. Up the hill to the crosstown trolley line at the crest on 116th Street, and down the hill to the Sunday-night recrudescence of the pushcart market that began at 115th Street, hawkers and shoppers leaving the carbide glare under the massive street canopy of the railroad, he drove his legs to 112th Street. Crazy to go, to defer his supper for the sake of displaying his whiskers to Zaida.

But for once Pop and Mom were in harmony. So to make them happy . . . let's go.

And around the corner west a block to Madison, and weakening with haste, railing even more sulkily at himself for having acceded to his parents' plea, he drove his legs another block to Fifth Avenue, and then another dozen houses to midblock, reached Mamie's house. Up the flight of stone stairs, and panting, he swiveled the ratchety doorbell key, and to his surprise the door opened before he removed his hand from the knob, opened to a medley of Yiddish and Yinglish voices of his relatives calling out, "Who?" "Hoozit?"

They were nearly all there, Zaida's progeny as well as the spouses of those who were married—and a few of their children, those who lived in Harlem, his first cousins, Yettie, four-year-old blond daughter of his aunt Ella, frisky red-haired Hannah, Mamie's brat, and Stella, blue-eyed, blond, and pudgy, glared at covertly, peremptorily, to compensate for her total inaccessibility, by Ira, who realized he had vitiated another ambush by this premature visit, burning ambush; no, the altered pun lacked pungency even when contrasted with the romance in whose midst he had been just a few hours ago. Hell, an option shot. "Hello. Hello," he called out without enthusiasm, and thrust open the door.

In various homely attitudes, they were gathered at the end of the long hallway in the front room about the large, square dining table under its multi-stained, taupe-colored tablecloth: a dozen or more people, all ages, relations, enclosed by wallpapered walls lit by the bright unpleasant light of the cluster of ceiling incandescents. Only Baba was gone. Ten years and a year more had passed since some of them had come here from Europe; uncouth, noisy greenhorns, they had charged into the kitchen in the house on 115th Street to gargle salt water, or something of the sort, and sent him wandering off in vast disappointment to Central Park to drink from a mountain rill. Bullshit. If he could wave a wand, make them vanish, as he used to wish at home with Mom and Pop so he could get at Minnie, he could give Stella, who was there with the rest, a real backscuttle, just what he needed. Jesus, all that pure romance charged up in him would have to find an outlet.

They gaped at him, more taken aback, startled, than even Mom and Pop had been. "Hollo, *mishpokha*," he greeted the assembly. He felt like Douglas Fairbanks adroitly, improbably, foiling the thrust of so much openmouthed cynosure with a single blade of jocularity. "*Vus macht sikh?*"

His uncle Saul, ever taut, suspicious conniver, scowled, "Who're you?"

"'Tis I. Don't you know me? Mom, your sister, asked me to come over."

And of all the people to recognize him first, it was his aunt Sadie, Mom's youngest sister, so myopic that Pop, in benign mood, called her The Purblind; but more often, his spite prevailing, he called her Der Blindeh. "*Oy*, it's Ira! *Gevald!*" she cried out. "It's Leah's son!"

Commotion and outcry throughout the room. "What do you say to that?" and "What's got into you?" from Moe's wife, sharp, disapproving, bleached-blond Ida. Ever-tactless Harry, Ira's youngest uncle, demanded, "Whatsa matter, you're such a *koptsn*, you can't afford a safety razor?" And "See, Father!" Mamie cried out. "Your oldest grandson, a Jew with a beard." And meek Ella, her meat-cutter spouse Meyer absent, gaming in a café on 116th Street, "*Oy*, is he handsome! Avert the Evil Eye!"

"Leah's son?" Gray-bearded Zaida, though his cataracts had been removed, still squinted. He had eyeglasses, but wore them only when reading. Invincible hypochondriac, he peered at Ira with histrionic squint. "I don't see well. Who? Is that Leah's son?"

Burly, affectionate Moe, now permanently Morris, stood up, came over, shook hands and laughed, "*Tockin, a yeet mit a boort*," he addressed the assemblage. "I used to carry him with one hand in Galitzia."

"Who doesn't remember? He was a tot," said Ella. "Smaller than you," she addressed little Yettie. "Just look."

"A *rebbeh*," Morris chuckled. He stroked Ira's beard with blunt fingers. "His *malamut* came to the house on 9th Street when I boarded there, and told Leah that God had bidden her son to be a rabbi."

"I don't like whiskers on a young man," Ida reproved, secure in her platinum-blond acculturation. "When I was still single, I never made a date with a man with whiskers."

"You didn't. Maybe he didn't want to make a date with you too," acute Max twitted. "Did a man with whiskers ever ask you?"

Ida ignored the innuendo. "He knew I would've turned him down."

"You?" Max replied.

"Don't be snotty. I wouldn't care who he was. I'm Jewish, but to go with somebody with whiskers? On an old man, a religious Jew, all right. But on a young man like you," she addressed Ira, lapsing simultaneously into Yiddish: "S'pahst nisht." Vehemence kindled the large wen on her chin into a fiery plug.

"No?" Ira said apologetically. "I wouldn't inflict it on you. It was Mom's idea. She wanted me to come here."

"Take it off."

"Oh, sure, sure, Ida. First thing in the morning. After Minnie sees it." Goddamn Delancey Street tramp. Ira looked away.

"Why should he take it off? Maybe he wants to become a rabbi, like Morris says," talkative and mettlesome Hannah drawled in Ira's defense. "We'll have a rov in the family. A real rov. He'll come to the family circle. He'll say all the brukhis for us—"

"Maybe he'll be the rabbi that marries us. He would learn all the Hebrew he would have to say." Stella's wit was whetted. "You hear, Mama? If Ira was a rabbi, he'd get the twenty dollars you pay for marrying."

"Kissingly I would present it to him," Mamie said with fervor. "Oy, I should see the day."

"I'd love to do that, Mamie."

"For my sake I know you would. Ah, the very thought serves me with a large helping of health."

"Mama's always worrying about marrying."

"What're you gonna be? A Reform rabbi? I like Reform rabbis. They talk in English," Hannah chattered on. "You could talk over the radio, too, like Rabbi Wise. He's such a smart rabbi. Everybody loves to listen to him—"

"Listen, local talent, children should be seen, not heard," Ida attempted to squelch her niece.

"Who's speaking to you? I'm speaking to him, not you. I got a right to talk to him. He's my cousin. You know why I'm only local talent? That's because Mama won't let me go to dancing school. She's afraid I'll grow up to be a you-know-what."

Almost everyone laughed at Hannah's retort. It might have been innocent in intent, but Ida took umbrage. Her wen glowed. She glared at Hannah. Ira had to admire the kid's crust, speaking in such tones to Ida.

"Where did you grow such a big black *boort*?" Harry demanded bluntly. *"Aza boort."*

"On his chin. Where else?" Hannah offered at once.

"Smart. You're so clever. You're local talent, just like I told you," Ida huffed. "Where else?"

"You don't think there's a where else?" Saul asked unpleasantly. "Max. Tell her."

"You tell her. Morris, you didn't show her already?"

"Not even once."

Laughter mingled with Hannah's sharp "Oh, shoddop, you and your where elses. I don't have to know. How long did it take you, Ira?" She defended her modesty staunchly.

"Only about two weeks."

"You hear? *Azoy!*"

It was time to go. He had been on exhibit long enough. Besides, he had come for Zaida's diversion, but the old man sitting cheerlessly at the end of the table across the room obviously understood nothing of the English repartee. Nor, in all likelihood, would he have approved: he existed in a lopped-off, truncated ethos.

"I haven't had supper yet," Ira said by way of prelude to leave-taking. "I hope everybody's had a good look." He mingled Yiddish with English. *"Noo,* Zaida, I'm going." He brushed by Stella to where Zaida was sitting—could feel raptor desire spread wing within him: Sinbad's roc. Who was Sinbad—apt word—who the roc? Lucky he had whiskers to muffle facial twitch. " 'Bye, Stella," he bade gruff-voiced, and neutrally, " 'Bye, Hannah, Mamie, Ella, Sadie, uncles and everybody, Morris, Max, Harry, Sadie. 'Bye, Zaida. Don't get up." He knew the kind of handshake to expect: the weak token pressure of the Orthodox Jewish handshake.

Instead Zaida stood up. Even without glasses, the old boy's eyesight wasn't really gone. The steadiness, nay, fixity of his scrutiny made Ira feel suddenly flimsy, a tatter of self, sailing erratically like a scrap of wind-driven newspaper in the street. Jesus, he hadn't come here for that; he had come here at Mom's behest to display two weeks' growth of beard, grown in another place, another world, for reasons they would never dream. "Yeah, it's really me, Zaida, Leah's son," Ira reassured him in Yiddish. "Your oldest grandson, Ira Stigman."

"I know, I know," Zaida said once. "I want to behold you close, as well as these feeble eyes are able."

The two gazed at each other. How antic his own whiskers compared to the millennial-seeming gray beard of his grandfather; it was the difference between a transitory caper and a covenant. Boy, everything was turning out altogether unexpectedly—thumping out unhappy meanings, when all he had anticipated was a jovial greeting, a display amid hilarity—and after a brief visit, departure.

"*Noo*, let me remember you so." The old man stretched out his short thick arms, encircled Ira within them. "A Jew as God willed. Blessed be the name of the Lord. Weak as my vision is, these eyes have seen my oldest grandson a Jew." He grasped Ira to himself, holding his grandson to his thick torso in strong embrace. They kissed each other, beard through beard. *"Barukh atah adonoi, elohainu, melekh ha oylum . . ."* Zaida began the traditional prayer celebrating the rare occasion when a Jew feels he has been privileged to survive to a supreme moment. *"L'hazman hazeh,"* he concluded.

And each one, affected in his or her own way by awe of the patriarchal invocation, all the assembled relatives, devoutly sealed his prayer with their *"O-omehn."*

"Gey gesinteheit." Zaida opened his arms.

"Thanks, Zaida."

"S'kimteh dir tockin a shekheyooni, Tateh." Whose voice was it that Ira heard behind his back as he turned to leave? Mamie's, ever solicitous, protective where Zaida was concerned, no matter how lacking in sign of gratitude his response. Obese Mamie, alacritous to attend to his wants—his loyal daughter. She followed behind Ira down the hall to the door. "It's a pity my Jonas isn't here to view your *Yiddishkeit* with the others. How he would enjoy it. He was here celebrating the first day of Rosh Hashanah." And as they reached the door, "The

partners thought of closing the cafeteria for the holiday, but the neighborhood is so *goyish,* Saul said no. So the others went in the first day. Saul took cash, Harry behind the counter, Max cooked, and later Moe—so Joe had to take cash the second day. All day, my poor husband."

"Always seemed to me one day was enough."

"Azoy id es shoyn."

"Yeah. G'bye, Mamie."

"Greet Leah for me."

"Okay. Thanks."

Once again into the street, and striding toward the carbide push-cart lights under the trestle on Park Avenue—*Oh, fare thee well, for ill fare I.* Housman's lines, spontaneous and succinct, welled up. Why did everything turn out so differently from what you expected? Jesus, it was supposed to be a joke, supposed to entertain the old boy. But it didn't. The Yiddles at the pushcarts when he got there wouldn't know the difference between him right now and another *ehrlikher yeet,* one who bound his phylacteries on his arm and brow in the morning, one who *davened:* swayed and prayed under his striped prayer shawl. He never expected to be reminded of it. Kid among the pushcarts on the East Side. *Cheder yingle,* commended for his glibness in making the right sounds to match the Hebrew characters on the page. Jesus, you met yourself all the time, really all the time. What did Hannah say about his becoming a *rov,* a rabbinical sage? Instead he was coming fresh from a *goyish* two-week holiday at Woodstock, with Larry and Edith, his English instructor-lover, older gentile woman from New Mexico. Boyoboy. Could you blame anyone for shaking his head in disbelief?

"Bulbas, bulbas, sheineh bulbas!" The bearded peddler stretched a hand out toward Ira, familiarly, enticingly, exhibited a large potato.

The guy's trying to sell you potatoes. The next guy, tomatoes. Moe's joke on himself when he first came to America: he took them for ripe plums: pomatoes. Ira began the ascent to 116th Street—you go to see Zaida to duck out of, you call it circumvent, Mom's nagging that you go with her tomorrow morning to show off her sonny boy's beard—and you lose the chance of a casual weekday gamble, yeah, gambol with Stella Monday night. But look at what it contrasts with:

all that courtesy and politeness and tenderness he was witness to just this very morning, when Edith and Larry parted. Figure it out, and the nerve of you, transfixed by lust for Stella, in the same second you took Zaida's kiss, his benison. Excruciating. No? The flesh wouldn't stop.

Away from the hustle and chalky light below, he climbed upward, heard overhead a train, its wheels muted by the solid steel trestle. He headed down the incline past the squat brick comfort station at the summit of 116th Street, where the trestle seemed to dip nearest to the ground, how wonderful to see from there the trolley tracks, east-west trolley tracks gleaming at night as they passed by a hundred stoops and stores and a thousand people out Saturday-night shopping. Listen to the drone, way deep, steady. Tenor you call it, right? Tenor of the city.

What star was that, he paused to wonder, visible after he crossed the sidewalk, in the dark again between the tenements and the trestle: the uptown star he called it, came up first in September in constellation Bronx—Jesus Christ, it was different being a Jew, alienated—as Edith had used the word on one of those strolls—from other Jews—which Edith said he was, and Larry wasn't. Alienated, not assimilated, alienated.

Nearing the show-window lights of Biolov's drugstore, the ruby and cobalt amphorae casting their glow on the corner, he was almost home at last for supper, barley-mushroom soup, chicken fricassee, for a festive night it was.

IX

Ever since Ira had come back from Woodstock and had told Minnie—lied to her—that he had had intimacies with Edith, laid her in Woodstock, Minnie's attitude toward her brother had undergone a change. And even though he later confessed that he had lied, and she laughed indulgently, and called him *ligner*, prevaricator, her attitude toward him had clearly shifted. Was it those few dates with Rodney, and the fact that he had wanted to propose to her? Or was it the beard that had wrought the change?

Suddenly, Minnie saw him as the man he had become, no longer her rapscallion brother, and affectionately she greeted her brother, not having seen him for such a long time.

"She hasn't seen her brother in two weeks," Mom explained Minnie's warm demeanor.

"Not so. What are you saying?" Pop gainsaid. "Can't you see? It's her *Yiddishkeit* surging up in her. *Noo*, Minneleh?" he addressed her humorously. "Whether you like him or not, it's his *Yiddishkeit* that appeals to you?" Pop chuckled again.

The transformation in her was startling. She disclosed a new, an actual fondness for him, in touch of hand, tone of voice, slapping his hand in homey caress. Her actions with him when everyone was home were impish, sportive—always traced with a slight, easing detraction of voice, or modified by her peculiar short chuckle, that ended in the faintest derisive snort, but still fond.

"Ira, I know it's only been a summer, but I've become a grown woman, an adult. I'm no longer a girl you can have your way with. I'm in high school, Ira. Sometimes I think you still think of me as an object, as your kid sister."

Reproach and sultriness mingled in her voice. "You only think about what you want. What about what I want? Did you ever think of that? Just when I'm starting to fall in love with Rod, my *goyish* friend, somebody I can't marry, and it's no use going on, and you come home looking like a man, like a real *mensh*. What d'ye think I'm gonna feel?"

He was silent.

"You know, my darling brother, I could tell you something, but I don't wanna hurt your feelings, but you're just like all the rest of the Farbs. You men only understand how to satisfy yourselves, nothing about love. Moe is different."

"I'm not a Farb. I'm a Stigman," Ira replied proudly. He paused as he drank another cup of coffee in the kitchen. "What about the Farbs?"

"Sadie Farb told Mama all about Harry: 'It's in and out with him, with my husband.' Mama had to laugh."

"Yeah?"

"And it's the same with Saul. As soon as she puts on her corset Saul likes, it's in and out with him. She thinks maybe he's different with *shiksas*."

"Mom told me about Saul too. So I'm not an athlete."

"Athlete yet!" Minnie scoffed, waved him away.

Disbelief and fond forgiveness connected raised eyebrow to moue. "All right." Minnie turned toward the bedroom door, unprovocatively. "Tell Mama to let me sleep a little. I'm really tired this morning."

He sat down in the kitchen chair over which he had draped most of his clothes the night before, meditating, dressing slowly. Mom seemed to be taking longer this Sunday shopping—or paying her visit to Zaida at Mamie's. His frustration was increasing. What if? Jesus, he'd break Mom's heart. He would if he got caught—or they got caught. Pop couldn't thrash him anymore. He was bigger than Pop. Order him out of the house maybe. Well, it almost didn't matter. He'd break Mom's heart. What the hell are you gonna do?

He should have gone out of the house with Mom on Sunday morning. Anh, he knew he couldn't do it. Besides, why? Mom would ask why. What a habit—some habit—to have gotten into—from the age of twelve. And now, Minnie with a crush on him. He had to be careful, careful. Try to figure. You're cool now, cool. In another three or four hours you wouldn't be. Figure, for Christ's sake, figure. It's a goddamn calamity. She went from taboo, the *goy*, to taboo you, Jew-brother. All right, you said that. Figure. . . .

Figure. . . .

A job maybe. Some kind of job. What kind? He had heard talk in the '28 alcove about jobs at Loft's candy store. Part-time work there after three o'clock . . . weekdays, Saturdays, he had heard: "a real sweet job," some sophomore wag had cracked. All day Sunday. They wanted clerks to substitute for the regular help on their days off. *All day Sunday.* He'd have to give it a try. Loft's or any job like that. Christ, with Minnie like that, if he ever tried anything like that again, he'd get caught, he couldn't resist it.

As he gulped down a third cup of Mom's coffee, his hands began to tremble, just a bit. As Minnie lay down for her Sunday-morning nap in the bedroom, he imagined what would happen if Pop ever caught them. Came in unexpectedly in his waiter's outfit and saw him in his underwear, barefoot. If he wanted to lay a hand on him, he'd go crazy. All those goddamn beatings the sonofabitch gave him, the dreams he used to have when he was a kid, after a beating, trying to pick a knife off the table to stab Pop with, but it was stuck there. Jesus Christ, he really would go crazy, hit back, grab anything, any goddamn knife. See Pop lying there, bleeding on the scuffed linoleum. Killed maybe, who knows? Dead. Cops. Courts. Jail and judges. Mom without support. Crushing disgrace. Bowed down by it, lifelong, like Atlas. And Larry thought he felt bad about his widowed mother. He wasn't like Ira. He hadn't *made* his mother a widow as Ira could his. Jesus, maybe the best thing, go in there where Minnie was sleeping, and bust her one—right now—bam!—right on the jaw. What an aubade. Cure her from being stuck on him. Cure her for good.

Slowly the terror crept over him, the deep, hair-raising horror he hadn't felt since plane geometry days—there it was, that fracture inside him, separating him within: murder. Murdher. While she slept in the bedroom on a Sunday morning, murder her. Oh, Jesus. He had to find a way out.

The nearest thing to death that the living can know of death is in the memory of old times once lived. He would soon be ninety, Ira thought. He would be ninety in eight months. Incredible, wasn't it? And how many times will you say it? he asked himself. How many times will you exclaim the petrified, old fact in wonder? 1995 this year, 1925 that. What do you want of me? He could hear the echo of Yiddish inflection in his ear, though *they* would have said, What do you want *from* me. Seventy years ago, and you ask me to recall all this? Or embellish it, trick it out with frill and fancy. Ach, for a guy who has mangled his life—or cooperated in the mangling—there seems so damned little use in setting it down, how much less in the re-creation, in the artifice of fable. But it must do for now, tide me over this low ebb. Who said he was supposed to or expected to present a unified piece of fiction, being crazed and cross-hatched as an old saucer?

When aging Dr. Newman, psychiatrist at the Augusta State Hospital in Maine, where Ira worked for four years as an attendant, finished reading TSE's *Waste Land,* he was convinced Eliot had gone through a "psychotic episode," as the good doctor phrased it, had suffered a brief psychotic interlude at the time he wrote the poem. Said Ira at the time: "I guess we were all more or less suffering from the same aberration, or the poem wouldn't have spoken so unerringly to us and for us."

The good doctor was unconvinced. He was still of a piece, the elderly man replied, and that was why he could recognize symptoms of the poet's psychosis during the writing of his famous poem. (Of course, no one at the time knew of the important role Ezra Pound had played in the poem's creation, or at least in determining its final form.) Born many years ago in Latvia, Dr. Newman was still of a piece; his psyche had stabilized firmly and satisfactorily *within his time,* and perhaps that was why he failed to understand what happened to succeeding generations of highly sensitive men and women of letters, increasingly fragmented in their diverse ways, and increasingly hostile to the society in whose midst they lived.

Four hours later. Autumn afternoon in 1925, in the kitchen, alone, desire as shriveled as his dick. Oh, Jesus, what a life. White oilcloth-covered washtubs, and brass-faucet sink, window on the gray wash-pole in the backyard, and door between window and washtubs to the toilet. College texts on the table. That was the worst of it, what a mix. He had told himself a hundred times before, if only they had stayed on the Lower East Side, if only he had gone to work, maybe everything would have been different. Well, make a compromise. Try to obliterate Sunday. Monday morning go to the Loft's employment office, the way he had gone to the P&T office, and fill out an application. Show initiative.

But think—Ira paused at the keyboard—you had never exorcised the violence, you had survived it, driven it underground, but not far. When Jess had just entered his adolescence, think of that afternoon he talked back to you: verged on insolence: sassy. You struck him. You didn't slap. In fact, you scarcely knew how to slap, had unlearned it after all those years, literally, of training to box, in the aftermath of that beating you took on the waterfront handing out CP leaflets. You hardly knew how to slap; you knew only how to hook, like a boxer, with thumb down and knuckles forward, even though your hand was partly open (ah, would that it had fallen off! fallen off before you batted one of your sons! Oh, those vain, Yiddish implorings). The kid was ungainly, seemed without instinct of self-preservation. Hershel, the younger, on the other hand, immediately dropped to the floor out of reach, out of harm's way, the moment his father lashed out at him. But Jess uttered a cry of pain, swung around—and struck his head on the corner of the newel post he was standing next to, struck his temple on the very corner, and grabbed his head. That was sufficient not only to cool Ira's wrath, but send him into a transport of dismay at what he had done: "Goddamn it, what the hell did you do that for?" he swore at his son. "For Christ's sake, you always do the goddamnedest things to yourself!" He sheltered his son's head, massaged his son's temple.

Now, whether *that* had anything to do with what followed, there was no telling; whether the subsequent symptoms were the outcome of impact of the boy's temple with newel-post corner, or simply the result of a change taking place in adolescence (Ira devoutly hoped it was the latter). His son developed what the doctor termed an *equivalent epilepsy*. With a strange, fixed expression on his face, Jess would take off his shirt and undershirt, because—he said—he couldn't bear to wear them—his skin was burning. What were the other symptoms? Ira searched the ceiling for some clue to memory, saw only the yellowish patch of the leak where ice had apparently forced the seams of the sheet-metal roof. He'd have to ask M what the other symptoms were. Not the typical petit mal seizures which he had come to recognize during his four years as a state hospital attendant, the momentary loss of consciousness, the brief period of disorientation, but something else. M took Jess to the Portland General Hospital for tests, encephalograms. They showed nothing conclusive.

"Why don't we just wait, and see if he grows out of it," M suggested to Dr. Thomas U, whose daughter Penny was taking piano lessons with her. "It's just my maternal intuition that he'll grow out of it," she added apologetically.

And Dr. U had replied, "A maternal intuition is sometimes more dependable than a medical one. Let's do nothing more for the time being, and see what happens."

Nothing did happen. Jess seemed to return to normalcy. But one day, he was washing his hands at the kitchen sink—the black cast-iron kitchen sink of their Maine farmhouse—kitchen sink with large, ever-reliable pitcher pump at the end. Done with washing his hands, he sipped a few mouthfuls of water from the pump lip. And in aimless, awkward fashion, his usual fashion, holding on to the pump handle, he reached over and touched the massive, old-fashioned "Dual Atlantic" stove, as it was called. It was a truly massive construction of cast iron (they didn't care how much metal they used in those days; oh, they were prodigal once!), with nickel-plated grille about the upper edge and just before the compartment for heating water, grates and firebox in which to burn wood or coal—which Ira adapted to burn kerosene. Gas burners on top (hence the adjective "Dual"), supplied by a tank of propane outside, just beside the back stairs—Yankee ingenuity the stove represented, Yankee ingenuity of the twenties and thirties, as weighty with nostalgia as with cast iron (and for all its bulk, with too small an oven to suit M). In every way, though, it was adequate: it warmed the kitchen winter nights with steady kerosene flame, during the long years the kids grew up, almost twenty in all; the long years of his mental depression, M's limitless constancy, teaching school and giving piano lessons for the only reliable cash income of the household. Meanwhile he lost so much money waterfowl farming that all her withholding taxes were rebated. Clear profit!

"Do you ever expect to show a profit in your waterfowl business?" The IRS person had called Ira and his daffy accountant, Quinner, into the IRS office.

"I hope so, sir."

"When do you think that will be?"

"I can't tell yet."

Holding the iron pump handle, the boy reached out aimlessly, and touched the stove—he uttered a wild shriek, and burst into tears: for no reason, no reason!

Oh, I've lost! The words sprang from within Ira's heart: I've lost! I've lost! The son he doted on. Maybe because of that blow he had struck him. Lost his temper completely—like Pop. Oh, anguish! The anguish beyond remorse, anguish of irrevocable, unbearable loss. "What's the matter?" Ira asked, numbed to the core, already bereaved, an automaton speaking—while M looked in utter consternation, and Hershel swung a disbelieving gaze from brother to parents. "What happened?" Ira pursued—without hope. He knew full well what had happened: the kid was off his rocker, out of his mind.

"I got a shock!" Jess wailed. "I got a shock when I touched the stove."

"Oh, yeah?" Ira humored him—with all the bitterness of futility. He was already reconstituting the self to adjust to this hideous catastrophe: his kid had gone insane. He had fallen prey to dementia praecox. "You say you got a shock when you touched the stove?"

"I did! I did, Dad. I just put my hand on it!"

Well, what harm in his trying to do the same, see if he got the same effect? The kid was so earnest, vehement; he sounded rational. But so did some of the schizophrenics at the Augusta State Hospital where Ira had worked for four years, and many of them had complained, raged about diabolic magnetism, baleful electric currents. What the hell . . . what was there to lose? Humor him, that's all. Ira arose from the kitchen table, went to the stove, rested his hand on the nickel-plated grille. Nothing. Just as he expected. "Is that what you did?"

"No. I was holding on to the pump handle. Like this." Jess leaned over, reached for the stove, but made no contact.

"All right. I'll do it too." Last chance. Last chance. Better be knocked down by a shock, knocked to the floor, anything to prove the kid right. What joy that would be, no matter the jolt, even if knocked cold—and sure enough, it came! Not a great jolt, but sufficient to make him recoil. "Well, for Christ's sake!" he cried out, this time shaken by pure bliss. "You're right! Listen, M, there is a—there's current in there. An electric current. I just felt it."

"There is?" She too showed her great relief. "I wonder how?"

"I don't know. There's a short somewhere. No doubt about it. Okay, Jess, don't touch the damn thing. I mean the two of them together, pump handle and stove—everybody. Let's see if I can't figure this out."

Eventually he did. They had had the supplier of their bottled butane gas install a new gas dryer in the hall, and the mechanic had attached the ground wire to the water-pump pipe under the kitchen. Ira called up the owner of the company from which he bought his bottled gas, and in no uncertain terms made clear his indignation at this instance of flagrant carelessness or sheer ineptitude. "One hell of a job!" he stormed. "Was the guy who installed it a qualified electrician?"

"Why, yes," was the answer at the other end of the phone.

Ira thought he detected a qualm. "Well, he ought to lose his license, that's all I can tell you. My kid got quite a shock. He's been going through a difficult phase in his adolescence and when he let out that yell, I thought he had gone completely off his pulley. I wanna tell you, that took ten years off my life. And my wife's too."

"I can sympathize with you," the businessman at the other end commiserated. "I know just what you feel. I'll tell you what I'll do. It's our mistake. We'll fix it right off, and we'll make it right with you."

"Yes? How?"

"The next five tanks of gas are on us."

"Well." Mollified. "It wasn't my intention to put the screws on you because of that."

"I understand. It's a mistake. And we made it. If five tanks of gas squares us with you, that's all we ask."

"Okay." Ira was a heavy user of bottled gas in his "dressing plant," euphemism for his waterfowl slaughterhouse. Five large tanks of butane at about ten dollars apiece, that represented most of a year's supply—free! "I appreciate the—" For him to use the word *gesture* would be too highfalutin. "I appreciate the goodwill."

"That keeps us in business."

X

Ira did as he had resolved, and always it seemed that if he really meant it, if his fate hung on the event, it came to pass. He was hired. He was assigned to the Loft's candy store on 149th Street and Jerome Avenue in the Bronx. The corner was an extremely busy one, a shopping mart of the populace, bustling, noisy, heavily traveled, the junction of trolley lines, the location of a large subway station, a train interchange with a large platform above the street. And everything below the platform, shop windows and window shoppers, throngs and vehicles, was shaded by it, submerged in the perpetual shadow of a subway station which in the Bronx became a stop on an elevated line. Located in the midst of a medley of storefronts was Loft's, and here Ira was assigned.

He worked six days a week: weekdays from three to ten in the evening, Saturdays, a full eight-hour shift from three to eleven at night. And Sunday, from nine-thirty to six. On Sundays the store closed early. Mom had to change her schedule on Sunday, give him some breakfast first, anything, fry a couple of eggs, serve up a roll and Swiss cheese with his coffee. He remembered what had hounded him, what had driven him off to work. It wasn't for the sake of the sixteen bucks a week, it was only that *goyish* boyfriend Minnie had had. It was that goddamn terror. When that crowded into him, preempted his psyche, it didn't matter if he told himself a thousand times he had been safe as hell—he couldn't dispel it, budge it. Guilt, guilt, guilt— as if he had murdered somebody: Minnie herself. Guilt, guilt, and more guilt. But enough of that! he told himself en route to the 116th Street subway station. It would soon be time to put on a big smile for the customers. That was why he had a job: to keep busy wrapping up the "99¢ Special," to keep the diffuse terror at bay.

Of the sixteen dollars he earned per week—and a dollar or two at the end of the month for commission on sales—he kept five, gave Mom nine—and with a great flourish, gave Minnie a dollar every pay-day, to Mom's beaming and Pop's grudging approval. A few times she secretly asked him for more, another dollar, which he gave her, without knowing why he was so generous, since he didn't get anything for it. How could he? Or hardly. To salve his conscience maybe, pay back, or because he was relieved she was going though a transition again, a kind of waning of feeling that allowed the return of ostensible attitudes, the safe and snippy Minnie. Giving her that extra buck was like a propitiatory offering to anxiety.

Why—Ira turned aside to ponder the question—why did he continue to demean himself so? Why was he debasing himself, the Jew, the serious writer, the serious literary man, the artist? Why didn't he just bowdlerize the story, please his critics, delete his amorous dalliances with Minnie and Stella, as easily as pressing control-Y on his computer? It would take a volume to answer that alone. And was this the place to try to find an answer to his question? For he was posing the question to himself, not in the time of his typescript, or the later time of his first transcription to the word processor, his IBM PC*jr*, sometime during the mid-eighties, but during the living present, this very moment as it passed. It was something he had earlier promised himself not to do, inject the living present, but remain within the confines of time in which he had set down his narrative. To do otherwise would load the narrative exponentially—and finally it would be out of control. Entanglements would become endless, become the briar wall around Sleeping Beauty. He would never be able to get through it to his narrative—his double narrative. But now he couldn't resist the diversion into the present moment, the living present.

He would only pause, he promised himself, just long enough to dwell on a few points, although even in doing so, he was breaking the rule, violating the canon. He was allowing room for precedent, for new departures—before the time he had planned to allow them. Well, the question had dogged him long enough: why was he doing this, demeaning himself—and perhaps Jews, the multitude of Jews who had transformed one previous novel into a shrine, a child's shrine at that—to the extent he was?

The answer seemed to be connected with the same frame of mind that had produced his first novel: anxiety, dread. But now much enlarged, involving his whole people, involving Israel, especially Israel. How and in what way? He feared for Israel's survival. The question hadn't come to him in that context, and perhaps the answer he found to it was simply rationalization. Before, in the thirties when he wrote that first novel, the Nazis were coming to power, did come to power. He had reason to fear. Now it was Israel's survival he feared for, Israel's viability he had begun to doubt. What his aspersions, his stigmatizings, meant was that to himself he was already setting the stage for, already justifying, Israel's and the Jews' disappearance. In other words, in the confusion and alarm in his soul, he feared he was laying a basis for a new Final Solution. Look at the scum these Jews are. Why should they not be annihilated? How else could he say it? It was in the old sense, in the Biblical sense, that they suffered—because they had sinned, because he had sinned. He had been guilty of abomination.

He would have to dwell on it at greater length later. But right now all he could do was to reflect the desolation he felt that Israel would not survive. Desolation like Jeremiah's. It wasn't only that the media took every opportunity, like a school of piranhas, to tear at Israel's flesh—Jew and gentile alike (Who owned the *New York Times*? Who owned the *Washington Post*?). Damned piranhas! But the facts—no, the *acts!*—the acts grew more and more brutal, the acts grew more and more insensate and remorseless, vicious tributaries that would join into a flood sweeping the Jews out of existence. He couldn't avoid, he couldn't evade, the conclusion: Israel was doomed.

Ira bought a tin of condoms to use on Stella, who was proving to be a damned good substitute. Stella could be counted on to be the same every Monday, his evening off, when he called at Mamie's house after supper. Always the same, blond and plump and simpering-ready for his lead, if he could connive a scoundrelly way with her assistance, improvise a subterfuge. She was always ready, ancillary to his opportunism. All he needed was a little luck. No beating around the bush with Stella, no sitting on the edge of a bed, or things like that, wooing against the clock, as he used to do, wooing like an alley cat on a fence. Nothing like that. He got into her first crack out of the box of contingency. Rare was the Monday he missed.

Oh, it was damn funny, and oh, the treachery of it, Iago. About once every other month he would arrive with Zaida's favorite—a two-pound box of glacéed fruit from Loft's (at a small discount for employees). Glacéed fruit were the only sweets the old man regarded as sufficiently kosher for him to consume. Perfect show of deference on Ira's part, perfect tribute, perfect pretext! And yes, the gift rewarded him with a durable vignette. The swift movement of the old boy's hands as he helped himself to a piece of glacéed pineapple, and immediately, with what astonishing speed, popping the box into his trunk. Yet Zaida's presence at Mamie's constituted a new hazard for Ira. One more person to keep an ear and an eye open for. But then, the race of heartbeat, the spindling of wit and senses to the pricking point, the rearing of a pinnacle, the rearing of a steeple of awareness, higher, higher, as if his flat, phlegmatic nature tapered to a singularity by the forces of duplicity, stealth, concentration, craftiness. If only—devoid of conviction, the wish merely flitted in and out of Ira's consciousness—if only he could invoke all that cunning and wariness, that acumen, foresight, playing cards, playing pinochle, poker, he'd be a shark, a world-beater. He'd clean up. The same in business, if he ever tried it. He'd be rich. If he were as intent on getting the advantage, as sharp, premonitory, in the marketplace, putting it over on someone—oh, hell—he'd be a millionaire! Or now that he was a collegian, if he paid that much attention in class, listened acutely to a lecture, acutely and with the same assiduity, as he took stock of the situation at Mamie's, he'd be a straight-A student, like Aaron H, or Ivan H. Straight-A, yeah, straight eight. Maxima come lewder. What the hell.

Despite all that, the job at Loft's, Minnie's inaccessibility, the furtive gambles at Mamie's, his sophomore year was a dreary one. Why this was so, Ira in retrospect was never sure. Perhaps because that fall of 1925 was a time of spiritual lethargy, the withering of an intended career, the realization, growing into conviction, that the withering was irreversible, irreversible because he had been deprived of nutrient interest. How could he be expected to pursue a career in biology when his schedule at CCNY was nothing more than an exercise in waiting, waiting while his interests drained and drifted into other fields, disciplines, and finally, the shadowy, nebulous art of literature? He would never, never be a zoologist, biology teacher, or anything of the sort. He seemed headed into a degraded future, a baneful void, with only an iota of luster to light it, a hint of aspiration whose sole credential was the CCNY *Lavender* in which the "term paper" that earned him a D had appeared—and which Mom kept as a souvenir.

Though he had again become her "stupid brud," Minnie tried, with utmost solicitude, to cheer him up, when she saw his evident despond. Mom and Pop were around, but her tenderness no longer made him scowl apprehensively. It was as if that same tenderness was always there, just took different forms. It was strange. The sisterly seemed to be winning out, sisterly concern, sympathy. Was that how she attained to maturity, something he had gloomy presentiment he wasn't capable of, wasn't anyway, and he was two years older? No matter his exaggerated pose of indifference, his slighting words, and what offended her most—his bored yawn—she persisted in her encouragement: "Don't worry. Don't get so downhearted. You'll write a book yet, and I'll type it, the way I did for *The Lavender*. You remember?"

He did. "Yeah," he said skeptically.

She stroked his arm. He kept his face dour. No point in arousing suspicions at home, when nothing was happening anymore.

Doldrums, that sophomore year, interspersed with, punctuated by, excitements that left him more hollow, more gnawed by tedium than before. His college work, with the exception of his Composition 2 class, was substandard. He was failing in Calculus; he was doing so poorly in Physics he had to drop the course. He was doing no better than C work in Qualitative Analysis. His instructor in Descriptive Geometry could scarcely conceal his vexation when he looked at Ira's mechanical drawing. His college career was a hopeless mess.

Ira felt he ought to drop out, quit college, apply to Loft's for an all-day job behind the candy counter. If it weren't for Mom's fixation on his having a career, he would. Christ, what a career! Except for Composition 2, Professor Kieley's course in descriptive writing, his college career was a disaster. It was like walking on a treadmill up in limbo. No future. No prospects. No preference in profession. High school teaching positions were reportedly harder and harder to obtain, especially for Jews, CCNY Jews—it was an open secret that they were being weeded out. And what would he teach, if he no longer felt interested in biology? English? Even worse. He already had a D in the subject, and even though he was doing A work now, standards were stricter—and worst of it was, he hadn't the least inclination to teach English. He already felt intuitively he had no aptitude either. So he would be left with elementary-school teaching by default. Pop was right. A *malamut*, that's all he would be: teaching grade-school kids, like Mr. Lennard, the goddamn fag, like Mr. Kilcoyne, the dairy farmer, Mr. Shullivan, the crippled public accountant, the only one who sensed that he had more than standard ability. Nothing with nothing, as they said in Yiddish, nothing but a wisp of hope that he might be a writer—someday maybe. Nah, he was ruined.

Ruined, ruined. Dumb. Sluggish. Shrinking. Sneaky. Abhorrent. Perverted, what else but perverted? He had fucked his sister, and when he no longer could, his kid cousin. Got a kick out of it, a double kick out of it—maybe not as vile, as violent, as with Minnie those special times, but good enough—like Joe, that sonofabitch who lured him way back when to Fort Tryon Park. He didn't have to lure Stella, but, ah, Jesus, that was good. Once a week, once a week, on a Monday, make a sordid tour to Mamie's. Right? Feel the exaltation, exultation of having violated, perpetrated—ah, the only relief he got: maneuver the fat little heifer into a half-minute of perilous privacy in the front room, precarious privacy, while everybody in the kitchen might be talking—what a tight squeeze, wow!—stick it in for a half-minute of furious, silent spraddle. He didn't give a goddamn what anyone would have thought, if they knew—and who knew? He ravened, he lusted for the prohibited, the proscribed—Jesus, what would the heinous be like? The really heinous, like what? What was heinous? He couldn't imagine.

But meanwhile he'd have to be satisfied by trampling on the deep shadows under the Park Avenue trestle on Monday night. The anticipation buoyed his climb up to 116th Street. He quickened his pace as he reached 112th Street, Mamie's street, and felt at least for a while alacrity, the elation of shaking off the staleness of existence, the insidious stupor of his aimlessness, his torpid despair that he was scarcely conscious of—but Minnie guessed. And instead of appreciating her sympathy, he could only recall the instances when he wanted to hook it into her. Jesus, no question he was ruined. . . .

But it was on those same Monday nights that Larry, now a classmate at CCNY, had begun to ask Ira to accompany him on his visits to Edith's, and more than ask—to urge. It was hard to decline, although at first Ira did. "Why don't you go see her weekends? I mean, you got all weekend," he had suggested.

"I know that," was Larry's smiling reply. "But I'd like you to be there. Edith would too."

"Edith would? You sure?" Jesus, his one chance at a piece o' tail. "When? In the evening?"

"Yes. Have supper at my house. And then we go downtown together. What say?"

Ira hesitated.

"Try it this Monday. You know, she hasn't seen you since Woodstock. Come on, show her you haven't disappeared. We talk a lot about you, and I keep telling her you're working after school, but she'd like to see you."

"Yeah?" He seemed to hear a rumor in the words "she'd like to see you," a tiny intimation of a future dimension, a promise. It was only at Edith's that some meaning toward a future might take shape. Only at Edith's, nowhere else. "All right. Monday."

"Fine!" Larry was genuinely glad. "Tell you the truth, I'm happy you're coming too. What's a few minutes gabbing in the alcove? Even my mother has asked about you. My family, in-laws and the rest."

"Yeah, well. You know how a job is."

So Ira went . . . sardonic, strangely morose—at the utter jumble of his own mind, its peculiar villainy, of which Larry could guess nothing, not the sacrifice of gratification at Mamie's. Oh, it was all so confused, so goddamn confused. He wasn't accompanying Larry for nothing; Ira sensed his ulterior motives: he came to Edith's with postponed lubricity, longing. There would have to be requital of some kind. Somehow. Someday. Or was it all just dumb fantasy? The dainty payoff for the foul. Nah.

From a pinnacle of purest enchantment, as Larry's affair with Edith had seemed to Ira in the beginning, to the high, dreamy, ambivalent valley of Woodstock, it now leveled into a more comprehensible, more predictable plateau. With the arrival of the long-awaited, polished and dazzling Rhodes Scholar, Richard Smithfield, from fabled Oxford, Edith and Iola began to go their separate ways. Soon after Edith's return from Woodstock, when the two women still shared their apartment on St. Mark's Place, Richard, with John Vernon trailing him animatedly, called—at exactly the time when Larry and Ira were there. Richard was faintly amused at Edith's sophomore lover, who was, despite all his urbanity, clearly at a disadvantage vis-à-vis the elegant Oxford graduate. As for Ira, he was totally tongue-tied. Completely abashed, Ira listened in awed silence to the other's felicitous speech, and watched entranced the graceful movements of the superb, clean-flavored gentleman, whose very perfection summoned up visions of Continental drawing rooms, elite and exquisite. Would Ira ever forget Richard speaking of the flavor of borscht, borscht which he had eaten at the Russian Bear restaurant?—that it was delightfully dill. Dill! Borscht! And when he took his leave, after his brief, demigodlike visit, he said, with such impeccable protocol: "It desolates me to leave you."

Yes—for once, Ira had successfully located a document in his files: it was from Richard, who had married Iola within a year of returning from Oxford, cordially acquiescing in Ira's request to visit him and Iola in Annapolis, where they lived in retirement after Richard's distinguished teaching career at St. John's College. "What a horse's ass I was!" Ira said aloud—and shook his head. He had had a chance to visit them, and hadn't. "Goddamn lazy bastard."

"Dear Ira," he read Richard's fountain-pen black but clear handwriting: "I hope it isn't too late for this to reach you. Iola and I would very much like to see you. We can't put you up. For different though similar reasons, we are invisible until about three o'clock in the afternoon, but we'd love to take you to dinner and travel backward with you to New York and forty-odd years ago."

That was in May of 1970, and Ira, lazy, cheap bastard, after first writing them he would go, canceled at the last minute. Ira still heard Richard's voice on the phone expressing his regret at hearing Ira's change of mind, the pause in conversation, and the regretful silence prelude to acceptance. Rue would consume him every time he thought of the lost opportunity. *Shlemiel, shlimazl.* They both had cancers. Both were dead in a couple of years. . . .

*   *   *

With unfailing altruism, Edith dictated that she would leave the St. Mark's Place apartment to Iola and Richard, while she herself sought, and found, another place. The new apartment was far less attractive—probably less expensive too—totally without any charm, even to Ira's slowly developing taste in such matters, a single low-ceilinged room, dingy, two steps down from the sidewalk and in the basement of a typically remodeled former townhouse—in the very midst of the turmoil of 8th Street's motley thoroughfare, its stores, traffic, eating places, window shoppers, trolley-car din and clang. It was there, in that dingy, low-ceilinged basement apartment, that Larry's inability to find lyric outlet, or to tap new sources of literary inspiration, became associated in Ira's mind as the place where his friend's frustration became chronic. Avowedly so. It was there he grieved over the loss, lamented his condition more than once; the last time, when Ira was there, Larry's voice faltered, became throaty, almost broke. Edith tried to soothe, to cheer. All writers ran into these "fallow periods," she said, endeavoring to keep incentive alive. Fallow periods were succeeded by recrudescence, she assured him: inspiration revived all the more vigorously after such periods of quiescence.

The weeks went by, but Larry's poetic impulse showed no sign of revival. It was as though a phase had passed. Something—a lyric, a literary surge, had risen on the tide of his early youth—and ebbed away with it. Why? What was this thing called imagination? This urge called creativity? What drove it; what was its motive force? What was this strange need that demanded outlet in a certain form, that could only be satisfied a certain way? Strange. And was it the need that left one, or only the ability to satisfy it? Or both? Ira pondered, and could find no answer. It happened, and as Mom would have added: *und shoyn.*

The Arts Club, in which Larry had been so active, too was disbanded. Larry was no longer an undergraduate at NYU, and whether he could have continued as secretary of the club or not had become moot. He no longer cared to be secretary, nor even cared to belong. And with Larry gone, and no one to replace him as student secretary, no one to accept the executive burden of arranging meetings, Edith and John Vernon found themselves too busy with other matters to afford the time necessary to keep the club functioning. They felt the club had served its purpose. The initial enthusiasm, the ferment of innovation, had also waned, or been permitted to subside. Ira also gathered the impression that the two faculty sponsors both felt more secure in their positions, and hence could safely slacken in their activities to win favor with Professor Watt by further devotion of time and energy to the enterprise they had initiated. Edith, especially, was sure she would be advanced to an assistant professorship the following year. The Arts Club was allowed a quiet demise.

The weeks went by, bringing the fall term of 1925 to an end. Having given up further attempts at writing, Larry turned to another art form entirely: sculpture. What a strange metamorphosis Ira felt he was witness to, on those Monday evenings when he accompanied his friend to Edith's basement apartment. Larry had enrolled in a private school of design, and was taking evening lessons in drawing and the plastic arts. Not only had his art form changed, but the whole setting of his love affair underwent a change as well, became different, in so many ways, and in so short a time. Truly, the pristine bloom that once had seemed to encompass the lovers had passed. That bright, airy, quiet apartment, to which Larry had taken Ira the first time, with white walls more radiant than reality, with trees outside the windows in a yard of verdant and flourishing vegetation, had now given way to a dingy, cramped, low-ceilinged room, one into which street noises intruded, past whose single, smudged window the legs and feet of pedestrians continually traveled. Changed, vanished, hard to define: the novelty was gone, the afflatus and promise of that first sense of new freedom, its bewitching latency and illusory horizons, all had dissolved like a mirage. "Romantic" was the word that described what it once was—ah, yes, now he understood, understood the meaning of the word—in *his* terms: the sense of a marvelous unfolding of the new, mysterious and boundless. He understood because he realized he had been under a spell, and the spell was broken. Drab clay now displaced all those airy sentiments, glamorous overtones, those allusions to books and *belles lettres*. Masses of drab clay dispossessed discussion of ideas, the New Criticism, the advent of Humanism, often, more often than not, insubstantial and fragmentary to Ira's intellectual grasp, yet all the more precious whatever

he succeeded in grasping—grasping and retaining. Ah, precious
to dwell on, to try to extend, extend the implications, mentally test
their application. The only thing that had the power of transfixing
him, like the power of plane geometry, seemingly long ago, the only
thing that sometimes could actually evict thoughts of sex from his
mind.

But changed now, changed. Terminated. Yielding to talk of
sculpture, sculptors, and techniques. Oh, hell, who cared? The
change in Larry's artistic medium seemed to have a kind of subliminal symbolism about it, graphic, maybe too, well, say visible. Drab
clay in a small, gray apartment had taken over the aspiring word, the
novel notion, the expansive oral prompting. Did the kind of transformation he saw occurring in Edith's dingy apartment take place in
his mind only? Did it mean a change in Larry's personality? Anh,
what kind of a dumb question was that? And yet he now actually beheld how the quotidian, the mundane, precipitated out of the romantic the way silver chloride precipitated out of solution. Facts
swept away illusions—one had read about that and reread about that,
but one had to experience the process, mull it over, and even then
still be puzzled about how the change took place, and what effect it
had, or what it indicated. Something mysterious about it, sad too, the
final settling into a mold, the hardening forever of the once protean
and iridescent, eternally cast in dingy pall. Jesus, he'd never get free
of his confusions; he couldn't think. Feel, yeah. How the hell do you
get ready for the change that will lock you into the settled and prosaic? Jesus, and you thought that out of the change something else
was going to emerge, something else come to fruition?

Brought in by Larry, a mass of clay on a modeling stand made its
appearance, modeling tools, large wooden calipers, other instruments of the sculptor's craft, an ample cloth throw as well. Edith was
to be Larry's model; a study of her face, a portrait or bust of her in
clay, his first serious project. And while Larry sculpted the image of
his lady love, Ira was left to his own devices, *more or less*. It *seemed* he
was left to spend the evening in any way he pleased. But little by little,
out of the vagueness of Ira's mind, the realization began to coalesce
that Larry needed, Larry craved, someone to admire him, to extol

him, that he brought Ira along as audience. For a time, Ira played the role expected of him: he watched and praised, and for a while it was diverting to watch Larry at work. As he did everything else, he sculpted with a flair. Nor did he omit any item pertaining to his role as sculptor. He wore a smock, he wore a beret. He exclaimed in delight as he traced the contours of Edith's features with his long white fingers. Praiseworthy and truly impressive was the facility with which he reproduced the contours of Edith's features in clay, reproduced them with ever-growing verisimilitude. It was clear he had talent, just as it had been clear he had talent as a lyric poet.

Edith meanwhile sat silently with a manila file folder in her lap, reviewing her lectures for the next day, or sometimes conversing with Larry and Ira as she posed. Two or three hours of the evening would pass while Larry worked on the bust. When he was done, and the session over, all signs of his artistry were concealed: the cloth was carefully draped over his work, and the unfinished sculpture again stowed in a corner of the apartment, to be unveiled and brought out the next time, a Monday hence.

What a bore that must have been for her. . . .

With fingertips together, Ira sat reconstructing scanty vestiges of recollection.

You hear, Ecclesias, what a bore. That mature, increasingly sophisticated (and undoubtedly discontented) woman sitting there patiently, while her youthful lover exclaimed in delight when his scanning fingers discovered a new curve . . . in the light of the floor lamps and table lamps of her small room. She should have posed bare-ass: the not-too-proper, risqué thought crossed an old mind. That would have been more fun, given the occasion more éclat and daring and reward, more exposure—

—Come along with you.

Mo' diversion, at any rate—who knows—though not for Larry, of course. He was an honest, faithful, and conventional lover; and she, as Ira was to learn in time, most enterprisingly unconventional and demurely clandestine: the way she smuggled in the *Ulysses,* the way her sober gaze perched on his fly. More diversion, for everyone but Larry.

* * *

As things were, Ira sat there, many an evening, Larry's inert retainer, wishing he were at Mamie's and then remembering why he wasn't: biding his time, biding his time in Edith's apartment, especially at first, when lamplight would contract to merest points, as if he were in a trance, biding his time, in suspended animation, biding his time. So that even Larry's sculpture phase seemed to add a listless increment to the doldrums of that sophomore year.

Still, there's one thing to observe, Ecclesias, a trait of Edith's, not too con-spicuous, but noticeable: a subdued—should one say?—a well-bred narcis-sism. Or what else to call it? A covert seeking out of self in the mirror, a culling, as it were, of every new fold and wrinkle. (Others too had noticed the trait.) Perhaps that accounted not only for her numerous, passing, amorous episodes, but for the seeming passion she had for initiating youth, friends of mine and strangers. Would I had known it—

—You did, eventually.

No, no. I meant known it sooner. Even, as I have already indicated, as early as Woodstock.

—You still regret?

Yes, the undone. Not to do again, but the undone. It is the undone that exerts a stronger grasp on the soul than the done. She would have been avid to lay for us both, to be vulgar, lay with us both, to be Biblical. I know. All the more so, since she was indeed dissatisfied, unfulfilled, by Larry as a lover, as I surmised at the time, and ascertained later. But more than that, she was given to treating the body, her body, as a kind of counter, not contour but counter, an existential pawn subservient to curiosity or to policy. For example, out of sheer altruism, she and another woman both undertook to induct a famous homosexual poet—well, what the hell—Hart Crane—into the praxis of ordinary fornication. The guy puked—

—Gossipmonger.

No. It's an illustration. We'll all be dust in a couple of years, Ecclesias. I daresay I'm almost the sole survivor.

XI

At Loft's, where in a surprisingly short time Ira became cloyed with even the choices of pecan "logs," as they were called, not to mention chocolates, however exotic the filling, the company promoted the regular evening clerk-cashier to assistant manager, and transferred him to a different branch. As a result, the duties of the clerk-cashier, by order of Mr. Ryce, the manager of the store, devolved upon Ira. Another clerk was hired in Ira's place, a young Southerner, lately come to New York. He was winning in person and manner, charming all and sundry with relaxed friendliness and native drawl. He and Ira worked well together; he was easy to get along with. He was a member of the Naval Reserve, to which he had to report for duty one weekend per month, and he filled Ira's ears with all kinds of agreeable tales of the uses to which he and his mates put the launch that took them—and often female friends and visitors—to the training ship and back. How varied and interesting must have been his experiences aboard the man-of-war, his impressions and manifold memories of life in Alabama, which he told Ira during those many afternoons and evenings they worked together. Most notably, however, to the vulgarly, no, perversely inclined Ira, was that he frequently and humorously referred to the naval launch as a fuck-boat. How Ira envied him.

And well you might, Ira thought, well you might indeed: how pitifully contracted already was the scope of your libido, how atrophied the spirit of play, of sport.

Working the same shift, afternoon and evening, was the soda dispenser, soda jerk, a Briton by the name of Jeffrey, with a peculiarly orange complexion and a penchant for telling the most pointless and

smutty jokes Ira had ever heard. One clung to Ira's mind particu-
larly—the attempted buggery by an English seaman of an Oriental
shipmate. "Hey, me Chinaman," the latter protested. To which the
nautical sodomist made retort: "I don't care if you're a charabanc,
I'm going to ride you anyway." And then Jeffrey had to explain for
the benefit of Bob, their Southern sidekick behind the candy counter,
what a charabanc was. No gag deserved the name more than his.

Known to Jeffrey was a speakeasy two or three doors away from
the store, and there at his invitation, Bob and Ira would repair Saturday nights, after the store closed, and quaff "needle beer," and listen
to more of orange-faced Jeffrey's jokes. Oddest damn thing though:
not so many years later, now a writer, and in the company of Edith,
Ira met the same joker tending bar in a restaurant. Franklin Roo-
sevelt was in office by then; Prohibition had been annulled; and
there was Jeffrey behind the bar shaking up a cocktail. "Hi," Ira said.
"How are you? You and I worked together at Loft's. Remember? You
were a soda jerk there."

Ira must have said all the wrong things in the world, all the things
that belied everything he told his employers. He gave Ira the blank-
est stare an orange could give, and shook his head. And somewhat
miffed, embarrassed too, and seeking to avoid further embarrassment, Ira returned to the table, sat down again next to Edith. "The
so-and-so was a soda jerk at the same store I was at Loft's," Ira explained. "And now he doesn't know me at all."

She laughed: "You may have changed since then a great deal."

But the guy kept his eyes on Ira, a little worriedly, all the time the
two were there. Why the hell didn't Ira ask him, "Hey, do you remember that story about the Chinaman and the charabanc?" Too
sensitive. But then again, what the hell would have been the difference? Ira shouldn't argue with a tangerine in a barkeep's outfit.

One night, when time came to cast up accounts, to turn in Ira's receipts for the evening, he was ten dollars short. Ira compared actual
receipts with the figures for receipts on the cash register, tallied and
totaled and retallied, with growing alarm—he was still short by a ten-
dollar bill. Ten dollars exactly! Not nine dollars and fifty cents, or ten

dollars and a quarter, or some other number, but exactly ten dollars, give or take a measly penny or two, a discrepancy of no small consequence. To account for so large a discrepancy as the one in his receipts for the evening was beyond him—and beyond everybody else, Bob or Mr. Buckley, the assistant manager, who took over in the evening. Neither Mr. Ryce, the manager of the store, nor the day cashier, Mrs. Deane, whom Ira relieved in the evening, could account for the shortage. No one could. Had Ira—so Ira and others reasoned—inadvertently given a customer a ten-dollar bill instead of a one when he made change, then he would be nine dollars short. Or if Ira had been guilty of some other carelessness in making change, then he would be short some other explicable amount. But in no case an *even* ten dollars. The mystery resisted solution. Ira was docked ten dollars from his weekly total of sixteen dollars per week.

Slim pay envelope that week: reminded him of the time Biolov docked him two weeks' pay to make up for the five-dollar bill he lost on his way to the wholesale drugstore on Third Avenue. Hard to cavil at the justice of the penalty, but hard not to, hard not to rankle at the sting, especially when one is certain of one's scrupulous honesty and unfailing attention to business.

A week later, the mystery was solved: concentrating on making change for the customer who stood in front of the cashier's cage, quick, vigilant Mrs. Deane spied—out of the corner of her eye—a youngster's very small hand slide beneath the acorn-shaped ferrules of the upright brass rods that enclosed the cage, dip into the open till of the cash register, and pinch a ten-dollar bill out of its compartment. They habitually kept bills of larger denominations in the compartment on the left (which was also on the door side of the store). In a flick, the little hand snapped the bill out of the cage, and before Mrs. Deane could move, the little scamp beat it through the door. Out and away he fled, and into the crowd on 149th Street.

"Thief! Thief!" Mrs. Deane screamed: "Thief! There he goes, Mr. Ryce!"

At once Mr. Ryce set off in pursuit, glimpsed his quarry an instant, but lost him the next, as the kid dodged among the moving throng and vanished in shadow. Now they knew why Ira's shortage had been exactly ten dollars. Together, Mrs. Deane and Ira signed a petition, which he drew up and Minnie obligingly typed, to the president of the Loft's corporation, requesting forgiveness of the ten-dollar loss: the money had disappeared not because of the crew's negligence, but because it had been stolen. The manager of the store himself attested to the fact. *Noo, noo,* as they said in Yiddish, it helped like cupping a cadaver. In her next pay envelope Mrs. Deane too found she had been docked ten dollars.

She fumed about the injustice a great deal. She was a slightly built woman, with shrewd, darting black eyes behind her eyeglasses. Angry, she seemed to condense into the very essence of outraged probity. But nothing could move the president of the Loft's corporation. He sympathized, but in management's view, Mrs. Deane and Ira had been wanting in alertness. Their carelessness was to blame for the loss of the money, and therefore they had to make amends. As a precaution against further thefts, a metal barrier was fastened to the bottom of either side of the cage, closing off the space between the acorn-shaped ferrules and the wooden ledge beneath.

For Mrs. Deane, after a few days or a week of indignation at the injustice the two had suffered at the hands of a great company, the matter ended there—Mrs. Deane sought to recoup the lost portion of her salary by flitting in and out of her cage to wait on customers. Staff were given a tenth of a percent on all sales they rang up. Whether in the course of time she succeeded in recovering her ten dollars, Ira didn't know. Ira did know that a little brooding over the wrong done him hatched another and speedier system of redress. The system, or scheme, went as follows:

The Loft's weekend special, three boxes of different kinds of candy for ninety-nine cents, was a very popular item and in great demand. With it, as with the purchase of any item in the store, came a little sales slip. The clerk behind the counter printed the amount of the purchase on the cash register, and issued the sales slip to the customer together with his purchase. The customer then presented the slip to the cashier, in this case Ira, and paid the amount of the sale printed on the slip. All Ira had to do was to retain the little sales slip, retain it absently, and instead of giving it back to the customer as proof of payment, simply hand the sales slip back to Bob. He would then issue it to the next purchaser of the ninety-nine-cent special, without ringing up a sale, who would then present Ira with the same sales slip, along with a greenback, usually a dollar, receive his penny in change, and go on his way—without Ira's having rung up a sale. The sales slip would then be returned to Bob for another round in the nefarious cycle. Would Bob agree to be a party to the scheme? Ira made discreet inquiry: would he? Of course he would, and with alacrity. His sense of justice too had been violated by the company's summary disposition of Ira's appeal, especially since the two would go half on the proceeds: "That bunch o' tightwads doin' yo' all outta ten skins. We only gettin' even."

They got even. If not in a jiffy, in short order: on two successive Saturdays, on the way to the speakeasy after work, they surreptitiously divvied up a little more than five dollars apiece. Ira was satisfied; he had gotten his money back. Justice was served.

Bob was not. His sense of justice outstripped Ira's. The ease with which they had redressed the balance, or, witticisms aside, mulcted the company of over twenty dollars whetted his appetite for more. His day off was Tuesday, the day after Ira's, and he was making it big with a honey of a beauty parlor operator, a blonde who looked like a million bucks in her black skirt and white blouse, and brother, could he use a little extra dough.

Ira too was impressed by how smoothly the stratagem had worked—not a hitch! How easily they had skimmed off more than twice the sum Ira felt the company owed him! Ira agreed to continue the ploy next Saturday. But nothing on the same scale. There were spotters, he warned. They both knew that: Mr. Ryce, the manager, had given Ira and Bob a report of the findings on their approach to customers: whether the two had addressed the investigator in guise of a bona fide patron with a properly obsequious "May I help you, sir" (or "ma'am"), and thanked him—or her—with due appreciation after the purchase. And of course—what went without saying—whether they were guilty of any irregularities in the way in which either, or both, Ira and Bob conducted the transaction, namely in the handling of sales receipts and cash. That was the main thing. And besides, Ira stressed to his cohort, Loft's had an accounting department, and if the manager himself couldn't explain the reason for a continued drop in the store's income on Saturday—yes, even ten bucks, Ira overrode Bob's skepticism vehemently—they would surely send somebody out to keep the two under surveillance.

Ira's prudence—or cowardice—prevailed: they limited their swindling to a couple of dollars apiece per weekend. Even then, Ira felt uneasy. "Let's cut it out altogether," he urged. "What the hell. For a couple of bucks. What the hell will it look like on your record if some big guy steps behind the counter and tells us we're under arrest? You say you hope to be a petty officer in the Navy someday."

"No, you don't mean to tell me one o' those fat I-talian ladies waddles in heah with three, fo' kids is goin' to step back heah and put the ahm on us. Yo got mo' sense than that, Iry," Bob blandished. "That's a safe sale, an' you know it."

"Yeah, but somebody else could be watching. The fat lady may be just a decoy."

"Aw, come on. Listen, tell you what ah'll do: instead of us going to that gin mill Saturday night, we-all go to my girl's place. I'll tell her to get one of her friends for you."

"Yeah? . . . Thanks."

"What d'y'all say?"

"No, I can get all I want."

"This one's a real cutie. I laid her myself."

"No, I'm cutting out the—" In the face of Bob's eager candor, Ira felt his shrug was churlish. He riffled the stack of white waxed bags on the marble counter. "I got my dough back, and more. I'm not takin' any more chances, that's all. I'm ringing up every sale. No more sales slips back."

"Suit yo'self." Bob was clearly miffed.

"You do a thing regularly like that, you're asking for it," Ira commented darkly.

"How come you so sure?"

"I'm sure, all right."

And it wasn't more than two weeks later that the clerks were agog with tales of a night-shift team like theirs that had been caught doing the same thing they were guilty of. Only they had gone Ira and Bob one or several better: they had a number of sales slips in reserve, sales slips with different prices on them, and the one they had been caught passing was for a two-pound heart-shaped box of fancy chocolates, with nuts and rich fudge centers, costing ...o-fifty. They were both fired, but not before they signed a confession of guilt, in lieu of being hauled into court to face petty-larceny charges.

"We were lucky," Ira said to Bob. "See?"

"A two-pound box o' nonpareils. They must've thought they were in business fo' themselves. Two-fifty a clip." His lips pursed in generous confession. "I'm just kiddin', Iry. Y'all were right that time. You're purty smaht." He moved away to attend to a blowsy woman just entering the store; she looked a little unsettled, to say the least: her hat was jammed all the way down to her eyebrows like a fuchsia bucket with a green flower on it.

"Yes, ma'am. What can I do fo' you, ma'am?" Bob's address was punctilio itself. "Can I he'p you, ma'am?"

She looked like a freak, but she could be just the type of customer who could put the arm on them, as Bob phrased it.

Ira went back to the cage and sat down behind the cash register. Idly, Ira watched Bob dig the candy scoop into the dark slope of malted milk balls under the glass counter, then into the mound of peanut clusters. No, probably not. The dame was probably straight, was just what she seemed to be: a mama, maybe some widow returning from the shop or factory, bringing home a treat for herself and the kiddies, bringing home "bong-bongs," as Ira had jested with Larry. No, Ira wasn't "smaht," though it flattered him that Bob thought so. Bob slid the scoop under the pile of paper-wrapped nougats, pale surfaces flecked with citrus. No, Ira wasn't smart. He just learned on his own hide, the only way he seemed able to learn. For a moment, a small cloud settled on the white-topped soda tables in front of the cage. Wherever his eyes roved, from the large double doors opening on 149th Street to the soda fountain tended by henna-skinned Jeffrey, the cloud roved; and embedded in it was a silver-filigreed fountain pen. The nightmare of Stuyvesant High School had taught him a little, anyway. Ira had quit just in time. But what a damned fool he was to run that risk for ten bucks. Oh, it was a lot of money, but compared to what might have happened to him— what a damned fool he was, and yet Ira had done the same thing in his bus-conductor days, swiped nickels; nearly croaked when the spotter in the car yelled at him. And this time to have the dick come around the counter and say "You're under arrest" would have killed him. Smart. Ira was smart in the other sense, when "smart" meant hurt.

Yet this newly acquired wisdom did not constrain him on his visits to 112th Street. He continued to use any imaginable ploy to visit Stella, growing bigger, plumper, at sixteen. She was his regular one, and he hated passing up a Monday visit that fall and winter. Larry could not understand why he refused to accompany him after classes on Monday evenings. Again and again, Larry invited him for supper in the new apartment on West 110th Street to which Larry's mother and he had moved. With Irma married, and the uncle traveling, they lived alone now.

Nonetheless, Ira adamantly declined Larry's invitation. "No, I gotta catch up on work," was Ira's unfailing excuse. "Can't do it. Thanks. Can't do it. Jesus, am I ever failing." Boy, give up his only chance for a nice piece of ass that week in exchange for a couple of lamb chops or broiled salmon and fresh peas—and have to listen to Larry's enthusiastic disquisitions about his latest artistic outlet: the stage, and the flair he had for acting.

The trouble was that visiting Mamie's was regular, every Monday evening, regular. Oh, he was great at maneuvering, keeping a straight face. He was a wonder when it came to that: maneuvering, waiting, stalling, stalking—hey, that was another pretty good one: stalking, he'd have to underline the stalk—what the hell was he talking about? It was the regular, regular, that's what he was talking about; that was what was gonna trip him up. With Stella, the same as with the fountain pens, regular, the same thing he had warned Bob about. Monday, one after another. Cut it out then. He couldn't. Couldn't. As long as he knew it was there. Christ, he finger-fucked her when she had the monthlies and she pulled him off. That was all right, as long as he had someone else doing it, someone else coming with him.

Better he took up Bob's offer of getting him a lay. Better, but he couldn't. That was the worst of it. He knew he wouldn't get a hard-on now. Scared with grown-up girls who knew all about it. That's what fucking kids had done to him, fucking Stella when she was fourteen, taking Minnie when she was eleven. . . .

Ruined . . . long ago . . . and that was why performance with words was the only option open to him, the only tramway out of himself. Conveyor belt: and on it, like chunks of ore cut out of a gloomy mine (mind): words, words, extricating himself from Joyce by Joycean means. Well, perhaps not words alone: anything innovative might do as substitute, anything exploratory, visionary, even quixotic: the thing Pop did when he was eighty-seven. He bought the old Turner farm on Church Hill Road in Maine above where the Stigmans had lived, an old run-down farm on the crest of the hill, and a horse and old buggy for transportation to town (the *Kennebec Journal* ran a feature on the old coot and his hay-burner)—and he died a year and a half later in Bellevue Hospital, the pathetic, damned old fool. . . .

The overwhelming notion of his own death now lay imminent in him. And he recalled the morning when M had smiled at him wisely. "If you're not all right, I can't be all wrong." And she had added something he couldn't remember now about either one not living if the other didn't and he had seconded the notion of not living, seconded it all too heartily. *L'chaim,* the Jews said when downing a libation: *to life.* Apart from the correctness of the Hebrew, the toast might just as well have been *L'met.* To death. It would serve him just as well: *L'met.* Well met.

XII

While Larry sculpted, continually imbuing the clay with greater detail, and Edith posed meditatively in the light of the floor lamp, Ira began to depart from his practice of just sitting there quietly, more or less patiently, under the light of the other floor lamp, augmenting the weak, wintry light of the basement room. Chatting with Edith too much tended to disturb her repose as model, so Ira began to delve into Edith's ever-growing collection of modern poetry, the proverbial slim volumes of modern poets: Aiken, Pound, Frost, Adams, Sandburg, Millay, Stevens, Wylie, Winters, Teasdale, MacLeish, Cummings, Taggard, Sitwell, Williams, Tate, Ransom, Robinson.

Edith never hesitated an instant to buy a book of poetry she deemed to have literary merit—and most of them Ira failed to understand. Oh, there were exceptions: Jeffers he could follow quite well, his long narrative poems. Ira could follow a story, and the "plots" of some of Jeffers's stories dealt with subject matter he had become too thoroughly and too shamefully acquainted with, and Jeffers's incestuous narratives aroused his interest all the more. And Sandburg and Vachel Lindsay and a few others, like Housman, were easy. Edith remarked when she saw him assaying their collected poems that they no longer addressed the modern mood. "Passé," Larry chimed in, and added, "That's me. Passé."

Edith tried to soothe him: "Oh, no. You haven't really come into your own yet, how can you be passé?"

"It's a feeling I have."

"Oh, lad, these things have their own pace. Poets find their own voices. And sometimes quite suddenly."

And then in Ira's haphazard way, he came upon T. S. Eliot. He had by now achieved major status as a poet, in vanguard critical opinion—and among the CCNY literary elite, of course. Once again, Ira felt as he had about Joyce, even though Larry, just as with Joyce, found no affinity with Eliot. Ira felt this was another case in which it was his duty, if he really wanted to get some notion of the age in which he lived, its attitudes and presentiments, it was his duty to read Eliot. No, not merely to read—Ira didn't grasp what he read, so reading wasn't enough. Ira had to strive to understand, to study, study as if he were applying greater and greater mental pressure to a problem before him, to try to make up by sheer, undeviating pressure of concentrated pondering, make up for his lack of the kind of sensitivity to the significance pulsing within a poem that Edith had, and Larry too, when he cared, though he no longer seemed to. Ira thought he ought to try at least in this one case, to comprehend the widely acclaimed poet, T. S. Eliot, this one case, to make up for his failure to resonate, for his limitation of response to delicacy, to subtlety of allusion. Perhaps his defense against an inner foe, his continual sense of shame, had become a barrier to the messages of other minds, modern minds, the messages of most of the poets on Edith's bookshelves. That was how it seemed. But Ira was determined to wring intelligibility out of this one enigma, T. S. Eliot.

And alas, Ira began to think he had performed the task too well. In the nihilism of spirit that his self-opprobrium had brought him to, in which Ira found himself now, odious and unspeakable to himself, Ira was all too susceptible to the meaning, T. S. Eliot's meaning steeped in crushing fatuity, in alienation, tortured anomie, despair, that he absorbed so single-mindedly, as Ira had never absorbed the content of the *Ulysses*—it was too large, recondite, and finned with irony. Ira absorbed the emotion of Eliot's poems, especially his two major poems, before he understood the meaning. Ira absorbed the emotion, *until much of it became part of him.*

Ira was all too conscious of the recurring Jew-mockery in a number of the poems: of Rachel née Rabinovitch tearing at the grapes, of the Jews in "Gerontion" sitting in the window, "spawned in some estaminent," of Bleistein, of Sir Ferdinand Klein, Sir Alfred Mond, and the Jew underneath the lot, and the *echt deutsch* Litvak in *The Waste Land.* He was all too conscious of the poet's anti-Jew bias, but he accepted it, shared it, even approved of these thoughts—since leaving the East Side and becoming conscious of himself, not as a member of a homogeneous folk, but as an individual Jew, distinct from his milieu, nullified, demeaned, experiencing the entire spectrum from sufferance through malevolence to violence. And with relatives all sordidly straining for success, and home life what it was—and the even uglier thing he had made of it—and of the wider family relations—eventually, Ira became averse to Jews and repelled by Jews. Eliot's clever aspersions and disdainful caricatures seemed no more than just. Deft and diverting and oh so apt, their contemptuous attributions didn't apply to him, for the simple reason that Ira *appreciated* them. Ira shared his repugnance, appreciated his wit, applauded his finesse. That excluded him from Eliot's gibes, as it did all other Jews who possessed taste fine enough to relish the supreme adroitness of his calumnies. Or to whom his ridicule no longer pertained, people like Larry, sophisticated Jews, the assimilated, the deracinated: Jews like himself. Those Jews were exempt, because they were the elite, more or less.

Sixty years later he no longer felt so elite, or so impervious to more common acts of anti-Semitism. In fact, he could easily become depressed. He recalled a sense of dread when M told him, as she lifted him to a sitting position in bed one morning, that according to the radio newscast earlier, an avowed Jew-hater by the name of LaRouche had won election to office—over the major-party candidates. The news haunted him all through breakfast: a Hitlerite sonofabitch had won office in the United States, a self-proclaimed Nazi—under his leadership, his political party had established itself in four or five states. Haunted him: with a flurry of memories and fears: storm troopers, the camps, the ovens . . . the cinema scenes of women lined up naked before the "bathhouses," and the kids lugging suitcases to the freight cars, and—mostly what came back was the days before World War II, when Jew-baiting was becoming the vogue, in higher circles, not just the slum street, no, no, had become a tactic—what had Dalton Miltz told him, co-lover of Edith, Dalton, when he treated Ira to lunch in a Chinese restaurant: that the class of '38 at Cornell—the very university Ira had won a scholarship to—had marched in jubilant file across campus, singing, parodying the song of the seven dwarfs in Walt Disney's *Snow White*:

> Yo ho, yo ho, we've joined the CIO
> We've paid our dues to the goddamn Jews
> Yo ho, yo ho, yo ho, yo ho, yo ho . . .

In the city parks too, provocateurs had taken up positions, lying so plausibly, debating so coolly, and with henchmen about them, Nazi shills to attract a crowd. And the fear and the helplessness and the hopelessness that possessed him. And Father Coughlin whipping up a pogrom over the radio, with his boyhood pal Farley as an acolyte. Perhaps it was that, perhaps it was that, that triggered his depression. He couldn't tell. And where would the Jews run now? Apparitions of Jews thronging in flight, cramming into planes, cars. Where now? And he himself, and M, and Hershel, his Orthodox son, and Hershel's rabbi's-daughter wife, and their three off-spring. Run. And what about Jess, half-Jewish son, and his son, Oliver, quarter-Jewish grandson—where would they run? Would they have to run? "We decide who is a Jew," said Hitler. By the time Ira had finished breakfast, gone into his study and switched on the computer, the very thought of re-suming his narrative had become intolerable.

So he had gone shopping with M, stopped her just as she was about to back the car out of the driveway, and gone along . . . to a new Wal-Mart west across the Rio Grande, and while he shopped for a scratcher such as he had seen his neighbor use a few days ago, to combat weeds, and a beaded chain-pull to extend the ones from the ceiling fan and lamp, which he could no longer reach, and two tubes of Magic Glue for the price of one, yes, a bargain in Magic Glue. What else? An old-fashioned apple corer that M had been hunting for for some time. The apple, he said to himself sardonically, now costs more than its corer. Chatted in front of a gas grill on sale for $125 with a burly old Western type, gray-haired under his cow-boy hat, who said he was a retired auto-body repairman. And when the good Lord gave him the call to stop smoking as He had already to stop drinking, he would. He was smoking over two packs a day, and it was killing him with coughing, but he couldn't stop. He had been smoking so long, he couldn't remember when he began, and he could remember all the way back to the age of three. His stepfather had given him cigarettes. "What do you do for a living?" he asked.

"Retired. I worked as a gauge-maker." Ira fell back on the old sub-terfuge. "I worked in a toolroom years ago."

"I thought you were some kind of an old perfessor," said the new ac-quaintance.

"Well, I happened to be a math teacher once. A tutor." One couldn't deny the man the satisfaction of his perceptiveness.

"Ah, I thought so." Vindicated in his appraisal, the other nodded con-tentedly.

They parted, smiling.

Meanwhile, M, who had stepped into Walgreen's for his Valium which he had ordered by phone, stressing: generic Valium (the difference was about twelve dollars), then shopped for groceries to swell the larder sufficient to meet the added demands of son and grandson, guests beginning tomorrow; met him at Wal-Mart. "Ah, I found you right away."

"Yeah?"

"I hate this store," she said. "Not that there aren't good things in it. It's so cluttered."

"What you hate is of no consequence. Look at the mobs in it. The clutter attracts the hoi polloi. They'd feel uncomfortable in a roomy, orderly store."

"I feel uncomfortable in Kistler-Kollister." She led the way to the checkout counter. "Even the clerks are better dressed than I am. I suppose that's more or less the same thing in reverse."

"That's right . . . The guy runs Wal-Mart knows what he's doing." And after a moment: "Personally, I don't give a damn what it looks like." And reaching the checkout counter, preceded only by a woman with a single cart, "They bait you into the place with a few bargains. That's the thing to beware of. Those Circline fluorescents cost twice as much here as at Allwoods. But once in here, you get into a buying furor."

They were out of the store, in the car again, M driving home.

"I've been thinking, what does my grandson mean to me, the little I see of him." Ira gazed moodily at the chocolate-brown waters of the Rio Grande. "And what do I mean to him? Either one of us could disappear, and not make much difference to the other."

"Oh, it would. It does." M shifted her eyes from the plastic orange tubs that marked the street construction on their corner. "I'll bet the El Vado Motel owner will be glad when those barrels are gone from in front of his place."

Father and son were to stay at the El Vado, where M had made reservations. The El Vado, cheaper by far than the AAA Monterey, less expensive, but very decent, as the new East Indian owner assured M over the phone. And she was pleasantly surprised by the neatness and attractiveness of the decor when she went there to make an advance payment for the room.

"Why is Oliver coming to visit us?" she asked after she negotiated the left turn safely into the multipronged entrance to New York Avenue.

"Custom. The thing to do. To see his grandma, obviously."

"Not his grandpa?"

"No. You love him. The best we can ever do is understand each other, and I don't believe there's that much time."

And when they got home, and began unloading purchases from plastic and paper bags, and spreading items on the kitchen table, he saw what M had bought by way of drugs, his poor wife: she had bought Valium, proprietary Valium. "Well, for Christ's sake!" Ira exploded. "I told them I wanted generic. Jesus Christ, on top of everything else! Don't you look at the price?"

"I'm sorry," said M. "I just gave them my Visa card. It never occurred to me to look at the price."

"It's just too much!" he stormed. "You can't take a goddamn thing for granted."

He went to the phone and called. "This is Ira Stigman. I ordered generic Valium yesterday, didn't I?"

"Just a minute, sir. I'll check," said the female voice at the other end. And after a short conference with someone else, the pharmacist, most likely, "Yes, you did."

"What happened? I've got the name brand."

"It was a mistake," said the voice.

"Yeah?"

"You asked for generic. But when we called Dr. Bennoah to okay the prescription, he said Valium. So then we called back to find out if you could have the generic. So he said, okay, generic. They were both down on the order, and we didn't notice you were supposed to have generic—"

The only appropriate reply that came to mind was Brooklynese: all right already. It took an act of will for him to limit himself to merely, "Yes."

"Please bring it in, and we'll change it," said the voice.

"Thanks." He set down the cordless phone on the typing table opposite the monitor, got up, went back into the kitchen, and recounted his dialogue for M's benefit.

"I feel I have to go change it," M said. "Get it off my mind. It'll just worry me otherwise."

"I'm afraid to have you go. I'm afraid of compounding mistakes into worse. You be careful."

He waited uneasily until she returned, about a half hour later. "Safely back," she called cheerfully from the rear door.

"Thank goodness." He waited until she came into the kitchen. "Big difference in price, wasn't there?"

"Over twelve dollars. No wonder they had that notice on the back of the prescription telling you how much you saved. They meant you saved by buying the generic."

"They make out a Visa credit slip for the difference?"

"No, they gave me cash."

"They did? That's a new one."

"That's what they did. Oh, I'm so dry. It's the excitement. I've got to have a drink of something: herb tea."

"And I'd better take half a Percocet, and get over this goddamn depression."

"Perk up with a Percocet." She reached a long arm to the shelf in the cabinet over the sink: a long arm in a blue knit sleeve with white and red stripes, of a knit shirt striped the same way. Ivory-gray hair with a gray fillet around it, a small yellow comb in back. In front, under her distinguished brow, dark, thick-framed glasses to conceal the folds under her eyes. With her, age took its toll in folds, rather than wrinkles.

While she set the splotched copper kettle over the gas flame, always too high—that's why the copper kettle was splotched: she roasted it—he took out a Percocet tablet from the small vial he kept on the wooden tray of his medications, snapped the tablet in half down the cleavage line. "Only two things in this world are worth a damn: love and a sense of creating something worthwhile." There was still a little cold coffee left in the cup on the table to down the half tablet with. "I'm going back to the computer."

Where the time went? he thought as he crossed diagonally, the darkened path on the buff carpet, entered the hallway to his study: you will ask . . . a year hence . . . ten years hence . . . just as others continually ask: where did the time go? Where did the time go? Not if you had a hundred secretaries, a thousand amanuenses, could you keep track of where the time went, act by act, each within its moment, glissando. If anyone asks—he sat down before the blue-dark monitor—tell 'em time went thataway. . . .

XIII

How protean "Prufrock" seemed at first reading—and at second reading, and at third. How utterly ungraspable. It was like learning to swim; nothing to hold on to, no firm medium to depend on. What the hell was the man talking about? It was not each separate part that baffled Ira. It was all of it. It was the meaning of the whole that tantalized, that he couldn't comprehend. He felt as if he would have to memorize it, commit it to his mind, or his mind to it, have it with him at all times, without need of the book, contemplate the poem until the meaning became part of him, and then he could understand it— the way he understood himself.

Finally that was what happened, or something akin to it: the sum of the meaning came into view: almost like moonrise, like a harvest moon, to wonder at, yet know it to be true. So that was what Eliot was talking about? It was how living in the modern world affected his spirit; how living in the modern world formed his mood, a mood made up of futility and timidity, frustration and emptiness, loneliness, misunderstanding, self-distrust. That was what all the parts added up to. Now Ira could sustain himself within the poem. Ira had made it part of himself. It was himself. The only thing missing that Ira thought he could add was his self-revilings, his cankerous, special depravity. Yeah. Kept him from feeling all that intolerable ennui Eliot felt, but otherwise Ira knew he was close. He was telling you life was a worthless, pointless, tiresome void, papered over by what d'ye call it? Formalities. Why had it taken him so long to figure that out? The poet didn't say it right out loud, the way an old gink like Longfellow might have said it: life is real, life is earnest. He didn't say life is vain, it's a lot of worn-out etiquette. He didn't have to say it. You were the one who said it. So . . . he was only saying what Ira felt. And now what Ira felt was a poem. He could quote it. Though he was speaking for the leisure class, for the gentry and for gentiles, and he was from the *koptsns* and the *shleppers,* and a Jew, still, Ira felt the same; funny, Larry didn't. All in all, if he had come out of the long moiling and groping through Joyce's *Ulysses* with the realization that the materials for literature lay in the plethora of the squalid and the banal all about him, Ira emerged from the "Prufrock"—much more than from *The Waste Land*—inoculated with disenchantment, immune to ideology, to allegiance, more prone than he had ever been before to alienation, courting it. Everything became mere counters for manipulation—inventory for a writer, if that's what he was ever going to be: pegs to hang irony on: religion, *Yiddishkeit*, immigrant ordeals and adversities, sweatshops and trade unions and "sotzialism," sordidness and Jew-baiting, penury and persecution, one's own enormities, one's own callousness and cowardice, everything was convertible to universal literary currency.

How strange, how strange in so many ways! So many fateful forces at work: the petering out of Larry's literary impulse, his interest too, and with it, as though his charm were draining away, his personal charm, his social charm, as if he had lost an inner grace, and in its place, in place of that freshness, originality of observation, that lyric bloom, as in genetics, a separation had occurred. The pristine feature became recessive, and the commonplace one dominant. The poetic imagist became the spinner of set jokes, the histrionic raconteur, luxuriating in tedious embellishment. At first, and more and more, as time went on, Ira would catch Edith's eye seeking his own, as if she were trying to transmit her patient indulgence, or her evaluation on the beam of her sympathy—at the same time as she smiled tightly at one of Larry's long-winded anecdotes. Just a week before Ira got the job at Loft's, she had intimated—and how he treasured that minute of privacy!—that she would always welcome a visit by Ira alone. How he gloated over that! Some time was to elapse before he could—and before he dared—take advantage of her invitation. But when he finally did, the bashfulness he felt at first wore off by the time the visit was over. Ira went away, urged warmly, earnestly, to return; he went away, gleeful in his treachery, feeling as if he were someone between a neophyte and a confidant. Ira was pledged to discretion.

Edith and Ira discussed Larry a great deal—that first time, and afterward. From the very beginning, she dwelled on her disappointment in the way he was developing. He was merely facile, she now realized: his talents were superficial—not as Ira's were, deep and serious; they would develop, she was sure, into those of a genuine literary artist. Larry would never grow as an artist, she was sure of that too, because he shied away from discipline, or lacked the stamina to cope with it, with the taxing and the unpleasant—as Ira was capable of doing, as she had seen him do, first in Woodstock with the *Ulysses*, and then by his poring over T. S. Eliot and his shy comments about "Prufrock" and *The Waste Land*; she found them very stimulating. Larry's taking on sculpture was really just another proof of failure. It was an escape. Instead of tackling the arduous, the demanding, and patiently, quietly, requiring all he could of himself, he had shifted to the immediately rewarding. That was his trouble: he craved immediate rewards, accolades. It was his family that was at the root of all this: they had made so much of his cleverness that he expected the same kind of instant applause and admiration for everything he did, and when he didn't get it, he turned to something else. She had hoped he could overcome their middle-class influence, their ideas of success, and for a while she had thought he could, but she was mistaken. Though he had shifted from NYU to CCNY, and had given up his dental career, he hadn't been able to break away from his middle-class ties and his middle-class standards. He was just too dependent on family, too attached, too given to basking in their admiration. He would become just like the rest of his family in time: conventional. He would surrender to their middle-class values: "I'm sure you've noticed how shallow he's becoming." Edith shook her head solemnly.

Shallow. What did it mean, he now pondered, having become—long ago—a lapsed writer himself. His springs of creativity had run dry, seemingly petered out, just as Larry's had done, the chief difference being that his depletion took place a few years later than Larry's. Did the same stricture that Edith had once applied to Larry apply to Ira as well? Was he too shallow? Once again, what did it mean? In that case there were dozens of shallow writers of that period, that time, each showing great promise at the outset, each producing creditable work, a novel, a trilogy, and then, silence or redundancy, Hollywood or academia—or premature demise, as

though they willed it. Salmon who fought their way upstream to breed—
Ira turned eyes inward, as if to examine the metaphor. Perhaps it went
deeper than he knew. Salmon fought their way up to their own origins,
their own native freshwater streams, to breed and perish. But that was only
an analogy; it told you nothing of the concrete forces at work, psychological, social. One could say they were like certain minerals, Ira told himself:
lead sulfide that fluoresced in ultraviolet light. They were on the beam
then, irradiated and radiant, and when it passed, they went dark. But
again, that was only analogy. What beam? How many writers and poets
who belied their early promise did Edith dismiss in the same way that she
dismissed Larry: they were shallow? What was it that gave out? It seemed
as if an entire literary generation, Ira's own contemporaries, had petered
out. Why had replenishment been curtailed for them, and what kind of replenishment was required, but absent? One after another of the writers
whose acquaintance Ira had made through Edith came to mind. Each offered a different explanation, or for each one a different explanation was
offered, to account for each individual's default in the face of early
promise. Here, one imbibed too freely, here, another suffered a psychological block, here marital and here financial difficulties . . . until Ira began to
suspect that all these explanations, or excuses, were so many symptoms of
a general malady that affected them all. It was a most peculiar malady,
more nearly like a plague, and today, Ira regarded Larry's case as one of the
earliest examples of how that plague affected them, the more susceptible
talents like his first, the less susceptible ones later, but all eventually. Initial
success virtually guaranteed that one would succumb to the plague sooner
or later. And why? Because the dynamic of the scourge lay coiled within itself: success tended to drive the artist from his source. To the degree that
he exploited that source, to the same degree was he divorced from it. Nor
was there any other source remotely as viable that could be annexed in
place of the abandoned one. Why? Did the transfer from a parochial world
to a cosmopolitan one negate the parochial one? Negate, yes, in an or-
ganic sense. But here was annulment, and therein might be the answer.
The two worlds were not organically connected, for otherwise the one
might have subsumed the other. Greenwich Village literati, growing excited about literature over a cocktail, were sterile as literary material—at
least to Ira. He didn't know these people, their origins, memories, motiva-

tions, patterns of thought. They were alien to the world Ira had fled from, but was informed by, as he was alien to the world they had fled from, and were informed by—and neither they nor Ira could any longer return.

There you have it. And Eliot before you. Ira slid dry fingertips over dry fingertips. Editing his prose of five years ago gave him an oddly unreal feeling, imposed a kind of surrealist duality upon himself, almost dangerous, in that he was at a loss as to who the writer was, who judged, who determined, whose emotion and sense of fitness was the more authentic, corresponded best with reality. Dangerous, in that he verged on loss of control. Or was it that writing under stress made the transcribing and rewriting seem surrealist? He had been depressed again this morning (new pains, new symptoms: osteoporosis, perhaps, from taking cortisone over so long a period). He had been hostile to existence, surly to M, and she had begun to weep: "Do you want me to give up writing music?" she had asked.

Perhaps it had been the visit of M's brother, Clive, and his wife, Mary, these last two days, that had had something to do with his grimness—unconscious maybe, who knew. Clive was well-to-do, with a winter home in Florida and a summer home in Michigan. A retired insurance consultant, he was tall, naturally imposing, and thoroughly American. Soon to be eighty, a bit florid of countenance, he had to watch his blood pressure, hoped to die on a tennis court, and addressed his placid wife—mother of their eight children, social register, though exceedingly versatile domestically—as Mrs. P. Clive was very cordial with Ira, communicative, as toward a member of the family. He was warmly affectionate with his sister, recalling old times when they tried to motorize a bicycle, and failed, and when they went out to the sand dunes with the outmoded box camera that took pictures on glass plates. "And who carried the covering cloth?" M reminded pointedly, just as a sister would. And therein lay the rancor, of that were the filaments spun.

From the time of her marriage to Ira, until . . . when? 1975, over thirty-five years, Clive had never communicated with M. And in what dire straits she had been once, back in 1950, when she had lain paralyzed with undiagnosable Guillain-Barré, she who had driven her brother, Clive himself, for radiation treatment when he developed a cancer of the colon—miraculously remitted. Well, what the hell . . . Ira had behaved boorishly, in the family's Cape Cod home, Jew Ira, after Father, executive secretary of Kiwanis International—and an ordained Baptist minister besides—in his

monumental insensitivity had remarked that Kiwanis International, that famous, public-spirited, public service organization, didn't want kikes joining
in. Ira had been asked to leave. And when Father himself was about to die
of a stroke a year later, he enjoined his wife to have nothing more to do
with M, cut her off from all inheritance (to their credit, M's siblings had ignored the paternal injunction). Well, the hell with it. What did Pop do, the
old sonofabitch? Left Ira and his two sons a dollar apiece, out of about forty
grand. To hell with it. What did Blake say? Something about running your
team and plow over the bones of the dead. There were other things more
important to consider.

Yes. Whose voice did the talking, whose was in the right? The one in a
previous draft arguing so persuasively, so convincingly, that he felt un-
moored from his own ego? Or his own later voice, almost diametrically opposed in view: that it was not separation from source, or truncation of
"roots," that was the cause of the deterioration of the talents, the cause of
the fading of the brilliant gifts of those whose advent as writers had been
so auspicious? He had argued that the cause of their failure lay in their inability—and his own too—to align themselves with the future. Marcia
Meede had said something akin to the same notion in one of her poems, a
kind of old-fashioned exhortation in verse, which Edith (in days of friendship still) had included in her first anthology: "We have no past for fuel,"
the young men said, as the first stanza began. And the second: "Cut then
your future down!" the old men said. It was an ingenious conceit, more
than a little forced, and like some of Longfellow's tropes, silly if pressed too
far. Who knew what to cut, or where? Who knew where that future lay? It
was a matter of luck, of conditioning, of alignment with the grain of that
future forming in the present. Moreover, he didn't like her metaphor of
"cutting your future down." It struck him as distasteful, lacking in nuance.
And further, it begged the question. Then so did he with his own idea that
he and others as talented as he was, or more, had failed because they had
been unable to align themselves with the future. Oh, hell, all he proved to
himself was that he was no intellectual, even remotely, was incapable of
dealing with abstractions. No philosopher. How many times had he looked
up the meaning of "ontology," only to forget it the next day. He learned by
rote; he learned through his muscles, he was wont to say. Plebeian: Christ,
anybody could see that Larry had clung to his folk, had not severed from
them, his sources, so called. But were they, were they? And if they were,

was that where the "shallowness" was to be found? Who were they, first- and possibly second-generation Americans? Then Edith was only partly right, partly right and partly wrong. Larry had the capacity—for feeling; he had the receptivity, the discrimination, the imaginative bent—but no pro- found source to draw from. Then he, Ira, was back to his original thesis: the same thing applied to him: his sources were the measure of his depth. Though deeper than Larry's they too had given out.

That was not all he could say about the subject. That was all he should say. Literary figures appeared at the threshold of mind, Joyce and Shaw, Synge and Sean O'Casey and Yeats—curiously, all Irishmen. Well, Faulkner then. But he barred them all. This was not the place to dwell on the topic any longer, even in his ramshackle fashion. It was strange, though, how contradictions within the self made you feel, as if you had lost all your sub- stance, were hollow. It had taken him a long time to oppose himself to himself, nor was he sure any longer he was right now and wrong then, but at least he had acknowledged the two opposing theses. He had tried not to ignore anything, blot out anything, fake anything. He had tried to be hon- est. And the answer he sought still eluded him. Still, acknowledging his own contrarieties reunited him within himself.

He sighed. Time to save: his electronic timer beeped a warning that the hour was up. And then the dreadful thought occurred to him. If his second thesis was true, could it be there was no future, and that was why so many bright spirits so suddenly dimmed? Nonsense.

I am Merlin and I am dying, involuntarily, the Tennysonian quote came to mind: *I am Merlin and I am dying. . . .*

XIV

They would be lying on the studio couch, Edith and Larry, after Larry had put away his sculpture, or possibly finished it, done all he was capable of in reproducing a likeness of Edith in clay. They would be lying on the studio couch necking, as it was commonly called: clinging, caressing, billing and cooing, giggling. That was how they made love, with a third party, himself, present, though why he should be present puzzled him—at first. Was it because Larry wanted to show off his skill in modeling clay? (Afterward, his being there seemed natural, and later still, in later years, the tripolar, if not more, seemed to characterize all of Edith's relations.) He knew only that he was welcomed by both, welcomed by Edith, invited by Larry. They didn't mind his being present, he explained to himself, because their lovemaking was so harmless, so innocent, so unsullied. Little wonder—he would reflect afterward—that he got all kinds of bizarre notions of how decent people made love, people not wrenched beyond recovery, not saturnine and self-despising, as he was by the despicable things he did—with a kid cousin. Unfortunately, there was an element of truth in his bizarre notions too: decent people weren't maimed by their early sex experiences as he was; quite the contrary, their early sex experiences may have been, as they were with Larry, one of memory's loveliest blooms. All this Ira discovered later.

But then, as 1925 pressed toward its wintry close, Ira would discreetly turn his chair sideways, so that his back was mainly but not entirely toward the lovers. Not to seem rude, as if he disapproved, the way he sat didn't preclude occasional glimpses of close embrace by the two figures stretched out full-length on the studio couch, nor erotic speculations—while he ruminated intermittently over passages in *The Waste Land*.

Why? Why? Why did Larry want him there—and Edith too? Was he, did he appear so safe, in their eyes, so sexless, so indifferent, that their amorous play wouldn't bother him? True, he feigned well, feigned unconcern, ingenuousness. Oh, but he had lots of experience dissembling: look at the way he had gotten away with it at home, under the noses of Mom and Pop; at Mamie's, under her nose—and Zaida's too, now that he lived with Mamie, under his very whiskers. Maybe because he appeared to be so phlegmatic, inattentive, abstracted, he gave the impression that he was unaffected by display of normal libido. That was why he had been invited to stay in Woodstock with them, that was why he was here. They were wrong, but they were right too. Something in him, that kind of normalcy, perhaps, had been stamped out, had been destroyed. Had something in her gone awry in Edith too? Would he still feel that way if—if, yeah, Larry rammed it into her, by some pretext, undercover flagrante? Yeah, that was it; why the hell didn't he? Why this dry simulation, this dry cuddling? Maybe they did the regular thing some other time, and Larry made no mention of it. But Jesus, that was funny. He had the same feeling in the 8th Street basement apartment that he had about Larry in the lovely stone house in Woodstock, the same feeling about why Edith was so tense: Larry wasn't satisfying her. All right? So if that was true, what difference did it make whether Ira was there or not? Okay, for Christ's sake, why didn't Larry satisfy? Why? You tell me. . . . *While I was fishing in the dull canal on a winter evening round behind the gas-house . . .*

Wasn't that good? It gave you the feeling of loneliness and emptiness, right in the midst of a great city, a sense of the forlorn, the drab and deserted. Who was that king whose death the poet mused on? The guy fishing in the dull canal musing on the king his father's death. Who the hell was that? Ira's gaze rested on the line of the open page: *And on the king my father's death before him—*

Edith, who lay on the outside edge of the studio daybed, sat up first. "Sometimes Ira looks like an ancient Hebrew prophet."

"Me?" Ira scraped his chair around. Now that the amorous séance was over, he could face them. "Me? I'm the raven never flitting."

"I was just thinking you missed your vocation," she said, still seated.

"Just barely missed," Ira rejoined with appropriate absentness.

And Larry behind Edith, still lying on his side, his white shirttails out, mussed, "What vocation? He's a bugologist."

"Oh, no, a rabbi," Edith countered. "He would have made a wonderful rabbi."

"What's the portion for the day, Rabbi Stigman?" Larry chaffed.

"I'd hate to tell you."

"Go on. Let's hear it."

"Something I read in *Walden Pond: What demon possessed me to behave so well.*"

"Did Thoreau write that?" Larry rolled luxuriantly supine. "I don't remember it."

"Yeah. *What demon possessed me to behave so well.*"

"Is that how you feel?" Edith inspected him with large brown eyes. "You do behave well, so loyally in every way. And so stable. Do you regret it?"

"Yeah." His lie loomed up before him huge as a genie from its vase.

"Poor lad."

"What would you rather have been?" Larry asked. "If you didn't behave so well? A what? A Don Juan? A trickster? Held up a stage-coach?" Larry grinned. "A highwayman, like Alfred Noyes's. 'The highwayman came riding, riding . . .' What's the next word, please? That was a scream, to listen to Salmanowitz in Mr. Donovan's Public Speaking 3. Everybody had to memorize a piece."

"Yeah?" Ira enjoyed the imagined scene.

"About every third line—'Salmanowitz: what's the next word, please?'"

"Do you have Public Speaking? Oh, yes, you told me you do. It seems so strange."

"I know. Ninety percent of CCNY is Jewish. It's compulsory. Four years."

"It's the only college I know of where that's true."

"You can guess why."

"I suppose so. It never bothers me, but then. Hamberg's accent was atrocious. But nobody seemed to care. What annoyed people was his bad manners, and of course his political views. I told you he was tarred and feathered."

"Unbelievable."

"How do you get rid of tar and feathers?" Ira asked earnestly.

"Cleaning fluid of some kind, I imagine. Naphtha. I really don't know. I never asked Shmuel what he did do."

"You expect to be tarred and feathered?" Larry sat up.

"Me? No. Worse."

"After telling us about the demon—that you behaved so well."

"What would you rather have become?" Edith asked.

"'A pair of ragged claws,' Eliot says. I'm dumb. I don't know. My mother told me I once wanted to be a janitor when I grew up, because that way we could get our rent free. Another time, the rabbi gave me a penny because I was so apt reading Hebrew. It was gibberish as far as I was concerned. Once he even came to the house to tell my mother I would make a great rabbi someday. So Mom gave him a glass of cold seltzer water out of one of those glass siphons we kept in the icebox."

"Where was that?" Edith asked.

"On the East Side. Boy, didn't I pity that poor deliveryman with the whiskers, panting and groaning up four flights of stairs with a wooden case half full of siphons."

"You two are so different. Your backgrounds are so completely different. People tend to think of Jews as being alike, but that's ridiculous. When I think of you two, and Shmuel Hamberg spluttering and ranting about Zionism and socialism those first years. And then of course there's Boris, my colleague, who's almost too smooth. Actually, I find him a little repulsive, you know, he's so *very* oily."

She had stood up. And now Larry followed suit: "Attraction of opposites in our case." He opened his belt and the top button of his trousers, then began stuffing his shirt under his waistband. Flat as a lath and boyish his waist. "It gives us lots to *shmooze* about." He had used the borrowed expression so often that Edith understood.

"I tell him about the wonderful beaches in Bermuda, the glass-bottom boats and the darkies singing, 'Aeroplanes up in the air droppin' bombs on Leicester Square,' and he tells me about living on Avenue D and the tugboats in the East River. Just now about the man with the seltzer bottles. I tell him about my father's dry-goods store in Yorkville, and the kinds of people who would come in there; and he tells me about his father's milk wagon. That's how we keep each other interested. I know all about manufacturing ladies' house-dresses from my brother, Irving. Ira knows all about hustling soda at the ballpark. I know how to sell housedresses; Ira knows how to sell Loft's candy. You're a better cadger than I am, though." Larry rubbed an eyelid.

"What do you mean?" Edith asked.

"Hey, wait a minute," Ira cautioned.

"There goes the prophet," said Larry. "Say, how should I spell that? With a *ph* or an *f*?"

"Aw, c'mon."

"I don't know what you two are talking about."

"It's a secret."

"Let me just tell Edith about the roll of quarters. Okay?"

"No. Some bosom companion you turned out to be."

"What *are* you two talking about?"

Larry smiled at Ira's discomfiture. "It has to do with the baseball park, the Polo Grounds it's called. I told you I worked there too for a day. It was awful."

"Oh, yes."

"The concession owner's wife, or daughter—"

"Daughter-in-law."

"All right?" Larry pressed for permission.

Ira remained silent: his tacit consent and curiosity about Edith's reaction . . . complex curiosity, like that about the cat.

"What was her name?"

"What's the difference? Mrs. Stevens," Ira conceded.

"Oh, yes. She gave Ira a ten-dollar roll of quarters by mistake when he asked for a two-dollar roll of nickels for change."

"Yes?"

Larry broke into a delighted chuckle: "Oh, you don't get the point at all, darling. You don't get the point at all!"

"Don't tell me you didn't return it, Ira?"

"He's a traitor, a low-down traitor. Wait till I get even."

"You really didn't keep it, Ira?" Edith was manifestly shocked. "I don't believe it."

"It felt so nice and round," Ira began—stopped, and sensed a blush rising to his cheeks at Larry's guffaw, and Edith's sudden high-pitched laugh. "Well, it's a difference in upbringing." He scowled, gesticulated. "Poverty has a—a different set of rules from affluence— maybe. I don't know."

"I never would have dreamed of taking anything that didn't belong to me."

"Well, you get funny ideas of impersonality," Ira tried to justify. "If it's from a company, or a corporation, it isn't so bad as from a person."

"I don't think it makes any difference."

"No? Well."

"Would you do it again?"

"You want me to be honest?" And meeting her large-eyed gaze: "Hey, that's a funny question a guy like me should be asking himself."

"I'm sorry I brought it up," Larry apologized. "I didn't know we would get into a debate on morality."

"I warned you," Ira accused. "What was the point, anyway?"

"I just thought I'd give Edith an idea of what we talked about. The demon didn't possess you altogether."

"I'm sure she knows by now." Ira could feel Edith's large brown eyes still searching, searching candidly, as if to penetrate the surface of the identity he presented. Seconds passed before he could meet her gaze, and then he did, and for the first time since they had known each other, though he could feel his lips trembling, he was aware of the steady harshness with which his eyes met hers. "Well, I'll tell you, the lady with the orange hair is smoking a cigarette in a long silver cigarette holder. And she comes up to the till with a big bosom, and condescends to swap your money for a roll of coins. You don't think of 119th Street, the cold-water flat you live in, and maybe," he hesitated a moment, "what it did to you, what it's doing to you. It takes over, a dynamic mass, you might say. Now that doesn't make the act any more honest, you know, doesn't justify dishonesty. Condones maybe." He fought against the grimness permeating him. "I've paid for it, over and over, for that lousy roll of quarters."

"I'm sorry, I'm so sorry, Ira dear."

"What a tempest I've managed to stir up," Larry interjected. "Never again, I promise on a stack of Bibles. Let's forget it."

"Do you still want to know whether I'd do it again?"

"Oh, no, please, Ira."

"You know, it's funny. Now that you've asked, maybe I wouldn't. Maybe I never would again. Two worlds get into collision." He could sense the trace of a faint smile easing the grimness of his visage. "I'm sorry, Edith. I'm just getting to know yours."

"Oh, no. I'm the one who should apologize," Edith said, compassionate in her contrition. "I keep being surprised all the time by the values other people have. I think everyone's values are like mine. I should know by now they're not. Especially in New York. In fact, I know they're not, but I still keep being surprised. The impersonality of the big city, of cosmopolitan New York, the very height of the skyscrapers, instead of the piñons and ponderosas of New Mexico. Instead of the desert and the cactus of all kinds, there's the noise and the crowds of the streets. I suppose they breed an altogether different outlook from my Western one. I'm just getting over my belated Western romanticism. We're about twenty years behind someone like you in the East."

Values. Values. Ira took a deep breath, studied the black-and-gray design of the Navajo rug on the floor. He seemed on the margin of some kind of idea that he couldn't quite compel into definition—as usual. He saw values as an agglomerate of tiny bits of experience, or tiny conditions of life, hers in Silver City, in the Southwest, sun-drenched, open, mountainous, and clean, a land he never knew—and his ghetto and slum values, like minute bits of shells and silt, held together into a mass. Where had he seen it? A mass, abrasive and crude, agglomerated by his inescapable East Side Jewishness.

"Where are you two going from here this evening?" Edith asked.

"To the apartment, I hope." Larry turned his head toward Ira. "Real Hungarian goulash. I heard Mama say this morning she hadn't made it in a long time." He adjusted his tie. "What d'you say?"

"What?"

"Have dinner at the apartment."

"I don't think so. I've got a bunch o' work to do."

"So have I. You've got your briefcase. We can practically have the whole house to ourselves after supper."

"I know."

"Okay?"

"No."

"Why not? You're not peeved about my bringing up that roll of quarters, I hope. I apologized."

"Oh, no."

"Then what?"

Ira burst into sudden strained laughter. "I don't like Hungarian goulash."

"Oh, come on. I know you do. And nobody makes it better than my mother."

"Well, the fact is I ought to visit my grandfather. My mother's been after me for weeks."

"Do you still have a grandfather?" Edith asked.

"Yes. On my mother's side. On my father's side they're both gone, both grandparents. It's one of those freaks. Mom was the oldest child of her parents, and Pop was the youngest of his. And I'm the firstborn grandson. It's the only night off I have," he addressed Larry. "Thanks just the same."

"Well . . . big galoot." Larry approached with grudging manner. "Dr. Pickens fired him out of the class for whispering. Both of us were at fault, but Ira was the big galoot. I can just see Dr. Pickens in his stage-acting days touring the country with a traveling company, and playing out West before an audience of big galoots. Back in 1890, I bet. You know, Edith, we used to have to learn gestures." Larry extended a long arm gracefully: "Left hand, middle front supine. Like this."

"Really?" Edith smiled appreciatively. "And he called you a big galoot?"

"Oh, I deserved it, I guess."

"Elocution 7," Larry added. "That's how we met."

"You know . . ." Ira looked up, embarrassed by the memory. "The funny thing is that *galoot* in Hebrew means 'in exile.'"

"Galoot in exile!" Larry bent over Ira's armchair. "Oh, my God, not again!" He looked down at the book in Ira's hands, inclined his head further to make sure. "Hebrew in exile. Edith, do you know what this raven never flitting has been reading again?" Larry wailed in mock despair. "He's been reading *The Waste Land*."

"Why not?"

"That's an obsession. An *idée fixe*."

"So it's an *idée fixe*. Next time I'll hide it behind a jogafree book."

"Hide it behind Sandburg, hide it behind Amy Lowell. Cummings, Aiken—now there's a lovely poet!"

"I think I ought to buy you a copy." Edith tugged prettily at the tassels of her brown dress, straightened up to regard herself in the large wall mirror. "Would you like a copy?"

"Oh, no, I've practically memorized it. Be a waste of money. Waste o' land. Ho, ho."

"Then why do you keep reading it?" Larry demanded.

"I don't always read it. Sometimes I read 'The Love Song of J. Alfred Prufrock.'"

"But why?"

"Something I need to know."

"Something you need to know?"

"Yeah."

"Why?"

"I don't know."

"Oh, great."

"I think I understand," said Edith.

"You do?"

"I think Ira keeps reading Eliot to find out what he feels about life—"

"Who's he?" Larry interrupted. "Eliot?"

"Oh, no. Ira. Isn't that so?"

"It comes close," Ira agreed.

"Do you mean to say," Larry addressed Edith, while he pointed at Ira, "he doesn't know what he feels about life?"

"It's quite possible."

"That's news to me. You don't know what you feel about life?" Larry demanded.

"I don't. That's right."

"I didn't either at his age." Edith interceded. "But I didn't have time to think about it. I was too busy being an A student, getting on the dean's list, honors, a Phi Beta Kappa key, and other things I don't think are anywhere near as important as I did once. And of course, earning my own way, playing the piano in moving-picture houses, at shivarees. I think what Ira's doing is far more important."

"Why? What's he doing? He reads *The Waste Land*. He reads 'Prufrock.' All right, then what do you get out of them? I'll ask you." Larry turned to Ira.

"Well, I'll tell you," Ira began slowly, paused.

And when he failed to go on: "It's not to be in the swim with the literati in the '28 alcove?" Larry suggested.

"Well, maybe. I don't know." Ira found a cove in his ear to scratch. "You're asking a multiple-choice question. I could either make a gag out of it, or tell you a tale that would make the hair on your head—what is it Shakespeare says, *snaky locks in horror standing on end?*"

"Well, we're all grown up. Go ahead."

"Make your hair stand on its head." Ira grinned in evasion.

"You've indicated something like that before," Larry persisted. "In fact, a number of times."

"It's like something I'm trying to find out. I won't know till the end."

Larry shook his head.

"Eliot is a bitterly disappointed romantic," Edith came to the rescue. "Completely disenchanted about everything in the modern world. He scoffs at progress. He doesn't believe in it, doesn't believe in our modern conveniences. Or says he doesn't. For him all our old values are meaningless or exhausted. Not necessarily middle class. Western values. They're arid. He compares them to the richness of the Renaissance, the grace of the Elizabethans. He juxtaposes them to show how mean and tawdry ours are."

"All right. But how many times do you have to read him to get a particular meaning? Once or twice would be enough. Ira reads him like a—what's the name of that book clergymen read?"

"Breviary." Ira shifted position, self-deprecating.

"Yes, breviary. Thanks. Why? Because he's become the fashion, he's become the vogue."

"No. Because there's more to it than that."

"To tell you the truth, Edith," Larry digressed, "I pity anybody with talent today. I mean any poet, especially if he falls under Eliot's influence. It's the undoing of their own, you might say, pristine sort of perceptions. That's what I think, anyway. I feel that even though I don't go along with Eliot, he has subtly undermined me."

"You do?" Edith regarded her lover with large, solemn eyes. "Darling, I don't think any writer can afford to neglect that part of his existence that a poet like Eliot is addressing, ignore it and hope to develop as a writer. I often tell my class: beauty is truth today in a way Keats never would have imagined. In fact, he might have been revolted by the way poets interpret beauty today."

"I wouldn't blame him," Larry said.

Edith tilted her head and smiled, as much to console Larry as to indicate that she was prepared for what he said: she was resigned. There was a lull.

"I do. Yes. I feel quite resentful about him. It's enough to feel his effect, the undermining of one's own romanticism. I don't think there's anything wrong with romanticism, with being a romantic. I mean, Eliot's destructive enough of youthful outgoing feeling, say like Millay's, without having to pay tribute, get aboard his bandwagon. And I—" He looked at Ira with a certain restrained desperation. Then his gaze fixed on a passerby seen through the window, at the same time as the window light illuminated Larry's regular features. "We seem to be very much opposed in this matter." The palms of his big hands opposed each other. "That's the chief reason I can't stand rereading him. I'm just repeating what I said. He does something peculiar to my psyche, my id, identity, whatever you want to call it." Larry grimaced at a vague unpleasantness, looked chidingly at Ira. "That's why I wonder why Ira keeps rereading him. It's not a question of bad faith, it's a—well, antagonism." He laughed at himself.

"I really think it's too bad." Edith shook her head commiserating. . "Something like Eliot coming between you. It's just too bad. It's odd too. And almost funny."

"That's what I say."

"I'm not arguing that. I'm not a poet," Ira tried to rebut.

"Then what in all that futile, yes, cheap, moribund world of today he makes such a point of appeals to you so much?"

"That's it. I see myself mirrored."

Edith sat at the edge of the couch, her tiny hands clasped in her lap. Meditatively her large brown eyes traveled from Larry to Ira.

"Well, beauty has gone out of style is what it amounts to. I still think it exists despite Mr. Eliot. I can put it in a word: he's undercut beauty." Larry pressed his lips inward against his vehemence.

"And I have no feeling for it. Somehow, it's not my world, that's all. You've been raised on Beauty as something to worship; I haven't. And when you turn Eliot down," Ira leaned forward in his chair, "it means you haven't been weaned."

Edith suddenly laughed.

"What's that supposed to mean?" Larry demanded.

"Oh, I don't know. Just a wisecrack maybe. Weaned into the lousy modern world."

"I don't think Ira is denying Beauty," Edith intervened. "I think what he's trying to say, and I think what he's looking for in Eliot, and Joyce too, is to find some way to make use of his city upbringing, with its many ugly aspects, to make it into something beautiful."

"Are you?" Larry addressed Ira.

"Vehr veist?"

"Galitz!" Larry's epithet was not altogether humorous. *"Vehr veist?* He means 'who knows.'"

"Although it may not necessarily be in Joyce's or Eliot's manner," Edith continued soberly. "I suspect he's trying to find some way of keeping the ugliness of modern urban life from overwhelming him. And us too for that matter."

"By doing what?"

"Almost by making a shield of it."

"And *I* can't because I spent so much time in Bermuda, where life was so peaceful and beautiful. Is that it?"

"It's not just that, lad. You were too gently reared."

"And yet you thought it wasn't advisable for me to break away from it. Or try to. Expose myself to some rough spots."

"And I still think my advice was right, darling. It would be the height of folly if you didn't go on and get your degree."

"Damned if I do, and damned if I don't. You got a good quotation for me, Ira? You generally manage to come up with a good one."

"Not this time."

"All right, then tell me: you pore over Eliot whenever you're here. You waded through Joyce, right? When we were in Woodstock? You admitted you didn't understand half of what you were reading about. The same thing is certainly true of *The Waste Land.* You need a lot of scholarship, literary background, not just English literature, foreign literature, Latin, Greek, all kinds of esoteric allusions. Frazer, for example. You haven't got all that any more than I have. So in what way are they going to help you? That's what I want to know. If you don't understand it?"

"What you say is true. I don't." Ira thumped his back against his chair. "It's a state of mind I get out of them. I don't know what that state of mind is. I couldn't give you a definition. But as I've said before, I can discern a compatibility. And I need it if I'm to do any writing. Maybe I can't. But you know, Larry, there's a lot of difference between us. I don't have to tell you. I'm a *shlemiel*, yeah, I am," he overrode Larry's gesture of objection. "Gee, the things you can do. You can turn your hand to almost anything: writing popular lyrics, skits, acting, selling, that modeling in clay over there you're doing. I haven't got a damn thing, excuse me, Edith, I mean anything except where my 'Impressions of a Plumber' in *The Lavender* points to. If I'm wrong about that, I'm, gee, I don't know. I could end up—" He wagged his hand in comic transition. "Dun't esk."

"And you think Joyce and Eliot will guide you toward realizing future literary ambitions?"

Ira shrugged. "I imagine I need more than just those two. But so far, I notice one thing: they both contrast a heroic or—or noble, maybe, past, chivalric pieces, passages, with an ugly present. Is that right, Edith?"

"I think you're making a better point of it than I did."

"Yeah? I don't think the past was what they make of it either. Not for the common guy. The nobility maybe."

"Is that what you expect to do also? Contrast the two?"

"I don't think so. Not explicitly, you know. It happens that I come from a past a helluva, I mean a heck of a lot longer than any of their *goyish* ones. I mean gentile, Edith. But in both of those guys, life today is a negation. And I demand an affirmation. Another point is that Larry makes unfair comparisons. You know what he does. We've spoken of it. He contrasts the inconsequence and sordidness of modern life with the great literary art of the past. He links passages of his own observations of the tawdry modern actualities with quotations from the classics. Well, if you're going to compare all the common ratty things of today with Elizabethan art and courtliness, it's a cinch to tell who comes out ahead. What about comparing like with like? Joe Blow who comes in off the street to buy the Loft's ninety-nine-cent special with Tom the shepherd who blows his nail, or the actual illiterate guy, probably, who lugs the logs into the hall."

"All the more reason for me to ask, why are you so smitten with them?" Larry queried.

"I told you. If I don't know who I am, how I can handle who I am, they come closest to telling me."

Despondently, he skimmed through the small stack of her Xeroxed letters in his possession. Years and years ago, in the depths of the Depression, he had bought for Edith a secondhand five-drawered metal filing cabinet—twenty-five dollars—had paid two bucks extra for delivery from the Jewish office furniture dealer's on Third Avenue to their place at 64 Morton Street.

And in this ample filing cabinet he had sorted out all his letters to her, and separately, all her letters to him. Of the ten-year exchange of letters, he had recovered none of his, only this little batch of Edith's letters to him.

Just the sight of these letters made him recall Edith, poor Edith, near the end, an alcoholic, a confirmed sot, and she had undoubtedly blabbed everything. Pitying insight posed the question: what had happened to her self-esteem? Edith's? So fine, so good, so generous, so tender. Oh, Christ, he had been just the right protégé for her. And had Edith also had incestuous relations with her father? A friend of Edith's, Daniel, had asked him. Shux. If that wasn't the morbidity of inversion.

Daniel had intended to write a biography of Edith sometime in the near future. But apparently the project fell apart when he learned about Larry. Edith hadn't told Daniel a word about her freshman lover, or about other young men she had initiated, and was inclined to be skeptical about Ira's assertion that Daniel's primary source of information was untrustworthy, until Ira's disclosure about Larry: "Well, how the hell did I meet Edith? I went to CCNY. Larry, my high school chum, went to NYU." Perhaps, after that, Daniel saw that Edith was making sure she would be seen the way Ira felt she always wanted to be seen: as the heroine of her own tragic drama.

Anyway, there they were, the Xeroxes of her letters, relics of Edith, of the living woman that was, the mundane, the matter-of-fact, the worried, the hurt, unhappy, intelligent, forthright, moderately promiscuous woman he had scarcely understood, and couldn't portray. Her voice in the typewritten letter was unmistakable.

I've been to Silver City twice in two weeks. The days are as I described before: just a setting and setting and a lifting Papa up and down, and getting his cigarettes or his glasses, and making and making conversation; and when he's to bed, then there is Inez, his housekeeper, who can't read, and making conversation with her till bedtime. I'm calming down now, was frightfully nervous at first, and have had little appetite, but sleep has helped, and I'm taking advantage of that at any rate.

So, to repeat, apparently things are awful out here. They are damned bad in Gallup too, I gather. I've decided I'm weird in one respect. All these people here around my age do is reminisce about the past. And how well they remember it! I've always pushed the past out of my mind; I don't linger on it, rather resent it, I suppose, and consequently completely forget it. I always think either I'm crazy, or these people are, when I'm out here with them at all, as I've been once or twice, and only out here. Moreover I've an inclination to want to shock them, which is purely childish on my part, and this shows I still resent them more than I should. I've outgrown everything I met, one thing at a time, but you're the one thing I'll never outgrow, that outgrows me all the time, and that therefore I adore, and sometimes could kick violently in the seat of the pants, because you're able to hurt me, and no one else is, and because most of the time you're right, though your youth makes you immature in knowing how people live and are, often. You'd better have more personal life soon, or you're going to need it badly, and whatever amuses you and feeds your imagination is all right with me always. Those letters of mine you're filing away will give you a good deal of dope, I think, with which your imagination can work. I've forgotten how many people have deared and darlinged me, and it doesn't matter, but what does matter is that most of them still like me, and take me for what I am without glamour. There is a terrific streak of emotional sentimentality in my family which I've always fought free of, but undoubtedly am possessed by at moments.

Much love, darling, and kisses for the beautiful black eyes, and go on a tear with a lady or a lamb or a man or a wolf now and then. Just don't get bit or hurt.

So . . . there she was, a trace of her. Echo, an echo. He stared at the pale keys until they swam, and he became melancholy with brooding about a past he strove so valiantly to re-create, about a past that he could feel, but that he could not resurrect from the dead.

Ira turned the doorknob, eased the doorknob, eased the door ajar, as he prepared to leave. "Gee, these glacial departures," he muttered.

Edith laughed lightly. "What did you say?"

"I said these glacial departures. In the hallway already."

"That's what I thought," she smiled. "Good night, lad." She lifted her face to Larry's, as he put on his coat as well.

"Good night, Edith." Larry kissed her lips. "I'll call you in a couple of days."

"Good night, Ira." Smiling fondly, she extended her hand.

"Good night, Edith. Thanks for all that toasted raisin bread and cinnamon."

She followed them as far as the street door, contracted when they opened it, caught her breath and shrank back. "Isn't it cold! Good night."

"Good night, Edith. You'd better get back inside," Larry called out.

They closed the door behind them, entered upon wintry, incandescent, hurrying, shifting forms on 8th Street: turned toward the Sixth Avenue El, amid the frigid stridor, frigid commotion of the crosstown trolley car, passing voices—and the ding-dong of the Christmas bell, shaken by the well-padded Salvation Army Santa Claus on the corner, tending the black iron pot hanging between the legs of the tripod.

"Oh, boy, it's sure snappy out." Ira quickened his gait, to keep abreast of the longer-striding Larry.

They forged ahead toward the murky dusk until the illuminated frosted-glass sides of the Christopher Street subway kiosk came into view.

"I wish you'd reconsider coming over to the house and having some of that lovely goulash with us," Larry urged.

For a moment Ira hesitated. "Gee, wouldn't I like to. But my poor old grandfather. It's long past time I paid the old boy a visit. Mom's been after me. You know how it is. I bet I'm missing something good."

"You are, believe me. I've told you, my mother makes the finest goulash this side of Hungary."

"What tough luck." Ira shook his head regretfully. It would still be early evening when he got off at the 110th Street station, early enough to make a homey call at Mamie's. Stella would surely be home by now. "I really mean it. Boy."

Larry pulled off a fur-lined glove to get at a coin in his pocket. "Next Monday, okay?"

"That's a far-sure as Pop would say."

J'ai fait la magique étude que nul n'élude. Was that approximately the way Rimbaud's line ran? He understood now. What was it he understood? The encompassing realization that he had slipped into his mind of its own accord some pages back, and been deferred. Edith would say, when he revealed his sorry history, first with Stella, then, as if torn from him, with Minnie, "I thought you were unawakened. I thought you were maternally directed, and still uninterested in sexual relations." She thought right, in the right direction, but not far enough. How could she? It had taken him a lifetime for the truth about himself to coalesce into the simple fact that stared him in the face, single fact with multifacets: that answered such questions as: why was he invited to accompany Larry and Edith on their tryst in Woodstock? His first conjecture had been that he was invited in order to play a diversionary role (actually, had they been discovered by people who knew Edith, they might easily have come to absurdly erroneous conclusions regarding her appetites). But the true answer, he now felt, went deeper than that.

He had been invited to Woodstock first, and later, with Edith's consent and apparent approval, he was invited to assist at those sculpture-cum-lovemaking sessions, because of what he was. Had he, Ira, been other than what he was, someone with developed masculinity, or with developed libido corresponding to his age, Larry would certainly have discerned it, certainly have avoided competition. Was Larry too wanting in that respect? Of course he was. As if it were a formula by which a number of seemingly diverse problems were solved. Turn where he would, the same fact stared him in the face from a score of directions. Even that—what did Edith say in her letter to him of which he had excerpted a part: ". . .though your youth makes you immature in knowing how people live and are, often. You'd better have more personal life soon, or you're going to need it badly. . . ."

Ira put the letter back in the file.

Ironic as hell! Two waves intersecting so casually: "your youth makes you immature . . ." and "You'd better have more personal life." Two waves that originated from the same source, two waves propagated at different times. For when he *did* seek that more personal life she spoke about, strove to break free of that which she called immaturity (merely immaturity!), there was hell to pay: Edith turned into a Fury. But what was this all leading up to? What was the underlying cause of this unifying fact that stared him in the face, that synthesized his diverse manifestations of behavior into a comprehensive realization, into a Joycean epiphany? Nothing other than his continued, his prolonged *infantilism*. It was that that made him a safe confederate at his friend's wooings, such as they were; it was that that had accounted for his own acts with Minnie and kid cousin Stella. Why the hell hadn't he seen that before—and chided Ecclesias for not revealing it? Why the hell? His infantilism. Safe as a child—ostensibly—safe as an "unawakened" juvenile. His puerility lulled everybody into trust, his own family, his shrewd aunt Mamie, predisposing Larry, perceptive Edith. Only the almost clairvoyant, mercilessly unequivocal Vivian, with whom he was to fall in love, saw through him at once: "You kiss like a baby."

You might swing around in your swivel chair, my friend, and ask, Why? Ask why of your mentor, Ecclesias. Oh, it wasn't necessary, Ira thought: he knew why, knew why without asking. He had been fixed in infantilism as deep as a bronze boundary marker was fixed in the ground, deep as a utility pole. A few genes might have been predisposing factors, a few of Pop's genes. But no use going into that now, Ira checked himself. Enough that he had abstracted at last the key to his behavior, a conception of the driving force of behavior he loathed—and in the end, had to counteract.

P A R T   T W O

The joy Ira had felt when Larry transferred from NYU to CCNY, the joy of having his closest friend in the same college, the same class, sharing the same alcove with him, had worn off by the time the spring term of 1926 began. Relationships had altered, and no longer was Larry the unquestioned, the well-nigh anointed guide he once seemed in realms of art, letters, and poetry, Ira his shy, abashed follower. It was not only that Ira had published a piece in *The Lavender* and Larry had stopped writing that changed attitudes and roles, but Ira had learned much from Edith, in the very presence of Larry, by whose wish he was present. He had learned much from Edith by merest hints and intimations, inklings, almost, of judgment, reflecting without doubt her changed feelings about Larry. Barely perceptible changes of mien transmitted all manner of subtle information concerning true feeling under a beguiling exterior. Whether Edith knew it or not, or Larry either, Ira's presence at these sessions enhanced awareness, capacity for perception; it increased his explicit evaluation too. All at once, as if stemming from early subordination to Larry, incipient rivalry grew, and then domination. Edith knew it. Larry knew it. His creativity seemed in retrograde remorselessly. He gave up sculpting, dropped out of the School of Design. The clay bust of Edith, the stand, and the modeling instruments disappeared. His enthusiastic descanting on Brancusi and Maillol shifted to talk about the theater, about the stage. Acting was nothing to look down upon, he declared. Many a well-known playwright had begun as an actor, and he intended to begin that way himself. He was sure he was endowed with a natural talent for the stage. Dramaturgy might well follow. A single term in a school for acting would be all he needed. He intended to apply for a bit part at the Provincetown Playhouse that spring, and if none was forthcoming, then a bit part the next fall when the theater opened with a new play.

Fortunately, Izzy, classmate and member of their small clique at the college, worked as a doorman at the Provincetown Playhouse, the famed little theater in Greenwich Village. Eugene O'Neill had made his debut as playwright there, and since it was the policy of the theater's ruling committee to try out plays by new and often unknown dramatists, avant-garde plays were to be expected, and did occur. Because Izzy's sister, who had gotten Izzy the job as doorman, was a combination cashier-bookkeeper and business manager for the theater, it would be a simple matter for Iz to keep Larry posted about new developments. Besides introducing Larry to Tom Wright, the stage director, Izzy could let Larry know when casting would begin. Flushed with hope of a new beginning, and the auspicious way expectations dovetailed with prospects, Larry already moved about like a seasoned actor treading a proscenium.

Edith and Ira applauded his new choice of artistic calling. Ira knew they both made the same appraisal of it, though Ira felt sure his was far less kind, far less generous, than hers. Ira's contained an element of gloating—because, knowing Edith so much better now, if only intuitively, and striving to conform to her standards, her values, Ira could guess how she must be comparing Larry in his new avocation with the promising young lyric poet who had so romantically entered her life only a short year and a half ago. So he'd found his true level—that of a performer and nothing more; Ira knew she wondered how she could have been so mistaken. Conjecture, and unkind conjecture, was all Ira had to go on—at first. Fancy, given play, became a kind of thermocouple formed by *her* merest hints of tone of voice and features and *his* wish fulfillment. And yet, the more Ira tried to reflect objectively on what was taking place, the more inevitable became what he had foreseen, even when presented with the

Ulysses by default the summer before. The present reverted to the past, but in a spiral. He and Larry walked again through 59th Street from DeWitt Clinton toward the chary shadow under the West Side El, in which the United Cigar store show window glared with incandescent beacons. How different the meaning in retrospect of Larry's singing those snatches from *The Pirates of Penzance* in which he had a small part: "A paradox, a paradox, a most ingenious paradox—" The enchantment Ira felt then had its current analogue in Larry's own bathetic parody: a pair o' socks, a pair o' socks, a most ingenious pair o' socks.

In keeping with his new choice of artistic avocation, Larry applied for the position of assistant entertainment director at the prestigious Jewish summer resort Lemansky's, in the Catskills, for the summer of 1926. He was granted an interview with the board of directors of the resort. Larry came away believing that he had made a very favorable impression, ad-libbing as stand-up comic, suggesting skits and partly performing them. A short time later he jubilantly announced that the board of directors had confirmed his appointment to the position of first assistant to chief of entertainment for the entire summer season. His summer, as he said, was taken care of. And not only *this* summer, but the next, and his prospects of a career on the stage greatly enhanced. For besides his functioning regularly as an emcee in the evening, he would have a hand in conceiving, writing, and staging all kinds of theatricals. True, it would be on a borscht-circuit level; still, it was a great chance to acquire professional knowledge of theater, from creating effects to scene-designing, costuming, and, of course, acting. Once again, Larry stressed, as if he were addressing himself to Ira's unspoken reservations, that even the position of borscht-circuit entertainer offered valuable grounding for a career on the stage. He again cited instances.

And then something happened, momentary and sinister, an omen so ephemeral that only after many years was it recognized as a kind of preamble of a fateful warrant. During exam week, after which, and without waiting to ascertain grades, Larry had planned to pack at once and leave for the mountain resort, he suffered an unaccountable brief loss of consciousness. He had just stepped out of the doorway of the high-rise apartment house on West 110th Street

"when all of a sudden I went blotto," said Larry. The spell of uncon-
sciousness must have lasted only a few seconds, for he recalled trying
to pick himself up from the sidewalk just as passersby were extending
a helping hand. He hadn't suffered any ill effects to speak of, just a
bruised shoulder and a swollen and lacerated ear. He was assured
later by the family doctor the cause had probably been a small blot
clot, nothing serious. Probably it would never happen again.

"He told me a little borscht would do me good," Larry laughed
when he met Ira in the '28 alcove at noon between exams. "I just
took the Mili Sci exam before, wouldn't you know it. If I'd taken it
with this bandaged ear I might have gotten an A-plus for the course.
I got a battle wound."

"Boy, all those bandages; that's some knob. What'll you tell 'em
up there in the mountains?"

"Oh, I still got a day or two left. I'll take it off. It's just there
against infection." He tapped the top of the bandage with long, white
forefinger. "They'd think it's a gag anyway: a comedian with a cauli-
flower."

He left the city without further incident.

Came the Tuesday following exam week. With Larry out of town,
and at Lemansky's, Ira took the opportunity to telephone Edith. She
would be delighted to have him over, if Ira didn't mind the mess. She
was packing her suitcases, she was getting ready to leave New York
and take the train for the three-day trip to New Mexico.

She was in the act of wrapping a pair of her tiny shoes in tissue
paper when Ira entered the apartment. A couple of her dresses were
still laid out on the bed. "It doesn't look too much of a mess," he
commented, after greetings.

"The cleaning woman was here yesterday, so it looks halfway
tidy," she said. "Would you believe I've sublet it for the summer? I
posted a notice on the college bulletin board, not expecting anyone
would want it. It's so dingy and noisy. And I told them about the dust
they could expect in the summer. But that didn't stop them in the
least. They were simply starry-eyed at the prospect of living in the
heart of Greenwich Village. It *is* near the university. I wish you might
have seen the two very proper schoolteachers who rented it. They're
here from Waukegan, Illinois, to get credits in education."

She invited Ira to sit down. No, she didn't need any help. She could do this in her sleep, she had done it so often—and please forgive her for not stopping; she hoped he didn't mind. "I loathe these ritual trips to the West," she said. "The long boring train ride. I'm sure to get constipated. But I haven't been there in two years. Last summer, of course, I went to Europe. It would break Papa's heart if I didn't appear. Mother could live. So could my sister, as long as I sent them a check regularly. But Papa is beginning to sound so old and defeated in his letters, it breaks my heart. I'm more attached to him than I realized. This daughter of his," she tucked the shoes into a corner of the suitcase, "not one of whose ideas he approves of. Still, there's a kind of unspoken affection that comes through despite our differences."

"That's how I feel about my mother. Not that she doesn't approve. She doesn't understand."

"I know. Your face lights up when you speak of her."

"Yeah? I guess you always love something you once loved," Ira ventured.

She smiled. "Scarcely."

"No?"

"I daresay you haven't been through as many of these things as I have. They've left scars, deep ones, and perhaps it's those very scars that have helped me get over loving. Anyway, I seem to have done that very well." She folded inward the shoulders of a dress, held it to her as she faced Ira. "Perhaps you're right." She studied her reflection in the wall mirror. "I may not be speaking of true love. And yet I don't think what I've been through, certainly not all of it, would be classed as merely encounter."

"Encounter?" The word made Ira think, or try to, and thinking interfered with talking. Encounter? He worried the word. It was that kind of subtle distinction Larry could handle, could comprehend at once, justly, properly, Larry and his kind, yes, his middle-class kind. Ira couldn't. Or was it that he had destroyed the true shape of that sort of word? Ira knew what she meant, he thought, but he had to translate it to himself—no, that wasn't right. He had to let the word resound, not to translate it: resound within himself until it became imbued with a kind of pragmatism. Wasn't that crazy? He knew that word, and now it was a stranger, or as if displaced. Which was the word, and which the parallax? Encounter. The same word used in a different world, one of the many Ira would have to relearn. And who would understand what he meant? How could he explain it?

"Oh, dear, I've forgotten to lay down a sheet of tissue paper. These linen dresses muss so." She laid the dress down on the bed, where in the basement dusk the pale linen turned putty. She spread tissue paper on the top layer in the suitcase, then picked up the dress again. "I shouldn't have bragged about being able to do this in my sleep."

"You were talking," Ira provided the excuse . . . waited until she patted the dress smooth on top of the suitcase. "You heard about Larry?"

"Oh, yes. He was here Friday evening."

"Oh, he was?" His aim was to say it as if it had no implication. Maybe it didn't, for all he knew. No more than that scream she had uttered in Woodstock. Nothing ever stayed simple with Ira. "Did he take the bandage off yet?"

"No, poor lad. His ear was still pretty sore. I believe that's a very, very serious thing—I know people will think I'm overly worried. They always do. But I've turned out to be right many times: his losing consciousness for no reason."

"The doctor didn't think it meant anything serious."

"I'm very suspicious of most doctors." With the last dress disposed of, she sat down on the studio couch. "Very suspicious. Larry's father died of a heart attack. I presume the doctor knew that too. There's always the danger. Unusual strain may bring it on, and it happened during examination week. I find that very disturbing. I think it's a clear sign he may be headed for trouble, poor lad."

"Yeah, but he wasn't worried about the exams, though. His courses were easy, you know, arts courses. I don't say they're all snap courses, but—" Ira shrugged a shoulder. "Larry does B work—almost without trying. He tosses it off."

"Well, how about that resort position? You don't think he was overanxious about succeeding in it? He had already given up trying to write poetry, the thing he seemed at first best fitted to do. Then the stab at sculpture. It didn't last very long. Again, he didn't want to work at it. I can't blame him if he tries different things. But he's got to learn, none of them can be mastered without hard work, without self-discipline. You can't substitute personal charm for achievement."

"No, I know. But I thought he was happy about this: acting and that sort of thing. The stage. Entertainment."

"That's how he seemed to me." Her bosom rose in an involuntary catch of breath. "I'm almost afraid to think about the possible causes. For one thing, they bring the matter so much closer to home."

As usual, intuition provided an inkling of her meaning, an inkling cruel in its inference as Ira construed it, yet avidly countenanced.

"The last things the doctors take into account are the psychological factors; they're always looking for physiological ones. I suppose they have to. That's all most doctors can treat. But I don't think I need to go the same route they do." Her dress had large, bronze oblongs strewn against a lighter brown background. Her hands pressed palm to palm in her lap were so tiny, they seemed like a wedge in one of the oblongs. "There's only one thing to do. Not show my concern. Or overconcern. And to be very careful."

"You mean *you* have to be very careful?" It seemed the safest thing to say.

"Yes. I'm afraid so. He may be suffering from an inherent weakness: his heart. But it doesn't change things very much. I mean, as far as my own responsibility is concerned. Even though nobody can accuse me of it. Possibly Larry's folks might. Still, I may bear a greater share of the responsibility than I care to admit."

"You mean responsibility for Larry falling down?"

"Yes."

"I don't see how."

"I'm glad you don't think so."

"If you'll excuse me, Edith, I think you're exaggerating. It was a blood clot. So?"

"I keep reassuring myself that's all it is—or was. And telling myself I'm being morbid. On the other hand, he *was* very young when all this began. I gave him all sorts of false hopes. As I said, the effect is beyond any doctor to detect. I can't wish that the same beautiful lad was in somebody else's English class, and see what would happen then. Would he have switched from dentistry into English litera-ture—into thinking he had any kind of substantial talent as a writer, as a poet? All of which, unfortunately, I encouraged. In that sense I do bear responsibility. I'm sorry beyond words." Her tiny fingers laced and unlaced as she spoke.

"Yeah, but there are other people who go through the same thing. Make big decisions that turn out wrong. You might say I did. They don't get heart failure right away. They don't even get blood clots."

She laughed. "Thank goodness you came over." Her nervous fin-gers came to rest. "Do you think—in fact—anything will come of his new enthusiasm for the theater?"

"I don't know," he hedged. "Larry's always liked to—well, play a part."

"And I've been foolish enough not to realize that trait from the very start. I've encouraged the poor lad to try to reach goals he never, never can reach. And there was Vernon with his homosexual designs to cloud my judgment even further."

"Yeah."

"Larry is a dilettante by nature. Perhaps he has to be, that may be how he saves himself. I know you think I'm hipped on the subject. But art does take a sturdy constitution. You notice how stockily Léonie Adams is built. Art does make demands on the body. His ef-forts to be a poet, or do anything worthwhile in writing, have come to nothing. I think because he loved me he was determined to show that he could live up to my expectations, and he couldn't. He can't. So his very love has frustrated the poor lad. The one thing he wanted most was to find meaningful artistic expression, and he's been un-able to. I think the pain has gone much deeper than he's let anyone know. And now there's the proof of it." She paused, regarded Ira with her large, solemn brown eyes so steady within her olive counte-nance. "There's proof of what's happened."

"Gee, just that one fall? We keep saying the same thing." Ira tried to avoid looking askance.

"Yes. But I'm sure that's just the beginning."

"So how do you know? The doctor didn't say so."

"And you know what I think of doctors."

"Then why're you to blame?"

"I've said. For encouraging him to do what he's not capable of. I think I encouraged him to overtax himself." She paused, moistened her lips. "Of course, I didn't know how serious it might be—how serious the consequences might be. But as I look back on it, I just know when the real heartbreak happened. Do you remember those last few days—or nights—in Woodstock when he would sit by candlelight trying to create the mood for a lyric, and couldn't?"

"I remember he said once that the lyric he was writing wouldn't go anywhere." Even as Ira spoke, inarticulate perception hummed in the background: how calamitous she was.

The dimness of the room accentuated the gravity of her features. "It's too late to do anything about that now. I've got to bring this thing to an end without his hurting himself any further. I'd never forgive myself if he did. I know I'm straining your loyalty to Larry, but you can see why, I'm sure. I'm deathly afraid of anything happening to him."

"I don't think anything will."

"You won't say anything, please?"

"Oh, no. I understand what you're saying. But I don't think you are—you're anywhere near as guilty—I mean as responsible as you, uh—" Ira tried a pejorative frown. "As you say. And holy smoke, you're accusing yourself of being responsible for just guesswork."

"I hope you're right." She paused. "Oh, dear." She seemed to encounter her anxiety in the window on the sidewalk. "You're sweet to bear with me."

"I don't mind. I mean, I'm glad. I don't know what good I am." He shrugged. "Anyway, nobody can tell. How can you tell? His father had a heart attack last year. And this is a year later that Larry fell on the sidewalk. So even if what you say is true, I don't see how you—you can blame yourself."

"I probably wouldn't, if John Vernon hadn't been in the picture. I might have acted a little more maturely. I was much too concerned, and needlessly." She raised a tiny hand to the back of her head as she spoke, absently fingered the bun of braided, glinting, dark hair, and brought a hairpin into view. "No use shifting the blame to John. I was just plain silly." She applied the round of the hairpin to the inside of her ear. "It's all water over the dam anyway."

Ira watched, fascinated. When she had apparently relieved the itch, she pressed the round of the hairpin between her lips—

"Gee!" Ira exclaimed, jerked his knees together.

She regarded him in surprise.

"How can you do that?"

"Do you mean what I just did?" She held the hairpin suspended.

"Yeah. I never saw anybody do that before."

"I'm sorry. I shouldn't be doing it either." She bent her head placatingly.

"Doesn't it have a taste?"

"Oh, no. It's just a bad habit." She restored the hairpin to its place in the bun behind her head. "I'll try not to do it again."

"It's all right."

"It isn't, really." She patted the back of her head. "Does it bother you?"

"Oh, no, no. I was just—" He shrugged.

She smiled. "I wish Larry had more of your directness."

Embarrassed, Ira was silent. To him, the incident had a peculiar metaphysical quality, a permanence transcending the transience and confusion of her preparations for departure, the shadowy walls, darkened by street dust, the open suitcase beside which she was sitting, on top of the mussed black couch cover. Reality seemed of another order, seemed condensed, the novelty of his being alone with Edith, here in her 8th Street apartment below the sidewalk. Her thoughts had apparently reverted to the difficulties of her situation.

"I'd thought even before Larry got this position of entertainer at the summer resort where he is now, that was where he was headed, and when he did get it, I was sure our relationship would come to a natural end. He was maturing so differently from what I expected. We were moving in such different directions. You must have noticed it."

"Yeah. I think so."

"Now I'm not at all sure how things will end, especially with his fainting so unaccountably, and this hint of heart trouble he's shown. I can no longer be direct with him, you see, at least not as direct as I might have been otherwise. And of course there's no turning back for either one of us, undoing what's been done. All *I* can do is hope and pray that some adoring young female at that summer resort will worship him to the point of diverting his attention away from me. From me, and all I represent. It's a rather slim hope, but it's all I have to go on. His weakness for adoration for its own sake."

"I know. He told me once."

"Oh, he did?" Edith looked at him questioningly.

"Something about wanting a woman to get down on her knees and worship him. I thought that was funny."

"I'm not at all surprised. Then you understand what I mean. I'm past that stage. I can't imagine how I could have been such a ninny in the first place. But I was . . . I don't suppose you know what it means to be a woman turning thirty, and someone as beautiful as Larry coming into her ken. Such an extraordinary Adonis comes into her life— so worldly, so cosmopolitan—in love with you."

"I was crazy about him too—that way, at first. He was wonderful."

"Yes . . . and I don't want to spoil your feeling for each other either. It's a very beautiful relationship."

A kind of rhythm went through Ira's head, as of a poem whose words he had forgotten. The two sat quietly looking at each other for a few seconds without saying anything. How could Ira tell her, he felt sorry for the guy, but it has to be? Tell her: *It isn't her fault at all. It's his.* He's up against a will that's so inexorable, he doesn't even have to exert it, a will that compels him. How did he know he hadn't overborne him step by step, overcome him? As if he had become some kind of elemental, insensate force, and Larry was somebody humane and mild and good. Tell her that he was like that hungry fighter you read about; you can't beat him. Not Jack London's hungry fighter either. But he said: "You want some help with those satchels tomorrow? I don't go to Loft's till three-thirty tomorrow."

"No. You're very sweet to offer. I'm going to telephone for a cab. Then I'll get a porter at Grand Central. There's no trouble in getting one, and they're always very accommodating. Do you work the same hours at Loft's in the summer?" She crossed her legs, so trim under the discreetly low hemline of the bronze overlay-patterned skirt. "You've given me a great deal of comfort just being here."

Ira tried to look away, find distraction in passersby outside the window. "Well. About Loft's, yeah. But I'm going to take a French course this summer. Every day, two hours a day. I didn't take enough credits, and I lost nearly a credit with the D's I got; I gotta start making up credits."

She shook her head wonderingly. "You're such a strange mixture. It would seem you would have no trouble at all getting good grades. You got an A in Composition this semester. That wasn't even your original interest."

"That was just my luck. Mr. Kieley's course was devoted to descriptive writing. You've told me yourself I'm good at that. Overall, I'm slow." Lowering eyes brought into view sleek ankles, calves. "Slow as molasses. And college . . . I daydream instead of paying attention. I can't keep up."

They meditated differently from men, women did, or at least Edith did. She seemed lenient, but was she really? "I'm going to have an early dinner with a colleague, Boris, you've met him. And I'm going to bed early afterward. Probably my last good night's sleep for the next two or three nights."

"Two or three nights," Ira repeated, shook his head in sympathy. "That's some trip. Then all the way back too?"

"Yes." There was a wry curve on her lips. "People still ask me whether New Mexico is in the United States."

He hemmed in appreciation, stood up.

"Please, don't feel you have to leave."

"No, I just—" He debated in himself an instant: he had employed the alibi only a short while ago. "I have to go and make my visit." At least, by semi-quoting, he obviated repeating prevarication.

"Oh, yes." She stood up also. Womanly figure, yet girlish. Bronze skirt bridged by neutral heathery sweater to olive skin. And after a glance at the mirror, "How *is* your grandfather?"

"My grandfather? He's the same. He complains and complains. His eyes, his legs, his sides."

Her charity was proof against Ira's flippancy. She shook her head pityingly. "He lives with your aunt, doesn't he?"

"Yeah, my aunt Mamie. She's getting so fat she can't cross her legs."

"Really?"

"Yeah." How different his world must seem in her view. "And right now he's complaining about how loud the girls play the new radio."

"Oh. I don't think you ever mentioned them before."

"My two kid cousins? Yeah." Boy, that was a boner. He felt as if he carried a tremendous pack on the back of his brain: a pack-Jew carrying a skull crammed with ugly articles he couldn't display. That would be a funny notion, if he could do something with it. But it had to be beautiful—to suit the *goyim*—yeah. They carried around beauty in the back of their heads—"What? I'm sorry." He had heard the question she asked but needed more preparation to answer.

"How old are they?" So steady her large brown eyes in her curiosity.

"Oh, sixteen, twelve. Something like that. One's blond, wants to be a manicurist, the other's a redhead, wants to be a dancer." Ira chuckled. "They're both taking commercial courses."

"Then they're younger even than your sister."

"Oh, yeah. Minnie's about—two years older. Eighteen. She graduates from high school next term. In the winter."

"I'm really sorry I have to make this trip, Ira. I think it's time we knew each other better."

"Yeah?"

"One more thing. Thank goodness I remembered."

He waited, puzzled, watched her rummage in her sewing box. "This ought to do the trick. I just plain *guessed* Larry's size, but your hand is so much smaller." She came dangling a yellow seamstress's tape. "Really, one ought to have those jeweler's sizing circlets, but—which finger do you prefer to wear a ring on?"

"Oh." Ira complied almost automatically. "This one." Ira presented the third finger.

"I'll try to measure as carefully as I can." She looped the tape around his finger, tightened the band, read the divisions on the tape, loosened it, then read the divisions again. "You can always get it adjusted afterward."

He tried to concentrate on what she was doing—to foil an incipient hard-on, first time ever in her presence. "You gonna get me one o' those?" He frowned worriedly. "I mean, Indian rings?" Jesus, he was on the verge of disgracing himself. Hell of a way to show appreciation. "Gee. That's gonna be nice. I mean thanks."

And he wasn't concealing the tumescence very well, wriggling in order to increase room of trouser. It was that encirclement of tape that did it. But what a bland way she had of observing one's condition: unperturbed brown eyes impersonal, and toying with the yellow tape around her dainty finger. "Larry's ring was very bold—to go with his big hand. I'll have to find something right for you."

"Thanks. We'll be the only two people in City College with Navajo rings." Ira sidled toward the door. That was the way to beat it: keep moving. "I just write the box number you gave me, and Silver City, New Mexico? Is that all I have to do? No street?"

"No. That's all. And do please write often. You have no idea how much I enjoy your letters." She followed Ira to the door.

"Yeah? I'm glad." He felt the offending member sink into reverse. "I hope you have a good trip."

"Oh, it won't be. They never are." So American, the way she opposed a cheerful demeanor against a disagreeable prospect. "I'll be bored to death. There's nothing more certain than that. And constipated, of course." Her expression changed to one of serious affection. Her hands stretched up, and held Ira's cheeks between them, drew his head down, and pressed her delicate lips against his, delicate yet firm. Ira could feel the cool shape of them. "You're very dear to me, Ira."

"Thanks." It was strange to be oneself, no more, no less, just honestly be oneself. "I've learned so much from you, I can't tell you."

"I hope it's a little more than the silly things I've done."

"Oh, no. I don't think you've been silly. Yeah, I know: you're too generous. And you worry too much. You blame yourself too much. I do something like that too. But I'm not generous."

"You've been that with me. All this time."

"Yeah, just listening."

She laughed. "Please take care of yourself, lad."

"I'll try."

"Goodbye. And write often."

"All right. And your letters mean a lot to me." He took her extended small hand in his. "Goodbye, Edith."

"Goodbye."

II

Ira attended a daily two-hour French class in the early *après-midi. Oui.* The course, the second half of the second year of French, all Ira would ever take, was given by a Professor Girain, a native of Gascony (D'Artagnan's country), a most astringent and delightful person. He bristled with gruff Gallic wit. Gallic wit it would be called—there was such a thing as Gallic wit, Ira reflected: no other people made those sudden reversals and ripostes (possibly the Irish). "I ask a man on ze corner where is Leo Nard Street, please. 'Leo Nard Street.' It is ze English langwahje wheech is crazy: you write Leo Nard, and pronounce it Lennard."

Ira relished his professor's jests and thrusts, relished them so, and was so receptive, he invariably caught their drift before anyone else in the class did, laughed before anyone else. And after a while Professor Girain's glance would veer toward this most appreciative of his students, as if Ira were a sort of connoisseur of the quality of the humor being purveyed. There was also one other bond between them: Ira's pronunciation of French. Out of the entire class, only two students consistently received a ten out of ten for pronunciation; one was Ira, and the other an upperclassman, Calvin Schick, who had spent the last six months in France on a scholarship.

Ira stopped typing. The damned memories of that college, the damned memories that college had branded on his mind, memories twined with his own folly, rashness, febrile sex as the *New Masses* reviewer, unwittingly euphemistic, called it—even now the damned past arrested its own re-counting. It was that same Calvin Schick that Ira had tussled with when he obstinately insisted on staying in the registrar's office until he was given his transcript, and the other, who now did part-time work there, tried to throw him out, physically. Ira resisted: the window in the office door was broken, and Ira's wrist superficially cut. The women clerks, alarmed at the sight of Ira's gore-smeared hand, quickly conceded. Ira received the object of his long trip uptown—his transcript—and exited the building shielding it from his bleeding wrist. Oh, hell, the memories that trooped back. It was Schick's brother, classmate of Ira's and with whom he had been on good terms, a *goy*, who upbraided Ira bitterly when he appeared in the very dec-imated '28 alcove on Yom Kippur: "That's your holiest day. Why don't you respect it like the rest?"

"Because I don't feel like it." A little more, and the two might have come to blows. Ira was to repeat the performance at a much later date, under dif-ferent circumstances, but with much the same reaction by a non-Jew. It meant, Ira dimly "divined," that refusing to observe his own religion in some way undermined the other's faith, undermined it, trivialized it, in short, was an affront to the other's beliefs. One would have thought, in advance, the *goy* would have said: Ah, here's a Jew who doesn't give a damn about Ju-daism. But no, it meant: Here's a Jew who doesn't give a damn about religion.

To return to his French course again, it was one of the few courses that Ira enjoyed, that bestowed not an element of pleasure in recol-lection, but an element in the formation of taste, an enhancement of discrimination, something, in general, that he had thought he was at-tending college to acquire, and in general didn't. Was it because an adaptation of Anatole France's *Le Livre de Mon Ami* was used as a text? Ira thought so. He still remembered the selection to be recited from memory as part of the final exam: *Soyez beni pour m'avoir révélé, quand je ne sais pas à peine de la pensée, les tourments délicieux que la beauté donne aux âmes avides de la comprendre.* "May you be blessed for having re-vealed to me, when I scarcely knew of the idea, the delicious tor-ments that beauty gives to those souls who are avid to understand her." How he loved to imitate the pronunciation of that gruff old

Gascon, the way he gargled his *r*'s in the back of his throat. And Professor Girain in turn seemed to be more than a little well disposed toward his slouchy, capricious student. Once, when Ira chanced to wander alone with his elderly instructor, without exhorting, Professor Girain almost seemed to plead: "Why are you not more serious? You are capable of excellent work. You have a remarkable delicacy for French, for its literature. Hein?" And was met by Ira's enigmatic—and probably insufferable—grin.

Get it over with, get it over with—Ira hunted an old acne itch under his shirt collar. Get it over with, goddamn 'em, those stupid years, all those intervening, feckless years—feckless? Understatement of the week—rotten years, until he met M.

Oh, one had to reconsider and qualify, Ecclesias, include those transitory, those illusory intermissions: when he became Edith's lover, when he began writing his novel. The years are like hounds after the roebuck, Ecclesias, tireless, hemming in the quarry.

—*E l'animo mio ch'ancor fuggiva*—until that sublime, ultimate, transfiguring instant of clarity, when nothing's left to be said, nothing's left to be done, save perceive, save contemplate. It's a kind of ineffable grandeur. . . .

Not that those years after he met M were so much better, or that he was any more judicious or wiser—he wasn't. But he had M to turn to, M to guide him, a Beatrice to guide him through a journey toward redemption, to steady him—what should he say?—moderate his manias with her clemency and her wisdom. Jesus, he had said to himself this morning, when his brain seemed like a lump of dough, and facing the monitor, utterly beyond him—

He had gone back to bed, defeated, stuporous, wishing he were dead: *apothanein thelo*; enjoining himself before he fell asleep. Remember, the thing to do is to shop around for the right-sized trunk, and begin packing away all your—lousy, he said and retracted—all your inane papers, stow them away, get ready for demise, for *peigern*. Did anyone leave more written trash behind, more documentary drivel, than the baffled scrivener? Nobody. Get things ready, in some arrangement, in order to depart leaving a minimal mess.

Ira contemplated the tangled, intangible skein of thought that seemed to lurk in the dark corner between monitor and system: the carnal component of his marriage to M, once so overriding in importance, had now sublimated completely into the intimacies of custom, of caring and sharing, the intimacies of intellectual companionship. But even as M had expected and received his total fidelity in the previous stage, so now she expected a monogamous mental fidelity. She wanted all of his mind; she opposed anyone else's partaking of it.

—And thus, what do you commit with me, dear friend?

Ecclesias? No, confiding in a reflection of what was, a window onto my only remaining future, is not infidelity—that is my survival, and a penance.

But he was flattering himself. His hypothesis would never hold up under any rigorous examination. Well, get on with it. How many times—he feared—would he tell himself that before the end of his testament, if he ever reached it. No matter, if spurring himself on served to help him reach the end, then as many times as was necessary. Get on with it . . . as expeditiously as possible:

But before that he had quit his job at Loft's, quit or was fired. In July. If there was such a thing as a gray area between, it was within that area that his job was terminated.

Mr. Buckley, the night manager, was on duty. A summer night. Warm, brightly lit, sweet-flavored interior of the store, with the wide-bladed fans circling languidly overhead. And customers coming in for sundaes and sodas, and seating themselves at the round marble tables.

A crowd of people came into the place intent on ice cream refreshments, and occupied the round tables. Bob shuffled over to Ira, turning his back to the front of the store. "Boy, look at them nigger customers comin' in, fo', five. Uh-oh, they're all settin' down at a table," said Bob.

"Buckley is lookin' this way. You know what that means."

"Oh, nuts! You mean I'm gone t' have t' play waiter to them niggers?"

"Nobody else but."

Bob turned back toward the front of the store, where children and their parents sipped on malteds and milk shakes, and young couples fresh from the moving pictures shared sundaes. As he turned his body, he rotated so that he hugged the cash register, effectively pushing Ira into Mr. Buckley's view. Ira was now the unoccupied employee who needed a task.

Mr. Buckley called on Ira to wait on the newly arrived patrons. Ira refused. Truculently, without doubt, he asserted it wasn't his job to wait on tables; he was a cashier as well as candy clerk, and that was enough. He intended to stay behind the counter; he refused to be a waiter. And Mr. Buckley, offended, probably more by Ira's manner than his insubordination, snapped that if Ira refused to do as he was told, he could go home. Ira took off his white Loft's jacket and cap and left the store. Bullheaded, caught in a loony consistency of his own making, as so many times before. He went home—and he stayed home.

He had been wishing for some time to quit, wishing subliminally to quit, and had never found occasion. When he went in a week later to get his pay for the previous week, Mr. Ryce, the manager, berated him in no uncertain terms for not reporting to work the next day— or days—for staying away so long a new clerk had to be hired in his place. What was the matter with him? That disagreement with Mr. Buckley was of no consequence.

"A college man like you, with all the experience you got in the store, why, they would have grabbed you when you graduated—even before, maybe, for a relief manager," Mr. Ryce fumed. "A young fellow like you could have gone way further than me—you could have got up there with them general managers."

Ira hung his head, trying to look more foolish than he was. "I—I thought I was fired."

Mr. Ryce handed him his pay envelope with the finality of one dealing with a hopeless case.

Just before Edith left for New Mexico, Minnie left her job at the five-and-ten store. She had succeeded in getting a job with B. Altman's, the department store, and worked down in the bargain basement, where she sold marked-down articles of all kinds—furniture, clothing, housewares. A few weeks passed. Near the end of July, she confided to Ira that she had met "a nice Panamanian fellow, and he wants to date me."

"Yeah?" Cool now, limp and detached, he listened with a certain degree of judiciousness. Curious, though his reaction was understandably ambiguous. He was aware that he felt benign, even helpful: "Well, you don't mind he's Spanish. Is he a nice guy?"

"Oh, he's lovely. He's so good-looking, I'm telling you; he's the floorwalker, in charge of all the different kinds of plants and flowerpots, all those things that have to do with houseplants growing in windows, and hanging from the ceiling. Vines. He knows all their names. He learned all that in Panama." She paused in amused reminiscence. "And he wears a white carnation in his lapel, just like you see in the movies."

"Yeah? How'd you meet him?"

"Oh, you know Altman's. In the elevator before the store opens. You see people. You hear them talk. I heard about the gorgeous flowers and plants on the third floor. So I went up there during my lunch hour. He thought I was a customer, and we started in talking. He asked me to meet him after the store closed. He took me to Schrafft's."

"To Schrafft's. Hey, that's high-class. How old is he?"

"Twenty-six, maybe twenty-eight."

"And you don't mind that he's not Jewish? You said last year you'd never again go steady with a *goy*. Or something like that."

"I don't care. I was a fool then. I'm not going to be a dope this time. So Zaida can say *Kaddish* for me. But," she stressed, "until then, I'm just talking. He gives me that feeling, you know?"

"Yeah?" Ira studied her: pretty, despite the thickened eyeglasses she now had to wear, lips parted, her eyelids arched, her fresh, dappled cheeks rosy with surge of tender sentiment, she signaled the kind of state he recognized, but would never know.

"Well, good," he said. "Good luck." He started suddenly to his feet.

A few days later, on a Sunday morning, he heard Mom leave. He lay in his narrow bed, unmoving, staring at the opposite gray-daubed bricks seen through the window of their air shaft. It was only a few weeks after the summer solstice, he reflected, and yet the sunlight would no longer descend even this far down at high noon—not that it was noon. Who was it? Eratosthenes, who had conducted his experiment to determine the earth's diameter by climbing down into a deep well. It couldn't have been any deeper than the bottom of an air shaft was from the roof. Even to the first flight.

Minnie had been out late last night, a sure sign she was out on another date. She had turned on the ceiling lights after entering the kitchen, shut the door to the bedrooms immediately after, but he had awakened. He said nothing to her when she went by on her way to her folding cot in Mom and Pop's bedroom. There could be no doubt in his mind with whom she had been out: Arturo—but she called him Artie, the good-looking Latin floorwalker in charge of the potted plants and the hanging vines. He felt strange; he felt almost sexless as he lay there in abject silence, trying to determine how he felt, since it was really over for good. Oh, hell, let it be over, and stay over. He'd sneak a quick one into Stella as he had at most other times. Needed only to raise half a hard-on, and he was done, hardly had a hard-on and it was over, and she was retreating from his knees—before anyone even guessed. Hell of a way to fuck, half a minute, half-backed, high speed.

Toss-up. She was sleeping, sleeping it off. Well, then, get up, get up and dress, if he really wanted to make this the breaking point. Show her. Oh, hell, he didn't know. Would the Latin romance go on? Would there be an engagement, the way other romances progressed?

Would she accept? Maybe. Would he attend to old Zaida, tearing his hair, *davening* over her *Kaddish* candle? But she would never begin with him again anyway.

So pay no attention to her. Get out of bed. Right. Jesus, start now. Right. Get your clothes on. Okay.

He got up, walked quietly barefooted into the kitchen. He was behaving so differently now, aware of it, for once not opportunistic, not halfhearted, or what to call it? Shilly-shallying. He felt almost like a somnambulist, sleepwalking in broad daylight, standing in the kitchen, Sunday morning, looking at the washpole out of the corner window on the backyard, and alone with Minnie—would that be the way Siamese twins felt if they tried to tear themselves apart?

He was about to shut the kitchen door to the bedroom, but he heard a bed creak, the creak of one bed, a few barefooted footsteps, and the creak of another bed. She was changing from her cot to Pop and Mom's bed. He eased the tongue of the lock into its aperture as quietly as he could.

"Mama?"

"No," he said gruffly. "It's me."

"So she went away a long time?"

"No. A few minutes ago."

"So what are you doing?"

Invisible point of the spinning *dreidel* on Hanukkah: *shim* when it came to rest, take all or lose all. Which? He had forgotten. *Gimel*, take all or what? Not since the East Side. "I was gonna get dressed."

"Let me talk to you a second."

"What for?"

"Sit down. I want to tell you about my date. It was wonderful. Oh, it was wonderful."

"Yeah?" Ira sat on the edge of the bed. Oh, Jesus, would it never end. "Tell me quick. All right?"

"You got time. We're not doing anything. He took us to a hotel room, you know. Just for a couple of hours. Oh, we had such a wonderful time. So easy—" Her hands came together rapturously above the white-fringed bosom of her nightgown. "I've been out on dates. But like this, never. You got a big bed, you got a wonderful room all to yourselves. Oh, you got ti-i-me."

"Wonderful. So why tell me?"

"He's got such a soft, golden skin. And what a wonderful lover. You feel like you could—" The hands at her bosom arose upward, spread apart. "You don't know how much you can stand. I'll tell you something else you should know. He's married!" Her head lifted from the pillow. "He's married, he's even got two kids."

"Well, I'll be goddamned."

"He told me."

"You know that, and you still let him fuck you?"

"Shut up, you dirty louse. Dirty. Dirty. That's all that you are."

"All right. Good."

"You stink."

"Yeah?"

"You oughta see somebody who can make love. Oh."

He turned on her, spewed vindictiveness. "You mean you with your spic feller. Why not?" He was about to dredge up more, but the viciousness of his own gloating stunned him, nay, intoxicated him— there was no telling the two apart, only that he was ravished by his own memories—and transfigured by the rapture of his horror at the abyss he had come to, untrammeled, the barriers he had broken down to the verge of depravity—that he had fondly imagined only minutes ago that he could somehow begin to restore. He barely heard her as through a corridor of selves in a mirror, the dark reiterated reflection of becoming nil.

"Shut up, louse. He makes you look like a *mensheleh,* you know that? What he's got you'll never have in all your life. He's got charm. And a build. He's beautiful."

She stung, the way Mom did Pop, when she taunted him. "So what're you blaming me for, you goddamn twat!" he reviled. "And with a Spanish *goy* yet! And married." He could hear himself, abandoned in his malevolence, saw apparition of summery gutter dust at the curb, the grated sewer at the corner. What of it? He could murder her.

"Better than a brother, better than a brother," she kept jeering in rejoinder. "Better than you. And don't scare me you're gonna tell Mom this time. I'm nearly of age. I'm a senior at Richmond. I told her myself I was going out with a Panamanian."

"Yeah? What'd she say to her little *rusjinkeh*? Did you tell her he was a married man with kids?"

"No, I didn't. I just said he was from Panama. She said—you know what Mom said?" Minnie scaled over his heavy irony. "She said, '*Noo*, do what you want. *Bist shoyn a groyseh moyt*. You're not a child. *Nur breng mir nisht kein benkart*.' You know Mom: don't bring me a baby."

"I hope you do."

"Go to hell. I could tell Mom I had learned from you."

"Go to hell yourself. I'll tell her it was her fault."

"Her fault?" Minnie was startled from rancor to perplexity. "Why was it *her* fault?"

"Never mind." He adopted an easy, lofty sneer. "I'll stay on the sidelines, okay? Till the end of summer."

"Yeah, I believe you," she parried sneer with contempt. "You'll stay on the sidelines, period. No more. Always with your nose in a book, a book. Go make some girl the way other fellers do. No, you're too lazy—a *folentser*. Her voice tightened, became almost a squeal, the way it always did when she was wrought up.

"Who else do you know who did it with his sister? You're my brother, and I was like your wife, like a hoor with you. Yeah, because I loved you. That's the whole trouble. I loved you and I hated you. Why? Because you were making me like you. I don't have to go with other boys. They rub up against me when we're dancing. I know what they want. I have to act like I don't. They wanna neck. Who needs to neck? I've missed all a girl should have, what other girls still have, all the excitement. Finding out and everything. All because of you, I missed the whole thing. That's all!"

Welladay. Little more was to be gained by laboring the point any further. It was the sense of exploration that drove him on, in the present as it had in the past. It was the word "exploration" that aroused him now, that still swung in his mind with something of the original lurch of feeling when he jotted the word down. He would be an exploration in debasement, his own, the soul of a twentieth-century first-generation American-Jewish writer, alienated from his kind by twist of circumstance, and perhaps, in part, justifiably alienated. But it would be exploration in vileness organically connected with the sensibility of one professing to be an artist. At least *Unity* would be attained, however reluctantly he had been driven to it. What if Saint Augustine had obliterated from his *Confessions* the pain— one could guess—the throes of his renouncing the two women, his paramours, banning his sensual appetites, even the most innocuous. Could one ever forget the old saint's self-reproach for yielding to the entrancing sight of a swift hound coursing a hare? He would have given us a docked Saint Augustine, and who would have cared for it? He gave us the whole man, something Joyce didn't. Joyce espoused the Unities, but eschewed Unity. Something that he, Ira, now strove to do while battling old age, and approaching the eternal.

III

The first of September 1926, Edith returned from the Southwest. She began a "furious" hunt for another apartment, an apartment "a little more gracious" than the one she had been living in. She found one on Morton Street, on the south side of Morton Street, a renovated town house, like others between Seventh Avenue and Hudson Street. It seemed odd at first that renovated town houses shared the street with two or three typical five-flight walk-ups. They were all undoubtedly relics of the past, before the Village spread into a formerly immigrant Italian neighborhood, even before that neighborhood became Italian. A day after the Labor Day weekend, Larry returned home from the summer resort. He looked fit, tanned. He had gained weight. Sanguine, successful, with every movement he belied Edith's calamity-ridden prognosis of the ills the future held in store for him.

As she had promised before she left, she brought back with her a Navajo ring from New Mexico for Ira, and while Larry stood by, his healthy countenance aglow with approval at this show of Edith's esteem for his friend, she presented Ira with the gift. The ring was altogether different from Larry's, which, as she had said, was bold, a large piece of turquoise held in a solid setting of silver. Ira's was far more delicate, and more elaborate, with nine turquoise beads held in a matching silver grid, and fretted at the sides with small embossings. She thought its approximate age was at least fifty years, from a time when Southwestern Indians still melted down silver dollars and made jewelry out of them.

And that was nearly seventy years ago when she presented it to him, Ira allowed himself the luxury, the luxurious dolor, of brooding: of time and vicissitude . . . fixed an instant on the enticing pun on the amber monitor: silver dolor. . . . He snorted, and went on.

The ring was a little too loose for his third finger, but any jeweler could adjust it to his size, Edith thought. Transported by joy at the novelty and the honor, Ira held out his hand.

"Beautiful! Beautiful!" Larry exclaimed. "Everybody at the resort wanted to know where I got mine. I bet that's what happens to you. Everybody in the '28 alcove will ask you where you got yours. We'll be the only ones at CCNY wearing Navajo rings."

"That's just what I told—" Ira swallowed Edith's name down just in time. "Just what I told myself. I wish I knew what to say, Edith. It's a beautiful surprise!"

She just loved giving; she showed her enjoyment in fond brown eyes, olive-skinned smile. "It's not very expensive. I bought it because it was so unusual. It seemed to be right for you."

"Yeah. Thanks." He looked down at the ring that rotated so easily partway around and back on his finger. What a strange gulf seemed to open within himself, so wide, so nameless. He fancied, always on the brink of a pun, that the beneficent gravity of her world was separating the wretched fragments of his. "Maybe I can help you when you move. We both can."

"That's right," Larry concurred. "We'll get Ivan. He's back from camp. He's got a driver's license. And Matt's got a car. He and Miriam are crazy about Ivan."

"Yeah?"

"Oh, no. You're both very sweet. I'm going to let someone else handle the mess. They know just what to do—"

"I was once a plumber's helper," said Ira. "If I could save you something."

She laughed, so merrily for once.

"And don't forget I was an able-bodied seaman on His Majesty's ship the *Pinafore*," Larry joined in. "Trust me. I can batten down the butter plates abaft the binnacle better than the boatswain himself."

Happiness was a short respite when well-being held sway. A bulkhead of euphoria—Ira recalled the Conrad tale—that held miraculously, in secrecy, against the unrelenting pressure of the future.

Ostensibly, Ira and Larry were juniors in college. Ostensibly. In fact, they were both wanting sufficient college credits to rate as valid juniors, juniors in good standing academically: Ira for the usual reasons, failures, insufficient number of courses, incompletions, poor grades, and Larry because he "lost credits" when he switched from NYU to CCNY, where credits were differently evaluated. Both faced the prospect of having to take summer courses next year. The three credits Ira had gained in a summer of French still left him woefully in arrears—and with little hope of reversing the shabby trend of attainment. College routines were now well ingrained, a familiar treadmill for both of them. Mechanical drudgery, most of it, drudgery resigned to, drudgery despised and shoddily performed. Floundering in mediocrity, Ira's career came close to foundering when he took on that most boring of banes, his first "Ed" courses, electives. He drove himself to read the pages of his texts on the subject resentfully, sullenly, cursing the career he had chosen for himself, more like a miserable fate than a career.

There were small variations in the collegiate rounds sometimes: hiking home with Aaron Hessman, classmate who lived a few blocks farther south—in Jewish Harlem. Not altogether dull, Aaron H, not altogether humorless, but already dried by academic overachievement, and wound up with a shoulder-hitch tic. He was well on his way to a Phi Beta Kappa key, well on his way to a tutorship in Latin: *Eheu fugaces, Postume, Postume, labuntur anni.* Crack breaststroke swimmer too, he had impersonated brawny Ivan, physics whiz, who swam like a plumb bob, swam as if he meant to thrash the pool dry, and walk its length instead.

Eheu fugaces, Postume, Postume, labuntur anni. Alas, how swiftly the fleeting years have gone by. How could so powerful a swimmer as you, Aaron, drown off Rockaway Beach a year after you won your coveted key and your *summa cum laude,* and your Latin tutorship? It seemed impossible—unless you intended to . . . to be the first of the class of '28 to go.

—And indeed you will be the last.

To have traded places with Aaron.

—To your narrative, my friend.

Delighted classmates, sitting about the large scarred oak table in the middle of the '28 alcove, stopped whatever they were doing to listen to Larry sing one of the skits he had helped concoct last summer at Kopake in the Catskills. As always, with his charm, his personableness, his air of worldliness, his facility as entertainer, Larry had already become a popular figure in the class. Many were drawn to him, as long ago many were drawn to Ira's childhood chum Farley. There were adulators who sought to curry favor with him, but as with Farley, only certain ones were allowed into the inner circle, of which Ira was the closest to the center. On the scarred alcove table, Larry, the sad little Jew, wearing his World War khaki uniform, swayed with stereotypical Jewish woe to the tempo of his song:

> *"Vot is life, dot's the quvestion vot I ponder.*
> *Vot is life, over here or over yonder?*

> *It's a game of chence, of circumstence—*
> *Oy, gewalt! I burned a hole in my only pair of . . ."*

Larry paused, and against expectation, instead of pants, sang: "trousers."

The alcove applauded, and Ira grinned, amused and sardonic as ever. Larry was certainly funny: with that fresh batch of gags, anecdotes, comic lyrics he'd brought back from Kopake, and now Lemansky's, there was no doubt about his ability to amuse. And there was no doubt the stuff was amusing, too. But it was—what was it?— the way Larry appraised it, the value he set on it, personal value, the way he identified with it, that was new, new and different. He no longer related to the stuff with a show of derision, a mocking counterbalance of appraisal, but as if it were stock in trade, a commodity of value to be purveyed in the marketplace of entertainment. A paradoxical change had taken place in him, as if this recent accession of comic triviality were an embellishment of his personality, an enhancement of it, not something he might advert to in passing, with absence of self-emphasis, an absurdity naturally apropos, but rather as if the anecdotal and the droll were prized substance of his character, his gift to any group. Ira had the most difficult time with himself trying to "figure out," as he would put it, just what the difference was between the Larry that was and the Larry now—and between himself and Larry—when it came to things of this sort, to humor in particular. Was it the performer taking over in Larry, was that the difference? The performer filling a vacuum left by the exhaustion of the poetic impulse that had burgeoned within the college freshman of only a couple of years ago? It was a strange thing, something to contemplate, a decline, a deterioration of sensibility, that at the same time as it seemed a matter of choice, seemed the effect of spiritual compulsion. It was like an optical illusion, the nugatory imbuing one aspect, pathos the other.

Ira felt a throb of poignancy at the unmistakable proliferation of the commonplace in Larry. How the constellation of personality could change, how it could alter—as Ira had read celestial constellations would change after many millennia—and the whole configuration of temperament scarcely be recognizable as what it once was. By intuitive modulations of affinity, he had taken advantage of Larry's temperament in an earlier phase. By a different method he was now ready to take advantage of it in the next. Inbred, alert predator, who could not be anything else, as if it were a matter of inevitability, he could only function by exploiting his friend, his benefactor, who had been so generous to his grubby, slum-misshapen chum, misshapen in more ways than Larry ever dreamed, who had instilled something of deportment in Ira, something of couthness: from that first dinner at Larry's home, of lamb chops and creamed spinach. It was a recurrent, ambivalent theme with Ira, his attitude toward his friend's bloom and blight. And even though Edith had attributed Larry's change, his petering out of poetic impulse, to his "shallowness," still, her dictum continued to leave Ira unsatisfied. While he profited by her disparagement, and stood to gain by it, it left him uneasy: something unaccountable about it, or if applicable, how wide was the scope of its application? If that was shallowness, what was depth? How deep did "depth" have to go to prove itself? Or did a guy burn out, the way Farley had "burned out," a schoolboy outrunning the foremost sprinter of his day, outrunning the gold medalist Abrams in the Olympic relays.

—You've already expatiated on that at length, my friend.

And so I have, so I have. But I suppose it's become an obsession with me, Ecclesias, because I traveled the same road as Larry did, and if I traveled it "farther" than he did, I'm no longer sure which one of us suffered more when the road ended in trackless morass. . . . I lived. His heart slowly atrophied. And something else has come to me in belated fashion, something I should perhaps merely make a note of at this stage, and reserve dealing with at a later time: consider that central trope of my first novel: why did I "choose" the central character's near-fatal contact with the third rail as a climax? The third rail that all but immolated the child, virtually gutted his future? And I was so oblivious I didn't know my seemingly detached fable *de me narratur*.

IV

It was in Ira's junior year that he was at last able to program into his schedule the Biology 1 course that he had been so eager to register for the afternoon of his first day inside the college—and that had become after two years mere memory of an aspiration and no more: desiccated and crushed autumn leaves trodden underfoot in the euphoria of sauntering along Convent Avenue high in blue sky above the city—before encountering the workaday, lackluster interior of the auditorium where he was to register, the chalked courses on blackboards, the crowd of competing students busy at their seats, or impatiently waiting in long files. No, there was nothing like that now—in registering for courses in his junior year. He had all the time in the world to make out his schedule, and do it in leisurely fashion without fear of seeing the course erased on the blackboard before he reached the desk.

But what the hell was the use? In two years' time, he had become nobody. And less and less every day. Together with scarce-known classmates, he walked out of the auditorium, through the dull halls, past the gray-white Gothic exterior walls, down the steps into the quadrangle among the trimmed ginkgo trees. . . .

And Bio—by the time classes began, the subject left him as cold, if not as clammy, as the pickled frog he shared with a fellow student, and dissected parts of as ineptly and lackadaisically as he drew the batrachian's innards, barely wresting a C from a quiz, and skittering toward a C for the course. Oh, he understood what Mendel was all about, the methodical monk in the apron and little eyeglasses, understood the dominant and the recessive in sweet peas, and what happened when they were crossed. So what? But this genetics business—why the hell did they have to wrack his brains with all these crossword-puzzle-looking charts?

Minnie was faring no easier than Ira. One afternoon she flung herself through the doorway, flung herself at him with a cry of woe, inarticulate with weeping, woe, a lamentation, loud and louder, disfiguring, eyes crimped together, tears in droplets and glistening in liquid braid down her cheeks as far as chin, her mouth open to its widest, red-curled tongue and tissue flaming, bawling.

"Shut up! What the hell's the matter with you!" Ira closed the door as quickly as he could—to confine her frenzy, her hysteria, to the kitchen interior. "What happened to you? For Christ's sake, talk!"

"Oh, my dear brother! Ira, dear! Ira-a-a!" Her sob soared from coherence to a prolonged wail, then trailed away into a moan: "A-a-a-ah!"

"For Christ's sake, I heard that!" Brutal with dismay, he yelled at her. "A-a-h, what? What the hell happened?"

"Oh, oh, oh, what happened," she wailed, and with the same hand that let her briefcase drop onto a chair, she stroked his. "Oh, Ira, my darling brother!"

"Well, what, for Christ's sake?" He yanked his hand clear.

"They didn't want me, they didn't wanna take me into teachers college," she sobbed.

"Into what? What d'you mean?"

"Into Hunter. Into the teachers college. That I was taking an academic course for. Taking Latin for."

"Why the hell not? What the hell's wrong? If you'll stop your goddamn bawling, I'll know what you're talking about. Why wouldn't they take you?"

"My *s*," she wept. "Wait, I'll get my handkerchief—I failed."

"Failed what?" He was beginning to surmise.

"The test, the test for normal school. The speaking test. I failed." It seemed as if her spirit were scourged, not her body. "Ah-ah-ah!"

"Will you cut it out and talk!" he shouted at her.

"Oh, Ira."

"Yes! Yes! Yes! Bullshit! You failed what? What *s*?"

"I have a lateral *s*," she moaned.

"You have a lateral *s*. What in hell!"

"That's what she said. The lady that came to test us. From the Board of Education. I don't talk right. She gave everyone something to read. A hundred we were nearly . . . so. Oh, Ira." Forlorn, she seemed without a will of her own. She pushed the briefcase from chair to floor, but didn't sit down, kept standing. "You know how I wanted to teach in the public school," she continued brokenly, fingers crooked above the collar of her gray dress, and chin drooping to rest on them. "If I could get my teacher's degree, we could move out of this dump. We could move to the Bronx. We could have a decent apartment. We could have a phone. Decent dates. Jewish fellers who could come to the house."

"All right. All right."

"You don't care. You're a man. You don't care."

"I do care. What the hell good is all that crying gonna do?"

"Oh, Ira, I can't help it. Oh, I tried so hard. I read every word. I knew what everything meant when she asked me. And I didn't pass. I didn't pass. They don't want me." She slumped into a morbid silence. When she spoke again, her sobs had dried. She panted rather than spoke, words arid with bitterness: "A lateral *s*. A lateral *s*. A kid's gonna know I got a lateral *s*. Who ever told me I had a lateral *s*? Nobody. No English teacher. That's how they took us out. That's how they got rid of us. I think it's only the Jews that they got like that."

"Yeah?"

"I could swear. It was only the Jewish girls that failed in the speech test." She brooded. "I'm glad you were here, not Mama, when I came home."

"I am too. Your shriek. You would have scared the life out of her."

"Oh. My darling brother. Oh."

"Aw, c'mon. For Christ's sake! Teaching isn't the only thing in the world."

"So why do *you* wanna teach?"

"Because I'm a *malamut*, as Pop says. What the hell's that got to do with it? I hate business. I don't want to have anything to do with it, and you don't. You've had—" He gesticulated. "Experience. You've worked in stores, in a shop. You've been in an office—you like people. You get along with people. You like to talk with people."

"But I wanted to be a public school teacher."

"Listen, don't tell me what you wanted to be. You got that half year left next term: then take business courses. Didn't I get all screwed up with those commercial courses in the beginning of high school, junior high school, that I didn't want?" He tried to talk as fast as he could, as forcefully as he could, anything to get her out of the sagging collapsed creature that sat as if dumped into a chair. "I'm telling you. I'm really sorry. No bull. But Jesus, Mom comes home and looks at you. You—you act like the end of the world. Immediately her ears are gonna start roaring. You're gonna get her all worked up. *Oy, gevald! Oy, a brukh is mir! Mein orrim kindt!*" He rocked in disgusted mimicry.

"That lousy supervisor. She should croak! I know it was only the Jewish girls."

"So we're up against the same goddamn thing. What're you gonna do? At least the other way you can tell her—calm. 'They didn't take me. I didn't pass the test. I'm going into all commercial courses next term.' Make it natural. You didn't pass the test, so—"

"My dear brother. Oh, you're so smart. Oh, I'm glad you were here. You make me feel better. I could hardly come home. I could hardly walk. I was so *fertsfeilet,* I didn't know where I was going. I swear I could have walked downtown from Richmond. I could have died. I wanted to die. You know what I thought of: the subway tracks."

"Listen, you didn't steal anything. You weren't going to get expelled from school." Harsh memory steeled his harsh voice, against itself, against sympathy.

"My poor brother."

"Yeah."

"I feel just like it."

"Like what?"

"Like you. When you were expelled from Stuyvesant." She lifted her face, nodded drearily several times. "When you came home, and gave Papa the stick to hit you with. I'm no good. No good, that's all."

"Aw, come on. The two things don't compare. I didn't fail. I stole fountain pens. I got caught. I was expelled. You didn't do anything wrong."

"I did. I did. I let you lay me. How many times? How many times did we go in the bedroom? How many Sunday mornings?"

"What the hell's that got to do with it?"

"A lot. Everything. Everything it's got to do with. That's why I'm no good."

"Listen, for Christ's sake, Minnie. Now, listen." With hands extended, he summoned full exigency of plea. "Try coming back to yourself, will you? You're way, way too excited. I mean, it's a shock you've been through. Come on. Be sensible, Minnie. You'll get over it." He gesticulated. "Listen, there are other girls failed that test."

Her hysteria blocked out the outside world, the world of Larry and Edith. In the preternatural light of the musty kitchen, Ira looked from the door back to his sister. Her hair disheveled, bronze locks hanging tear-drenched in her tortured face, she looked more like a Bacchant than a sister. The evident madness of his own horror contrasted so vividly with Larry's descriptions of his shipboard romance, of the sweetness of salty-aired love: firm, cool, and far removed from this frenzy.

At last, she did go to the sink and wash, freshened her appearance, brought the dapple back to her cheeks, combed her reddish bobbed locks, primped. Fortunately another half hour passed, and Mom and Pop still hadn't come home. By that time she seemed completely recovered, presentable, engrossed in a textbook, as he was.

"Do I look all right, Ira?" she asked. Her voice was humble.

"Huh?" He raised his eyes from the genetics chart he was trying to decipher, the small squares and symbols that hung like a screen before vision for a moment as he surveyed her: his sister, nothing special: serious, determined countenance. Red, curly bobbed hair, thick nostrils, hazel eyes. "You look all right. Some difference from before."

"You know what?" Minnie smoothed the bosom of her dress. "Don't say anything."

"No? About what? What do you mean?"

"That I failed in the oral. My crazy s."

"All right, if that's what you want. Why?"

"I'll tell 'em tomorrow. They're coming home happy for a change. They saw a vaudeville show. What's the hurry? I'll tell Mom tomorrow. I won't lie. I won't say I didn't fail. I'll just say, so if I'm teaching public school and I get married, what's the difference if I'm in an office and I get married? I'll feel more like that tomorrow. You know what I mean? It'll be better." She paused to let the thought sink in. "I'm getting a little hungry. You? I wonder what Mom's got ready. I don't see anything to warm up. Must be a big can of salmon to chop up with an onion. But maybe she'll buy something on the way."

*   *   *

The image, the episode, the whole passage of it, grew to a peak days after it should have receded, became more immanent in his mind the next day and the next, immanent, became a revolting progression. It wasn't as if he were haunted by some wrongdoing, specific offense, as in the past, cringing before imagined execration and worse in store for his miscreant self, discovered. More grievously, he was aware that he had tainted her forever, and that her recent failure was inextricably related to him. He would sometimes sit smirking when he felt out of danger, sounding the Yiddish epithets his parents would have hurled at him: *Paskudnyack! Meeseh chaiye! A meeseh mishineh auf dir. Zus verfollt veren!* Oh there were dozens, fantastic extravagant dozens. And Pop, what could he do? Now that Ira stood a head taller than his father? And as for little Jonas, Stella's father, even shorter than Pop, the little erstwhile ladies' tailor, cafeteria partner—Jesus, it sometimes made Ira chortle—when he was out of all danger. And Zaida, well, spewing Yiddish curses. No, he wasn't the least filled with remorse for *that* act, guilt, burden of the sordid, consequences of taboo violation, disgrace. He almost wished it was as simple as that, as though they were the good old days, when he at least knew how he would feel, what to expect. The feeling he had now was general, altogether different. It was not the horrible twist of terror that wrenched his whole being, that terrible, that permanent crimp of plane-geometry days when she didn't have her period, or any other time when she was late. Don't think of the past, that's all. Get over to Mamie's. That didn't do the same thing, even if she was still a kid, kid or no kid, and not such a kid, either: sixteen. And you had to walk eight, nine blocks, take a chance, act a part, wait, hang around, look dumb—and maybe lose. But it was outside, and if you won, as long as you were sure you didn't knock her up, boy! But so what if you won, that was the trouble: winning, winning, no more winning.

He recalled a short address that he had given nearly a decade before, in which he had expressed his genuine perplexity that he should be so honored. His fame, the tributes he received for his first novel, never ceased to seem unreal to him—that he was the one who should be the object of these accolades. He felt that there was something freakish about it all, and he honestly felt so: a fluke. And he would quote from a biography of John Synge that he had read some years ago, that talent was not enough, that the writer, the artist, in order to achieve greatness, had in some way to tap something universal and permanent in his time. And he followed this quotation with another by the late Georgia O'Keeffe—one he had within easy access, contained within one of the poems of his rheumatologist, David B. "I might have been a better painter, and no one would have noticed, but because I was in touch with my time people saw something in my work that they knew. . . ." She was saying the same thing as John Synge, whom Ira idolized.

So it was a fluke, he would reiterate, he would stress: he was acquainted with much-better-endowed writers than he, far more intelligent, brilliant guys, witty, acute, original. But it was as if they had tried and failed to align themselves with the lines of force of their time, and so if he were to name them, he was sure few in the audience would know them. And the strange thing was, in his opinion, that it was not given to the individual to align himself by an act of will to the lines of force of his time: one couldn't choose to or refuse to. Genes and circumstances either made him do so, made him an eligible candidate for the canon, so to speak, one of the elect, or did not. It wasn't in his hands. So if he was the one so chosen, he actually deserved very little credit. Only that of striving to develop the most preeminent, if not the only, gift he had . . . which was what the others did, also . . . those more gifted than he, who yet failed to win universal appeal. It was all a Calvinist fluke.

V

"Back safely," his dear M announced when she returned home from a performance in Roswell. She had played selections from her latest composition there, a work for the piano. "I feel guilty leaving you alone all day, but I had such an exciting time." She went on to tell him about the program given by the New Mexico Women Composers Guild, about the beautiful concert grand Baldwin on which she had played excerpts from the piece she was working on, and how well both her composition and her performance were received by the audience. "Though I did play a few wrong notes," she smiled. "My eyes simply aren't up to playing in public anymore—and isn't that the longest stretch of nothing between Vaughn and Roswell? I'm glad I didn't have to do the driving. My attention would surely have begun to wander. The ranches must be way back in." And then she noticed that he hadn't eaten the frozen dinner she had so solicitously provided for him.

"Too much trouble," he said curtly. "I had a peanut-butter-and-jelly sandwich."

And then without asking, and without further comment, she knew he was depressed. . . .

Things had come together that morning, before she left for Roswell, adverse things, of little or no importance, except for the state he had been in—and still was. He had wondered aloud, as they shared a last sip of coffee, how soon they might invite John Keleher and his wife, Marie, over for supper. John was a young artist, devoted to Ira, a virtual surrogate son. M had heartily endorsed the idea.

"We might get four of the Le Menu frozen dinners, save you work," Ira had suggested, and went on: "I'd like him to do an illuminated inscription for me, a couple of Greek words."

"*Enteuthen exelaunei,*" she quoted cheerily from the *Anabasis,* and then inquired: "May I ask what words they are?"

He put her off with: "Just a couple of words. Happen to be meaningful for me. I'd like to frame them." It wouldn't have made much difference probably if he *had* told her. They were included in the epigraph to *The Waste Land,* which Eliot himself had borrowed from the *Satyricon* of Petronius, and Ira with minuscule remnant of Greek, and the aid of a dictionary, had succeeded in translating them from the original: they were the Sibyl of Cumae's reply to the youngsters who asked her what she wanted: *"Sibylla ti theleis?"* Sibyl, what do you wish? *"Apothanein thelo"* was her reply.

I wish to die. He would like the Greek words framed and hung on the wall of his study.

Things had come together that Sunday morning, things of little or no importance, as he had said, except when he was in that state of mind. Goddamn it, stuporous. Would anybody believe that the onset of daylight

saving on the same Sunday morning that M left for Roswell would have so
adverse an effect on him as it had? He loathed the damned change of time:
it threw everything off for him: sleeping and eating and the other established nodes of existence.

"Why don't you just accept it?" M had counseled. "Why do you have
to keep referring to the old time, telling yourself it's really an hour earlier?
It would be so much easier if you didn't. You make things so much harder
for yourself that way."

"I always do," he had answered. *"Apothanein thelo."*

"You really did look awful when I got home from Roswell," M told him a
day or so later. "You look better now, but you looked awful when I came in.
What were you so depressed about?"

"Just depressed," he had answered evasively. "Frustrated maybe. You
know how my goddamn neurosis takes its toll every so often."

But afterward they had gone through a brief estrangement. She
chided him for twitting her before company, dinner company, something
he almost never did, deplored when others did, something she never did,
and reminded him she never did, which was true. What was it this time he
was guilty of? Because he was, and was ashamed of himself (and pondered
deeply why, found insidious, subterranean reasons to account for his
anomalous behavior). But what was it made her say, "You know how I feel
about husbands picking on their wives before others. You hurt my feelings.
I never do that to you. I'm going to fight for my rights." He would have to
ask her what it was he said or did specifically. . . .

Specifically . . . he sat down before the keyboard. Scenario: Action!
Camera slowly pans big blond John Opa, tubist with the Albuquerque
Symphony, and his Jewish wife, Leslie Heil, bassoonist, and presently pub-
licity director for the orchestra (and most important, proficient at the computer; she has just offered to turn over to Ira a program that would allow
his PC*jr* more memory). They are seated with Ira around the Stigman dining table in the evening, partaking of a quart of Baskin-Robbins vanilla ice
cream in celebration of the tender of a better-paying position to John by
Florida University. While M is at the gas stove brewing decaffeinated coffee, Ira jibes: "My wife frequently turns the gas flame to high, and as a result she often roasts a pot—not to be mistaken for pot roast." Smiling at

HENRY ROTH

the amusement of his guests, he adds jocularly: "That's been the grounds for many a divorce."

Trifles. Minute modulations of the quotidian, Ira reflected moodily: how anyone would allow them to take precedence over the catastrophic explosion of the nuclear reactor near Kiev, which at that very moment was impregnating the atmosphere with lethal radioactivity, perhaps threatening the existence of whole populations, he didn't know. But most people did, they did, and everyone knew they did and why they did: the petty immediate concern took precedence over generalized impersonal peril. Platitudes. He felt the same way about politics, political crises, social controversies, reformist clashes: for him they were most often mere eddies of concern, superficial and ephemeral.

And yet, he had been a zealot once, he reminded himself, the supercharged missionary of revolutionary change, proclaiming the messianic new, peaceful, just world order, the Socialist utopia around the corner, all in accordance with the tenets of Marx, whose true disciples were members of the CPUSA. He had a mystique once, to fill the void left by that all-encompassing ancestral mystique he had left behind on the East Side. But what a mystique the new one had turned out to be! What a mystique! A hideous personal debacle—though he was still half convinced that the principles on which the mystique was based were sound and were bound to triumph in time—which made the debacle even worse. It was all a great mystique.

Only one force of a social and political nature had stirred him in the last decade, had ruptured the tight shell surrounding his self-absorption, disrupt his "explorations." That force was *Israel*! Only Israel had sundered his well-nigh impervious preoccupations with his psyche, burst open the pod of his self-engrossment, and had sent predilections flying—as if his partisanship were an accelerator. And even then, when anxiety about Israel's welfare or some latest report of menace or outrage against Israel had breached his habitual introspection, it had done so only temporarily—though violently—the way the Red Sea parted, only to close again after the Israelites passed.

But it was like the parting of the Red Sea. The waters returned (alas, without engulfing the foe), returned, and once again rolled in their wonted way, and once again from the great deep to the great deep he went. Oh, the mind of man, how could one express even a whit—of its,

yes, wit, express admiration comparable to its capacity, versatility, suscep-
tibility, its epiphanies, Joyce called them: that resentment of M's against
her husband's facetiousness at her expense went deeper than a principled
criticism of his behavior—justified though her protest was. No one could
deny that. But there was an even deeper justification for it. The music she
was writing now, the music she had begun writing in the last few years,
was music she should have been writing, she said, years ago. Spoken in
calm and even tone of voice: "Music I should have been writing years
ago." He didn't believe it, but he didn't say so, he believed she had to live,
to experience, to be seasoned by the innumerable hardships she went
through—teaching in a primitive one-room school, building the fire in the
schoolroom stove on bitter-cold Maine mornings, caring for their two off-
spring, living near the rural school in a dilapidated farmhouse where she
had no sink, had to haul up water by pail from the well in winter, water
that froze in the very pail itself even when in the kitchen, all this while he
was away working as an attendant in the Augusta State Hospital. She had
to be changed by their living together, tempered to a greater maturity, as
he was changed and tempered by their living together to a greater maturity. By living and striving and suffering, by forgetting and learning, by the
forging of vicissitude, only then, and only at the last moment and with
many waverings, had he built up the confidence to endure the shifting demands of serious writing, of coping with new and untried and question-
able forms.

She had been a musician of acknowledged attainment when he first
met her in Yaddo. His spiritual and artistic breakdown, his mental turbulence and fits of near madness, had no counterpart in her life, her career.
So if she believed that the music she was composing now she should have
been composing years ago, what had stopped her? It was obvious what
had stopped her. He had. His neuroses and his foibles, his defects of character and judgment. And his impecuniousness too. But obstacle above all
others, obstacle that stood in the way of her realizing her gifts, was his inability to earn the kind of living a man of his status, his education, his potential, was expected to earn, as a rule did earn, and at some respectable
social calling. Of course, he was a Jew, a factor not to be forgotten. Still, it
was his impracticality, his aberrant impulse, his vacillations and flaccid as-
sertiveness, that had precluded his realization of his potential, rather than
his Jewishness; and so their standard of living and her musicianship were

both forfeit to the flaws of his mind and temperament. Therefore, instead of a composer, she had been the breadwinner, the one-room-school teacher, school principal, the piano teacher, the steady cash-income earner, and he auxiliary, working as a hospital attendant four years, raising and "dressing" waterfowl four and more years, tutoring math—ever frustrated, at a loss, ever in need of her steadiness. It was he, he, who had barred her from her rightful profession, her art. And now her resentment was coming to the surface . . . like that bit of pavement he passed on his way to the dumpster with the day's accumulation of trash, the asphalt crumbling above the welling up of ground.

Oh, you're crazy, he told himself, crazy as usual. But no. He might be right, for a change: why shouldn't she be resentful, and with resentment intensified by failing eyesight that robbed her of her former superlative facility at sight-reading? Threat of blindness, when at last she had the opportunity to write music again. She no longer trusted herself to perform in public, and especially to read and perform her own music, with its greater strain on vision because of its novelty, its modernity of approach. A cataract in one eye dimming and discoloring the notes on the page; in the other, in the eye with the lens implant, far more ominous symptoms: hemorrhages around the macula propagating molds in vision. Laser treatments hadn't helped, or only partially: blobs of darkness still interfered with sight. He looked at her in astonishment in the evening, when after the supper they read a paragraph or two of the Hebrew textbook, an account of Shalom's ordeal in emigrating to Palestine in the early part of the twentieth century. She misread continually, not that Hebrew was easy to read at any time, the damned print with its *gimels* looking like *nuns,* and its *beths* like *kaphs,* and its *daleths* like *reshes* and its *khets* like *hehs* and its *vahv* like *zion,* but she even confused the more distinct letters, the *tets* and the *mems,* the *mems* and the *sameks.* He regarded her with astonishment—and with grief and apprehension—when she misread the obvious, as she held a hand over the eye with the implant to block out the blots that seemed to be hovering there, while she peered at the print with the other eye, its lens clouded by cataract. How old she looked, wrinkled and old, under the unsparing white light of the new circular fluorescents they had recently installed in place of the previous bulbs in their hobnail globes softening the light.

Dear M, dear, patient, steadfast, objective M, weighing her options, deciding on her priorities, bravely abiding by them—abiding *him* these many, many years; was there any reason why she shouldn't be resentful?

But then, who could tell, perhaps that remark of hers simply indicated that she had reached a stage where she no longer needed him to the degree she had before. Far-fetched? Possibly. But the fact was she *had* matured, both as person and as artist; she was by then deeply engrossed in her music, in composition. And she had scored undeniable successes, both in the Babi Yar threnody and the unaccompanied cello rhapsody. She was as modest a person as he had ever known, devoid of affectation, devoid of self-aggrandizement, so when she said that her compositions were the event of the evening, stood head and shoulders above the others, he knew he could take her statement at face value, for she was a composer to be reckoned with. His decrepitude, his self-involvements, made inroads no longer merely on her time and energy, but on her creative time and energy. He was, or thought of himself as, a creative writer. He knew how he would have felt having to forgo his work to take care of another. He would have resented it; why shouldn't *she*? Especially in view of the limited number of years she then had at her disposal. It was only natural. To the past impediment of her art that he had posed in comparative youth and health, he continued to add present ones in old age and infirmity. In the past too, he had never given her the least occasion to doubt his total devotion, to fret over the least deviation from his total fidelity. And suddenly in senescence, in unworried impotence, he seemed to transmit all kinds of faintest, involuntary signals that, given her sensitivity, she was responding to, construing them as signals of changed attitude, diminished affection. Thus, she now had to bear the burden of his chronic ailments aggravated by a chafing of mistrust.

What did he mean, for example, or rather what did *it* mean, his inquiring whether he could get John to do an illuminated rendering of *Apothanein thelo,* the Cumaean Sibyl's reply? It meant that his attachment to M then was not, as he once believed, as strong as his desire to die. Living with rheumatoid arthritis was an ordeal, to be sure, but it was one he was determined to endure because M needed him, because he was the one who watched over her, exactly to prevent her from harming herself with oversights she never could seem to guard against, yes, to keep her from roasting a pot or a kettle. But his previously constant affection must have waned, to some degree: his wish to die indicated that. And without his ever having to say a word, she knew it, even then—and with the sagacity that had been her distinguishing trait all their married life together, she had ironically prepared herself for his qualified departure, for quasi-widowhood, for certain eventualities.

"Please, don't sing," M requested later that evening, while he was at the sink washing the supper dishes. "I'd appreciate it if you didn't sing while I'm at my desk writing music."

"Oh, sure, sure," he replied. "I understand."

It was interesting though how many times as he continued washing dishes he had the impulse to hum a few notes from this or that snatch of music. Habits were deep, head vacant seeking to alleviate tedium with a few notes of a remembered bit of song. But what did it mean that she had asked him not to sing while she was writing music, what did it mean beyond the request itself? That he was in the way, ought to be dispensed with, since she had begun to win musical and artistic acclaim? That or a hundred other things he misconstrued because—undoubtedly because the miasma of his damned past warped clear conception of everything.

But he had M, his M, from whom nothing could part him, he thought, only his death in due course. She was his M who had set Babi Yar to music, his tender, pitying M, who knew the Jewish plight, had set it to music. Levelheaded, judicious, merciful, lenient, she knew his plight, too, better than he did, his kinks and crazes. He had to hang on to her, the one sanity always available, the one sanity he could always count on.

"Any more dishes?" He looked about. "Coffeepot done?"

"Yes, I did it this morning." She too had a swivel chair at her desk, and swiveled about, sitting thin and gray, her dark-rimmed glasses that masked the wrinkles under her eyes contrasting prominently with hoar hair and distinguished, fretted brow. "I'll put the dishes away later, they can drain for now."

He bowed his head to lessen the distance—and the pain—arthritic shoulders had to overcome lifting the loop of his apron free of his neck. "Tomorrow is Mother's Day."

"What are you getting me?" M teased.

"Well, I tried to buy you a plastic ketchup bottle. One that would squirt."

"Only the cover didn't screw on very well."

"Yeah. So I left it on the bread counter."

"It doesn't matter. As long as you love me."

"That I do."

But he didn't know just how much he loved her, he said aloud to himself, listening a moment to the piano notes from the living room. And continuing to himself in silence. He hadn't known it at the outset, hadn't known it would turn out so, that his conclusions would be the very opposite of his imputations at the start.

"Oh, yeah." What with his emendations and interpolations, RAM was 91% full (and thereby hung a tale too: why, when he had gone to the expense of having the IBM technician install another captain's card, didn't the system acquire more RAM? He would have to do something about it.). At what angle, when fingertips of one hand touched those of the other, like a gable, did the thumbs lose contact with each other, the pinkies, the forefingers, when the pitch of the gabled roofs approached the horizontal? What a problem. He shouldn't have any bigger ones.

98% full.

How now, Ecclesias?

VI

And as they had often done before during an idle hour and a fair one, Ira and one or another of his college cronies strolled along the sidewalk next to the main building of the college. Across the street was Jasper Oval, the playing field. There, in fair weather, freshmen and sophomores, "frosh" and "sophs," attired in their World War uniforms, marched and countermarched over the bare ground to the command of junior officers; by column right or left, or by the right flank or left or to the rear. With their Springfield rifles, the cadets went through a manual of arms: port arms, present arms, order arms—just as Ira had done exactly a year before, in the spring of his sophomore year, and as Larry did still. The Gothic gray-and-white college main building on one side, the bare ground with the Mili Sci cadets marching on the other, both shared the unstinting sunlight of

rejuvenating spring. Drawn up in close order, in platoon, led by the
colonel as choral master, they could often be heard singing the in-
fantry song:

> *"Oh, the Infantry, Infantry, with the dirt behind their ears,*
> *The Infantry, the Infantry, that never, never fears.*
> *The Cavalry, Artillery, the Corps of Engineers,*
> *Will never catch up with the Infantry in a hundred thousand years."*

That was fun. But what a pain it seemed to give the blond staff
sergeant; he stood so stiffly at attention, he gave the impression his
skin would have rippled otherwise with embarrassment. The junior
officers also stood by much too politely, as if they too were enduring
a minor ordeal.

"The old shithead hopes he'll build up *esprit de* corpses that way,"
Larry imparted sarcastically. "Honest, isn't he the biggest joke on
campus?"

Everyone agreed.

The first campus rebellions, pacifist rebellions, against compulsory ROTC had already begun the year before in the spring of 1926,
and would reach a crescendo in the three years that followed with
the signing of the Kellogg-Briand Pact and all the naval disarmament
treaties. There was even talk that the League of Nations would outlaw
war. Suddenly, the junior officers lecturing on the elements of military science deported themselves in a very defensive manner: "We're
not here to promote war," Lieutenant Jacobs repeatedly argued.
"We're here to train you how to prevent the enemy from massacring
you in the event of war. If you didn't know how to deploy your troops
against enemy machine-gun fire from lower ground, or how to deploy them against a cone of fire from above, then you'd be massa-
cred. And that's what we're here to prevent."

The tall, sandy-haired major, soldierly even in civilian clothes, de-
fending Mili Sci in CCNY's largest lecture hall, packed with quiet
though hostile students, interrupted his address when the redoubtable Professor Morris Raphael Cohen entered, entered like a
Jewish thunderhead. "Of course I'm no match for Professor Cohen
in a debate," the major smiled deferentially.

"Then you shouldn't talk!" snapped Professor Cohen—to tumul-
tuous cheers from the assembled undergraduates—and Professor
Cohen took over the forum. Ira felt a twinge of embarrassment—and
then and afterward, a sneaking wave of sympathy for the major. He
found himself disavowing the renowned professor's tart riposte (as
well as any ethnic allegiance with him). What arrogance, what intellectual intolerance. Strange and paradoxical too that involuntary demurral, mere sympathy and emotion, should better limn the shape
of things to come than a highly touted intellect.

That spring too, a memorable occasion for Ira, Edith gave a cocktail party in the evening, to which Larry and he were invited. Chief
guest was Marcia Meede, the same scintillating personage whom a little more than a year ago Larry had so proudly escorted to her seat,
together with her enigmatic friend, at a poetry reading of the Arts
Club. Spiky in brilliance the lady was, unanswerable her retort and
epigram. Fortunately, or unfortunately, she was snub-nosed and
homely, affording fantasy no leeway to stray, though attention often
did. What long dark stretches of homage he had to maintain for the
honor of being there. A short time ago, she had returned to America
after completing a study of the mores and customs of the natives of a
South Sea island. It was a spectacular, a daring and pioneer venture
for a young woman, a venture—so Edith informed Ira later—that Dr.
Boas, the eminent head of the anthropology department at Columbia, where Marcia was studying toward her doctoral, was very reluc-
tant to have her undertake, gave his consent to only after much
trepidation. Needless alarm, Ira snickered to himself, after Edith told
him. She had been under the protection of a U.S. naval base there,
to which she retired at night. Besides, who would have dared assail
such spiky brilliance as Marcia's? It was like a spiked collar on a mas-
tiff. She could quell anybody, anybody's incipient hard-on, with the
swift deployment of her sharp rejoinders backed by her invincible
homeliness. Jesus, he had such vulgar thoughts, but he couldn't help
it. How could her husband stand her? He was with her at the party:
Lewlyn Craddock, tall and engaging, wearing greenish tweeds, a genial, pleasant man with a ready chuckle that often punctuated his
dry, nasal tone of voice. He had just been appointed to an instructor-
ship in the sociology department at CCNY—Edith laughed at the

slight awkwardness of introducing a pair of CCNY undergraduates to a CCNY instructor—and he laughed too, agreeably and warmly, when he shook hands with them, showing not the least condescension, but asking them about their intended careers and favorite courses and whether they felt the college answered their needs. And he listened with a kind of self-effacing gravity to the replies. Though abashed at first to be on such equal terms with a CCNY instructor, one who didn't keep his distance the way the others did, Ira soon felt at ease with the man, talked freely to him, and listened to him in turn. He had been to England on a grant from his theological seminary, during his wife's stay in Samoa. He spoke glowingly of long jaunts through the English countryside as a relief from his research into European methods of birth control, the purpose of the grant.

"Are you a—are you still a—" Ira gesticulated. "You're a clergyman?" Thank God he remembered the proper word.

"I'm an Anglican priest."

"A priest?" It was hard to suppress that start of surprise. "So excuse me, how is that?"

"Are you referring to the cloth or the collar?" Lewlyn chuckled.

"Color? Oh, collar! No. I mean—" Ira thumbed in the direction of Marcia. "You're her husband. You got a wife."

"Marriage of priests is permitted in the Anglican Church," said Lewlyn. No chuckle accompanied his reply, and he seemed thoughtful. "We resemble the Catholic Church in most ways, except for obedience to the Pope. And we don't take vows of celibacy. Does that answer your question?"

"Yeah, thanks. I don't know much about the Christian religion. Just what I've read, and that's not much. So if somebody says priest, I think of the Catholic Church. Around where I live, almost everyone's Irish."

"Where is that?"

"In East Harlem. On 119th Street."

"119th Street!" Lewlyn exclaimed. "We do too."

"You do? Where?"

"In an apartment house near Columbia University."

"Oh, that's different. Gee. Some difference."

Lewlyn chuckled. "I suppose it is."

Drinks in hand, a mix of grapefruit juice and bootleg gin, delivered by the Italian janitor of the house, the two had moved into a corner of the room. Sitting on the burlap-covered couch, Marcia was speaking to an admiring group of Edith's colleagues at the university, Boris and John Vernon among them, and two or three others of the English faculty, whom Ira knew only slightly, and poets, friends, Léonie, who had given the reading at the Arts Club the same evening Marcia had attended. Ira could hear her say that Scribner had paid her a handsome advance on her doctoral dissertation to be published as a book. And there was Edith across the room, smiling her indulgent, amiable smile, speaking to Larry, while her eyes searched for Lewlyn; then catching Ira's gaze, answering with amused, deprecating expression, as if sharing something.

"Otherwise the forms are much the same," Lewlyn continued. "And of course so is the ritual appeal. I'm on the inactive list at the moment."

"Oh." Ira felt completely out of his element. "Because you're gonna teach?"

"No, for other reasons, I'm afraid." Again, Lewlyn failed to chuckle. "I'm no longer sure of my mission, to tell the truth."

"Oh." The distance between their worlds made Ira feel a little dizzy, and yet Lewlyn seemed unaware of it, as if Ira shared his background, or was conversant with it.

"I think the twenties have much to do with it," Lewlyn went on in his dry, unaware fashion, this time interspersing remarks with a chuckle. "No other decade has seen such an upheaval of accepted ideas. In all fields. Anthropology, social science, psychology, the physical sciences. In the arts. Innovations are taking place on every side. No other decade in recent history has seen so many. We're really fortunate to be alive at this time, aren't we?"

"Huh? Yeah." Ira was glad to see Larry threading his way toward them. It was too much to cope with, generalizations of that kind, too much was expected of him, by way of knowledge and thought, to hold his own with a practiced mind, accustomed to forming generalizations.

"Edith just told me you're going to begin teaching this summer, Professor Craddock," Larry said.

"Lewlyn," the other corrected. "Yes, I am. Not a moment too soon, either, before I'll be reduced to borrowing."

Larry joined him in chuckle. "Are you going to be teaching an elementary course? I mean Sociology 1?"

"Yes, indeed. A new instructor could scarcely escape Sociology 1."

"That's fine. You wouldn't mind if I took your course this summer?"

"By all means. Glad to have you. I just hope you think it's worth your while."

"I've got to make up credits." Larry caught himself and smiled apologetically. "I didn't mean that. I meant I'm sure it will. Is there a standard text for the course? I might as well get it now."

"No, I intend to mimeograph leading ideas. The course is compressed. I feel I ought to keep it as open as possible, and a standard text won't do. Besides, concepts are changing so rapidly, standard texts are becoming outmoded. You might find it useful to go through Abernathy's *Social Institutions*, if you have time. It's easy on statistics, doesn't stress measurements as much as some of the other texts, and makes good reading. Again, a little outmoded. I think—they say there's a revision due out soon. You might want to wait—"

"I've gotta make up a pile o' credits myself," Ira chipped in—and then noticed Edith was staring at him fixedly. Did she want to speak to him? She made a motion with her arm, and he realized that all this time she had been holding something in her free hand that looked like a strip of cloth. He made his way toward her.

"I don't think you've seen this before, Ira, have you?" She displayed the coffee-colored, foot-wide strip, on which there seemed imprinted a dark green, flowerlike design.

"It looks like tree bark," he said. "What is it?"

She was looking at him intently. "It is. It's made from the bark of a tree, a mulberry tree I think Marcia said. It's called tapa."

"Tapa?" Ira scratched his ear.

"Marcia brought it from Samoa."

"Oh. What do you do with it?"

"Tack it on the wall." And with fixed smile, "Or the door." Then with altered voice, "Do you think you could come over alone sometime during the week?"

"Alone?" He knew she didn't mean for him to tack the thing up.

She actually turned slightly toward the apartment door. "Can I trust you to say nothing to Larry?"

"Sure."

"Some evening."

"I'll come right over after supper, if you want. When?"

"Monday, if you're free. Tuesday."

"I can come Monday."

"I'll expect you then." She displayed the tapa again for Ira's appraisal.

It had all the makings of the plot of a mystery story, except that it wasn't. Ira felt elated that Edith wanted to talk to him alone, but she already had before once or twice. It was something personal; it was probably about Larry again. He knew how she felt about Larry, and he had delved in his mind for mature suggestions he might offer to her problem: how to end the affair without hurting Larry. Ever since Larry had lost consciousness and fallen, she had dreaded the consequence of wounding him. Ira had no ideas. Not even zany notions. How do you end a love affair, painlessly or otherwise, when you've never had one? Hey, wait a minute: suggest to Edith that she tell Larry she had had . . . intimacies with Ira. What an idea! Oh, stop it, you cuckoo.

But things turned out to be utterly different from what he was prepared to hear when he came into Edith's apartment. It was altogether different, a new development, a disappointing one too, imparting a mild chagrin, ruling him out for good, sap that he was, proving what he was for the nth time:

She was having an affair with Lewlyn.

"Oh." And after recovering, Ira asked: "I thought—he's married to Marcia, isn't he?"

"Yes. I know you'll be discreet." Edith's large, solemn brown eyes rested on him.

He felt almost disgruntled, thwarted, waited silently for her to explain. They were no longer happy together, Lewlyn and Marcia, and Lewlyn had taken his own apartment in the Village.

"No?"

"Marcia had become restless and dissatisfied with their marriage."

"I didn't know."

"She believes their marriage was a student type of marriage, at a student level, and she could do much better, accomplish much more work, with a husband in the same field she's in: someone in anthropology."

"So how can that be?" Ira felt a certain grimness come over him, perhaps because he had lost all hope. "How d'you—I've never been in love. How do you pick somebody else out just like that?"

Edith laughed. "You're priceless."

"Yeah?" And now he felt shy.

Edith told him what had taken place. Instead of taking a ship directly to Marseilles where Lewlyn had agreed to come from England to meet her, because of a seamen's strike, she had taken a ship to Australia, and aboard she had met a young and brilliant anthropologist, who had also been studying native customs in another part of Polynesia, and the two had fallen in love.

"Oh. That's different then."

He was of noble descent, could lay claim to a title if he chose, she went on.

Suddenly he was reminded of the fact that Edith had the nicest calves, and the smallest feet, such a trim figure, and she was even fond of *him*. Shucks. Trim figure, the way it was molded out from the waist to her bottom on the gunnysack material covering the bed on which she so habitually sat, like a vase with legs projecting. He was the natural pretender, wasn't he, now that Larry was about finished? Natural heir apparent. Instead, Edith had gone and fallen for another man: a usurper. Nice guy, sure, Lewlyn. If only Edith didn't have such an appetite, such a gusto for someone else's hard luck, calamity. So it was the guy's hard luck. But then she wouldn't be Edith. And then he wouldn't be here. Hell, no use looking sullen. Shine up sympathetically. Even if you didn't like it, what the hell.

"How come Lewlyn's a priest?" Ira snagged the question out of the air.

"I doubt he'll remain one much longer." Edith smiled.

"I think he said something like that, about becoming inactive. Why?"

Explanations followed, to which Ira listened restively, distracted by Lewlyn's recurrent hum of disappointment. For one thing, Lewlyn had lost his faith in the efficacy of his priestly office—he saw no efficacy in prayer, in the mass, in any of the sacraments. Beauty, yes, often, but no efficacy, and hence no real meaning. Salvation was an illusion. And so was religion in general: a crutch. And on and on, about what a bunch of rigmaroles anybody should have known religion was, as Ira had learned when he was fourteen years old.

"He's been going through a great deal of soul-searching," Edith said cheerfully. "It's been something of a crisis for him."

"Yeah, I see. Is he over it?"

Edith gazed at him. "Not quite. For a while he considered remaining in the church as an as-if priest, if you know what I mean. As if he did believe, because that way he would comfort others, his congregation, his flock." She tilted her head, charitably smiling. "But in the end, he's decided against that too. He wouldn't be true to himself. And if Marcia sues for divorce, as she undoubtedly will, he'll have no alternative except to resign from the priesthood."

"Why?"

"He won't contest it." She went on to say something about the church's not tolerating such permissiveness on the part of one of its priests.

"Where does he live now?" Ira asked.

"In the Village."

"Down here?"

"Yes. On Barrow Street."

So that was that, that was about as much as he needed to know. Well, what else could you expect. Lewlyn was a grown man, an adult, steady, presentable, self-sufficient, a man with a Ph.D., a man with a teaching job at CCNY. Boy, the way his own fantasies ran away with him. Wasn't he a *lucksh* though, a *lymineh golem*.

"She can't make up her mind," Edith was saying. "He's been trying to counsel her—"

"*He's* been trying to counsel *her*?"

"Yes. Console her. Quiet her down. She gets quite frantic when she doesn't receive a letter from Robert."

"Oh, boy, is that the guy she's leaving him for, the guy she met on the boat? Robert?" It would take a year and a day before he understood, before he could really comprehend that world. Maybe he never would: priests that married, consoled their wives when they cast them off—

"He's still quite in love with her."

"This Robert?"

"Oh, no, Lewlyn. He actually speaks of Marcia's beautiful body, her white breasts."

"To you? He tells you?"

"And to others of their former friends, other women. Léonie has told me. And about his devotion to Marcia. It's touching, in a way, his trying to help her do the thing best for her, make the right decision."

"It's touching. That's what you call it?" Ira stuck both hands in his pockets, heard the wicker chair creak loudly as he pushed against the back.

"You're such a strange lad," she said. "So blunt and so sensitive. So mature in so many ways, and so withdrawn. You're the only one I've spoken to about it. Of course, Léonie knows, and one or two others of Marcia's friends know." She referred pensively to her reflection in the mirror across the room.

"I don't know how mature I am. Maybe I've been through a few things. But to tell you the truth, I don't understand most of this. It's not the way the people I know would have done."

"What would they have done? He's moved out of the apartment."

"Well, that isn't all. Gee. Moved out of the apartment." Ira shook his head. "Boy." He placed his hand on his cheek. "I guess that's the way you should do it."

"If you're at all civilized."

"Yeah?"

"They've remained on perfectly friendly terms—needless to say. Marcia promised Lewlyn when the two went on their separate projects last year that she would never leave him, except for someone she loved more."

"And what about him?"

"It wouldn't have mattered. He would have remained faithful to his vows, no matter what."

"Because he was a priest, you mean?"

"Quite probably. But I think that was his nature."

"You mean he's like that. Is she in the same church too?"

"Oh, yes, Marcia's family has always been Anglican. It was she who convinced him to switch from Lutheran to Anglican."

"She convinced *him*? Why?"

"The Anglican ritual is much more beautiful, has so much more sensuous appeal, than the plainer Lutheran one, in fact, the Protestant ritual in general."

"And that counts. I get you." He jerked his head suddenly. "Humph!"

"Why?"

"I was just thinking of a synagogue. Not that I've gone there very often. Especially of late. But talk about lack of appeal."

"I went to a newly consecrated one in Silver City. It was quite attractive. In fact, it had a new organ."

"Yeah. The one Larry's folks go to on the high holidays is very fancy—I understand. But the only ones I ever knew were little stuffy dumps—you know, three-room flats on the ground floor. Anyway, she feels free to get a divorce. He doesn't."

"He won't contest it."

"Because he's a priest. Or something like that. Boy, I get about thirty-five different ideas running through my head all at the same time. She convinced him to leave the Lutheran Church and join the Anglican one. Convince a Jew to quit the synagogue for a Christian church, no matter how beautiful. Wow. How'd I get out on that topic?"

"I'm afraid I led you astray."

"No. Well. I better keep quiet awhile."

They gazed at each other in silence while she toyed with a yellow pencil. Silent, while all about were the tools of her trade, or profession, whatever one called the clutter of learning: the massive Underwood typewriter with its black cover on the floor next to the desk, brown briefcase too, and manila files open and closed in haphazard fashion, carbon paper, letters, magazines, *The Nation* and *The New Republic*, easily recognizable, the *New York Times Book Review*. A desk drawer protruding. . . . A quiet place too. Outside noise was almost inaudible.

"You're very dear to me, Ira." Her tiny hand suspended the pencil at either end. "I know I can trust you completely."

"Thanks. You've got no idea what I've learned through Larry and through you. This is where I've really learned. CCNY is a washout. I've told you that before." He waited, while he scratched his brow. "Mind if I ask you something?"

"What is it, child?"

"Does Lewlyn know about Larry?"

"Yes, of course."

Again a silence, solemn.

"We both understand this is a friendship. We're not bound by any vows, if you wish. It's the kind of relationship in which we're both free. It's friendship." She paused, leaning forward winningly. "We're both mature enough to know we can't rule out sex, the last step in intimacy between a man and a woman."

"Yeah." Ira hunted for his pipe in his jacket pocket.

"It's the thing missing from my relation with Larry, and why I have to protect him. His attachment was romantic from the beginning, and remains so."

"I think I understand. I think I do." He probed the bowl of his pipe, rubbed forefinger clean of char. He wished he could say something wise, appropriate, could make a plausible forecast into the future; but the future offered no more outline than the inside of his pipe bowl. Dense, he was dense, that's all.

"Of course, if two people intended to have children, that would change things," Edith said. "It's difficult to imagine having children without a marriage license." She smiled. "Of course you can."

"Oh." Why hadn't he said that? "That's how it goes?"

"Yes." And then blithely, "I might as well tell you Lewlyn is taking me to visit his parents' home next weekend."

"Where do they live?" Ira asked.

"In Pennsylvania. In a small town. His father is a country doctor there."

"Oh. Like that." He finally realized that she was talking about more than a mere visit: the contentment on her face, the look of anticipation, that was it. Jesus, they didn't tell you what they meant. You were supposed to understand. And now he understood. He felt almost proud of himself, despite the absurd end of an illusion.

"Lewlyn becomes quite poetic where his father is concerned. About their rides together in winter to pay a call on a patient. His father is evidently a very unusual person, knows the name of every tree in that part of the country, can recognize animal tracks in the snow. Lewlyn says he himself had a beautiful childhood, and I can well believe him." She sighed suddenly, arresting Ira's attention. "He feels, unlike myself, that life has borne out the promise of his upbringing. I could very much wish I had that kind of stability too, that kind of satisfactory sense that what I had been inculcated with was realized when I grew up."

"Life has borne out his upbringing," Ira repeated, to hear the words again. Well, you can't be a sore loser. She had been so nice to him, kind to him. "Gee, I hope it goes well," he said.

"You're very sweet to say that."

"No," he deprecated. "What will you tell Larry—I mean, what will you say to him if you and Lewlyn want to—well, make a permanent relation together? You get married?"

"That's another reason I wanted to speak to you. What do you think I should say—if it came to that? Or how should I say it that would hurt him the least? You know Larry, perhaps better than I do. What would hurt him the least?"

"Tell him." Ira shrugged. And at her laugh, he spread both hands before him. "Explain. The way you just did to me. You know, if it was like what it was when you came back from Europe, maybe it would be different. I don't know. But it's hard to say now the way things have changed. I don't know myself. It's just a feeling."

"Then you think I could tell him, safely tell him about the new relationship with Lewlyn? You think he'd see the necessity of it?"

"Listen, I don't know what you'd do before you're sure, you know what I mean? But if you are sure, why not? It's your life. What else can you do? Now that I know, if you tell him, he'll tell me. I can—well." He shrugged again. "I can tell him, 'Listen, if you love her, you want her tc be happy, Lewlyn is her best chance.' You know what I mean?"

In an instant she was up from the couch, with mirthful countenance, advanced on him in three quick steps, bent over and kissed him. "I'll treasure that always." She lingered a moment, body in brown dress near, returned to the couch and sat down—and shook her head: "You're like no one I've ever known. Ever will know probably."

Ira sat mutely. The high pitch of his visit had been reached. His thoughts were too flurried between gratitude for the sign of her favor and certainty at the end of his usefulness. He debated, eyes on his gray fedora occupying the other wicker armchair, just under the tail of Paisley shawl that followed the curve of the small grand piano she had recently bought.

"I know you have a great deal of studying to do," she said.

"Yeah. My ed courses." He smirked in disparagement. So he had guessed right. It was time to leave.

"Oh, no, no, please, Ira. Can you stay another minute?"

"Oh." Now it was time to hunt a place on his person to scratch. "You really want me to stay?"

"Yes. I won't keep you long. Do you mind?" She smiled her wonderfully winning smile.

"No, it's interesting. Honest."

"I wanted to tell you about one other thing—Cecilia." She tilted her head as if in expectation of his puzzled gaze. "That's the name of the woman Lewlyn met in England. She's a secretary of some social service society there. He saw a great deal of her."

Her voice had become so matter-of-fact he couldn't help sense the overtone of significance in her restraint. What? As always, implication lagged behind: but it was somebody, no? Another woman. A worry. "Yeah?"

"They correspond a great deal. He's obviously formed quite an attachment to her."

"She's in England?" Redundance helped him orient himself.

"Yes. And she's a spinster. I imagine she's one of those many British spinsters left behind by the war. Probably a Victorian in her outlook. I don't know. I'm judging by what Lewlyn has told me, when they were together, on walking trips through the English countryside. I'm sure that was just as delightful as he says. And by a letter or two."

"He showed you?"

"Yes. He gets one every ten days. Perhaps oftener. She writes well. He finds her wistfulness very attractive."

"Oh." Wistfulness. Something made his mouth water—the word, or the edge of bleakness it had when Edith pronounced it? Wistfulness. A whisper of trouble. Maybe more. Look at the way things were, in two directions—like Janus: one for you, one for me. Dope, he's taking her to Pennsylvania. Ira licked his lips.

"Her father is dying, which of course makes her more appealing. She *is* devoted," Edith was saying. "There's no question about that. But I should think he'd take very much into consideration the large difference in their ages. There's no getting away from that: a woman ten years older than he is. I'm sure it must be all of that. I wonder if she's passed child-bearing age."

"How much older you say?"

"At least ten years."

"Ten years. Oh." As if there were no question Edith had nothing to fear.

"You never know about men, and their need for mothering," Edith countered his unspoken reassurance. And with tiny hand in tiny hand, her head upraised, she added, "And that, sad to say, is very important to some men."

"Yeah?" He could sense his own uneasy identity.

"Lewlyn is especially vulnerable at the moment: he's lost his faith, he's lost his wife—or been rejected by her. He'll probably soon lose his priestly office. I don't see how he can do anything else."

"Than what?"

"Resign from the priesthood."

"Yeah, but—what's—what do you mean, vulnerable?"

"Cecilia. Cecilia means protection to him. Comfort. Men are such babies sometimes."

All he could catch was a little, little hint of meaning. If he could only think it out. All of a sudden she was talking about *him*, his motives, his traits, instead of just herself, Lewlyn, Marcia, and holding up a picture in front of him of what he surely was—and wanted. She thought being that way was unworthy, and yet he couldn't break free of what he wanted. What the hell. "He's taking you to—where? Pennsylvania?" Ira asked.

"And I hope his parents think well of me. He's so undecided himself."

"Yeah. And Marcia knows all about this too?"

"About Lewlyn's affair with me? Oh, yes, of course. He's under her influence more than he realizes, and I don't trust her." Edith became quite animated, seemed to dismiss the image she spied in the mirror. "I simply don't trust her. I know she favors Cecilia more than she does me. I can tell by the things Lewlyn repeats from their conversation—oh, I know. She took a dislike to me the minute she heard Lewlyn was seeing me. It's quite obvious why, but it doesn't put me in a very happy frame of mind to know she's doing all she can to change his opinion of me. And she may very well make all the difference. To have someone like Marcia opposed to you—well, you've met her. You know how overpowering she is. It would take an unusual person to stand up against her." Edith stopped speaking, looked at Ira, and laughed, commiserating in the midst of her own worry. "Am I wearing you out? You look so much older."

"No, I was just thinking." He found a subterfuge. "It's all so symmetric."

"What is?"

"He was in England, she was in Polynesia, and each found a different one."

"And now they advise each other. Is that what you mean?"

"Something like that." Actually it wasn't what he meant, though he wasn't sure that what he meant was true or not, or stemmed from his wish. "I mean—I hope I'm wrong—it's easy for Lewlyn to keep up Marcia's courage about this Robert if he cares for somebody else."

Edith sat up, sat perfectly still, intensely serious. "I'm afraid so. I'm afraid it's something I keep hiding from myself."

"No, I was just saying," Ira mitigated. "Maybe he is like that. If he's a priest and wants to help her."

"Oh, no. It very much needed saying."

"But he's taking you to Pennsylvania."

"Yes." She was no longer exhilarated at the prospect, she seemed remote, profoundly reflective, then shook her head. "A woman ten years older than he is." She watched him stand up, and pick up his hat from the wicker chair.

"I didn't mean to—" he faltered.

"Oh, no, no." She got to her feet. "I don't know where you get your maturity." She seemed quite severe, so unlike her usual indulgent self. "I keep thinking of the story Lewlyn told me about the poppies growing under the washline, where his mother hung up his brother's World War uniform after he had returned from fighting in France. Poppies grew under it—just a minute, Ira."

He already divined what she was doing, long before she reached her purse on top of the chest of drawers—just as he divined what Mamie was going to do when she asked him to wait.

"You must not refuse me, do you understand? It's not charity. It's not a gift—it's a very little return for my indebtedness. A little token of what I owe you for bearing with me. I wish it were more." She tendered him a greenback: the numeral 5 in the corner puffed out visibly, almost haughtily.

"Edith, it's a five-dollar bill." Ira drew back.

"I want you to have it. It's little enough."

"Gee, it's too much." There was no use gainsaying, only observing formalities of reluctance. "You shouldn't."

"Of course I should. You're very dear to me, Ira. I hate the thought of your going about without any money."

"I know, but—" Superfluous the saying. She held him to her purpose inflexibly. He took the greenback from her hand, and there was her tiny hand floating between them. He held it, and kissed it. As if space converged into the act, it seemed more than his own doing. And then he ran his knuckles over the suddenly moist recess under his lip. "Thanks, Edith."

"You're very welcome, lad."

"Gee, Edith. I hope you have a good time in Pennsylvania."

"Thank you, Ira. I hope I do too. Good night."

"Good night."

* * *

—Well, Stigman, how step by step you've been drawn into the web that seems to be of your own spinning.

Aye, father Ecclesias. What is it I do? Make life follow art, as I've said before? The actuality follow the narrative? It's the damnedest thing how the conceit, the fancy, lures on the deed.

VII

Lo, it is summer—almighty summer! How Ira loved that invocation of De Quincey's—and De Quincey too. *Lo, it is summer—almighty summer!* But instead of the everlasting gates of life and summer thrown open wide that De Quincey glorified so eloquently, final exams were near at hand, finals in two ed courses (yech), Economics (ditto), a dull Psychology 1, where only once did the professor know Ira was alive, when the results of a vocabulary test were in. And a disappointing English course in the essays of Addison and Steele, which he was taking with Professor Kieley, who had been so admiring of Ira's descriptive pieces in Freshman Composition II. He would have to take at least two courses in summer school—two evening courses, if he hoped to get to a job during vacation—in order to make up for credits lost over the past three years. He had a deficit of credits, he joked sourly with classmates. And for all of De Quincey, it still wasn't summer; it just felt that way in mid-May. Real summer meant not oceans, tranquil and verdant as a savanna, as De Quincey phrased it, but humid night classes, his stifling, sweltering tenement bedroom, and who knew what kind of a vacation job to make enough dough to buy clothes and shoes to get him through his senior year.

Hadn't that five dollars felt good while it lasted, that five dollars Edith had given him. "A fiver in my wallet, a fiver in my wallet," he hummed inwardly to the tune of "A-hunting we will go." "I got a fiver in my wallet. I got five bucks in my poke." He no longer felt, what with Edith's affections and Stella's pliancy, the need to try to tempt Minnie with a buck, or even two. She was finished with him for good—adamantly. She'd be getting a job soon anyway. She was getting ready for graduation.

Friends of Iz—not friends of the coterie, for they were seniors—in exchange for his admitting them free into the Provincetown Theater allowed him and a selected friend or two to slip into Carnegie Hall, where they were ushers. For the first time, Ira heard the New York Philharmonic, saw Feuchtwangler press his hand to his heart, heard Beethoven's Fifth—while he waited behind the last tier of the uppermost balcony until legs began to wobble, until it was clear no one was going to sit in the empty seat he kept in view. Sunday had settled into a usual routine, even without the compliancy of his sister. He would chafe through his texts till afternoon, and then hike to Mamie's on 112th. With luck or without it, he could count on coming away with a dollar—hence an easy nickel for subway fare to the CCNY recital hall where he could listen to Professor Baldwin of the Music Department boom out the "Pilgrim's Chorus" from *Tannhäuser* on the college organ, or other Wagnerian selections. He loved that high linky-linky-link from *Tannhäuser,* especially if he had been lucky; it fitted in with the way he felt, dispelled that last little cloudlet or worry about whether he'd pulled away in time.

He did good turns also, something like a *mitzva,* except he was usually rewarded for it: tutoring Leo Dugonicz in plane geometry. Leo, the Hungarian, had lived a flight up in the small three-story house next to Ira's, at the same elevation as Ira. They could—necks outstretched—talk to each other, leaning out of their respective windows on the backyard, and they became fast friends. Leo, of course, had gone to work with the bulk of the graduating class of P.S. 24, and had found a job as a lab assistant in a materials-testing lab, and had worked there ever since. At his invitation, Ira had visited him there, watched Leo subject a bar of iron to huge force, heard it snap with awesome bang. Meanwhile Leo's mother, widowed when her husband was crushed between freight trains when working for the Pennsylvania Railroad, at first kept house for a Jewish dentist on 111th Street, a morose and taciturn bachelor. Leo mimicked him endlessly, especially his gait and floppy pants cuffs, and called him the admiral of the Swiss Navy. Afterward Leo's mother married an Italian second cook in a large hotel, and she and Leo moved to their new dwelling on 111th Street and Lexington Avenue. It was because Leo sought out Ira, and because Ira enjoyed Leo's untroubled puckish nature, that the two kept in touch with each other. Leo demonstrated for Ira's benefit, and to Ira's alarm, how nitroglycerin exploded when wrapped in tinfoil and struck with a hammer. And he took Ira for a wild drive in a used car he had bought and was learning to operate, and wrecked while he was at it.

Leo was short and stocky, thick-lipped, pug-nosed—good-humored and amiable. He was in his twenties now, and eligible to take the examination for municipal steam-boiler inspector, a sinecure of a civil service job, with no few prerequisites on the side. He was both eligible and eager to take it, his years as lab assistant acceptable in lieu of formal studies. He felt he could easily pass the written part, except for one thing: he needed a smattering of plane geometry. He had tried boning up on the subject by himself, but his head began to swim as soon as the book dealt with proving the simplest propositions. Could Ira help him out? Of course he could. Plane geometry was his beloved forte, his savior.

So Ira would walk over to Leo's home an evening or two a week and endeavor to tutor him in the rudiments. It was a relief to be with him, on that plebeian level Ira felt he should never have left, the unadorned, uncultivated, unlettered, to which he could never return. It was a relief to be superior to someone in *something,* to be looked up to for something other than words, something demonstrable, tangible, that liberated one from that everlasting fretting and disapprobation that mind had become.

Leo was the worst dub at plane geometry Ira had ever known, would even have dreamed possible. He would look earnestly at Ira as he proved a theorem, or applied it to the solving of a problem, look at Ira soulfully with his blue-green eyes, his thick lips parted in grateful, humble admiration. But the simplest question would reveal that he had grasped not an iota of what Ira was so fervently striving to impart. His ignorance discovered, Leo would laugh—contritely. How could you get sore at the guy? Ira would begin the same problem again from the beginning, allow no latitude, take nothing for granted, but raise his voice and demand answers at each step. And at the end, maybe a little of the subject stuck, a little of Euclidean light entered. Q.E.D.

Because Ira would accept no cash payment, Leo would take his tutor afterward to the local seafood bar, with sawdust-covered floor— on Third Avenue under the El near 95th Street—and treat him to oysters when the months had *r*'s in them, and littleneck clams afterward with lots of ketchup and horseradish and a bowlful of small round oyster crackers. It gave Ira that mixed nostalgic feeling of the lost paradise of the uneducated, sitting there at the marble table on top of the sawdust, watching the pimply Greek youth, son of the owner, whack off the end of an oyster shell and pry it open.

Long ago, so it seemed now, when he first came to live on 119th Street, Ira remembered surveying these delicacies, on 125th Street, surveying them with revulsion, grotesque, rocky-looking fare fit only for *goyim*. Introduced to them now, as with other deviations from kosher food, he enjoyed them. How he had changed, from 1914 to 1927: thirteen years. And how Harlem had changed too in those thirteen years, imperceptibly, until you suddenly noticed. 125th Street, which had once appeared high-toned gentile, had become shabby, much of it. Where were those stores and shops that once seemed so fancy, and those ladies in white dresses carrying parasols who once patronized them? Ladies coming from the suburbs or from estates in Connecticut, and getting out at the 125th Street station of the New York Central on Park Avenue? And where the self-assured, freshly shaven gentlemen, often with a black porter behind them, carrying their suitcases, sometimes sample cases—they looked so large—and hailing a taxicab? Gone the way of Park & Tilford, the way of the sedate brownstones that once bordered Mt. Morris Park near the library. How secretly, relentlessly, change took place: like the replacement of gas-lit lampposts by tall electric-lit ones, like styles that people wore, like long pants for knee pants, and socks for long black stockings—now only men wore knee pants: knickers. Like the Irish moving away, so many, and the Jews moving in, with even a kosher butcher store across the street with a wide green blind in the window, above the Italian iceman's cellar—he was still there.

Except for a few who still lived in the big cold-water flats through most of 119th Street, the Irish had retreated as to a last enclave to the few three-story redbrick houses near Lexington Avenue. And across the street on Lexington, a wholesale cheese store had opened, Kraft's. Across Lexington, the stable on the other corner in which Pop had boarded his old nag during his brief period as entrepreneur milkman had gone up in flames (arson, it was rumored, since you rarely saw a horse anymore). In its place now stood a funeral home.

And the colored people were moving in, moving south from uptown Harlem. The colored people, Negroes, they were called when they were referred to politely, slowly moved south from uptown Harlem, at the same time as Puerto Ricans settled at the other end of Harlem. Several Puerto Rican families now occupied Mamie's houses in 112th Street west of Fifth Avenue. The twin six-story walk-up apartments weren't really Mamie's—or Mamie's and Saul's. The banks had repossessed them. (One of shifty Saul's unsuccessful finaglings.) Instead of being part landlord, Mamie was now only superintendent and rent collector. That way she got her apartment rent-free.

Not only in Mamie's houses but all through West 112th Street, all through mid-Harlem, Jewish tenants were moving away—to the Bronx, usually—and Puerto Ricans were taking their places: Spanyookels, Mamie punned, tartly bilingual. Ira had just finished screwing Stella in the front room, standing up, hurrying up, when to his consternation, lo and behold, two young Puerto Rican youths leaning out of the third-story window across the street were having a gala time pretending to be viewing them with opera glasses: peering at them through rounded fingers—and pointing and laughing. Jesus! How humiliating. On the other hand, what luck! Supposing they had been Jewish. Yi-yi-yi and *oy, gevald.* Undoubtedly, they would have told somebody else who was Jewish, and that somebody else might have known Mamie—and told her! The long-dreaded exposure would have erupted. Revilings and recriminations would have been the least of his penalties. His disgrace would have spread like a wildfire throughout the family: the abominable doings of Leah's college-boy son. And then what? Who knew? Certainly Mamie's door would have been barred to him forever. Mamie's door and her dollar bill. *Aza Paskudnyack! Aza Parsheveh shmutz!* And he was. He was. Anyway, what luck, it didn't have to come to that. East was east and west was west, and the "Portorickies" across the street were scarcely on speaking terms with the Jewish superintendent on the "first floor" of the house where her daughter was getting reamed. Woof. Didn't he beat it away from that window fast.

Indeed, the whole cosmos was changing: island universes and spiral galaxies could arrest one's breathing thinking about them. He never tired of repeating to himself that bit of floss he knew was anything but great poetry—about the great star Canopus—he had read in the Untermeyer anthology Larry had loaned him—"I meditate on interstellar spaces, and smoke a mild cigar . . ." He didn't even remember the poet who wrote it. And events crowded out events: Coolidge was President, and prosperity was going to last forever. The League of Nations was at the height of its ephemeral power, Stalin had taken over the USSR, and Mussolini ruled Italy. Mussoli-i-ini, the Italians pronounced it. There was socialism, and there was inchoate Fascism, and anybody knew that socialism was better, because Fascists gave dissidents castor oil. But in Russia, wrongdoers and wreckers were shot, which was only right. And everywhere, the Sacco-Vanzetti case aroused passions pro and con—everywhere—and the names of the two anarchists appeared in headlines in all the city's newspapers: from the tabloid *Daily News* to the *New York Times,* in the Hearst press, in the *Sun* and the *Globe* and the *World,* the *Herald,* the *Tribune.* And in the liberal magazines which Ira saw so often on Edith's desk, *The New Republic* and *The Nation.* Everyone who wasn't biased against Italians, anybody who knew enough to call an Italian an Italian and not an Eyetalian, knew they were innocent, and were condemned to die in the electric chair just because they were wops or dagos and anarchists. *"Orrimen Talyaner,"* said Mom pityingly. And Mom, who always followed the call of her feelings, was rarely wrong. Poor Italians, especially Vanzetti with his long, drooping mustache. Of course they were innocent, but why, why would a president of the most distinguished university in the whole country, President Lowell of Harvard, still agree with the prejudiced judge, still find the two innocent men guilty? Emotions rose to a fever pitch, as the newspapers said, as the day of their execution in the electric chair drew near. Fever pitch. Ira himself was so moved, had become so involved, so outraged at the patent, gruesome injustice of putting the two men to death, just because they were foreigners and opposed to big fat corporations (what if they were foreign-born; he was too)—so they were anarchists; that didn't mean they had scraggly whiskers and threw bombs with lit fuses in them the way the Hearst newspaper caricatured them—that he made the case the subject of his final address in Public Speaking 6, which would account for half his grade in the course. He went to the New York Public Library on 42nd Street and Fifth, and read as much about the famous *cause célèbre* as he could—and came away more convinced than ever that the two men were innocent of killing the paymaster of the shoe company in South Braintree, Massachusetts, as charged.

Mr. O'Tealy, the young, handsome—and Irish—instructor, didn't seem pleased with Ira's choice of subject matter; in fact, the more Ira put his heart and soul into his address, the more Mr. O'Tealy's jaws tightened, the more Ira could sense the other's antagonism. How could he be that way? It was the first time Ira had been gripped by anything political, the first time he spoke with conviction, spoke the truth about discrimination and oppression, and Mr. O'Tealy was practically frowning at the end. *Irisher hint,* as Mom would say. And all Ira got for all his trouble and effort was a C.

The old man at the keyboard sighed. Sometimes he pitied the youth: not because the youth had once been himself. No, he might have been anyone else's youth. But so naive, so vulnerable, so lacking in ordinary judgment, foresight, unable to envisage consequences until they were upon him. A child, that was it: he was a child, long after he should have attained to at least a sophomore's canniness. And a child he would remain, long, long after childhood was over.

Mr. O'Tealy previously had directed every student to choose a piece to recite from memory, a moving poem, a prose selection, an excerpt from a drama, but something by means of which he could convey a play of powerful emotion. And Mr. O'Tealy himself had demonstrated the sort of thing he expected from his class by delivering Shylock's speech in answer to the question about what he would do with a pound of human flesh: "To bait fish withal." Mr. O'Tealy's entire demeanor changed, and by the time he was done, his chest was heaving and his nostrils flaring for breath.

So tempestuous had Mr. O'Tealy become that Ira felt embarrassed. But instead of emulating, instead of choosing something approximately as impassioned, Ira chose three short poems that he liked: T. S. Eliot's section of *The Waste Land* entitled "Death by Water," John Masefield's "Ships," and Walter de la Mare's "Lady of the West Country." Mr. O'Tealy expressed his dissatisfaction in a voice and gesture keyed low with hopelessness.

A nar, the old man at the keyboard thought, *a nar und shoyn.* No savvy. It would take fifty years before he acquired a little acumen, a little *khokhma.* Still, child though he still remained in spirit, the kids in the street had begun calling him Mister. When a rubber handball had gotten away from them, and was rolling toward him: "Hey, Mister, will you stop that ball. Hey, Mister, please! Don't let it roll down the sewer." From Fat, Fat, the Water-rat, he had too outwardly changed, had evolved, into Mister. And boyhood, and the East Side of early boyhood, were as remote as *where the remote Bermudas ride,* as Marvell wrote.

Mom now suffered severely from what the family thought then was merely chronic catarrh. She heard noises in her head, sometimes loud, sometimes soft, sometimes so loud that she would ask Minnie or Ira to put an ear against hers to hear the sound, as Uncle Louis had done. They heard nothing. Now a loud roar, now a soft piping, the volume of the sounds she heard she was convinced depended on the weather. "The weather is about to change," she would say. "The engineer has begun to drive the train like one demented."

"What did they tell you at the new clinic, Ma?" Minnie asked, after Mom had been guided downtown by Mamie to the New York Polyclinic.

"Chronic catarrh and chronic catarrh, and again chronic catarrh. In that hospital especially they tell you nothing. Every word costs them too dearly. To a doctor—I won't say all—a pauper is a pariah." She hung the dish towel above the sink, blew her nose between her fingers, and flushed them clean under the running water of the faucet. "A Jewish woman waiting her turn there told me if I could go to Kholyerada, to a sanatorium on a lofty mountain, I would hear only a thin whistle. Who knows whether it's true, and who can go to Kholyerada?"

"Colorado, Mom," Minnie corrected gently.

"Kholyerada," Pop lowered his Yiddish newspaper long enough to mimic.

"I thought it was Kholyerada. *Kholyeria* means plague, that's why it was named Kholyerada, so many consumptives went there."

"No, it's like color, Ma. Color, like this." Minnie pinched the cloth of her blue dress. "It doesn't have anything to do with *kholyeria*."

"And I always thought it did."

"Because you got that kind of head. You're here twenty years, and you still speak like a greenhorn," Pop jibed through his paper.

"My clever spouse. How did you learn? By going to work. How would I have learned? By going to work. Just as my sisters did, Mamie and Sadie and Ella. In the shops."

"Who kept you from working?" Pop queried. "Not I. You were entirely at liberty to bring home wages had you chosen to."

Mom sat down. "Go dig your grave," she said calmly. "Married and with two children, to go to work."

"Mrs. Shapiro goes to work," Pop reminded her. "And she has a husband and three children."

"The kind of work she does, I could only have done too: wash floors, clean windows, dust, stand and iron shirts. Much English I would have learned that way. The mistress of the house where she works doesn't know any herself."

Pavlov: dogs and salivary glands, bells, and synapses: Ira looked up from the psychology text he was trying to bone up on. "Did you ever think of trying it, Mom, I mean plain housework?" What a complex, yeah, more than Freudian complex, his own question brought into being. A complex of contradictory filaments simultaneously weaving in and out of awareness: earnest wish and guilt and desire, fantasy and remorse. Why hadn't *he* gone to work with most of the others in his class in 8B? How much easier it would have made life for Mom, and been better for him too. But if he hadn't, if *she* had gone to work, the house would have been empty all day long, as empty as the day was long.

"Besides, I become so bewildered when I step out of the subway into the street. I don't know where I am, where is uptown, downtown." ("Optom, domtom," she pronounced it.) "The whole neighborhood reels about. And if the person you ask—with my *Engalish*—is a *goy*, he, she, it doesn't matter even a child, laughs in my face."

"Well, sure, if you have no head—"

"I could have taken you in the subway the first time. Or the second," Minnie interrupted. "You could have gone by signs. You know how you do? Here is a wallpaper store, here is a tailor shop."

"I become so panic-stricken. *Noo, ferfallen.* Chaim," she addressed the barrier of newspaper, "you'll do me a great favor if you give me the last two dollars of my allowance now. You still owe me—"

"So I owe you." Pop folded the newspaper. "I'm not fleeing town." He flattened the Yiddish newsprint on the table.

"Flee into your grave."

"Money! Money! Money! Forever harps on money."

"Aw, please, Pop!" Minnie intervened.

"Yeah, for Christ's sake, let's not get started on that!" Ira added reinforcement.

"Spare me your for Christ's sakes," Pop rebuked. "Right away it's for Christ's sake. Here live Jews."

"No foolin'."

"Don't mix in," Mom urged. "Study. Apply yourself."

"Yeah, try."

"Another wife," Pop continued, flattening the newspaper, "another wife, if she isn't earning herself, would think: how can I help my husband? How can I help him succeed: to be a businessman, an owner, a boss? Mamie fussed and frothed so for her little Jonas that Zaida finally commanded the brothers: you must take him in as a partner. Now he's a partner in the Jamaica cafeteria. From a little ladies' tailor, now he's a *makher*, a boss—*soll mit im gibn a tremoss*," Pop rhymed his spite into Yiddish. "But she, my good wife, she thinks only how much lucre she can wrest from me—"

"Oh, Jesus," Ira muttered, and tried to concentrate.

"Lucre!" Mom mocked. "*Oy, gevald!* You hear?" she implored all and sundry. "Twelve stinking dollars a week to run the house he calls lucre—"

"Out of which you manage to skim off enough toward a Persian lamb coat. My fine lady with a Persian lamb coat."

"So that the neighbors won't know how afflicted I am—"

"Please!" Minnie exclaimed. "I want to study too. I'm gonna get finals. And I'm gonna have to take the Regents exams!"

"She's afflicted, you hear?" Pop nodded in disbelief.

"Why else do I dress up in my finery, squeeze into a corset before I appear in the street? That happy Mrs. Stigman, the neighbors should say. See how stout and prosperous she looks. How fortunate she must be in her husband. How well he must provide, and with a lavish hand—"

"*Gey mir in der erd.*"

"*Gey mir in kehver.*"

Ah, to be a timber wolf! To lift up his muzzle, like a timber wolf, and howl.

VIII

108 East 119th Street
New York City, N.Y
July 17, 1972

Dear Ivan:

Yesterday it rained and rained, and everybody said it would then be very cool, and since everybody said so, even tho I am sweating as I write this, I suppose it is. And talking about sweating, I have already gained a reputation at the place I work for being the champion sweater there. But you don't know where I work, so come closer, and listen, as Mel Klee, the black-face comedian in vaudeville, used to say when I was a kid and worked in Fox's Theater on 14th Street.

The Irishman who lives with his termagant wife downstairs in the ground-floor flat, one Reb Mahoney by name, assistant timekeeper at the IRT subway system (once he was chief timekeeper, and I don't know whether it was drink and the devil did for him, or his health gave out: he's absolutely cadaverous)—Reb Mahoney, having been apprised by his wife, who was apprised by Mom that her son Ira neither toiled nor spun, suggested that I apply for a job at the Interboro Rapid Transit Co. I acted with alacrity. Of course they were going to make me assistant to the assistant timekeeper. On the strength of Mr. Mahoney's recommendation to the fat— and Jewish!—personnel manager, I was hired—despite the disgust of the doctor who examined me: "You don't have a single scar on you," he said. "Where did *you* ever work before?"

Hence, for the past couple of weeks I have been working at the IRT repair barn nine hours every day, except Saturdays, until noon—for $28.50 per week. Instead of assistant to the assistant timekeeper, as I fondly dreamed would be my job, I was hired as pipefitter's helper. That means like everybody else there, I'm always fiddling around in the vicinity of "old red mule," as the third rail is called. I have learned, not by experience to be sure, not by hearse, but by hearsay, that a very brief contact with the 550 volts of the third rail doesn't kill you as a rule, provided you've been endowed with a fairly sturdy constitution. What it does is play a percussion solo on your teeth, or cause them to play it; and since I'm not partial to that kind of music, I am very careful to keep my distance.

Another thing, I work just over the repair pit beneath the subway trains. And the first day there, I kept wiping my brow with my sleeves, which were filthy with grease. *Freg nisht.* When I came out from under, half the place, from the superintendent to the lowly sweeper, went into a fit of laughter. I felt peeved at first to be taken for such a joke, but when I looked in the washroom mirror, I understood and forgave. I had two black horns of grease sticking up from my brow, and the rest of my features had those strange, eerie shadows on Dr. Caligari's visage beat all hollow. The work is damn hard, but when I get that pay envelope, I'm satisfied.

At CCNY, which I attend after work, I am taking Government, Geology, and Public Speaking, the last-named course attended by Larry too, who's also taking Sociology with Lewlyn, whom we told you we met at Edith Welles's. I'm taking Government with a Mr. Benno. The guy is a scream. He has a lisp beyond anything you ever heard. And when he lectured us about the invalidity of *ex post facto* laws, "You can't fool me, your honor. I thtudied ex potht facto lawth in Thity College too!" I had to duck down behind the seats ahead to hide my convulsions.

I see Larry twice a week in class, sometimes meet him before. Iz I haven't seen until now, but I hear that while the Provincetown Theater is closed for the summer he sells programs at the Lewisohn Stadium concerts. He's probably written you. So has Larry, I imagine.

You certainly got your driver's license just in time for that boys' camp job. You sound busy, picking up supplies from the railroad station, and taking kids on excursions. Hey, what's this about your learning to ride horseback? Let me advise you: don't ever say "Need any ice today, lady?" or the nag will stop so abruptly you'll go over his head.

Please write soon, and tell me all about the women counselors, especially the attractive ones. Take care of yourself.

Ira.

It was the first time in his life that Ira had ever worked in so huge a plant, the first place that he learned about the transcendent power of the third rail. The plant structure itself was immense, an entire square block in size. And within it, hundreds of men, divided into crews, and every type of machinery and equipment, all there for the same purpose: the maintenance and repair of the IRT subway trains. Every morning, eight lines of trains, ten to a line, waited to be serviced, outside, inside, and underneath!

The first day that Ira was conducted into the huge "barn," he quailed before the fury of motion and din that assailed him. Crews of burly men boosted thunderous timbers onto high, massive wooden trestles at each end of the train—while gargantuan steel hooks, dangling from a great horizontal hoist on tracks *overhead*, held that end of the train aloft. The work was perilous, to say the least, and the brawny Italian roustabout with bandages on his face as puffy as a pillow, who had been struck by one of the swinging hooks, was evidence to that fact. Appalling, the turmoil and the noise: airbrakes soughing, rheostats clacking, hammers banging, drills whirring. Acetylene torches blinded and smoked, kerosene reeked everywhere, cut through by the acrid odor of ozone. And as if lurking silently and unseen behind the overt turmoil brooded the greatest menace of all: the menace of high voltage.

The foreman, Mr. Kelly, beefy and tobacco-chewing, impressive in his striped, clean shirt, assigned Ira to help Vito, expert in the installation of brake rods, who would "break" Ira in on the job. Ira was more than a little apprehensive at the proximity of 550 volts. "The juice is off right now," Vito advised. "But never touch here, here, here. Never take chance." The propinquity, the seeming ubiquity, of 550 volts, and the uncertain footing, the narrow ledge just below the aisle between trains, and above the repair pit—his sheer lack of muscle in coping with brake rods that were anything but rods, egg-shaped slabs of steel that had to be held overhead while they were lined up by drift pin to mating parts, and a connecting bolt driven home—rendered him unequal to the task. Before the morning was over, he was shifted to a genuine "grease monkey" job: that of assistant to a diminutive Italian named Quinto in charge of servicing and maintaining brake cylinders.

The new job was actually more hazardous than the other, because the pistons were heavier than the brake rods and required two men to remove them, which in turn necessitated a degree of cooperation between them. Quinto was cooperative enough: he kept to the level aisle between trains, and stationed Ira on the ledge above the pit, when the pistons were to be removed. And once Ira even slipped from a greasy ledge down into the pit unscathed, much to Quinto's amusement. Still, Ira felt more at home on the job. Quinto showed him how to unbolt the brake cylinder facing, and Ira had toughened enough to apply effectively the hefty open-end wrench to the hexagonal nuts—the wrench slid off once, and kissed Ira rudely on the lips. With Ira balanced on the pit side, the two removed the heavy piston and examined the large leather gasket; and if it was still in good condition, Ira, not Quinto, slathered great gobs of fresh brown grease inside the well-buffed cylinder wall, and then replaced the piston, with Ira, not Quinto, retightening the bolts. Ira noticed, as his muscles developed, that his shoulders and arms could thrust far more than his relatively small hands could endure. It was a mindless job, or nearly so.

"What the hell is a white man doin' on a ginzo job like that?" asked Burgess, stoutly built, bronzed young family man. "Why don't you ask Kelly for a decent job?"

"I'm happy," Ira assured him. "I don't mind."

Summer of his twenty-first year, summer of 1927, still vivid after almost seventy summers, still printed on memory: the straw-boss worker, near day's end, proceeding from aisle to aisle, like a town crier, warning all and sundry: "On the juice! On the juice!" Now that all the trains had been lowered down to the tracks, ready to roll out of the barn, unaccustomed quiet prevailed, and the sunlight, sloping on the high smudged glass roof, hinted of evening. Because smoking was forbidden, those who craved a cigarette crouched in the gloom of the pit beneath the lowered trains, as in a tunnel. Cigarette tips glowing, the smokers took hasty, furtive, heady drags. Tobacco smoke mingled with smell of unwashed bodies, unmistakable stench of unwashed feet. And once again, member of a group, sharing the risk, squatting with the others, Ira felt the claim of nostalgia: of a fraternity missed, a communion lost.

From a distance in the tunnel, his kerosene flare rising, falling, as he ducked under train axles, disappearing when he poked the torch into crannies to examine newly done work and metal tags, the long, lean inspector approached—to be stopped sometimes by someone lagging in the shadow who wanted to light a butt off the yellow flame: tobacco aroma, kerosene stink, musty body odor.

* * *

Ira could scarcely continue. Ah—the regretful wish kept coming back and back—if only you had written of this while you were engaged in it, or soon after, never mind the unpolished prose. The freshness of it, or perception, sensation, experience, would have more than made up for lack of finish. Why didn't someone say, Hey, sit down and describe it. Why wasn't there someone to assign it as a theme for a course? Why wasn't there a course? Why? Don't blame anyone else for your own lack of gumption, your idler's ways. Instead of supinely taking those deadly ed courses at CCNY, if you had enrolled in one of Edith's courses at NYU, perhaps with Edith's assistance. . . .

There were eighty trains at a time in the shop every day, eight rows of ten each. Quinto, the lead man, though illiterate, would be given the work sheet. Their stint for the day consisted of eight cars whose brake cylinders were to be maintained. Before work began, with list in hand, Ira would lead the way, traveling from aisle to aisle, and pointing out to Quinto the cars on the list. Eight cars in eighty; they were like separate points in the huge rectangular quadrant determined by a pair of coordinates. Eight points in eighty, and yet Quinto's ability to remember them afterward was all but uncanny. It was Ira who was more apt to make a mistake in location than he. They got along quite well, after Ira learned to do most of the work. They horseplayed now and then, after work, especially at Saturday noon, during wash-up, in the euphoria of the remainder of the weekend off: Quinto initiated the practice of dousing his workmate with kerosene-soaked wads of lint: *"Managia chi ti battiavo"* was the sound of the words Quinto baptized him with. Ira followed suit, without benefit of clergy—and dashed kerosene into Quinto's eyes. They almost came to blows.

They loafed a great deal together, as did most of the crews. The practice was one of the things that puzzled Ira at first, and he was never really sure later why it was so. The company would rather have them—and the other workers in the place—loaf, than reduce the hours of work down to the time it would actually take to finish the assigned task.

* * *

Oh, hell—he lifted his eyes from the monitor—it was obvious now (showed he was growing more practical, finally, nearly ninety).

Keeping the work force on the job longer than was necessary reduced the hourly rate of the work—that was at least one good reason.

So they loafed a good deal, especially after the half-hour lunch break, when full of food, and lethargic with summer heat, they seemed unable to contend with drowsiness, and yielding, fell into stuporous sleep—on the straw-covered subway seats of a train lifted up on its wooden trestles, and safely out of the way of foreman and superintendent. At other times, their stint finished, or all but finished, they lounged in the lifted trains along with others whose work was almost done and were killing time. One could smoke up there too, take a few drags discreetly, or gab about anything under the sun. Usually talk was about sports: racehorses, and the odds on them, the jockeys, and the favorites, about baseball, the standing of the home teams and the ballplayers, for Babe Ruth was nearing a record in home runs. Or about women: what tight lays the new wave of German nursemaids were. And about wages and working conditions. This was where Ira came to life.

A union, that's what was needed. Instead of the company union whose meetings nobody attended except the bosses and their stooges. Instead of a company union that was as phony as a three-dollar bill, the subway workers needed a bona fide union of their own, one that would win them an eight-hour day and higher rates of pay, pensions, sick leave, paid vacations—it was obvious as hell. Ira preached with fervor: all they had to do was organize.

"Muz be a union." Padget, whose task was to change the advertising cards under the train ceiling, looked up from his green racing form. "Muz be right away a union," he jibed.

Young family-man Burgess, dark-haired, serious, assistant electrician, had been telling the others about fishing for flounder: "Sure, we ought to have a union," he said to Ira. And not challenging, not hostile, but stalwart and practical: "Who's gonna do it? You?" And relenting when he saw the effect of his words on Ira: "It's a good idea. Nobody's against that. But how're you gonna do it? That's what we wanna know: How?"

Their job was their livelihood—Ira had the queer feeling that the murkiness of his callow thought was being parted by realization, the way the dark waters of the East River foamed before the prow of a tugboat. The job was their rent, the meals on the table for themselves and their family, clothes and shoes and a pack of butts and an outing once in a while. They couldn't depend on words, on good intentions; they had responsibilities, pressing ones: wife and kids depended on them. How mawkish he was, urging them forward, onward, out of the security of a summer job. Why should they risk what they had for just words? No wonder. They had to know how the thing worked that would improve their lot, just like their tools, concrete, visible. He could feel his insights float away afterward, but something remained: a notion of practicality, bare though it was: of necessity, necessity.

As if to punish him for his impulsive harangues about the benefits of organizing into a union, when a brief strike did break out, a strike called by the motormen, the operators of the subway trains, against the company in the shape of the city-appointed IRT board members, Ira and a half-dozen other expendable workers in different departments of the system were culled out to attend to the wants of the strikebreakers. "Scabs," hired to replace the striking motormen in the event the strike was a prolonged one, they were herded onto the platform of a marshaling yard spur deep in the Bronx. So Ira, great proponent of trade unions though he was, confronted with the choice of being fired or submitting to the new assignment, Ira went meekly along. It wasn't hard to compromise with principles, such as they were, Ira discovered, and he enjoyed the irony of the adventure.

Everything was adventure. He no longer reported for duty at the car barn. Instead, he rode all the way out to the last stop of the Bronx line, got off, and walked over tracks and covered third rails to the spur. Under the supervision of a surly Italian cook, Ira and his fellow "caterers" prepared the ingredients for beef stews, chowders, and the other entrées that met the cook's criteria for a strikebreakers' menu.

Sitting perched on the steel stairs leading to the platform, the kitchen hands pared and peeled vegetables. An Englishman from the El station maintenance crew, probably singled out because he *was* an Englishman, had been a steward aboard transatlantic liners before he settled in America. Never did Ira see potatoes peeled as the Englishman peeled them: they had as many facets as a fine gem. Ira tried to do the same; he wasted potatoes like mad, but not once was he able to produce anything resembling the exquisite polyhedra of the other.

After the kitchen crew had prepared the food, and it was cooked, they served it. Once, as Ira reached over to set a plate of stew before one of the scabs, the plate in his other hand tipped slightly, spilling gravy on the shirt of another scab. He sprang to his feet, snarling fiercely. And scared and quaking, Ira cried out, "I'm sorry, mister. You can see I'm not a waiter!" Thus mollified, the man sat down again.

The culinary and dining area occupied the space where the ticket booth and turnstiles usually stood. The dormitory was the station platform. On it were double rows of canvas cots, and the scabs slept there in the open air. They were a seedy bunch, especially in the morning, when Ira came to work to serve them their breakfast of bacon and eggs, a seedy bunch who sat blearily or groggily on the edge of their cots, sat yawning in their blue work shirts and dungarees. Where did they come from, where would they go afterward? To another strike-torn place? Ira could almost pity them—perversely—though he knew he wasn't supposed to, and that he was no more scrupulous than they were, but they looked so surly and withdrawn—just like condemned men might look, he thought. Sometimes he thought he caught the glint of a hypodermic needle. They shot craps in the afternoon.

"The strikers won't maul you?" Mom asked anxiously, when Ira told her what his new duties were. "I fear greatly."

"Don't worry," he assured her. "They won't maul me."

"You're mixing into a strike," said Pop. "You don't know what they'll do. They'll open your head."

"Maybe you better not go to work," Minnie worried.

"And get fired?" Ira retorted. "Nobody's gonna open my head.

Nothing's gonna happen. What am I? A scab? I'm not gonna run the trains. *They're* the scabs."

"*Oy, vey,*" Mom moaned. "It goes ill with me. The first one they'll pick on will be the Jew."

"They won't pick on me. I'm not running the trains," Ira maintained doggedly. "If one of these scabs went into a restaurant where you're a waiter, will the strikers beat up the waiter?"

"That's right," Minnie agreed. "Ira's right. He's only a waiter."

"Indeed." Mom remained stubbornly unconvinced. "Would that I never knew that shrew downstairs, Mrs. Mahoney. Evil befell me that I had to gossip with her."

"Don't worry," Ira rebuked Mom wrathfully. "All I do is hang around, for Christ's sake, and peel potatoes. It's a cinch. And I'm making twenty-eight fifty a week."

"We'll see," Pop said ominously. "We'll see."

And Minnie pleaded, "Yeah, please be careful, Ira." She approached him, patted his shoulder tenderly. "Please watch out." She clucked worriedly. "Maybe you shouldn't go to work. Say you're sick. You got flu. You can go to Dr. Weiner. He'll give you a letter."

As suddenly as the strike had been called, it was called off. Mr. Quackenbush (what a moniker!), the comptroller, came to terms, the newspapers all proclaimed, with the motormen. They again manned the trains. All subway services return to normal, the newspaper said. All trains running on schedule. Before quitting time on Wednesday, Ira and the others were told to report to their regular places of work. He gave scant thought to the fate of the strikebreakers: they were still standing around, sitting on their cots, or striding on the platform, waiting for their pay, some rumbling about the bastards wouldn't even give us our supper, and some went to find the Italian cook for a handout or a sandwich, but he had disappeared. They'd like to wreck the goddamn station, they said, heave the cots onto the track—but they hadn't been paid. And there were a couple of cops around—somewhere.

It was back to the subway barn for Ira. Nobody seemed to have missed him. Mr. Kelly smacked his lips when he glanced at Ira.

Quinto said: "Hey, what'sa matter for you? You seek?" Maybe he pretended he didn't know.

Ira answered, unsuccessfully nonchalant: "No, they wanted me to work uptown."

Only Burgess seemed to take the measure of him with calm survey—without a word, quizzically, his brown eyes level, as if he were committing a thought to memory, or an object lesson: affirming the compulsions of reality. Who knew? No one said anything.

And at home, everything returned to normal also, to Mom's great relief, to Pop's noncommittal "*Noo,* it became nothing out of nothing." Fervently concurred in by Mom's "*Got sei dank,*" and Minnie's terse "You gave me a real scare."

Because Quinto was illiterate, and his command of English very poor, Ira would go on errands to the toolshed, in the charge of a cross-eyed, redheaded Irishman (the Irish were in the ascendant, needless to say), and fetch a leather gasket, new bolts, or other components needed to replace worn ones on the brake cylinders. Sometimes his errands took him to far corners of the barn, remote, almost mysterious places, visited once and not again, and as a result, imbuing the senses with imagery as vivid as they were pristine. He beheld with the eyes of childhood, with wondering gaze, the great emery grindstones truing the flange of a rusty car wheel, sending a comet's train of sparks into the gloom of the workshop, starchy and ozone-laden. He loitered whenever he had a chance: how like a dawn lighting up the smithy were the heavy, white-hot forgings brought from their crimson beds of fiery coke. And the two brawny, bare-armed Irishmen hammering the white forging on the black anvil, rhythmically, like the automata of a clock beating out the hours, spoke to each other as if out of a trance. Said one: "Do you mind the time we were in Cork?" And the other: "'Twas a day like this."

With eighty trains in the barn daily, eight rows of them, gobs of grease from the work of maintenance and repair fell in splotches everywhere, and mainly in the aisles: a hazard to the men traversing them. For safety's sake, the sweepers broadcast clouds of slaked lime, "to cut the grease," they said: to dry the smear left by the lubricant after it was cleaned up: to cut the grease. To cut the choking dryness of the clouds of slaked lime, men chewed tobacco. Ira soon got the hang of the vile habit. Ever impressionable, eager for every new sensation, he bought his package of cut plug chewing tobacco, and was soon squirting tobacco juice everywhere with the best of them, and proud of his ability to do so. Work made him oblivious of the cud in his cheek, except when time came to discharge a mouthful: *Chew Star Navy. Spit ham gravy.* It was easy. Wait till he got back to college. He'd show them. It happened he had a wide gap between his upper incisors, and could force a stream of brown fluid between them to arc over a considerable span. Also, chewing abated the craving to sneak a smoke. Quinto, who neither chewed nor smoked, was impressed. *Chew Star Navy. Spit ham gravy.*

IX

Ira dreamed at night, strange verbal, literary dreams. He often walked with literary and historical personages through the car barn, explaining the work that was being done: once with Mark Twain in his white suit, once with tense General Sherman. Again, in the company of George Gordon, Lord Byron, Ira took the poet on a tour of the place. Work was at an end, trains had been lowered down on the rails—and the barn was quiet and somber. Byron looked just as he did in Moody and Lovett's *Outlines of English Literature,* handsome and sleek, with tousled hair above a fine brow, and shirt collar open at the throat. The two talked as they walked by the ends of the long lines of brooding trains. Suddenly the atmosphere darkened, became sinister—trains stretched away in ominous perspective. And turning to Byron, Ira said, "You see, Lord Byron: the Aisles of Grease, the Aisles of Grease, where burning Sappho loved and sung." Byron laughed. A jubilant light spread over the entire car barn. Ira woke. "You're priceless," said Edith when he told her about the dream one evening early that fall.

From Edith he learned that Marcia had definitely made up her mind to sue Lewlyn for divorce. Proceedings began apace, and Lewlyn refused to contest the suit. And though it was all much too complex, too involved and unfamiliar, for Ira to grasp in all but haziest fashion, he gathered that Lewlyn was suffering acutely: from the ultimate rejection by his wife, from the disapproval of his bishop in the church for declining to contest the divorce, from his own renunciation of holy orders, the collapse of his religious beliefs and aspirations, and especially from the negative mood about life that had overwhelmed him of late. Life had become empty of almost everything worthwhile, empty of everything except sensation—how did Edith phrase it? Love had become glandular relief. He was profoundly disenchanted and pessimistic. How could she not help but comfort a man so dejected? She had, and, of course, intimacies had followed. She refused to assign undue importance to the body, Edith asserted, and both understood that physical intimacy was a consummation of friendship between man and woman—without binding commitment. And now even more than before, Lewlyn's affections were torn between Edith as a potential permanent mate and the woman he had met in England, Cecilia. The question of who was going to win out was the predominant issue in Ira's mind—it was simplistic, but he knew no other way of formulating it; and he was sure that, brought down to simplest terms, that would have been the way Edith would finally have expressed it. What other way was there? That was the paramount question: Ira could sense it: through all of Edith's altruistic, objective presentation of the triangle, within all the restrictions of cultivated behavior, all the restraints of propriety and fairness, she wanted to win, she wanted Lewlyn to marry her. Well, he had been through all that before, Ira mused, heard all those circular, subdued hopes before . . . and had so little to offer by way of practical response, by way of anything except sympathy, sympathy and attentiveness, until the subject became so attenuated it floated off beyond him. Yet even so, inadequate though he felt his response to be, Edith seemed to hunger for it, cleaved to it, sought for more. In fondest, most earnest terms she besought him to telephone at the earliest, to call. Twice she pressed a five-dollar greenback on him. She now had the utmost faith in his discretion.

It was encouraging to Ira that the body didn't mean too much to Edith, that she felt—aside from necessary physiological precautions, for the sake of health—like eating cooked fresh vegetables and other smooth bulk—the body deserved no special consideration. All the fuss made about it, preserving its "purity," chastity, was nonsense, nothing but a ridiculous carryover from stuffy Victorianism. No modern person would abide by such, or could abide such silly prudery. No emancipated woman would, certainly not after Freud had shown the grave emotional disorders puritanical repressions brought on. It was too tenuous for Ira—not entirely, but most of it, grazing him like a mist, and drifting off. Two clouds of thought interpenetrated within his mind though—the solution to the oft-posed problem (his wits roamed out of contact, mooning on the irrelevant): answer to the oft-posed problem: what happens when an irresistible force meets the immovable body: they interpenetrate—two clouds of thought all but fused inseparably, solipsistically, and in customary fogginess. Was he an example of a repressed person? If he screwed Stella whenever he got a chance, even though she was a kid cousin, true, not such a kid now: he was twenty-one; from that minus four left seventeen. Did that indicate repression? Of course, he couldn't ask Edith, that was the worst of it. He might fantasize as usual by telling her, describing the "first-floor" apartment, with its gewgaw onyx electric lamp in the parlor front room, the lamp Jonas got by opening a savings account with the Harlem Savings Bank, so heavy that as tart Hannah said, you could get a hernia lifting it. And the new Stromberg Carlson Heterodyne radio pouring out Black Bottom or Charleston music, anything to drown out the act, but boy, did your ears have to be honed for the least sound—no, no, it was a fantasy-urge to tell her. But was that repression? He felt like a felon, no, like a falcon, successful, fierce, the osprey rising with the live fish in his talons. Now there again, that sense if only he had the nerve during those few walks with Edith, if he told her his intimations, but he didn't, and maybe because he didn't the mind kept coming back to it. Did all that indicate repression? Of course he was repressed. Look at Leo, he even offered Ira a chance at the coffee-dispensing divorced friend of his mother, a regular hunky *yenta*, with eyeglasses and big tits and a box like the tunnel of love in Coney Island. Of course he was repressed. Leo with his fat nose and thick lips wasn't. He was always making jokes about it, pretending he was laying one of those hallway whores: Ow! Ow! Take your quarter back! Of course he was repressed. Why did he prey first on Minnie, and now on Stella in his aunt's house? Why didn't he go hunt up a piece of ass like a man?

No . . . all right. If she didn't propose to accord the body undue consideration, as she said, why was she so careful about her skirts, about the way she sat, so primly, hem down well below knees, always decent, never gave him a chance to look up, why? He didn't know, but that was how she was reared, inbred modesty, as they said, but it didn't give him much encouragement. Anyway, most of the time he'd be afraid to try to raise a hard-on with her. What would she think of him, although once or twice—was he crazy?—he could have sworn her large, steady, noncommittal eyes rested on his fly, as if appraising, as if appraising the bulge next to his crotch were the most natural thing in the world. He could have bet a dollar, but maybe it was just absentmindedness. Jesus, the things he was keeping from Larry these days, things like that, things he had learned: surmises and confidences. And only yesterday, it seemed, Larry was standing on the fine green carpet in the living room of the empty apartment by the crank of the Victrola, saying with a shining tear in his eye: I'm in love with her, with Edith, my English instructor. And the world toppled. But now he, Ira, was miles ahead of Larry in confidences, in revelations, maybe in chances too, if he ever got the breaks. Jesus . . . goddamn it, he had the rawest, unfettered sense of humor—that was the worst of it; how the hell did it get away from him, range at will with no trammel? He could—in imagination—ask Larry the filthiest questions: Hey, Larry, did you ever try back-scuttling Edith? I have to back-scuttle my kid cousin Stella most of the time—she's so short, you know? I never did with Minnie, didn't have to, across the bed on weekdays and along the bed Sunday, you know what I mean: regular. Who's Minnie? he might ask. You don't know? My sister. What about you and Edith? Ask him for advice. Ad-Vice. Ha, ha, ha! *Absent thee from felicity awhile,* said Hamlet. So what do you do? And why did she nearly jump out of her skin in Woodstock when the cat brushed her leg?

Come on. Come clean. I'll swap you smut: no holds barred. Not what
did you do; what didn't you do? Ha, ha, ha.

You bastard. *Le poète est semblable au prince des nuées,* Iz could quote
from Baudelaire's *Fleurs du Mal.* Prince de nuts, Ira could quote from
Stigman. . . .

If only Marcia would keep her hands off the affair, it might develop into something permanent, a life together, Edith told Ira for
the ninth time: a life together. She and Lewlyn had so much in common, love of nature, love of beauty, love of poetry. He was so sensitive
to loveliness of flower and leaf and country road. And now that he
had taken up living in the Village, they saw so much more of each
other, had dinner together, breakfast on the weekdays. And he was so
gentle, so very gentle and considerate of her; even though he knew
all the tricks of sex, and they tried every kind of play, his hands were
so gentle. They were strong, but gentle. And he was so steady, for all
the terrible suffering Marcia was putting him through, and the crisis
he was going through in reordering his life. If only Marcia would stay
out of it, if she didn't interfere, their friendship could ripen into a
permanent relationship.

"How does she interfere?" Ira asked, though he had a vague notion he had asked the question before, in another form, and could
derive the answer from Edith's manner and tone of voice.

"She keeps trying to influence him. She's so smart. And of
course, he's still enough in love with her, under her spell, he listens."

"Against you?" Ira asked the safely obvious.

"Against me, without a doubt."

"Why?"

"She still has his interest at heart."

"That's what she says?"

"Oh, yes. That's her way of saying she's not going to lose control
over him. She'll keep her grip on him. She'll manage his life as long
as it suits her, as long as she pleases."

Man-ages, Ira watched the word break apart. "But why, if she's
got another man, this Robert, I mean, to keep her busy? She's in
love, isn't she?" He stoked edification with candid simplicity. "She's
getting rid of him. I mean Lewlyn."

"Oh, yes, she will in time—get rid of him, as you say: when it pleases her, or she finds other things more important—other ambitions to satisfy. But she's always intent on *power*—that's what she's most interested in: power over people. It doesn't matter who. I think the same thing will happen with Robert. I don't envy him." Edith was clearly unhappy—with back against the wall, primly sitting on the gunnysack-covered couch. "She's going to get Lewlyn away from me if it's the last thing she does."

He broke the narrative in midstream, unable to repress the memory of his own behavior eleven years later, when he returned from Yaddo, and told Edith of his intention to leave her for M. He had used Edith basely at that, to gratify his sexual urge—and in front of a mirror to intensify his gratification—and she, poor woman, had more than acquiesced—had urged him on. Poor woman was right. Poor *women!* So many of them, they would do anything—first Mom, then Minnie, then Edith, even M—they would do anything to try and hold on to the guy, at all costs, the guy who wasn't worth holding. Nothing so bizarre about it. Nothing to prate about, no need to prate about it. Edith had mothered him, was mistress and mother both; but she had abased herself, for the sake of holding on to him, as Mom, the voices ringing in her ears as echoes of unforgettable assaults, had done with Pop and also him.

Indeed, Ecclesias, the grave is a barrier to all redress, but I must continue with this fable.

"Why does Marcia have a problem with you?" Ira asked. "I mean, what's so wrong with you?"

"Oh." Edith's knees drew elevated an instant—only. "What's wrong with me is that Lewlyn and I are lovers, something she wasn't prepared for—had none of her blessings. And was none of her business either, but she soon made it so. She never expected he would find someone else so soon, and I think she's more than a little jealous. She thought he'd curl up and die when she left him, and he hasn't. Her ego is—well, ruffled. It's a huge one anyway, if I know anything about such things. Lewlyn didn't pine to the extent she expected, that's certain—I wish he would pine even less—I'd feel much more encouraged. Truth is he found somebody else compatible, and I suppose that's hard for her to swallow. And she's so religious about these things, to put it mildly. Straitlaced—"

"Huh? Marcia?"

"Marcia is a practicing Episcopalian. She believes in God, in the sacraments, and all the rest."

"Yeah?" Ira became genuinely alert. "After her husband gave it up? You mean she's religious? I guess that's where he made a mistake." He grinned deprecatingly: "The idea just came to me that as long as Lewlyn was a priest, he"—Ira gesticulated, sought facial areas to rub—"he was superhuman. Godlike, you know? He had a speaking tube like the captain to the engine room—" Ira giggled. "So she felt something like awe. No?"

Edith laughed with him. "You may be right. It's simply that she abides strictly to religious doctrine in matters of sex. She's guided by the dogma of the church. She absolutely won't countenance sex without marriage—she won't allow sex before marriage."

"Yeah? Not even the trial marriages they talk about today?"

"Oh, no. Heavens, no."

"And she's an anthropologist?"

Edith radiated amusement.

"So you're sinning."

"It amounts to that. Only I'm the temptress, I suppose, and therefore the guiltier party."

He knew it was anything but funny; but, cracking a smile, he skimmed excess of levity with a sober "Gee."

And expectedly, she remarked, "It would be funny, if it weren't so serious—"

"I know."

"They never had sex before they were married—in fact, she was frigid, Lewlyn told me that. It was several days—or nights—before she relaxed. 'Your body is more honest than you are, Marcia,' Lewlyn told her."

"More honest than she was," Ira tried to fathom. What the hell did that mean? Get a breast drill and an auger bit. Boy, you had to give Lewlyn credit, though—

"Of course you won't mention this. It's very confidential. I trust you. I'd tell no one else but you."

"Oh, no! I'll tell you, Edith, I'm dumb in a lot of ways—"

"You're not."

"I am. But the little common sense I have tells me that once she found a man who loved her, and they became—what d'ye call it—compatible, Jesus, she should have stuck to him—"

"Unfortunately—"

"No, no," Ira interrupted. "It wouldn't have been good for you—"

"That's hard to say. What I was going to say is that's not Marcia's way. She's determined to become the foremost woman in America—in the field of anthropology. That comes first. That's what she's made up her mind to build toward. Not a husband, not a family, but a career. She's ready to sacrifice anything to that. And that's why Robert—" Edith raised her chin to stress: "He'll be the perfect foil for her in building her career. If he isn't, she'll do the same with him as with Lewlyn."

"So how the hell—" Ira caught himself. "How did he get along with her all this time? I mean Lewlyn?"

"By laughing at her."

"By what?"

"Laughing at her when she said something extreme. Of course, she eventually came around to recognizing it herself: that she was wrong. But you can be sure it wasn't often."

"No. I guess not," Ira admitted. "Not somebody as brilliant as she is."

They were both pensive. Did he dare—no, he didn't dare—tell Edith, though maybe she might like to hear it, if he could say it right, phrase it politely, summon up drawing-room politesse, which he couldn't do anyway, like Richard Smithfield, or only rarely, by imitation, which was a wonder anyway, considering 119th Street when he was eight, and the barber's son mocking the mick kid with "You gargle a weenie," and though incredulous about the reality of what he said, knew what he meant: I wouldn't fuck her with a wooden prick. All he could think about Marcia was dark asshole and bristling eyeglasses. Well, he was ruined; so what're you gonna do? And a nice guy like Lewlyn working her around. Jesus Christ, he'd sooner have Larry's homely Hungarian maid, and they didn't come any homelier than that; what a pork-nose: oink! Throw a blanket over 'em, said impish Leo. Then they all look alike. . . . Yeah, maybe.

Over forty years later, Ira's image of Marcia had not changed, but had crystallized as he observed her while waiting for her in her spacious Central Park West apartment, where he spent an hour or so, and where, after his fat omelet and two drinks previously imbibed, he dozed off in the vacant living room, while Marcia was occupied elsewhere. With age, the lady had become grander, being ministered to by her companion-lady-in-waiting-amanuenis-body-servant, who bound up Marcia's injured ankle, a little self-consciously. Then, with Ira her escort-in-tow, the two attended the memorial services for Louise Bogan, the poet, svelte of yore and presently deceased, svelte of yore in a peach dress when Ira last shyly eyed her queenly sensuousness at Edith's place. Svelte once, but dead now: she had said of Dalton, Edith's later lover in a second, or even third, love triangle, that he screwed like a rabbit—what these women talked about. Quit caviling: what did *you* talk about? Oh, hell, there was scads of copy—for a prudent guy in his right mind to write about, at least as valuable socially, and as enlightening as that which Ira dwelled on—or rather was restricted to.

He recalled two taxi rides, and in one, the Jewish hackie recognized the great seeress, and treated her with all the deference that Jews reserved for the learned and the intellectually endowed (and financially also didn't hurt). Surely, a weighty matter or two had been discussed on the way, broached and enlarged on; the gathering itself required extra chairs, he recalled, since she had been a famous poet, and many significant associates, including William Who, the editor of *The New Yorker,* clean-cut gentleman, running the show, looked fittingly grieved and gravely concerned.

Most telling was the inescapable fact that, while Léonie Adams read Louise Bogan's poems, Marcia slept off her steak tartare and two martinis, specks of lip skin—or was it crumbs of steak tartare?—stirring like tiny hackles to the current of her breath. There was Marcia snoozing away, while Léonie read Bogan's poems. "You wretch!" Léonie denounced Ira the following day when, seeing her off on the train to Connecticut, he told her that Marcia had slept through her reading of Bogan. (Hell, Bogan never stirred either.) And then Léonie went on to lament the fact that a once fetching huskiness had disappeared from her voice, ever since she had given up smoking. Fancy that! The service provided other memorable insights, not the least of which was when the celebrated poet W. H. Auden, sitting in the window seat of the chapel in the back, tapped Marcia's shoulder and said, "Hello." At which she was looking very pleased. And you sat there like a goddamn block looking up at Auden, glaring up at Auden, neither standing up nor seeking introduction. Why? Because the bastard had published, had allowed to be published in some late and unlamented ephemeral magazine, a piece of disgusting erotica, or homosexuality, of fellatio in clever rhyme. Talk about pubic smells and phallic sights unholy. So you glared up at him, never made a move to rise, introduce yourself, shake hands.

—Do you conveniently forget your own incestuous excesses, those acts of carnal behavior you have rendered so? Have you not eschewed the interactions of the polite world, as well?

Treat, Ecclesias, but not drooling about it in an amatory paean.

"We were quite good friends until this." Edith pulled a hairpin out of the tight bun in the back of her head and probed her ear delicately with the round end, licking the wax off in her unbelievable habit. She probed the bun with hairpin again. "But now I know she disapproves. Very. Her antagonism is evident in every word of hers Lewlyn repeats to me."

"Yeah?"

"Especially, do I resent"—the channel of brown dress between thighs narrowed, and Edith tossed her head with unusual abruptness—"her constant reference to my negativism. My negativism. I'm no more negative than she is, if I were happy. She makes it seem as if I'm incapable of anything but a destructive tendency toward life. That shows how stunted, really stunted, her sympathy is—no matter what she says. Or prates. Or pretends. She simply doesn't know what

I'm about. I wonder if she knows what anybody is about? She paints
me as being in love with defeat. It happens that I think Man is ulti-
mately defeated. And I'm not alone either. But that doesn't mean I
don't like people, I don't sympathize, I don't enjoy the simple things
of life, that I shun happiness. It infuriates me."

"Yeah." Something was coming through to him beyond the tepid
roil of slackness and his lasciviousness, something about Edith's
plight, Edith's longings, her endearing traits too: a glimpse. Something more than Stella, a woman, a person, a complexity with a mind,
and above all with feelings, capacity for suffering. Vast matrix of
synapses: mind, reflection, trying, worriedly trying, to peer into the
future. The realization was sobering: not whether she'd slip him five
bucks, as she did before he got a job, not whether that carnal opportunity would ever come. But Edith, the troubled woman, existing with
her dilemmas apart from himself, in her own right. How rarely he felt
that; how often others, sensible people, seemed to—and he ought to.

"I was just thinking I couldn't do anything for you," he informed
her, penitently.

"I don't expect you to do more than you're doing. You're very
dear to me, Ira, just by bearing with me."

"I know. You told me that. But it's funny." He shook his head, and
suddenly caught his breath. "I just got an idea: what can you do? In-
tervene!" The word made him jerk, thrust his legs out spasmodically.
"That's what I mean. You've been good to me—" Like bilge he felt,
putrescence; it suddenly silenced him, and he lost hold of the thread
of the idea, sought to stimulate it with fingers stroking temple:
"Good to me. I mean what can I do? Is there anything I can do? Gee,
I feel as if—" He hefted fate in half-closed hand. "If I could do something it would make all the difference. But what? I'll get a regular
aura in a minute, like Prince Mishkin, or somebody."

With tiny hands in her lap, she listened—so receptive, solemn, as
if deliberating. "I don't think anyone can do anything, change any-
thing—I'm not fatalistic, or am I? I can't change myself. Neither can
I change Marcia, certainly not Marcia, any more than a juggernaut.
Cecilia is far away in England—not that I would hope to change her.
The key is Lewlyn, his will, his character, his decision—his character,

to say it all over again. He's the one going through a very critical phase, and it will all depend in the end what he decides is best for him."

"But still you talk about Marcia's influence on him."

"That may just tip the balance. She's a very strong person."

"Still, he's here with you. Somebody else would have told her beans. I mean, wouldn't have told her."

"We, Marcia, Lewlyn, and I, have friends in common. He's spoken to all of them about his treatment by Marcia. They all know about it, and of course they're friends of hers—primarily. It's a big joke among them. They give him tea and sympathy, Léonie said."

"Only you."

"I'm afraid so."

"Boy. I don't know." Ira drew arm against the hand gripping his wrist in awkward stretch of skepticism. "Everybody's got someone to fall back on but you."

"Wouldn't common sense indicate that a woman closer to his own age would be a better mate than one ten years older?"

"Yeah. Sure." He shrugged.

And the tiny hands remained quietly locked in her lap, and there seemed to be a kind of drooping in her demeanor, something akin to resignation—no, more than that: it registered with no more than blurred observation: she had a kind of lien on defeat—what a crazy idea! Something within her ran contrary to winning, even if she wanted to. She fed on it. No wonder Marcia charged her with negativism. Oh, no, oh, no, he could hear within himself: oh, no, she's gonna lose. She's got to lose. Well, for Christ's sake. His hand fell from his lip to his thigh. Be goddamned. Which came first? That he'd have that trim body there for his? Or was sorry for her defeat? It was written as clearly as she sat there. Yeah. All he needed was Prince Mishkin's aura. The way the whole thing was building up. Ira squirmed around in the wicker armchair. Look, the way he was being drawn in here, as if preordained. Look. Look. And could you change it? Never come here again. Disappear. Larry might invite you, but too busy, pal. Or any goddamn thing. Would that make a difference? Who knew? He was forcing destiny. Drop out of sight, drop out of college, go over to the steamship companies on the Hudson River, the way Mannie Levine did on 118th Street, when Ira went with him: bedbugs on the mattress under the blanket on his bunk, but he got a job, pot walloper. Get a job as oiler, anything. Disappear. Do something decent in your life, quit pratting Stella, forget about Minnie—would that make a difference in Edith's life? Would she win, despite herself? He was making her lose, helping to prepare her to lose, so he could gain. Jesus Christ, did you ever see such a cuckoo?

Or just the reverse—when was he going to say something instead of sitting there mulling glumly like a stick? Go over to her and say: Hey, Edith, how about a lay? Hey, Edith how about a frig? Hey, Edith, how about a piece of ass? Would that make a difference? It would break the spell. What spell? Vortex spell. Free things—free her from the web he was weaving. So I'm a prick, all I want is a piece of ass. That's all I've been wanting all along. Nah! Goddamn it, she wouldn't be horrified; she'd probably laugh at him. What if she said: here. You cuckoo. Can you foresee consequences? Yeah, yeah, yeah, instead of this closeness continually binding them together, that mental web he was helping her spin. Nuts. Drool and swallow, drool and swallow. Only difference between chewing tobacco in the car barn: what's the use? You chew tobacco and spit the juice.

"I forgot what I was going to say," he finally said, shrugged hard: "I can't figure it out."

"It's not surprising," she said. "Only Marcia thinks she can, and probably will. Are you still doing the same work at the repair place?"

"Yeah. Grease monkey. Look at this." Ira rolled back his sleeve. "I wash and I wash and I wash. And there's one place I keep missing: right under the elbow. See that black smear? It keeps escaping me. It hides."

X

Flashing his IRT pass at the change-booth man in the subway station, Ira grabbed a train home after quitting time. Oh, he had to rush, there was so little time between jumping into the tin tub of tepid tap water in the bathroom, scrubbing with pumice soap (and leaving the grime he couldn't get off ingrained in fingers and deposited under nails), so little time between bolting supper, to Mom's cries of dismay, and Minnie's pleadings to slow down—though Pop chortled in rare show of pleasure: his son was earning wages for a change. So little time to trot to 125th Street, in the shadow of the New York Central trestle, iron parasol against the slant sun, and, sweating anew, climb aboard the Third and Amsterdam trolley, and clang, clang, he was on his way to CCNY evening classes. He was twenty-one, and inexhaustible, tough and inexhaustible. If anything was immortal, it was twenty-one, more immortal than De Quincey's summer: twenty-one. By the shores of the Gitchee Goomee, twenty-one I heard a wise man say. And that last time Zaida and Mamie gone, he had to hold Stella up almost, she went so slack afterward; he grew bigger and bigger coming, scared he'd get stuck like a dog inside her, cock swelling up like a bottle.

So off at 137th Street, and hurrying. There were times he overtook Larry on the way to campus—and once or twice in the company of his sociology instructor, Lewlyn. Oh, that was ironic. One had to have a flair for irony, to enjoy it to the fullest, the overtones within overtones, endlessly propagating: rarer and rarer, evanescent. They made you grin: *From bush and bar, from brack and scar, the horns of elfland faintly blowing.* The *horns* of elfland! What did Quinto say, index finger and pinkie spread under his nose in imminent goring of mimic horns? *Cornuta.* Ha, ha, ha! Eager Larry doing his utmost to entertain his sociology instructor with the latest salesman's jokes, win a dry chuckle of appreciation, unaware the guy was cuckolding him; nah, he couldn't be cuckolding Larry; he wasn't married to Edith: just laying Larry's lady fair, laying his lady love. Now that was ironic, or wasn't it? Sitting in the classroom sopping up sociology from the guy sinking a shaft into the same woman you were. Only, Lewlyn really sank a shaft, and Larry just bunny-hugged on the couch. Why the hell was that all he seemed satisfied to do, so innocent he didn't mind having Ira there? Mystery . . . mystery.

Ah, loyalties had long ago shifted, hadn't they? Now it was all waiting, waiting, long waiting and wondering. No other way to de-

scribe it. Waiting for what? Wondering about what? Whether the way
for him would someday be cleared: by Larry, by Lewlyn. Ira didn't
have to gloat over it, he ought not; Larry was his friend, but it was a
fact. Larry was just hanging on by sufferance, as they called it: she
didn't want to hurt him, Edith said, dreaded his harming himself. If
she was unnecessarily drastic, it might affect his heart. The other, ah,
there was the rub, the toss-up. Negative, Marcia decreed: Edith's outlook on life was negative. She and Lewlyn would destroy each other,
if he joined his life with hers in marriage at this time. Why would they
destroy each other? Can you think that one through? Ira asked himself. On a magnet, poles that are like repel, but hell, they weren't
magnets. He wasn't afraid of Edith destroying him, and he was more
negative than Edith was, a damn sight more, Ira told himself. What
was Edith's negativism compared to *his* negativism, Ira heard himself
echo a quotation he couldn't place. Biblical maybe. His world had
been twisted right around, dislocated by woe, and not by self-pity either, twisted around all the way to murder, murder Minnie, his own
sister. What contemplation of an act could make one more negative
than that? Lot's wife had turned to look back at burning Sodom and
Gomorrah, and been turned into a pillar of salt (if you believed it).
But what it meant was that horror petrified her.

And so resolve to murder had petrified him, unhappy forever,
though an assignment in plane geometry saved him a split hair away
from killing. "Woe, woe, unhappy," Jocasta's words crossed his mind,
"this is all I have to say to thee, and no word more forever." That's
what negativism meant: unhappy. Lewlyn couldn't stand the depth of
Edith's unhappiness. The guy was normal, the guy was sound, opti-
mistic in disposition; that was it: he was affirmative in outlook. He believed in Man's future. That was why a permanent union with Edith,
marriage with Edith, would destroy him. She was too sad for him, she
was too tragic in outlook, that was all there was to it, Marcia or no
Marcia. Bet a buck Lewlyn only listened to counsel he wanted to
hear, and Marcia's was the counsel he wanted to hear. Even though
Ira nodded his head in agreement when Edith accused Marcia of
prejudicing Lewlyn against her, that was just good tactics to agree. Instinct told him Lewlyn was more and more inclined to do what Marcia advised him to do. So . . . go along with her interpretation. What

use saying no? Besides, he couldn't be sure. She was older, smarter, a hundred times more sophisticated in the ways of the polite world than he was or would ever be. Who the hell was he to gainsay? Gainsay and lose-say. No, let it unfold.

Privy to it all, wasn't it strange? Grease monkey working over a pit under a subway train, so engrossed with what was going on in Greenwich Village, so bemused about Edith and Lewlyn and that brilliant, brilliant anthropologist pitted against poor Edith, so in the grip of speculations about the future, he felt himself at times like a link, an odd human turnbuckle, fastening the most delicate of people to the grossest, the poet and professor to subway repair barn crews, where nobody would have dreamed as he started to loosen the bolts on a brake housing, when working alone by old red mule, while Quinto faded off to take a leak, nobody would have dreamed, when, wham! Jesus! Someone was in the motorman's cab checking the brakes. The sleeve snapped back within an inch of his cheek. But he was battle-hardened, he was twenty-one. What the hell was a brake sleeve, as long as it didn't hit you? Nothing. Except on his part: "Hey, for Jesus' sake, *you* up there?" To the answering cry of: "Hey, for Jesus' sake, *you* down there? Why didn't you tell me?"

So downhill toward campus of a late, sunlit afternoon, with Lewlyn between them, Ira and Larry, talking of this and that, Ira's subway job, Larry's salesman's job, Lewlyn saying that his father expected each of his sons to grow enough wheat during the summer to pay for his tuition at Penn State. Ah, how different, how healthy, wholesome in the best sense. . . . Downhill past Lewisohn Stadium to the campus quadrangle in tranquil shadow. There they separated, Larry to Lewlyn's sociology course, Ira to Government or Geology, or once a week another way, Larry and Ira to Public Speaking 7. Larry had applauded vigorously, his big hands smacking together noisily, when Ira finished delivering his defense of Sacco and Vanzetti. It was a rehash of the same defense he had delivered in Public Speaking 6, but tolerant, old (and more politically sympathetic). Dr. Dranon didn't know that. Anything to get by in the summer.

Why hadn't he taken some junk course—Economics—instead of Geology as a crash course that summer! Geology, the one course he truly enjoyed, the one class he looked forward to attending. Why

hadn't he saved it for a full semester? Those field trips, Saturday afternoon. He sometimes had to join the group already on site, he had
so little time between quitting on Saturday afternoon and getting
there. But even so: to view the potholes in Bronx Park, potholes
bored in the rock by thousands of years of glacial eddies. Eons of the
past intoxicated him. The mind reeled ecstatically contemplating
metamorphic rock, just plain metamorphic rock. Ah, what entrancing ages had gone by, gone by and left their parallel glacial scoria
on the mica schist outcrops in Central Park. Who would ever have
guessed those scars were gashed by glaciers? He never knew just
where the fault was that separated Manhattan from the Palisades, but
what matter. He climbed the sedimentary rocks of the Palisades, the
shales and the slates, so different from the mica schist and the gneiss
of Manhattan. Just knowing the fact alone was heady, climbing the
Palisades. "And did you know?" he asked Minnie. "Mt. Morris Park is
a monadnock? A pile of rocks and boulders left by a melting glacier."
That fact alone all but reprieved "Porkpie hat," the man who had
molested him thirteen years ago on top of another hill, on a monadnock's sister, of a summer day. All but. . . . The rise of the hill under
the trestle on 116th Street and Park Avenue a monadnock, the hill
he had panted up so many times on his way to Baba's as a kid to
scrounge a few coins—on his way to Mamie's to scrounge a piece. So
that was a monadnock with a new comfort station on top, and rows of
pushcarts below.

　　"My clever son," said Mom. "*Alles veist er.* Ah, would I be happy if
my head didn't roar so."

　　And he found himself reflecting a great deal more that summer
than he ever had before, seeking deeper explanations than the ones
he thought already explained. The realization came to him sneaking
a smoke with the others under the lowered trains at day's end. It
wouldn't have made any difference if he had gone to work with the
rest of the graduating class of P.S. 24, at age fourteen. He no longer
belonged, he no longer belonged even then, at fourteen. Why? Minnie, and the guilt of his incest? Nah, he hadn't thought a great deal
about it, didn't know much about it: it was gratification. Even before
he lost the glimmering thread under the train before the quitting
whistle blew, he had parted from the rest somewhere, somehow—

when? What was all that "speeching" he did, way back on the East Side? Poems he recited in the public school assembly that Mom came to listen to: about the east wind, and the color it had, and the west wind, and the flowers it brought. Even then, even that far back, the separation had begun—quick, another drag or two, and he'd have to crawl out—separation from Yiddish to *goyish,* no, to beautiful, beautiful English. "Kelly around?"

"No, he's in the office."

Oh, long ago, he had parted company with the rest, long ago before he was fourteen. Before Harlem. In the very heart of the East Side. Before he was eight years old. When he learned to read. Yeah, yeah, yeah: 1912 on the calendar. Hard to remember—

Whe-e-e!

"There she goes. Quitting time. Another day, another dollar."

They clinched their butts, broke the glowing embers of tobacco off, stamped on them, and climbed up to the aisle.

Some sort of large rhythm ran through his head as he joined the rest trooping to the washroom, a declamation without words. Another day, another dolor. Stuff that in your literary calumet—no. "I have lost the great—what?" he could hear himself say. Was he trying to remember a quote—from whom? Shakespeare? Othello? "I have lost the great—Damn."

"Kolly," said Quinto at his elbow. "Kolly biga cockasuck."

"Yeah?"

August sunlight splayed on the great sullied skylights overhead, filtered through the smudged glass and spread over the shop, train and crane and aisle and workbench. Here and there, where a corner of windowpane had broken, or a piece of mullion weathered out, crystal spikes of sunlight flashed through, stabbed with radiance of splintered diamond. Bright, bright, ah, forever. You'd think the glitter was tangible.

The shop was hot. De Quincey, the shop was hot. Always August seemed summer's last assault, and with a vengeance. Sweaty, and snorting everyone against the weight of thermal torpor. Wilted: "Hot enough for youze," exchanged for mirthless: "It ain't the heat, it's the hoomiliation." And: "I ain't sweatin' bullets, I'm sweatin' minié balls."

Ira had been tempted to give his notice that week, and with the heat, he regretted he hadn't. But another week—or two, if he could hold out, another two weeks at $28.50, with gray fedora and second-hand oxford gray suit and "it's like new, I should live so," a Chesterfield overcoat with black satin collar, and yes, brand-new, tooled brogans, all bought for his senior year. He was all set: he'd have a few bucks in his pocket a few weeks longer at CCNY. He'd give Mr. Kelly notice in September, a week before college opened that fall of 1927, and give himself a week's vacation. Doing what? Turkey trot, as they used to sing. You know? He squared off against himself within his mind: now that Stella had enrolled in that business school on Union Square, he could hang around there a free afternoon from CCNY until her school was out. And then? Yeah, and then? That was the whole trouble. Nowhere to take her. To the park, Centrum Pock, as Mamie called it. But they'd have to hike all the way past the lake, up the hill, genuine mica schist, and find some dell or dingle, what the hell ever that was. But that would take too long, and somebody might see them, meet them. That was the worst of it: somebody might see them. They'd know he wasn't taking that little bimbo for a Platonic nature study in the bosky groves. . . . You know? What a villainous idea he just had! But that would take nerve. And a little dough, too. Well, he'd still have some. Take her to Fox's Theater on 14th Street, where he worked when he was fourteen. Fourteen, fourteen, remember? First balcony—you could smoke up there. Third balcony, the projectionist's booth. Second balcony, dead and dusty, vacant, empty, empty as a—what did Andy Marvell say? *None, I think, do there embrace.* But it had two toilets in back, like the other balconies. And in the back, and in the back—which one would he use? The ladies' or the gents'? With a low sweep of his new fedora like Sir Walter Raleigh: ladies foist. Oh, what a villain! . . . Nah, he couldn't, wild Indian, he couldn't. But nobody could say that he didn't have injunity—enginu-ity. *But that two-handed engine by the door stands ready to smite once, and smite no more.* I betcha it was the executioner's ax. . . .

* * *

Edith invited him to attend a cocktail party at her apartment on the following Sunday. A singular honor: alone this time, without Larry. "I know I can trust your discretion," her note in the old brass mailbox said. It was the second such "solo" invitation of the summer. That first time he felt himself balloon with pride like the frog in the story when she sat next to him on the couch across from Lewlyn. You could smell how delicate she was: "You mustn't be so shy, lad." And he had agreed, but was tongue-tied just the same. All those writers and poets and colleagues circulating around, who wouldn't be awed? Larry wouldn't, Larry wasn't, and that's what was so damned funny about it: he wasn't invited, and the party was kept a secret from him. "He simply doesn't fit into a gathering like this," Edith confided, forgetting she had already confided the same thing the time before, but it was nice to hear just the same. Traitor. Yeah, he found himself pondering a thin segment of his mind, as if it were a slide on a microscope. *Traditore,* they sang in *Aïda*—that's what the word sounded like on the phonograph record at Larry's: *traditore.* Talk about irony. Wind up the crank, and the two were going to be walled up together, Larry said.

"People aren't interested in his long-winded anecdotes. People are interested in ideas."

"Yeah."

"He's amusing sometimes. If only he didn't demand to be the center of attraction always."

"No. That's true."

"Lewlyn has observed the same thing. He told me he liked your brief descriptions of people in your workshop much better than Larry's stories. He took so long coming to the point."

"Yeh?"

It was funny that first time, funny and strange—and embarrassing. After two big drinks of bathtub gin and grapefruit juice, he didn't know what he was talking about, especially when everybody got on the subject of Sacco and Vanzetti; still, Edith accompanied him into the hall when he left, squeezed his hand, and said he was wonderful. What did *he* say that was so wonderful?

Said the statuesque dame, statuesque, Edith called her, not

dame, just statuesque, in a peach frock—poet too—Louise? Louise
Who? Boy, you'd have to be six feet tall or nearly, have a cock three
inches longer, like Guido up in the stifling lifted train, putting eight
quarters on his lazy hard-on. "Animahl!" said Russo. In Italian. Not
animal. "Animahl!" So what did she say in the peach frock after Edith
introduced them? "What do you do, if I may ask?"

"Me? I work in a car barn." He just barely got the words out,
nearly inaudible with self-consciousness.

"A cow barn!"

"No, a car barn!"

"Oh, how delightful!" And then she suddenly laughed—not at
him, but at the thought. Laughing made her beautiful too. Boy, what
a goddess. "You herd trains into a barn. What rare human touch in
our mechanized existence. It becomes almost livable."

And then five or six clustered around him, unwilling center of attention. What do you do? You do, really! Oh, tell us! Tell us what you
do. They sat down on the couch, women, men, and Edith, her olive
skin even more luminous with pleasure, made room, and left him.
And that was when it all started about Sacco and Vanzetti. "We're
sure the men are bitter about it," one woman said.

"They hardly even talk about it. Maybe the Italians."

"They don't? What do the others talk about?"

He had finished his first drink, and giggled, "Who's gonna win in
the Aqueduct races. The odds. Babe Ruth. God, what else do they
talk about."

"The very worst thing in the world to romanticize," said the poet
in the peach frock. "A cause. The very last thing a poet ought to write
about. It's sheer sentimentality. There you have it. What did the Irish
nationalists do about Yeats and about Synge's plays? They excoriated
them, they blistered them. Please!"

"You're absolutely wrong!" declared the short, stocky man. "In
fact, I'm glad you mentioned the Irish nationalists. Who wrote, 'A
terrible beauty is born'? And on what occasion was the poem written?
On the occasion of the Easter Rising. Was that a cause?"

By now Ira had glugged down his second drink. He began to feel
a little at ease with the short, ladylike poet, Léonie, whom he had met

several times, although he still venerated her. She had read before the Arts Club when Marcia and her enigmatic friend had attended, and what lovely poems she wrote, lyrics, said Edith; Ira had read them when she and Larry snuggled together on the couch. And Larry was the first to agree they were lovely. What figures of speech they were—although she didn't have much of a figure herself: torso and face above like a Dresden doll, and a poly-solid build below. She was the one who just kept opening her lips to say something, and never said it, her mouth forming words without voice. What a wonderful way to talk; you never got into an argument. "What do you think of all this, Ira?" she said softly, so that almost nobody heard. And that was when he got started.

"You can't break the writer apart," he said almost sullenly—didn't care who listened. He didn't care if he made sense, as if he had a ventriloquist talking inside him. Hell with them, they didn't know what he knew; their beings hadn't been wrung the way his had. "You can't break him into this and that. He can't write like a doctor writes a prescription. It comes out of one piece—all his sickness too. That's the way I keep thinking about it when I'm under a train slopping grease in a brake cylinder. If I was to write, how'm I gonna separate it? I can't." Neither could he check his gesticulations. "He's supposed to use everything if he's a writer, a poet, I don't care what he is. We had some of Milton's sonnets in Survey of English Literature: he could write so beautifully reaching in a dream for his dead wife"—the words began to choke him—"and he could write, 'Avenge, O Lord, thy slaughtered saints.' He didn't divide himself up. That's what I mean."

"I agree with you entirely," said smooth-featured, attentive John Vernon. "But how many writers can be so completely holistic?"

"Huh?" He was being taken seriously. What the hell was holistic?

"Not even Milton was entirely whole," said John. "The only two that come to mind are Shakespeare and Rabelais."

"Plautus might be included," said Berry Berg.

Ira knew he was over his head. And worse, other guests had stopped to listen. He was flighty with liquor, he ought to shut up. "You can be just as involved as you wanna be!" he burst out.

"You can?" asked blurry Juno in peach. "Can you illuminate further?"

"You can!" He couldn't stop himself. The words seemed visionary within him. "If you had something inside you that kept *you* together, anything you write *you* can keep together." The guy he was, all twisted to hell, and only something to hold on to: holistic? He'd have to look it up. Mystical, mystical, and he didn't believe a goddamn thing. Jesus Christ, he must be disgracing himself. "You have to believe and not believe. You have to use everything like counters, you know what I mean? Did Melville believe that sky pilot's sermon? I don't think so. You use everything, I think, the way a kid uses blocks. Any kind of blocks. Any which way suits you."

"Go on," urged the poet in peach.

Instead, suddenly bashful at his temerity, he grinned in silent appeasement.

Edith offered him coffee, but he declined. He said he had to leave. And then she followed him into the hall, and squeezed his hand, almost looked as if she wanted to give him a kiss.

But you'd think that was enough. He got into the subway train uptown, and what did he start doing? He began to doze—and the next thing he knew was the trainman shaking him: he had already removed his necktie and jacket and was unbuttoning the top button of his shirt.

"Hey, bud, wake up." The blue-uniformed trainman shook him again, while everyone else in the train focused eyes on him.

"Oh, Jesus, I thought I was home."

"Well, you ain't. You're in a subway train." Still watchful, the trainman removed his hand from Ira's shoulder. "You all woke up?"

"Yeah, yeah, yeah." Mortified, Ira stood up, hung on the straps till he got to the cubicle next to the train door. Braced in a corner, he pocketed his necktie, put on his jacket. He skulked there, out of sight, until the train reached the 96th Street interchange for the Harlem local, and then he got off. He'd better stand up in the station, he told himself, stand up in the train for Harlem too, all the way to 116th Street. And then sober up walking from Lenox to Park Avenue. He paced groggily back and forth on the platform, waiting for the local. He was like somebody coming from one world into another. Was that the world promised him in that aureate moment of beatitude when he stood on the street corner in West Harlem?

Oh, Jesus, maybe he ought to try puking after he climbed up to the street.

The spikes in the chinks of skylight had become lances, smoky lances, like a moving-picture beam, only narrower and all impregnated with floating, powdery lime. Time for a siesta. They had only two more brake drums to do, and most of the afternoon to do it. Quinto looked guardedly about, beckoned to Ira, and mounted the ladder to one of the hoisted trains. Ira followed.

"Hey, wait a minute, you guys. Hey, you, Ira." It was the short, barrel-built chief electrician, Eakind, never without his blue racing form in his shirt pocket. He didn't seem to care about Quinto, but Quinto came down anyway. "Hey, Vito." He leaned under the train. "C'mon up, will ye? You there, Padget?" he called up to an adjoining train. "Okay. Will you give us a hand, Padget?"

"That ought to do it," said Burgess.

Vito climbed up to the aisle, pocketed his drift pin. Padget, with a sheaf of cardboard ads under his arm, looked out between trains, climbed down a few seconds later. One glance and he recognized the hitch. "That fuckin' thing holdin' up the parade again?"

The trouble was familiar to Vito, and here came Quinto, bobbing his head in recognition. Ira too could surmise. It was a heavy-duty cable, probably carried all the amperage to the motors right from the third rail. Heavily insulated, heavily lubricated, it had to be drawn through a length of steel tubing that protected it from damage under the train. A long wire, taped to afford a better grip, projected from the end of the tube. A "tail" it was called, and it was interconnected with the cable. Most of the time, Eakind and Burgess could pull the cable through by themselves, but sometimes, perhaps because of a slight kink in the tubing, the cable proved balky, and to slide it through took more muscle than the two men could exert. Besides, it was hot.

"All right, grab hold," said Eakind, "and get yer ass behind it."

All did as they were told, tugged manfully at the taped tail. With Eakind at the other end, guiding it, the thick, dark cable slid a few inches into its metal sheath. "Give us a little more, fellers," Eakind directed. "That's it. She's comin'."

"So is Christmas." Padget popped a shred of tobacco from the tip of his tongue, puffed at the heat. "Jesus, you'd think they'd have some kind o' goddamn winch for this by now, some kinda gimmick—a half-horse motor."

"I told 'em that fifteen years ago," said Eakind. "I told old man Haverly when he was superintendent. He said you'd pull the cable windin's apart."

"Bullshit. They're not goin' to spend the dough as long as they got a buncha stumblebums like us with strong backs and weak minds. Right, Ira? Muz be a union."

"It's only once in a while they're tight as this," said Burgess.

"*Fica stretta*, eh, Vito?" Quinto prompted.

"What the hell does that mean?" asked Padget. "You ginzos are always talkin' to yourselves."

"Let's go," said Eakind.

"*Fica stretta, gatzo duro*," Vito explained.

"Yeah? What's dat?"

All took hold of the tail.

"*Acqua fresca, vino puro*—" Quinto rhymed.

"Pull! For Christ's sake!"

"Oh, my achin' back! Hey, Red. What the hell're you guys doin' here?"

Newcomers: a moment ago they were out of sight—nowhere to be seen. Now they stood at the end of the greasy workbench, guys in overalls, vaguely known, the way fellow workers in a big shop are known, by gait, by purpose more than visage, as they strung along the street dangling paper bag or lunch box, to enter the shop, in the endless commutation of punching the time clock in—or out, flocking toward it at the end of the day, as if to render rough noisy obeisance before it, to escape home from the shop. Mostly anonymous, except Red, the cross-eyed keeper of the tool crib and spare parts. Everybody knew him: Red. Gingery Red, with a cushy job and Irish as Mrs. Maloney's pig. He had a tabloid in his hands, the *Daily News*, August 23, and he was evidently the leader, the spokesman of the several men with him. "Hey, how d'ye say dis name?" He held out the open front page to Ira's view.

"Vanzetti," Ira obliged. "*They'll* tell you. Right, Vito? Vanzetti?"

Vito said nothing, only looked—obliquely. Quinto couldn't read, but somehow gave the impression he sensed something unfriendly. What the hell? Padget grinned, and stocky Eakind waited indulgently, while he ran a thick, nicked thumbnail between chin and lip. Only Burgess stared at Ira, a level, dark-eyed, almost forbidding stare. What the hell?

"Not that one," said Red. "How do ye say de udder one?"

"The other one?" Ira could scarcely believe his ears. "Anybody can say the other one. You don't mean the word 'executed' at the end, do you?"

"No, we know dat. Dese guys are callin' dat foist name 'Sayco.'"

"Hell, yeah, dat's right." Red was seconded by one or two of his group.

"We want to know how you say it in American. You're a college guy, ain'tcha?"

And now Ira knew there *was* something wrong. A ruse, but what? He had a sense of the others hemming him in. What the hell could be loaded in the word "Sacco"? He stared at the big block headlines: SACCO & VANZETTI EXECUTED. The black scare headline seemed about to bolt from the page, held there as if leashed. Vito had begun to glower, Padget snickered, Eakind seemed on the point of pulling out the blue racing form from his shirt, scratched his chest instead, and Burgess looked hopeless.

"Can't you say that?" Ira hedged.

"I told ye, everyone was all sayin' it different. Wuzn't we, Feeney?"

"Yeah."

Ira knew he was trapped. But how to get out of it, whatever the trick was? Shinny up the sunbeam slanting right down to the lime-powdered cement slab: Jacob's ladder. "It's simple," he said, backing away toward Burgess.

"Yeah, what?"

"'Sacco.'"

And the avalanche fell. Six tightly rolled-up paper truncheons appeared from behind backs of Red's henchmen, and a guffaw went up as the truncheons crashed down. "Socko!" They flailed away at Ira's head. "Socko-o-o!"

Arm overhead, holding his glasses in place, and forcibly grinning, Ira retreated past Burgess out of range, but not before he had taken a dozen or more hard wallops. "Oh, so that was it?" he said.

"Yeah." They were bright with glee: "Socko! Right?"

"Managia," Vito muttered out of the side of his mouth.

"Let's go," said Eakind; and to the roisterers, "You guys wanna give us a hand with this cable?"

"Not us. Dat's too much like woik."

"Okay, you'll have Kelly around here in a minute askin' what it's all about. So let's go."

"Fuck Kelly," Red blustered. "We ain't afraid of him." Nonetheless, they moved off in the direction they had come from. "Socko!" They slapped their paper truncheons against their palms as they went through the aisle. "Socko!" They disappeared around the end of the line of trains.

"The fact is," Ira muttered the first words audibly, as he so often did when vexed or in quandary, that the transition he had envisaged, the second party alone at Edith's, felt anticlimactic. He had already told all that mattered: it was an open-faced sandwich—it didn't need that upper slice of bread. He had gotten his lumps in the shop, lumps on the coconut, and that settled the matter—and contrasted with the cultivated cocktail party at Edith's that had gone before. The two episodes balanced each other— he hoped: were poised in dynamic equilibrium, or should be. Besides, many of the same people were there—the short stocky lawyer too. And this time there was Lewlyn, and the young, tender-looking, freckled doctoral student in philosophy from across the hall, Amelia, sitting quietly by herself, and stealing a glance at Ira as he at her. Was she what you called demure? Or vulnerable? Or wan with study? Or . . . what? Philosophy: Plato, Aristotle. How could she be so much smarter than he was? That Philosophy 1 course he had taken as a freshman, one of the few courses still open when the classes on the blackboard were closed, what a fiasco that Philosophy 1 course had been. He didn't know a categorical imperative from a jelly bean. Hey, go over and tell her that. I Kant—ooh, *mamma mia!* Yeah, but she's a cinch. You can see, your brain tells you, but you Kant. Anh, what a shame. Everything had to be on the sly—first with Minnie, then with Stella—talk about a hit-and-run driver. Spoiled, that open, candid, natural self—ah, what the hell was the difference? Behold, Juno-Louise in a pink dress instead of a peach frock, clinging all the way up from calf to tous-tous. A vous tous-tous avez a vous? Pig French that meant "Where do you hurt?" in Yiddish.

Anticlimax, Ira told himself. The two anarchists were dead as doornails, and history seemed to mark time with disjointed postmortems.

Ira took notice of Dalton, the short thickset man, a lawyer, Ira learned, who was drinking a glass of bootleg gin. "I find the purport, the message, if you wish, objectionable," Dalton loudly interjected about Edna Millay's poems. "It's wholly negative and despondent. The death of the two martyrs hasn't ended the fight for civil liberties. It isn't over."

And Louise, tall, goddesslike, and certain, responded, "That's entirely irrelevant. It's a bad poem."

Which elicited from the thickset man a heated: "You've just made me realize it's bad because it's limited to her own emotions."

"And just whose emotions should it have come out of?"

"It concerns us all. It's not a private matter," Dalton continued. "It's of epic proportions. All who worked so hard on the case, and made so many sacrifices for the two men, and often at great personal risk. Men and women at every level from a needle trades worker to a history professor." He became vehement. "We may become discouraged at times, but we're not demoralized. *She's*, Millay's, demoralized. I can assure you the seed hasn't been planted under a cloud, as she expresses it. And it hasn't been planted in sour soil, as she says. And we haven't forfeited our patrimony."

Disjointed postmortems. Ira felt gloomy. He didn't know why, either. It wasn't just the execution of Sacco and Vanzetti that made him feel that way: more grumpy than gloomy. His own thoughts maybe, his everlasting hemming himself in with what he was. Last time,

liquor had freed him temporarily—and even then, look what happened: he had begun to take his clothes off in the subway. Suppose
he had started unbuttoning his pants, before the trainman shook
him awake—in front of everyone!

Anyway, he wasn't going to let the bathtub gin get the better of
him on this occasion. He nursed his drink, sipped a little—now and
then—and tried to forget his glass altogether, put it down on the
floor next to his chair, when his fingertips chilled. Yeah, history felt
as if it had gone to pieces, had exploded, slow-motion shrapnel floating around in ugly unidentifiable scraps. And yet nothing really
stopped—Tunney was still going to fight Dempsey again, Chaplin was
still getting divorced. The newspapers were just as full today as they
were when he was conked on the bean with newspaper bludgeons:
my head is bloody but unbowed. Baloney. Maybe he felt let down because he had given Mr. Kelly notice he was quitting next week. That
was part of it. He had told Burgess too.

"I'm sorry you're goin'," said Burgess. "I wish they was all like you."

Who was the "they"? Ira teased the tiny hint absently: Jews, who
else? That seemed to put an end to things. Nice guy, Burgess. You
wished what he wished for—and then you didn't. You knew it
couldn't be, and you knew what you were. And Ira had looked forward so to the evening at Edith's. He had a haircut at that strict
German-Jewish barber's on Park Avenue, scrubbed and washed
leisurely, with no geology field trip to take up the afternoon—all his
summer courses over—walked as slowly as he could to Lexington Avenue and 116th Street, and then to the West Side shuttle, leisurely,
not to sweat up again.

Ha. Arrived. Introduced. In the room the women come and go,
talkin' of Bartolomeo. . . . The guests seemed steeped now in twilight. How pleasant the living room was without busy electric lights.
The guests waded about in the sepia twilight with glasses in their
hands, shadowy, two-dimensional silhouettes, moving or standing or
sitting languidly around an urn, you could say, an urn containing the
bones of the two martyrs, if your imagination was as crazy as his was.
Bet he'd remember that beautiful half-light, long after he forgot
about Sacco and Vanzetti, that beautiful half-light: late afternoon's
chiaroscuro, and all figures in it two-dimensional. Serene notions

about things that weren't serene drifted around in the twilight, if you could forget sex for a minute—it—what'd he call it? Id? Spikes of sunshine through chinks in the shop skylight, and old red mule dozing on its paws beside you, like a sleeping dog. They didn't crucify you, they electrocuted you was what it meant; if only he were a poet. . . . Came Juno in darkening pink—there was a poet, flesh and blood and svelte, and with long gams. Followed by tall, proper Professor Berg, breaking away from John Vernon. Boy, try to connect John Vernon, not-a-bad-guy homo, with Larry, whom Edith had not so long ago tried to rescue, Larry who wasn't here, and with himself who *was* here, and boy, figure that out. And now Lewlyn teetering between Edith and the other woman in England—how could he dream such a thing? Ira couldn't, and yet he did; he watched his own future teeter with Lewlyn's. Boyoboy—

"Oh, it's quite possible, even for one with Puritan inhibitions like mine, given the incentive." Professor Berg elevated his glass.

"To be silly."

"To be imaginative."

Louise laughed incredulously. "You!"

"Yes. I can just see you with your nipples stained a deep purple." Ira could feel his toes curl.

"Berry, you must have spent half the night thinking that one up." Louise looked around, in the tranquil sepia, at the other silhouettes. "Did anyone else hear that? Berry is becoming gamy. Berry, how bawdy."

"I thought it was rather felicitous, you know: tit for tat. Ha-ha-ha!"

"Oh, no! To what depths have we sunk."

"I definitely do not think Longfellow is a modern poet."

"I didn't say that." Louise moved off purposefully in search of an ashtray, though there was one at Ira's side. "I only repeated Tom Wolfe's taunt. And I spared you his four-letter words. Why carp at me?"

"He's so much bigger than you are. And a male besides. It so happens I'm heterosexual."

"You may be, but your chemistry is all wrong."

They moved out of range, as Lewlyn crossed the room and sat down beside Ira. "You've been very quiet."

"I was just listening." Ira grinned weakly. "I'll tell you the truth. I'm afraid—after the last time."

"The last time? Edith told me how eloquent you were."

"Yeah, but was I ever stewed. I started to take my clothes off in the subway."

Lewlyn threw his head back and laughed into the soft gloaming of the room. "Did you?"

"I only stopped because the trainman shook me."

"Not because you discovered your pajamas were missing."

Should he say "I don't wear pajamas"? Ira debated. No. And aloud, "No."

Lewlyn's chuckle tapered to seriousness: "I came over to find out what the men at your shop said about the executions."

"They didn't say. Gee. This one bunch didn't say. They just—" He interrupted himself when he saw Edith approach.

Lewlyn stood up—and belatedly, almost forgetting, Ira got to his feet.

"Oh, please don't," Edith said.

"I'll take the piano stool," said Lewlyn.

"I probably can't stay more than a minute," Edith said. She didn't look as radiant as the last time, even though Lewlyn was present, but solemn, despite glint of gold-and-ruby earrings. "Isn't Berry a scream? Poor Berry. Trying so hard to break through his straitlaced New England background."

"What was that Tom Wolfe said?" Lewlyn asked.

"Oh, he shouted across the faculty desks at Berry—and I wouldn't be surprised if Dr. Watt heard all the four-letter words in his office: 'You still think Longfellow is a modern poet.' Louise *would* get wind of it. Am I interrupting you two?"

"Oh, no. We were talking about the men in Ira's shop. I was interested to know how they reacted to the executions."

"I started to say I got banged on the head," said Ira.

"You did! Why?" Edith asked.

Intricate twilight seemed to swathe the three from the others in the room. What a fathomless moment, as if something fateful were—but Edith was waiting for an explanation: "They yelled 'Socko!' and whacked me with rolled-up newspapers when I read the name 'Sacco.'"

"Oh, for pity's sake!" said Edith.

It was Lewlyn's silence that revealed to Ira what it must be like to be—to have been—a priest. He remained unshaken, calm and grave and forbearing. "It's not surprising. Cruelty is a form of ignorance, and always seeks a victim. How can they know any better, when they're so misled by people in power, people who speak with authority. It's a wonder any *do* know better."

Ira felt as if he had been gently chided, felt that way, not overtly, but as if his raw resentments were being addressed. He could never feel the way Lewlyn did, gently damping indignity—or indignation—with charity. So, that was a priest?

"Ira, are you ready for some coffee?" Edith asked.

"Yeah, but I hardly drank anything tonight. Thanks."

"I hate to turn on the lights, but I'll have to in a minute. Lewlyn and I would like to ask you something."

"Me?"

"Lewlyn is taking the steamer to England next Sunday. Do you think you could accompany us to the pier?"

"I'm taking a Cunarder," said Lewlyn. "It's berthed in Hoboken. Do you think you could come?"

"Sunday? Sure. What time is it leaving?"

"It's late," said Lewlyn. "After midnight."

"That's nothing. I gave my notice on the job. I can sleep all day Monday if I want."

"I can't, unfortunately." The smile on Edith's olive skin merged with the dusk. "I have classes the next morning."

"That's right. You got the second half of the summer session." Ira was beginning to feel sidetracked, puzzled. "So what are you going for?"

"To see Lewlyn off. The point is, Lewlyn would like me to have an escort when I go home."

"Oh, oh. You wanna go to the ship anyway."

"Yes. Very much."

"Would you?" Lewlyn asked Ira. "It's going to be quite late by the time Edith gets back to New York. You're sure you want to do it, Edith? With classes the next morning?"

"They're not till ten. Oh, yes, that's all been decided, Lewlyn. I do want to go."

Ira thought he detected a slight shift in Edith's tone of voice, slight, stirring, something that made him feel nonplussed. He'd have to defer thinking about it. "I'll go," he said. "If you want me to go, sure."

"I'd appreciate it very much," said Lewlyn.

"Ira, you're an angel to let me impose on you so." Edith stood up. "I'll write you a note reminding you. Or do you want to tell me? Or both—I'd better go turn on the lights."

"You understand: that's Sunday a week," Lewlyn said as Edith left. "Not Sunday tomorrow."

"Yeah, that's what I thought. Gee, that's already in September—and you can go to England and come back before?" Ira gesticulated. "Before college begins?"

"I've arranged with one of my colleagues in the department to hold down my classes for a couple of days—that makes quite a difference," he chuckled dryly, as the lights came on. "Interesting. We really have no idea how dark it's getting until the lights are turned on."

"No." Ira felt as if everyone had tumbled out of condoning twilight into an unsparing, a utilitarian reality held between walls: a fluid twilight that clotted into concrete things and people: Amelia freckled and so flaccid, and tall John Vernon, and short Boris, and tall Berry and tall pink Louise, and Edith with a large aluminum percolator—and a set smile.

Lewlyn seemed to linger—deliberately. "How were your grades this summer?"

"I got all C's in the first session. I still have to write a paper for Government tomorrow. But C's, for me that's good."

"And you had to hold down a heavy job besides," Lewlyn extenuated.

"Not so heavy." Ira lolled his head. "Greasy. Yeah."

Lewlyn arose from the piano stool. "I'd better go to the assistance of the lady." And bending down toward Ira, discreetly: "I'm sure she'll tell you when and where we meet. We have to take the Hudson Tubes to get there."

"Oh, yeah? That's right. The Hudson Tubes. Hoboken."

"It's an easy walk from the station. It's practically across the way from the steamship pier, fortunately."

"Yeah? I've never been there." Ira took advantage of Lewlyn's momentary pause. "Mind if I ask you, Lewlyn? Do you remember how Larry made out? I didn't see him all week."

Personable, strong and tall in his heathery tweeds, Lewlyn chuckled in his boyish way, short, high-pitched, ushering in humor: "I'm sure he must be amused. I gave him an A-minus." He chuckled once again. "Excuse me, Ira, won't you?"

It was a convection. Ira felt that he was a feather, blown around in a tremendous chamber he didn't know the bounds of, without any control of what he would hit, or what he would graze. Yet he knew that the currents were of his own making: Lewlyn taking a steamer to England, Ira escorting Edith back from the pier. He couldn't defer the thought any longer. Lewlyn's choice had been made, Ira knew, without need to refer to Marcia's judgments or advice. Did Edith? Did she acknowledge it? Or could she even see it as a choice for Lewlyn to make? All that existed for Edith within this tremendous wind tunnel was the currents, the zephyrs, and the hurricane winds of the tragedy she felt inevitable.

So that was that. Now it was up to Ira. No more telekinesis, no more telepathy, no more malicious subconscious connivings. He had to turn his id toward action, had to bring to bear the things that he had made possible by dastardly wishings. If only he could know the bounds, the powers, of his own breath, blowing Larry away from Edith, Lewlyn too, and leaving open a great passage, a wide corridor toward something like salvation, toward something that could lead him from bondage.

So don't blame me. If I gave my body to be burned for the poor, as Paul says, and the flakes went up the chimney in Auschwitz, they'd still bear the curlicues of abomination, am I right, ole mole? You'll never budge the flukes of that anchor, Ecclesias, buried in the protozoic, briny slime of the seafloor, no matter how powerful the capstan. Am I right, old mariner?

—You're right. But mad. Mad with the realization engendered of reality. . . .

PART THREE

I

Two days after the party at Edith's, just as the final summer session was drawing to a close, Ira stared at the cream-colored wall at Aunt Mamie's house, where preparations for the Days of Awe had already begun. It was that time of year when a crepuscular haze had already signaled summer's end; the orange, grayish tones of twilight appeared earlier over the western skies, and cooler air, while only at night, necessitated the removal of sweaters from the higher reaches of Mom's closet. With the knowledge that the school year, this being his last, was about to begin, there was a twinge of sadness that tempered the party atmosphere, perhaps a recognition that his student days were clearly waning. Ira knew he was no closer now to a career, or soundness and evenness of mind, than he was the day that he first walked into the CCNY auditorium staring up at the board trying to establish an academic program.

Ira took the last of the typed sheets out of the machine, and after switching off the ceiling lights, stood in this stuffy little bedroom that Mamie had converted into her apartment house manager's office. Should he roll up the typewritten sheets, having finished the job, or should he fold them, Ira debated. He ended by folding them, and shipping them into his jacket breast pocket. The scribbled sheets of loose-leaf notebook paper that had been his guide all afternoon he crumpled and tossed into the wire wastebasket. It was done. His term paper for the second summer session was about new immigration quotas and their effect on employment in the United States.

The bright Indian-summer sunlight of midafternoon, which had still shone when he first addressed himself to Mamie's ancient, grimy Underwood, had palled hours ago to an ashy dusk on the single window of the bedroom office. For an eternity, it seemed, he had pecked away, erasing and cursing his mistakes, and erasing again. Toward the end, something of that touch system he had been so cavalier about learning the year he took typing in Mr. Hoffman's class in junior high began to reassert itself. His typing had improved immeasurably. He recalled how Mr. Hoffman had clouted him alongside the head for being remiss in slipping a sheet of paper for a dust pan under his erasures to catch the errant crumbs of rubber and prevent them from going into the machine. What the hell, he had finished the course, and now this. A trained typist would have taken maybe an hour to do the job, but who could afford, who could even deem the work worthy of the offices of a professional typist. Ira had even considered asking Minnie, but after how changeable she had been, how quick to fly off the handle at him, he thought why bother. He even considered asking Larry if it would be possible to enlist the services of his sister, a private secretary, to do the typing. She was more reliable than Minnie. She had typed Larry's short story, "The Graveyard." But then, the thought of exposing his crudities—and possibly, his embryonic political leanings—checked him from carrying out his first impulse: he hadn't realized to what a degree the simple act of putting words on paper in one's own way placed one's personality on trial. No, he would perform the task himself, in the privacy of self.

So all that long Sunday afternoon and into the early evening, hours after he had halted restlessly before the dark, metal-sheathed front door of the "first-floor" apartment on 112th Street and turned the brass key of the cranky doorbell, he had labored in the office. Mom was there as well, visiting with Zaida, when Ira arrived, and was surprised to see her son, who, after greetings, explained the purpose of his visit.

"About everything else he's shiftless," Mom remarked to the others in her fond, disparaging way. "Only this he cleaves to without stint. It's a—something of a novelty."

"I'm trying to get a good grade, that's why," Ira emphasized. "And all I got is today. It has to be in tomorrow. All right then if I use your typewriter, Mamie?"

"Mit gesundheit," she accorded her terse blessing on the enterprise. "I have paper there near the rent receipts and the plumber's bills, and the heap of bill-of-fare paper which Stella types for the cafeteria. You're welcome to use it, if it's useful."

"It's useful. Thanks, *Tanta. Noo.* Zaida, *vus macht sikh?"*

"One makes do," the old man replied with predictable unhappiness, "one gets along without teeth, with worthless bones, and worst of all without eyesight. Such clouds I have in front of my eyeballs. As if I walk in a perpetual fog. And the doctor tells me that to remedy my condition, I shall have to enter a *goyish* hospital—"

"Tateh," Mamie assured him quickly. "There's a rabbi that will see that your meals are kosher. I swear to you."

"Among nuns a rabbi," the old man said despondently. *"Noo,* as the Almighty wills, blessed He, so be it." And to Ira: "Old age is a boon, my son. You know to whom? To the ground."

"I'm sorry, Zaida."

"Noo, go write, go write," Mom urged.

Ira needed no further prompting. He left the front room, went through the long hall to the first room after the entry, Mamie's office, settled into a chair, laid his penciled draft down on the frazzled green baize of the old rolltop desk, and began transcribing handwriting to typescript. Time passed, an hour or two. Mom took her leave—entering the little office first to bid Ira goodbye, but not before reminding him that Mamie had cooked a potful of *pirogen,* potato *verenekehs,* this morning, of which there would be enough and more than enough to go around. "And don't be bashful," she enjoined. "She'll serve you lovingly with sour cream."

"Yeah." His mouth watered. "Thanks for telling me, Mom."

"My handsome son," she said by way of departure.

"'Bye, Mom." He kept pecking away at the keys.

Mamie's two girls came home, lithe, carrot-topped Hannah, the younger, prancing and gabbling in pert, tireless dither; Stella tubby in comparison, though merely adolescent plump, and seemingly stolid, though actually she was not—she was judged a good dancer. It was simply an air, an effect she had, an unfortunate one, that Mamie took at face value, which in turn produced unfortunate results in her daughter. It drastically diminished her self-esteem, and at present he gloated at the ineffable proceeds of that diminished self-esteem, the easy gratification afforded him by her lowered sense of self. Ironic, wasn't it? Oh, boy!

Evading the quick, rash quips of her younger sister—Hannah's glib, derogatory thrusts—Stella spent much of her time reading. She read voluminously, read indiscriminately and without taste, every new popular novel to appear in the public library, every new romance she could lay hands on (in fact, he once, in heat, went looking for her in the library, to bring her home). So curious that she never developed taste. And musically—she had only to listen for a few seconds to any popular dance band on the radio, and she could identify it. Something wrong, something denigrated, something stunted. *And his prey!* Blond, round *zaftig* Stella, his prey, his peremptory, his summary lay. No hesitation here, no Edith, no subtle banter, no forlorn eyes perched on his fly, no friendship. For a minute, while she stood next to her chaffering, flighty sister, he burned, burned. But hell, there was no chance. And he *had* to finish his term paper. Maybe he ought to pull off, go into the bathroom and get it over with. No. Burn, you bastard. Keep on typing till you're done. Fortunately, Stella kept her distance in the doorway, and only Hannah skipped into the office to pry into what her cousin was engaged in doing. "What are quotas?" she exclaimed. "Why aren't you writing another story?"

"Bye-bye, chatterbox. Yes, that's what I'm writing about for college. Quotas, immigrants, workers, greenhorns. I'm working on my college term paper." He dismissed her with a supercilious wave of the hand.

"Collegiate, collegiate." Hannah exited, snapping her fingers, while her sister laughed her vapid laugh. "Yes, we are collegiate. Nothing intermedgiate. No, sir!" Trailing song, they went down the hall, leaving him to himself, to forget himself in his typing.

Three times he had to retype pages, or parts of pages, twice because his interlardings and his crossings out—X'ings out—of words were so numerous as to seem like a rank growth on the page, and once because his digression from his penciled guide left him at the end without feasible return; it had to be abandoned, and a fresh start faithful to the original made. At length he was done. He would look at it again before class, give the typescript a last inspection before handing it in. He got up, aware of a slight cramp in the region of the abdomen, broke wind, tapped the ashes of his pipe into the cracked soup plate Mamie had brought him for an ashtray, turned off the ceiling light, and walked through the long hall to the kitchen. The kitchen was this side of the sconce-lit front room. All the other rooms, the bedrooms of the apartment, opened on the hall, except two, one of which, Mamie and Jonah's bedroom, opened off the kitchen, and the other, Stella's bedroom, opened off the front room the same way. He felt played out, depleted. He didn't think, even if the chance were presented to him on a silver platter, he could work up enough interest in a sexual go-round with Stella. Uppermost in his awareness was the feeling of being spent; his very breathing, chest heaving, seemed jaded. All he wanted to do was thank Mamie, say goodbye to Zaida, and beat it for home. He wasn't even hungry, though he was sure once he traipsed the eight or ten blocks from Mamie's to his house he'd do justice to anything Mom set in front of him. Odd: he had been struck by the accidental mistyping of the word "stud" when he meant to type the word "study," and its meaning as applied to the vertical two-by-fours between which water pipes were installed in a wood-frame dwelling. Stud, with its further, its associate meaning pertaining to virility, to breeding, to sex, all suddenly dispersed by the simple correction, the addition of the letter *y*. That was what it seemed to have done to him. Where was Zaida?

His little, bare, and cheerless bedroom, the next room after the office, was vacant. Where was Zaida?

A few steps farther along the hall, and Ira could guess: Zaida was behind the frosted, wire-reinforced window of the bathroom, illuminated when occupied. Ahead of Ira in the front room, he caught sight of Hannah and Stella executing the latest dance step—to the muted band music of the family's newly acquired Superheterodyne console radio. In the darkened bedroom at the rear of the lighted kitchen, he could hear a window close. Mamie came in, short, obese, broad almost as the bedroom doorway.

"Hollo, bhoy," she said affectionately. "*Noo*, have you prevailed?"

"Yeah, thanks, *Tanta*. I think so."

"And the machinkeh served you well?"

"Better than I served it. The mistakes I made, *gevald*!"

"It's the first time since I bought it secondhand from a *shikker* who came to the door—only the Founder of the universe knows where he plucked it—the first time that a collitch bhoy has used it for his collitch work. Who would have thought it would be so honored? Bills of fare were all that were written on it before. *Goyish* fare: puck chops, hem, such things. And now and then, something Jewish, but *treife*, you know, even if Jewish: *shav*, potato *lotkehs*, borscht."

"Yeah?"

"And when needed, an eviction notice, you understand. Stella writes out on the machine an eviction notice that I have to hand a Portorickie sometimes. *Ai*," she groaned. "Rarely, rarely. I don't like adding to a poor man's woes. But often to repay your pity, they'll play you a trick: they'll steal off in the dead of night with their belongings. *Noo*, saves taking them to court." She soaked a rag under the brass hot water faucet, wrung it out, and wiped the enamel front of the sink.

"Have you become acquainted with these Portorickies? Who ever heard of them before? A peculiar people." She turned to face Ira. "Sit down."

"Mamie, I just came to say goodbye, that's all. It's after eight. And thanks for the typewriter."

"And Zaida? Won't you bid him goodbye?"

"I meant to."

"Sit, sit. Every minute you spend talking to him is another *mitzva*."

Ira sat down—reluctantly. "But he's in the bathroom."

"A minute, just a minute more." She transferred the damp rag to the oilcloth-covered washtub lids, and bending her heavy, Slavic, sober face under mousy topknot, mopped the green-and-white-figured expanse. "What can you do for a man who no longer cares to live? His shoulders hurt. He can't see. His haunches ache. His feet pain. *Noo*—mine do too. Still, I run for him twice a day every day save

Shabbes, to fetch him fresh, crisp egg biscuits, and every morning fresh rolls, a half a quarter pound sweet butter. Nothing pleases. Nothing wins thanks. Neither my soup, my veal cutlets, my fricassee, my strudel. Neither dairy or *parveh,* nor flesh. What can you do?" She bunched the gray rag and left it at a corner of the washtub lid. Then she sat down, ponderously. "Ah!" she relished her relief with a loud sigh. "*Oy!* I'll tell you: his life soured too early. He was scarcely thirty when your mother, Leah, was already a child, Genya a girl too, I was an infant, and Ella was born—four daughters! *Gevald,* he foresaw a desperate future. Somehow he would have to make a fortune. The dowry alone, to defray that for so many daughters, *oy,* where does one find a panacea? It happened that he knew that they were going to hew down the count Tatevsky's forests on the mountainside nearby, among the Carpathians, for lumber. Morris, your uncle, worked there awhile."

"I know." Beguiled, Ira encouraged: "He told me once he lost his crayon that he marked the ends of logs with. So he slit his finger, and marked the ends with that."

"*Tockin,* that's Moishe." Mamie folded thick hands on her wadded belly. "'*Noo,*' Zaida thought, 'hah, the count will need huts for the woodcutters. And with what do you chink the cracks of a hut? With mortar made of lime.' His little *gesheft* would be the purveyor. With all his money, and some borrowed, he ordered three great dray-loads of lime—three, and *goyim* to cart them. Didn't the Almighty send down a deluge from the skies, that mired the wheels, a deluge that fell hour after hour after hour. And the lime, *freg nisht,* worth nought but a curse. He took to the Talmud after that. He would scarce tend the little store. 'Minkey, this,' he would call Baba, may she rest in peace to eternity, 'Minkey, that. The *goy* wants kerosene. The *shiksa* wants half a loaf of sugar.' And so it went. Do you know Baba once loved him dearly? But little by little his selfishness killed all her devotion."

"Yeah?"

Mamie pushed her snub nose upward with the heel of her hand. "It is indeed so. He'll be out in another minute."

"Who's there? Who's talking? That's not Zaida." Hannah's voice rose above the radio announcer's. "We keep hearing somebody." A moment later, she presented her carrot-topped lissome self in the kitchen doorway. "Oh, it's you. Our college cousin. You finished?"

Stella wasn't far behind. "Of course he's finished. Can't you see? Now he has to dance with Mama."

"Always serious. Always his mind is somewhere else. On something important, something high and intellectual," Hannah said with customary effrontery. "You typed and you typed and you typed. Now you can dance. Why don't you dance?"

"I don't dance."

"You don't wanna, or you can't?"

"Both."

"Come on, we'll teach you."

"I said both."

"Oh."

"You know what it is." Stella slid by her sister through the doorway. "He doesn't wanna, because he doesn't know how." She approached Ira, lifted a flirtatious shoulder. "And he doesn't know how because he doesn't wanna. He's too intellectual, he's a real college man."

"At least waltz," Hannah enticed. "It's such an easy step. Come on. We need a partner."

"That's right, a male partner." Stella leaned against him. "We always need a male partner because Zaida won't let us have one in the house. To him men can only dance with men. And women can only do the *chardash* at weddings, when there's a big crowd." She tittered, leaned against him more flagrantly, bearing down on his shoulder with musky heft. "If he sees you dancing with us, he can't say anything. We're first cousins." She straightened up brightly. "It's in the family."

"No!" Ira shied away.

"How can you be so selfish?" Hannah scolded. "Your own cousins. We'd be so thrilled. All you got to do is hold us in your arms." She gauchely mimicked: "Ah, you hear it? Listen, it's dreamy. Come on. Before Zaida comes out, one little glide around the front-room table."

"It's not fair." Stella nudged again, bold in the patent innocuous-ness of her seductive teasing. "Men can do all the picking when they want. And we girls have to wait. If we were both boys, and you were our girl cousin, you'd have to wait and then you'd find out." She bumped Ira again for good measure.

Greatly diverted, Mamie's girth shook at her daughters' antics. "Let him be, you're nothing but hoydens. He has more on his mind than dancing. He didn't come here to dance."

"No, he came here to typewrite a term paper—a college term paper," Hannah said with mocking asperity. "About quotas. A college man, no less."

"I better leave." Ira tilted away.

"Stop, girls," Mamie reprimanded. "He's waiting for Zaida. I don't know what's keeping him. Go, go back to the radio. And turn it down. I don't want any quarrel. Zaida is going to bed soon."

"Oh, him," the two sisters chimed together in resentful unison. "Everything is for him."

Then Stella solo: "If you think he's in the toilet long, you should be here on Friday, *erev Shabbes*. Till he bathes, till he cuts his nails, till he wraps up every toenail, God forbid the rats shouldn't eat it, you could *plotz*—"

"Do me a favor, daughter—both of you. Leave."

They departed sulkily for the front room.

"And turn the radio down," Mamie called after them. "Even if it doesn't run on batteries now, it's electricity, it costs. You hear?"

"Ye-e-s," came the grudging drawl.

Mamie sighed—and yawned. "The old man to cater to, my daughters to look after, to rear them in true Jewishness, a *glatt* kosher home to keep. And *two* apartment houses." Mamie held up a vee of two thick fingers. "My brother Saul with his evil temper. Thank God he's no longer my partner. He thought I had nothing to do but collect rent. If he ever calls me a sonofabitchekheh again, I'll spit in his face. So now I'm manager of the two houses for the bank. What more can I do than I am doing? Nothing. And rent I get free." She rested her heavy arms on the table. "The neighborhood is becoming Portorickie: one has to know how to deal with them, and I do. I treat them like human beings. What else are they? I'm not afraid to live here with Portorickies. Other Jews are afraid. They move out. Everyone warns me, my husband, Jonas, warns me: don't go in the back-yard from one house to the other to collect the rent. He read in *Der Tag* how they felled a landlady, and tore her rent receipts from her. *Noo,* the white *goyim,* those Irish, don't do that too? I'm not afraid."

"No?"

"I fear only one thing, I fear the Almighty."

"Yeah?"

"Only Him."

Her blunt expression of faith was moving, a faith long lost to Ira, but still capable of resonance: the new radio softly churned out some popular instrumental number, Charleston, Black Bottom, jazz, who knew? Stella was in there too, object of his remote, his academic dawdling, nothing more. He smirked at himself—and at Mamie, his obese aunt, too obese to cross her legs, a balloon of faith. It made a curious design, a pattern, woven together with sardonic woof, and ambivalent warp. And Zaida, the figure Ira had all but forgotten, in the bathroom off the hallway, in the bathroom, opening the door, at last—

"Here he comes," Mamie announced.

"Will he come in here?"

"No, he'll go into his bedroom. He must be in his underwear already."

"Then it's late," Ira demurred. "Isn't it?"

"Go bide with him a few minutes," Mamie pleaded. "His life is so bitter. He's purblind. And the little sight still remaining to him he'll soon hazard under the knife."

"All right." Ira arose to his feet, frowned in resolve.

"It's a *mitzva,* indeed, that you perform," Mamie urged. "His eldest grandson, and an educated one, to comfort him in his loneliness, in his last years."

"I don't know whether I can."

"You can, you can. Come back afterward, and say goodbye."

"I'll be back in a minute." Farewells to Mamie usually paid off, even though he was in the funds for the nonce, thanks to Edith, and the end of his summer job for the IRT. Ira made for the threshold. On the one hand, in the direction of the house door, he saw the harsh light from Zaida's bedroom streaming across the narrow hallway; on the other side he saw Stella in the front-room doorway, Stella reading a magazine at the large dining-room table, blond, cuddly, insipid quarry to his sudden onset of rut. He had never experienced that before, a kind of erotic second wind; he never had to wait that long, hadn't thought of the time spent here as waiting, until this moment. . . . Nothing doing anyway. They exchanged glances through the harangue of a saxophone and timpani. Remarkable, almost incredible, that at so young an age, she could act so completely apathetic, and was not; she could seem so completely unconcerned, and was not. Hell, he'd been all right till now, quiescent. He'd better try and stay that way. His weekend was used up, even if his weak end wasn't. He trudged toward his grandfather's bedroom.

In house slippers, baggy, mussed trousers, and long-sleeved underwear, black yarmulke on his gray head, his back to the doorway, Zaida was plumping up the heirloom pillows on the bed.

"I came to say good night, Zaida." Ira counterfeited mien of contrite deference. "I've hardly talked to you."

"Who is it?" Squat man in his waning sixties with a bulging paunch, and the gait and flaccid flanks of a man much older, Zaida swiveled his gray-bearded visage—and peered. True, Zaida had cataracts in both eyes, but confirmed hypochondriac that he was, he missed no chance of exaggerating his ailments. "Oh, Leah's son. Are you still here?"

"Yes. I was talking to Mamie."

"Your mother was here this afternoon."

"I know. She said goodbye to me when she left."

"*Noo,* come in and sit down."

"I'll only stay a minute. It's getting late. I'll be keeping you up."

"Then I'll sleep better for it. How are your studies in the college going?"

"About the same, Zaida. Not too wonderful." Ira wagged his head in humorous belittlement.

"Then you should try harder, even to your utmost," the old man counseled. "You owe your mother that bit of joy at least for the sacrifices she's made for you—and still must make, no?"

"I guess so," Ira replied.

"What?"

"You're right, Zaida. It was just that first year that was hard, getting used to college. Now that I'm nearly a senior, as they call it in English—"

"What bliss will alight on my poor Leah when she sees you finished with your studies. How much longer do you have to go?"

"Another year. I hope no longer than that. I'm finishing summer school to make up credits. I won't have enough of what they call credits to graduate this next summer."

"I hope so too." Zaida apparently caught the lack of enthusiasm in his grandson's tone of voice. "It's time you thought of her, no? How many years still have to pass before you begin earning money and begin to lighten her poverty? How many have already passed? My afflicted Leah, with her chronic catarrh and her sorrows, and her lunatic husband." Zaida rocked back and forth a little, as if *davening*. "Woe is her. May the Almighty take pity on her—and on me, no? That I have to behold my daughter enduring such suffering? On me as well, on me, believe me, with my cares and my plagues, my shoulder joints and my hips, all racked—and my eyes, it goes without saying. And soon to be imprisoned in bed: they say with a bag of sand on each side of my beard. *Oy, vey, oy, vey.* Each day brings a new ague, a new grief, and no one to abide it but myself." He indicated the direction of the front room. "Dancing and springing, *that* they know—to that ugly music. It's called music. When they play it loud, a terror smites me, as if savages were at large. And these I have for granddaughters."

"I'm sorry, Zaida. I don't like that kind of music either. It's called jazz. What can you do? That's today."

"What? I don't know?" Zaida reproved. "May it be destroyed, as it destroys me. What it makes of Jewish children, and of Jewish girls." He nodded significantly. "If this is today, tell me, what need of a tomorrow?"

They were both silent, Ira in his straight-backed chair, the only spare one in the small bedroom, Zaida in his high armchair next to the rectangular black table. Brass studs about the tall horsehide headrest framed his discontented, humorless features, those visible between yarmulke and beard: brown eyes oppressed, lips between tobacco-yellowed mustache and beard downturned and cheerless.

He sighed often, his broad paunch straining the pearly buttons of his dingy underwear. He pitied himself so ostentatiously, Ira continually felt torn between compassion and exasperation. Protocol required about five minutes of restive, stereotyped commiseration, and then he'd be off. No use spending any more time than that in giving plausibility to deference.

"You care to smoke a cigarette?" Zaida picked up the square blue box of Melachrinos. He held up the box rather than out, unopened and close to himself.

"No, thanks, Zaida." Ira brought out his pipe. It would be a crime to deprive his grandfather of his budgeted and hoarded butts.

Zaida found a cigarette stub on the ashtray, struck a match and lit the charred end, then felt about for the quill-and-paper cigarette holder. He fitted the stained tip of the butt into the scorched holder. "It's not good, it's not good, that's all."

"No?"

"I tell you we live in botched times. Botched, ruined. Fit for burial, no more."

"But if you're Jewish, you're not supposed to look at life that way." Ira tried tilting with the weak lance of his own skimpy lore. "Aren't you? A Jew is supposed to have faith in life."

"Faith in the Almighty who gave him life. That I have, blessed be His holy name. But if the mill won't turn, the millers quarrel. I'm not speaking of my life alone."

"No?"

"No. Though I pray it would please the Founder of the universe to gather me unto Himself. I mean the lives of Jews everywhere in the world. Immeasurable the menace that hangs over them, the woe in store for them. Except here in America, where we are tolerated— barely, but tolerated. In a small compass. Didn't my son Moishe tell me that when he first came to America, he applied for work in a company that makes these *betterien* for automobiles? 'You're strong and I like you. I can tell you'd be a good worker,' the owner said to him. 'You don't look Jewish either. But I can't hire you. There would be turmoil in the shop.' So Moishe told me. And *noo*: his officer after the Great War urged him to stay. 'You've learned how to command, and your men trust you.' *Noo.*" Zaida puffed frugally on his cigarette.

HENRY ROTH

"Why are we tolerated today? Why was Moishe raised in the ranks, and given those stripes to wear on his shirtsleeves when he was in the military? Because true piety is ignored, because Orthodox observance is ignored—one in a thousand is observant. My own sons—the very ones who support me—pay for my room and board in a kosher home—which of them dons phylacteries in the morning, which eschews work on *Shabbes*? None. *Noo*. I have to live, and live off their earnings. Do as you see fit, I say. What else can I say? A pious existence is for you to choose. Or not to choose. So at the expense of observance, they go unmolested, here in the Golden Land. They barter holy living for livelihood. *Noo*. I can see the day when the Jews will be hounded, sooner than later. Mark me. Soon they will not be permitted to earn a livelihood at all. I've seen it before: open Jew-baiting increases from day to day. And in Russia, no? They don't hate Jews? It doesn't matter whether observant or not, Jews they loathe."

"I don't think so, Zaida, from what I've read. Jews are treated as equals in Russia."

"Go, don't delude yourself. Why is Trotsky running to escape from Russia? From whom is he running? He's running from the Russian *goy*, the *khlop*? What is Stalin but a *khlop*? You can see it in his face. And a *khlop* is a pogromist. He was for centuries a pogromist, a *khlop* under the Romanovs, under the czars. So he'll be for God knows how long a *khlop* under the Bolsheviks. Why have they expelled a Jew from his high post in Russia, one that he shared once with Lenin? Heed me, were he a *goy*, it would be a different story."

"You think so?"

"I know. And I know you won't believe. The Jew is hated with a bestial hatred the wide world over."

"Well, what do you do about it?"

"Do? You pray to God. May He send us aid. As the Jews in Russia when the czar oppressed them prayed that the next czar would be more merciful. Was he? He wasn't. We pray that a new day will bring relief." His cigarette holder had begun to reek with the proximity of the burning tobacco ember.

"Zaida, the end of your cigarette holder."

He dislodged the butt, poked at the live end with a house key. "I won't cite Talmud since you believe in nothing of *Yiddishkeit*."

"I do, Zaida. Some of it."

"It seemed to me, when we first came to America, that you were truly growing up in Jewishness. A child, I thought, blessed by the Almighty, my firstborn grandchild goes with me to the synagogue on *Shabbes*, on *Shabbes* at night as well, for the *Havdalah*."

"*Shabbes* at night, oh, sure," Ira humorously parried his grandfather's censure. "They used to have a little spread in the synagogue at the end of *Shabbes*: black olives and wine, brandy, fresh rye bread."

"*Noo?*" Undiverted, the old man pushed his yarmulke back over grizzled gray hair. "They still do."

"I don't want to hurt your feelings, Zaida, but if I'm not the Jew I might have been, it's because we left the East Side when you came to America. You know why: my mother wanted to be near you and Baba."

"*Azoy?*" Zaida's tone sharpened. "Because we came to America you're not a Jew—and your father didn't have crazy ideas of becoming an independent milkman?"

"I didn't mean that was the only reason," Ira hastened to palliate.

"Live among the *goyim* because he thought he would be closer to the railroad where the milk came into the city. Because you were living among *goyim*, you should have been more a Jew than before. Here was I, in this Harlem too. We could have expounded all of Talmud together."

"It didn't work that way. Here was Harlem. Yes. But here were the Irish—here were the other *goyim*: the Italians. They were in the street, and where else did I have to go?"

Zaida was becoming aroused. "Is it my fault? That my poor daughter has such a lunatic for a husband—I shouldn't tell you that. He's your father—"

"Oh, I know."

"He could have lived in Jewish Harlem, like the rest of us. But instead he wedges himself on 119th Street, to save a dollar or two in rent. Live among the *goyim* at twelve dollars a month. Here on 112th Street still are Jews: 114th Street, 115th Street, 116th Street. He failed as a milkman. He becomes a busboy, thanks to Moishe. He learns to be a waiter. So don't be a lunatic; show the proprietor of the restaurant the respect due the owner. No, he has to be Chaim—look at Chaim askance, and he's enraged. Mamie lived across the street from us on 115th Street, and we came here from Galitzia, and from a cap-maker Jonas became a ladies' tailor, steady, quiet, decent. They lived among Jews. Do I dare go into your street, a Jew with a beard? That's where he crawled to—119th Street, to live with Esau, and he dragged my poor daughter with him. Woe is me."

"Well, we lived here too, on 114th Street east of Park Avenue when you came to America, Zaida. 114th Street. A Jewish neighbor-hood. But Mom didn't like living in the back. No window on the street. It was too much like Veljish, she said. So it wasn't his fault alone—even though I know he's a *mishugeneh*," Ira conceded.

"It fares well with me," said Zaida. Contemplation accented the distress in his eyes and lips. "*Sis mir git*. Let God be my judge, how ill I fare."

Unhappy and irreconcilable, they were silent again, in a silence coated like a pill by soft, cloying dance-band music that drifted through the long hallway. Should he leave; had he paid his respects sufficiently? Queer, how one had to estimate the just duration of a forced protocol. Or was all protocol forced? Another minute should do it. Then stand up and say goodbye. His eyes ranged about the room: bare and cheerless bedroom. Not dingy, the light beige walls looked recently painted—Mamie had probably had them painted over the summer for the New Year. Not dingy, no, but cheerless, with only a complimentary calendar from the Harlem Savings & Loan Bank hanging from a brad on the door of the closet. Calendar on the wall and mezuzah on the doorframe. What else did the reverent Or-thodox Jew require? It was as if decor were consigned—or con-fined—to the mind alone—decor of justice, of righteousness, decor of divine sublimity, without a single tangible attribute. It seemed im-possible of realization now, but he had known it long ago, when he was eight years old, and attended *cheder* on the lost and irrevocable—and unwanted—East Side. Decor of the invisible—well, no, not en-tirely: hanging from a hook on the other side of the closet door was the lambent sapphire-blue velvet bag containing Zaida's prayer shawl and phylacteries. Ella's work, no doubt, Mom's fourth-oldest sister, placid, painstaking Ella of "the blessed hands." It was she who had embroidered in gold thread the two lions rampant either side of the Tablets of the Law. Lions of Judah, they shone within the shadow of the closet, as if the gold thread of the design were informed with its own light.

"What is there to say? I am like one besieged. I am like one beset on every side," Zaida finally said. "I have only the Almighty to turn to, blessed be He."

"I'm sorry, Zaida." Again he had expressed his commiseration in English, and again corrected himself. There—now all he had to do was to wish his grandfather's pending cataract operation a success: *"Zol gehen mit mazel,* Zaida," Ira said on the point of arising—he had fulfilled his obligation.

"Do you know who I am like?" Zaida asked. "I often think I am like that bishop among the Christians, that Augustinus."

"Who?"

"That saint among them: Augustinus."

"Oh, Saint Augustine."

"Is that how you name him?"

"Yeah. Saint Augustine in English." The fact that his grandfather had said *Christlikher,* instead of *goy,* indicated respect. "You know about Saint Augustine?" Ira lingered.

"Noo, vus den? I don't read? While I could. I don't know?"

"You do?" It was already late on Sunday evening, almost nine-thirty, on Zaida's open gold watch on the table. Terminate as fast as he could, Ira told himself. "Yes?" He began adjusting his jacket.

"His city was besieged by the barbarians, the Goths, the Vandals, the Teutonim," Zaida hebraized.

"The Teutonim." Ira itched, scratched. What was it Eliot said in his notes on *The Waste Land?* "To Carthage then I came . . . unholy loves sang all about mine ears—" "I think he was supposed to be black, an African."

"Black, white. Whatever he was. After weeks passed, and the barbarians were still outside the walls, he prayed the Almighty to end the siege. Or to end him."

"Him?"

"Augustinus."

Ira got to his feet. "I ought to say goodbye to Mamie, Zaida. It's getting late."

"Well, go in good health."

"Thanks."

"And greet your mother for me."

"I will. I hope you see better after the operation, Zaida."

Zaida nodded—with invincible skepticism.

Ira took a last look at the tranquil blue phylactery bag. Boy, those gold lions rampant, they reared up around the Tablets of the Law, shining. He paused in the doorway. "And I hope the siege lifts a little for you too, Zaida," trying to instill a little humor into the parting.

The old man smiled at last: "What are you saying?"

"I meant I hope that things get a little easier, Zaida."

"*Oy, vey, vey.* You're still a child. Can the siege of existence ever be lifted? How? Never. Wish me what happened to Augustinus: that the Almighty would do as well by me as He did by him."

"Why?"

Zaida laughed—shortly, but for the first time. "You don't know?"

"No." Ira felt slightly annoyed to have Zaida laughing at him, and about a gentile subject too. "What happened?"

"What happened was that Augustinus never lived to see the Teutonim, the Vandals, sack the city. That's what happened. He never saw the havoc they wrought. You can imagine what wild barbarians are capable of: the cruelty, the slaughter, the violations, the atrocities. None of that he lived to see. What a blessing. Would the Lord favor me likewise."

Frowning, Ira tried to separate chagrin from confusion. "Is that what you meant?"

"What else?"

"Good night, Zaida."

II

Cryptic. . . . His grandfather's laugh echoed in Ira's mind, as he walked past the now darkened bathroom door toward the lighted kitchen and front room. Did they or didn't they lift the siege? Enigmatic. Wonder where the old boy gleaned that bit of ancient history? Probably from *Der Tag*. Didn't the old guy want to die, though. Maybe that was the answer.

Apothanein thelo. Ah, how I understand today, Ecclesias.

His mind reverted to *The Waste Land* again. Funny—he smirked—a barrel of unholy loves buzzing about my ears: too late, though, for him to have a chance at Stella. And for Christ's sake, he adjured himself: make it snappy. Bid Mamie "adJew" and be off, whether she rewarded him this evening with a buck or not. Stella was no longer in sight, and the radio was turned down to a barely audible floss of dance band as Ira entered the kitchen.

"Good night, Mamie. I gotta go."

"Come in. Another minute won't hurt."

"Oh, no. I've been here long enough."

"Come in. Sit."

"I've *been* sitting."

"Come in. Sit."

Ira came into the kitchen, dropped into a chair.

"*Noo*, was he complaining?" Mamie asked.

"Zaida? Well, he's an old man."

"He isn't so old. Baba of beloved memory used to say that every part of her husband Ben Zion's body failed him early, save one."

"Did she?" Ira couldn't resist a grin.

"After the disaster with the lime, he suddenly grew listless. 'I'm wearying of watching the stones grow in Veljish,' he would say. But appetite he had—the best was saved for him—and when it came to meting out punishment, blows he could deal out not a few. I sometimes think Leah married a man just like her father."

Ira shook his head.

"'The stones, only the stones thrive in Veljish,' he would say. 'Only stones prosper here.'"

"Yeah?" A hamlet he may himself have seen in earliest infancy, before he was three, Ira reflected: all the sights and sounds the toddler's wondering eyes absorbed, absorbed from the vantage of his stout young mother's arms. The Galitzianer hamlet of Mom's girlhood, with its village anomie and stagnation, of which she had given him so many intimations, must have weighed down the young spirit to intolerable melancholy. Little wonder she inveighed against living in "the back" of a tenement.

"Did Zaida ever go to a doctor for his disorder?" Ira said soberly. "You know, they have a name for it in English. Did he ever go to a doctor?"

"A doctor?" Mamie scouted. "In Veljish they called a doctor when you were dying. That's when you saw a doctor, and that's when you saw an orange."

"Neurasthenia," Ira suddenly recalled. "That's the name in English."

"Don't give it fancy names." Stella's voice preceded her. She had apparently overheard, and was coming from front room to kitchen. "New rasthenia, old rasthenia. Believe me, you don't have to go to college and use fancy words for him. I can tell you in plain English." In buff dress, always with that bland misleading unconcern, she leaned against the doorpost.

"Yeah?"

"Yeah, you wanna know?"

Jesus Christ. He felt like shutting his eyes. Get your ass out of here, and go home. You don't stand a chance. What was he waiting for? His shoes scraped the linoleum as he abruptly shifted his legs. Don't give yourself away. The little *knish*, the little twat, knew he was beginning to smolder, and she basked in his heat at a discreet distance from the—yes, the skewer. Helter-skelter libido swirled the associations about: associations with just the right prefix. His behavior had to be more than noncommittal; he had to overcompensate. A grim appearance was the only one he could rely on. "'Neurasthenia' isn't a fancy word," he said severely. "That's the word for Zaida's condition."

"That old guy?" Stella scoffed. "He likes the misery, that's all."

"Daughter dear, you know what? You're turning into an anti-Semite," Mamie reproved—but without conviction.

"Of course he likes his misery," Stella reiterated. "Ira, listen, if you're sick, and you tell everybody about it, doesn't it mean you like your misery?"

"Well. I don't know . . ."

"My daughter," said Mamie. "May no harm ever come to you, and enjoy a thousand blessings, but sympathy for another person you never had."

Stella was not to be put off so easily. "Look, Ira, your uncle Gabe, your father's brother, came here from St. Louis. When did he see Zaida before? Never. Maybe in Galitzia. Maybe. So what's the first thing Zaida begins to tell him? How mean his granddaughters are, with their radio and their dancing and springing, how lousy they make him feel, Jewish girls, and how rotten life is. Now if you talk like that right away to strangers, it must mean you like it."

"Go, you have no heart," Mamie rebuked. "Go back to your moving-picture megglezine that you're reading." She sighed—like a great bale of something, kind, obese woman. "Comes an old Jew to the door, an old Jew with a beard and a *pishkeh,* collecting money for the yeshivas or the poor in Eretz Yisroel. She gives him a penny, one penny."

"I gave him a penny, and that's enough, but *she* gave him a dime. Why? Because he's got whiskers."

"A fortunate thing your grandfather is in bed in his bedroom," said Mamie. "Go back to the front room, Stella, and let us be. It will soon be your bedtime."

"That's right," Ira said, and stood up—as Stella left the kitchen.

"Sit! Sıt!" Mamie's vehemence halted him. "I hardly have a chance to talk to you. We've been interrupted at every turn. One minute more. Be a good child."

"One minute." Ira dropped back in his chair.

"I have such good *verenekehs;* they smack of paradise," she cajoled. "Before you go, eat some. Tell me if they're not the best *verenekehs*—the best *pirogen* you ever tasted."

"Oh, is that why you want me to stay?"

"Well, isn't that a good reason?"

"That's what I thought. It so happens that I'm hungry."

"And that's what *I* thought," Mamie said, triumphantly tapping her large bosom.

"God, why do you have to tempt me, Mamie. I'm going home. Mom'll give me some supper."

"*Nein. Nein.* I have a whole potful of *verenekehs*, more than twice what Jonas and I will eat when he comes home. They didn't please the old man. The children avoid them, makes them fat. Why should they go into the garbage?" Mamie moved quickly for so heavy a woman; she was at the stove in an instant, wooden ladle in hand, stirring the white enamel pot on the stove lid that she used for a simmerer over the low gas flame. "A few. They won't harm you, believe me." She began the transfer of *pirogen* from pot to platter. "You'll still have a bit of appetite when you get home."

"I won't need it."

"You'll see. Appetite comes with eating."

"That's enough, Mamie! Gee, that's my weakness. You're a pasta masta too," he said ruefully.

"A what?" She brought the plate of gently steaming *pirogen* to the table and provided him with a fork. "What means a 'pasta masta'? Wait, I'll bring you bread."

"Oh, no! Not bread too."

"And a little sour cream. I have good heavy sour cream I bought this morning on Park Avenue."

"No—oh, all right," he capitulated. "Thanks, *Tanta.* Boy! That's enough sour cream." What a transmogrification took place when humble mashed potatoes were laced with sautéed onions, then clad in a jacket of boiled dough and drowned under sour cream.

"You are hungry. You swallow them whole."

"I'll say. Jewish oysters. What time does Jonas come home?"

"Another two hours. Twelve o'clock, sometimes a little earlier. It depends on the train from Jamaica after he leaves the cafeteria. And sometimes on my brother Harry too, how promptly he gets to the store to relieve Joe. Are they good?"

"Are they good!"

"More?"

"No, no, no! Well, maybe a couple more."

"Aha." Mamie spooned out half a dozen. "I told you: appetite comes with eating."

"And I thought it went!" he guffawed with zany mirth. "Ooh, if I'm not a goner!" Ira assailed the fresh batch with a gusto that made the *pirogen* seem to blench.

"You should know that with my poor husband I had to move heaven and earth," Mamie said as she rested the pot on the simmerer, "until I got my fine brothers to take him in for a partner. 'A cap maker, a tailor,' was their cry—Jonas was a good ladies' tailor too—'what has that got to do with the restaurant business? How can the one go together with the other?' So they said."

"How will they suit?" Delectable, the warm, slippery Jewish *pirogen*, lubricated by sour cream, and skidding down his gullet on an English pun. "Aah!"

"What?"

"A match," he chortled.

"A match," Mamie repeated, puzzled. "You know, they're dairy. You can stay and sit a little longer. Have some coffee with milk afterward, keep me company awhile."

"No, thanks, *Tanta*. Please!"

"I know why they didn't want him in the cafeteria. Jonas is not very imposing. Jonas is little. He is short. So? He can't hold his own at the cash register? If it weren't that Zaida intervened—'you must take your brother-in-law in as a partner'—I would be bickering with them still."

"Go ahead. Why does Jonas have to eat at home? He's got a whole cafeteria to get his meals in—to get his supper."

"Is it kosher?" Mamie tacked question to question.

"Oh."

"They said how will a cap maker, a tailor, be of use in a restaurant, how will he—"

"Fare?" Ira giggled.

"What?"

"Never mind. Just joking. Bill of fare."

"So I said, how did Harry become a *makher* in a restaurant? He was a furrier's apprentice. How did Max do it? He was a sign painter. He was a glove maker—"

"And my father." Ira tried to slow down his rate of consumption out of courtesy to the dwindling remnant. "My father came right from driving a wet-wash wagon, after he stopped being a milkman, and in no time at all, he was a waiter."

"Indeed, after he broke the mirror in Krug and Zinn's vegetarian restaurant with a water pitcher, he would no longer hear of being a busboy," Mamie nodded.

"Yes, I heard about that. He got his diploma."

"He's a madman," Mamie dismissed Pop. "But speaking about my brothers again, to me they wouldn't listen. It was not till Zaida ordered them—ordered them to take Jonas in for a partner into the business, that they did. You hear?"

"I hear." Ira speared the penultimate *pirogen* on the right. "Boy!" he complimented his aunt again. "*Verenekehs* like these are fit for the thirty-six Righteous—what'd Zaida call 'em?—*Tzaddikim?* For whose sake God spares the world."

"Better than your *goyish* macaronkahs, no?"

"Oh, much."

"A few more," Mamie wheedled. "*Nokh a bisseleh, nokh a shisseleh,*" she rhymed.

"A tureen, you mean, I'll fall away to a ton," Ira said in English.

"Such a small appetite you have."

"Ho. Ho. No, I learned my lesson. Mamie, I really have to be going. It's getting very late."

"You eat and run?" Mamie reproached.

"Eat and run. It's ten o'clock."

"Hear only this last thing. You're a learned youth. Perhaps you can give me a *khokhma.*"

"Me?" Ira dropped back into his seat. "I couldn't give you chicken *shmaltz.*"

"Go, I know better. Hear me a minute. I'll tell you." She wagged her tuberous finger at him. "With Zaida, a pious Jew, and my two American daughters, how shall I reconcile them? It's a difficult thing to do, no? You understand?"

"I should think so."

"I'm glad you understand." Mamie took the plate away, immediately began washing it. Rinsed, she set it on the drainboard, went to the stove, lowered the gas flame still lower, to a bare fringe under the simmer baffle. Then she came to the table and plopped down into a chair.

"To please both them and him is impossible. What they crave, he opposes. 'Father,' I plead, 'it's America, it's not Galitzia.' How did I meet my husband, Jonas? Through a marriage broker and photographs as in the old days? I met him in the same loft building on Delancey Street where we worked together. I worked at a sewing machine. In the shop next door he sewed the visors on caps. Both of us greenhorns. We ate lunch together. We joked together. We told stories of our Galitzianer hamlets. Then he asked me to go with him to a Yiddish theater on Second Avenue on Saturday night. I don't know: maybe Tomashevsky was the leading actor. Who can remember? And so, little by little, we became acquainted; then we became engaged. 'A girl has to win her own suitor in America, Father,' I said to him. 'But she can remain a good Jewish maiden, for all that,' he said. 'No, but your daughters are *hulladrigas,* both of them,' he said: 'Plain wantons. You at least had to go to work,' he said to me. I said, 'To toil as I did in a sweatshop all day over a sewing machine I won't send them.'"

"Mamie, I really have to go."

"Another minute and I'll explain. Why did I buy a new radio? Cost me a full whole hundred dollars, that they're listening to this minute—and that the old man loathes the sound of. To hear Rabbi Wise on *The Jewish Hour?* No, I bought it so that the two girls could entice youth into the house, young men, swains, you know, to learn how to deport themselves with boys, with young men. The time isn't far off when they'll have to think of suitors, no? One is seventeen, the other has turned fourteen. So what do you think he did?"

"I can just guess," Ira said laconically, and got his feet under him.

"Hear!" Mamie preempted. "He comes rushing into the front room, yarmulke in his hand—in his *gotchkis,* mind you, without trousers—flailing and shouting: 'Out, *trombinyiks,* out, scamps, out, wastrels!' Good Jewish boys. It vexed me so. Here I am, right here in the house when they're here. What harm can they do?"

"That's right," Ira said reassuringly, as he stood up.

"Well, ready to go to bed?" Mamie asked.

"Me?" Confused a moment by his aunt's deflected gaze, Ira looked over his shoulder. "Oh."

It was Hannah. Posing in twiggy sulkiness, rusty-haired, skinny-shanked, she slouched in the doorway. "I'm so bo-o-red," she said.

Shreds, transient husks winnowed from desire: not for Hannah, though. How the chaff swirled up between the time Mamie said, "Ready to go to bed?" and he turned his head expecting to see Stella in the doorway. What would it be like, with a whole night to spend pumping her . . . in a bed—whole nights? Whole days, to have her at his beck and call, every time he had a hard-on. Why not resign himself to being a shlump, a ne'er-do-well, with his witless piece of ass, and let Mamie and Jonas support him, while he did what? Read, mope, moon, speculate—and screw his onetime kid cousin as the swift seasons rolled. Never mind the stately mansions. Just be what he always was, except for a ready, steady, statutory lay. At least it was more tenable than belated fantasies with Minnie, impossible, murderous fantasies, though this was too: what would his family say? To hell with them. Or his college friends? Edith? Nah, unthinkable—then why did he think about it? Just scrub it from your mind, if you've got a mind. And what the hell good would it do you to satisfy what you wanted now? None. All you wanted was about thirty seconds alone. Thirty seconds. A thirty-second lost cause. Stella in the front room knew it was a lost cause too, undoubtedly she knew it. It would have to be a mackerel, said the Jewish *yenta*, when she meant to say "miracle," for him to get a chance to exercise his cod unimpeded and legally. He interrupted the exchange already taking place between Mamie and Hannah with an absent: "I guess it's time I went to bed too." Which passed unnoticed.

"Go to bed, go to bed!" Hannah squirmed at her mother in quirky indignation. "That's an answer to a maiden's prayer? What am I gonna do in bed? Sleep?"

"What else? You should listen to the old man." Mamie indicated the hallway. "You would know what a broken sleep means. He groans and he moans and he bewails his unhappy lot. Even in sleep he haggles with the Almighty. Like a Lubavitcher."

"I'm not an old man!" Hannah retorted. "I'm a young girl. And a girl should have dates. She should have something to look forward to. Dances. A nice party."

"Live. Only live," Mamie rejoined. "You'll have dates. You'll have parties without measure. You hear, Ira? A Jewish girl, little more than fourteen, she has to have dates, she has to go to parties."

"Why not?" Hannah countered. "Christian girls have dates, even when they're twelve. Isabella Martinez upstairs has dates. She goes to parties, lots of parties, in fancy white dresses her mother buys on 125th Street. She doesn't have to live, live, she's living already. Only Jewish girls have to live, live—till a *khusin* comes along. I wish I was a Puerto Rican!"

"God forbid! Go to bed!"

"Go to bed! I want to be a bridesmaid!"

"Again? I said no!"

"You don't have to buy me anything. No white dress. I have a pink dress already."

"I don't care whether it's a white dress or a pink dress. It's a *goyish* wedding."

"Oh, such *goyim* as they are," Hannah disparaged.

"I don't care. Catholics they are. If the old man heard a whisper of it, he'd take his stick to you. And your father—he'd box both your ears."

"They don't have to know. It's nothing, Mama. It's fun. Puerto Ricans are so happy. They sing and they dance and they play the piano and they play the guitar. They have such nice parties. Isabella wants me to be a bridesmaid with her for her older sister—oh, Mama please."

"Her older sister is only a little pregnant." Stella bulked behind her sylphlike sister. "You hear, Ira, whenever they get married, the bride is only a little pregnant."

"Oh, shut up. So she's a little pregnant. I'm only going to be a bridesmaid. You—" Hannah turned angrily on her sister. "Give me back my *Silver Screen*!" She tore the magazine from Stella's hand.

"*Oy, gevald!*" Mamie lamented. "Go to bed! Both of you! Go bathe, go wash. Leave me alone!"

"Say I can go. Please, Mama. It's in a week next Sunday. I have to tell Isabella. She's maid of honor. You liked fun yourself when you were a girl." Hannah was close to tears.

"Go! Stop tormenting me. You wish to mingle with *goyim*, with Portorickies—go! May it not be as Zaida says: little by little—"

"It won't be, Mama. Just this once, I'm going to be a bridesmaid. I'm going to carry a bunch of pretty flowers through the aisle—"

"*Noo, noo*, carry pretty flowers, but let me be. Only beware," Mamie's thick arm swayed menacingly. "Breathe the least word to your father—"

"I? Never! Oh, Mama, I can go? Oh, Mama, thanks. You'll see nothing will happen. I'll still be Jewish." Hannah kissed her mother's cheek, pirouetted. "I'll tell Isabella tomorrow. I'm so happy! I'll take my pink dress to the dry cleaner's. Oh, I'm going to be a bridesmaid!" She stood erect, ruddily radiant.

"Be a bridesmaid." Mamie's reluctance clear.

"Today a bridesmaid, tomorrow a bride," Stella said unpleasantly. "Maybe you'll be a little pregnant too."

"Maybe *you'll* be a little pregnant." Hannah fired back. "Just because they don't ask you, you're jealous."

"I don't have to wear three pairs of stockings on my skinny legs."

"Shut up!"

"Hush! Both of you! You'll wake him up!" Mamie raised her voice. "And then you know what will happen, don't you? A doom. Go wash, go bathe, go to bed!"

"Go wash," Stella ordered Hannah. "I have to bathe after everybody else," she informed Ira testily.

"Is that so?"

"Of course. After Zaida, I take his ring off the tub. And after she washes, because she's younger—"

"*Oy,*" Mamie prolonged her yawn. "Were you as tired as I am you would have gone to bed long ago, washed, unwashed, bathed, unbathed. *Ai, gevald.*"

The skinny and the rotund. The skinny red-poll, the chubby blonde. The one slipping by the other out into the hall. Well, a lost cause, to be sure, but now that her sister no longer blocked his view, there she was, in a vision once he saw, fair, short-throated damsel without a dulcimer, bare-legged in baby-blue house slippers with pom-poms, Goldilocks with glisten of goldy hair on her calves. So beheld her he, delectable nigh-tubby she, nubile firkin of seventeen.

He'd better get the hell out of here. But lingered instead, welded to the spot. That was how lost causes were won, but what they did to you, winning, you were better off with them lost.

"Tell me, Stella, what have I denied you?" Mamie chided wearily. "What have I denied you that you pout at everything?"

"Because that's the only way I can get anything," Stella rejoined. "I have to yell to get anything. If I don't yell I don't get anything."

"*Azoy*? Pretty spectacle you made of yourself. You hear, Ira?"

"What?" Pretext to stall, this one of being caught in the middle, not that his guile would do any good, but—

"Big as she is," said Mamie, "she threw herself on the kitchen floor, and lay there kicking up her heels, until I consented to buy her a new gray coat that she saw in the window on 14th Street. A grown-up maid having a tantrum like that. Wasn't that shameful?"

"Did you?" Ira asked judiciously.

"Of course I did. Why shouldn't I? I went into the store after I got out of business school. It's on Union Square. So I went into Klein's, and I fitted on the coat. It was perfect, Ira, it was just perfect. So why shouldn't I get it?"

"Not whether I can afford it or not," Mamie demanded.

"You can afford it. You can afford it. You don't pay rent. You take care of two houses—and you let Papa and Hannah go to the mountains every summer—"

"You know why I send Hannah along: Jonas should behave himself. He likes to chuck the girls under their chins, and give them a little pinch and a caress—"

"Anyway, you send her to the mountains."

"And she doesn't like to go. I'm telling you. The chairs in the train scratch her legs. She has tender skin. And she doesn't like walking on the roads there in the mountains, with cow *dreck* to step in. Ask her."

"I don't want to ask her."

Stella advanced into the kitchen. "You know what it is, Ira? Mama says I pout. You know what the real reason is: she won't let me be what I want, she won't let me go to school to learn what I want—"

"No!" Mamie exclaimed. And then added immediately: "Shah! The old man, he's gone to bed."

"You see?"

"What is it you want?" Ira shifted patiently from one leg to the other.

"I want to be a manicurist."

"Never!" said Mamie. "You know what a manicurist becomes?"

"Ira," Stella turned to him as toward final appeal. "Does a manicurist have to become a you-know-what?"

"I don't think so." Ira had never been there at an hour as late as this. Ten o'clock already—past ten—Jesus, this was funny—if it wasn't so combustible—what the hell did they do in Spain during the Inquisition? He was burning at the stake, his stake. Jonas would be coming home in a couple of hours, and that hemmed him between limits.

"Stella, let him go," Mamie commiserated. "The poor youth is worn out. *Noo,* go, go," she urged compassionately. "I don't want your mother angry with me."

"You're right," Ira squeezed eyelids together. "Just one thing I'd like to know before I go, Mamie. Are you really afraid she'll become a you-know-what if she learns to be a manicurist?"

"No, I only say that. I brought up my daughters to be good Jewish girls. But I admit, I'm a bit afraid."

"Why?"

"Hannah, you know, wants to be a dancer. Do I allow her to take dancing lessons? No. Why? Because I'm afraid she'll become a you-know-what? A dancer has more temptations than a manicurist to become a you-know-what. Still, that's not the reason I won't let her become a dancer. Or Stella to become a manicurist. You are a student. Were they boys, I too would send them to college. But they're girls. And in today's world, which is better for a girl? To be a manicurist, or to be a bookkeeper? To be a dancer or to be a secretary in a tall office? For that reason I send Hannah to Julia Richmond to learn commercial subjects. And Stella I send to the Union Square secretary school also to learn commercial subjects, because everything today is commercialize, commercialize, as Saul, your uncle, says."

With gross hands clasped in front of her bulging abdomen, Mamie folded infelicitous English into Yiddish.

"Yeah, because he reads that writer in the *Daily Journal*, so he knows more than everybody else," Stella heckled.

"Tell me," Mamie quelled her mutinous daughter, "which will they need more, when you go to earn a living, a dancer or a book-keeper, a manicurist or a secretary?"

"And you think you can't be a you-know-what in an office, too?"

"Go, you speak nonsense. I didn't ask you that. You hear, Ira? Did I ask you that?"

"No, of course not." Damned idiot, he cursed himself. Go yowl on a goddamn fence like a tomcat. Get the hell out of here!

"You look dejected," said Mamie.

"Yeah, I am. I don't have much hope for the future myself."

"Why?"

"My college career is *kaput. Farshtest?*"

"Go, you're just tired. They say in Yiddish, everything depends on will. He who wills achieves more than he who knows."

"Yeah? I don't know much, Mamie, but I sure will a lot," Ira said in Yinglish—and chortled wickedly.

"Azoy doff sein." Mamie got to her feet. "Money lost is nothing lost. But will lost, then is everything lost. Keep on willing." She went to the gas stove and tried to turn the fringe of flame under the stove lid still lower. The fringe winked out. *"Noo, ferfallen,"* she said. "I'll light it again when Jonas comes home. Another hour and a half. Maybe two. It'll stay warm." She returned to the table, turned her back to the kitchen chair to sit down—her knees lost control of her bulk, and she tumbled heavily onto the chair seat. *"Oy!"*

"She ruins all the sofas that way, my dear mother," Stella observed coolly. "Plop, the springs go."

"What can I do? I dearly love to eat. I'm only waiting for Jonas to come home to have a few *verenekehs.*"

"So why don't you give Ira some? He's looking so sad."

"I already had some," Ira rejoined.

"Oh, then it's a wonder you're sad. My mother cures every kind of trouble with eating. If my father says business in the cafeteria isn't so good, she eats. If that drunken *shikker* upstairs doesn't pay his rent, she eats. The trouble with you is you cure everything with eating."

"Very clever of you, Stella. Go bathe."

"You know, Ira, my mother can finish a whole pound box of chocolate cherries in one hour."

"I told you to go bathe!"

"Hannah's in the bathroom."

"And that's where you should be, too."

"I have to get my clothes off first, don't I?" Stella retorted.

"Then go into your bedroom. And turn off the front-room lights. Is the radio off?"

"Ye-e-s. O-o-f. Can you hear it?" Stella drawled petulantly, gave her mother an angry look as she left the kitchen for the hallway. "You'd think we still had batteries in the radio. She *tsitses,* my mother. It's a penny—electricity." She disappeared. A moment later the front room's electric wall buttons could be heard clicking.

"Something today," Mamie said to Ira. "I don't know what. Aggravations. Between two daughters and their grandfather, between the tenants and the bank, *oy,* what one has to bear."

"I bet." Time to go. Time to have gone—long ago. Hellish tedium. How could he be such a goddamn horse's ass? Jesus, all for the sake of a half minute. Was it even a half minute? All these sanctimonious preachers prating the same thing: was the soul's salvation or damnation worth a half minute? No, that wasn't what they said. Risking hell's fire worth the pleasure of a half minute? Evidently.

"That one, especially," Mamie spoke through a wide, prolonged yawn. "Till I see her under the canopy, the hair will creep out of my head." She passed her grubby hand before her eyes. Flesh rimmed the gold band on her finger. "Oh, I would so dearly love to lie down a few minutes."

"Well, why don't you? I'm leaving." Ira really meant it.

"Jonas may come home a little early today. Harry was off yesterday. So he may relieve him earlier. That's the way we have a few minutes together."

"Oh, yes." In the midst of his thwarting, a ray of pity made its way: for his gross, ponderous aunt, her immigrant striving, limitless, limitless sacrifice to climb out of her steerage arrival in the *goldeneh medina,* servant girl and indentured drudge paying off her passage to Granduncle Nathan, the diamond merchant. That's the way we have a few minutes together. Pity. The rays opened wider, like Blake's calipers. "Well, good night, Mamie." Ira stepped to the threshold.

He remained there, for down the hall, the doorbell whirred. Ira gaped in astonishment at his aunt.

"*Oy, gevald!*" Mamie sat transfixed, upright.

"Is it Jonas?" Ira asked.

"No, no! He has a key! It's too early." She thrust herself to her feet. "They'll wake the old man!" She squeezed past Ira into the hall.

Again the doorbell whirred.

Mamie's speed was again surprising; solicitude drove her shuffling down the hall. "Who?" she challenged at the door. "Whozit?" And then apparently reassured by the answer she heard, she withdrew the bolt of the lock, swung open the door. "Mrs. Gomez, it's you?"

With Mamie's girth filling the doorway, the newcomer couldn't be seen, only heard: a woman's voice excitedly sputtering a medley of Spanish and English. Then a small girl's treble, supplementing the first voice: something about little Teodoro. "Little Teodoro no can get out."

"How? *Vie zoy?* In the closet?" Mamie demanded. "Is not no locks on closet doors, Mrs. Gomez."

High-pitched protestations in Spanish. The apartment doorknob was rattled, as if in demonstration—which was followed by an admonitory "Sh!" sounded by Mamie.

"He break," said the woman's voice. "He cry inside. Cry! Cry! 'Out! Mama!'"

Mamie apparently understood. "Ver is Isabella? The other big sister? Ver is Mr. Gomez?"

"He night man Horna Harda work."

Horna Hardon, Ira coughed with weary, hectic mirth: Horn & Hardart, the Automat.

And the child's voice: "Isabella go with my big sister. Gonna marry."

"And a neighbor? The next *doorkeh?* Somebody. It's a nothing with nothing. A scrooldriver can open it."

"Scrooldrive?"

"A pointig knife you put in de hull und give a *drei*— Sh! *Oy, gevald, der alter.* Pliss comm in de hall."

Perhaps he could help, whatever it was, Ira wavered. He ought to try. It couldn't be very much of a job: a screwdriver can open it, Mamie said. Maybe it was just a— Oh . . . he hadn't heard her, Stella, and no shadow thrown before her as she came out of the gloom of the front room into the muted light in the hallway from the kitchen, juvenile, voluptuous apparition: "You!"

She simpered.

"O-o-oh," he purred. His hand under the green-striped bathrobe sought her rump in rapturous turpitude, digits seemed to sprout eyes, spread their width to clutch: "Ooh, if only I had a hand twice as big." And marched around to her mound with forty thousand men. "Get back." He nudged her toward the dark of the front room. "Jesus, maybe Mamie'll have to go upstairs."

"Hannah's in the bathroom. She'll come out."

"Oh, nuts! I forgot." Checked, goddamn it, checked, mated, checked, not mated—he didn't know enough chess. "Let's go in the kitchen."

She lagged behind him as he withdrew toward the kitchen, speaking as she followed: "These Puerto Ricans must never have lived in houses. They don't know what to do in a house. Give them the sidewalk. They love the sidewalk. There's nothing to fix there."

How could she prattle so inanely when seconds mattered, prattle away a prat. "You think she'll come out right away?"

"She's out already. She must have heard Mama."

Down the hall a door creaked. Seconds later, bosomless Hannah, boyish in petticoat, pattered in, barefoot. "I heard the bell," she said anxiously. "Is Mama outside?"

"What else? She's outside with your Puerto Rican friends," Stella informed her sister. "She's telling Mrs. Gomez how she should open the closet door without knobs. They fell off."

"Poor Mama. Why?"

"Mrs. Gomez doesn't know how. Her little Teodoro is inside."

"Oh, my poor mother," Hannah fretted. "Everything she has to do. Give instructions on how to be a handyman."

"They're *your* Spanish friends," said Stella. "So why don't you go help her? That's why Mrs. Gomez came here. She could've gone next door."

"You're so shallow! I'm not even dressed!"

"You'll wake up Zaida," Ira arbitrated.

"He's used to it already," said Stella. "As long as we're in the kitchen, and the radio isn't playing."

The apartment door was heard opening, was closed quietly, and quietly locked. Mamie's heavy, careful tread brought her into the kitchen again. *"Oy, aza shver leben!"* Her voluminous bosom heaved as she made for a chair—and thudded into it.

"Did you tell her what to do, Mama?"

"Oy! She was frightened." Mamie panted. "Nothing more. A mother, don't you know. But three flights of stairs I would have had to climb."

"You didn't!"

"Am I crazy? In a minute she understood. An old scrooldriver she had. And pointig knives she had—from Horn and Hardot, borrowed, no doubt. Up she ran, with the little one after her."

"You took so long, Mama," Hannah chided solicitously.

"Your friend, the other bridesmaid, and her older sister, the bride, they came just'n a just," Mamie drew on her stock of English. "Just'n a just, I tell you. So I had to explain to them also. But she'll know herself now what to do, Mrs. Gomez."

"Poor Mama." Hannah kissed her mother's cheek.

"Indeed. *Noo,* to bed. Tomorrow is school. *Oy,* cry havoc, it's late. *Noo,* Stella, the bathtub?"

"Good night." Studied annoyance marked Stella's departure.

"Good night, Mama. I'm sorry," said Hannah.

"Good night, my child. Sleep well."

"Draw a long line down the middle of the bed, I'll sleep better," Hannah said after her sister.

"Uh. Do you want a cot?"

"No, I don't like cots. I've told you that, Mama. Good night, Ira."

"Good night, Hannah." Ira waited until his red-polled cousin disappeared past the doorway toward the front room. "I thought I might help if I stayed another minute, Mamie," he explained his presence.

"Noo, a handsome thanks. It wasn't necessary, I already know this business," Mamie remarked. *"O-oy, gevald,* would I had the strength

for it as I know it. I'm exhausted. Today was wearisome without measure." Her head bobbed from side to side. "No help for it. I have to lie down."

"It would do you good, *Tanta*. It's too much," Ira encouraged. "I don't see how you stand it." And moving toward the doorway, "Good night, *Tanta*," he said partly over his shoulder. "Get some rest."

"Wait." Laboriously, Mamie groaned to her feet. "Wait." She seemed almost as if talking in her sleep, somnolently plodded toward the bedroom in the back of the kitchen, and got her handbag from the other side of the doorknob. Soughing aloud with fatigue, she turned, opening the handbag.

"Mamie," Ira reproved. "I didn't come here for that."

"I know, I know. Poor boy." She brought out her small leather purse, snapped open the brass prongs, and from a roll of greenbacks peeled off a dollar bill. "Indigent student, don't say a dollar doesn't come in handy?"

"Mamie, no!" Ira retreated.

"Take. Take. Don't protest. You waited so long."

"I didn't wait for that."

"Take," she insisted. "As one gives, take. After you amass a fortune, you'll repay me."

"Thanks, *Tanta*."

"*Noo*, give me a kiss."

Ira kissed her soft, flabby cheek. "Thanks."

"I'll have to leave the door open." She plodded back to the small bedroom. "I won't hear him come home otherwise. *Ai*, these Portorickies." She hung up her handbag. "They wear me out so. Only one thing they care about."

Ira paused obediently.

"*Nur dem* fuck," said Mamie.

"*Tanta* Mamie!" Ira was genuinely shocked.

"Truth is truth. Nothing means more with them."

"Well," Ira deprecated. He had used up his last shred of temporizing. He fixed on the Yiddish print of *Der Tag* on the washtub as he moved toward the hall door, lingered.

"You can still read Yiddish?" With one hand on the bedroom

doorknob, Mamie watched him drowsily from the darkness of the bedroom.

"I just wanted to see if I can." Another step, and Ira advanced to the hallway threshold.

He heard the bedstead creak, then Mamie's moan of relief. He couldn't stall any longer. *Ferfallen,* goddamn it. There she was, behind the oyster-gray glazed light of the window in the bathroom door, as he stepped into the hall. If only he had half a chance—

"Child," Mamie's voice followed him.

"Me, *Tanta*?" Ira retraced a step or two.

"You're still here?"

"I was going." Oh, Jesus, had his loitering alerted her?

"Do me a favor."

"Sure. What?" He reentered the kitchen.

"Can you pull the door."

"So it's closed, you mean? Oh, sure."

"No, keep it open a bit so the light is in my eyes."

"How much?" A polymorphous surf began pounding within him.

"A little open, so I can hear Jonas come home."

"This much?" He pulled the bedroom door slowly toward him, inches ajar.

"*Azoy, azoy.*" Sleep furred her voice. "Indeed so. A slit. Blessed . . ."

He stood irresolute, listening: heard his aunt's breath thicken, snag into a snore. Do what? Improvise. Safeguard. Rearguard. No, he didn't have any stratagems. Flurry of pink flesh, *que ce cor a de longue haleine, que ce cor, que ce cor,* pale safeties. He drew his term paper out of his breast pocket, tiptoed over to the washtub, laid the term paper conspicuously on the Yiddish print of *Der Tag,* scowled at the typed sheets as if to fix them there, and stepped into the hallway. In three strides he was at the bathroom door, opened it onto full banana-light on her smooth, wide, droplet-glistening back above the waterline. She pivoted small-titted, soapy torso. She smiled guiltily.

"Listen, Stella. I'll be right back. Get out, will you? Soon as you can."

"Now?"

"No, I'll be right back!" It was all he could do to keep impatience from raising his voice instead of intensifying its harshness. "Five minutes. You hear me?"

"So where's Mama?"

"She's asleep. Yeah. I left my term paper here by mistake-on-purpose, in case she wakes up. Get it? That's why I came back." He overrode her look of bewilderment. "Just make it snappy, will ya? Get out as soon as you can." He was already shutting the door.

At utmost speed that stealth allowed, tiptoeing, he passed Zaida's closed bedroom door, quickened gait past the little office doorway framing the dark, to the apartment door—retracted the tongue of the lock, slipped the little brass nipple up to hold it. And out. Shut door. Raced down the flight of marble stairs, to the lit foyer. Out the open double doors to the night street, deserted, row of roofs cleated on night sky, planet-star a smear east. Cool and late and eleven the hour. Maybe later. Get going. By ebon-windowed storefronts, from stride to brisk pace, he broke into trot. Faster. Soles of shoes smacking the pavement. Oh, so many memories: Farley's trained legs driving over the armory boards. Ira quit running at Fifth Avenue, slowed to a walk, at his best clip. Walk a block, in breezy September air, to 113th Street, he counseled himself. You can't go into that goddamn drugstore all out of breath. He'd think you're crazy, the druggist would.

You *are* crazy. Crazy is as crazy does. Cracked sidewalk percussive in street-night, your drum heartbeat. Get there, that's all. To the corner lamppost, high o'erhead . . . whew.

He rounded the unlighted haberdashery, up above it, as if in contrast to the quiet, the loud crack of pool balls cracking out of the break on some pool table in the pool room on the second story. Faster, but don't get out of breath. One block. Take a deep breath. Slow down. One block. So . . . "I forgot my term paper. I came back." His lips moved in audible self-cross-examination and self-exculpation.

"Why did I take it out of my pocket? Why did I take it out? My pocketbook, that's why. The dollar bill you gave me. I—" He had an alibi. Great. The bright light of the drugstore was like a tangible barrier he had to force his way through.

In the clinical brilliance of the interior, reflected on myriad hues of jars and vials and tubes of patent medicines, lotions and salves, herpicides, fungicides, soothing syrups, shampoos, toothpastes, laxatives, behind the glass tobacco showcase that served as his counter stood the pharmacist—

—No. Where's that insert?

I lost the goddamn thing, Ecclesias. I thought I saved it, but I didn't.

—Too bad. Both the fact and the moment require it. If you fail to insert it, your omission will gnaw at you till your dying day.

Oh, shit. I'm at the very peak of narrative form. Ecclesias, have mercy.

—I am merciful. I'm saving you an endless wrenching of future regrets. You know as well as I do, the contrast—which happens to be actual—is needed. Are you an artist?

Oh, shit!

The marble counter of the store had been divided into two parts: on one side was the pharmaceutical part, on the other the small soda fountain. Goddamn it, Ira swore to himself on crossing the threshold. *They* had to be here: two young people sat in front of the counter, straws in the froth of chocolate soda. A young man and young woman. On the other side of the counter the soda jerk.

Round-faced and wearing glasses, pleasant and alert, the young woman was saying: "I wish we had somebody like Hutchins for president. Old Nicholas Murray Butler is such a fuddy-duddy. Not a progressive idea in his head."

And Ira approached the pharmaceutical side of the counter. "Right," replied her escort. He was all but albino in the absence of pigmentation of his hair, his wisp of mustache invisible, until Ira reached the counter. "That's what we ought to have at Columbia: a Great Books program, the kind of thing Hutchins has introduced at Chicago."

Oh, hell, rub it in, Ira thought. That's what I ought to be, but I ain't. That's what I ought to think about but don't. Great Books program, my ass. Now, listen to this, boys and girls, good boys and girls.

He waited for the pharmacist to put down his newspaper and rise to his feet—

As the young soda jerk said: "Hutchins has got the right idea. Who needs football? A college is a place of learning. Intramural sports involve everybody—"

Ah, nuts to you.

Iatrically clad and composed in his white medical jacket, the pharmacist rested on his fingertips, awaiting Ira's request. Humane, brown-mustached, wearing a bow tie, and recognizably Jewish. Near him, yet oceans away, two different-size slick, white rolls of paper promised a prophylactic wrapper. "Yes, what can I do for you?"

"Trojans." Ira tried to keep his voice low. He canted sideways to dig out two bills. One was Mamie's, the other Edith's five-dollar bill.

"Yes. How many? A dozen?"

"No, no. The smallest package."

"Two. Two for a quarter."

"Yeah." Ira laid the dollar greenback down on the glass. "For now."

The conversation on his left hand lapsed noticeably. Go ahead, listen. I give, I give a fuck. Rancorously, as if he had uttered brutal derision aloud, Ira glared at the soda jerk eyeing him diagonally across the counter. You too. Jesus Christ. The guy had a wad of hair that looked like a hirsute raft supporting his ludicrous white soda jerk's fatigues. Goody middle-class. I'm going to screw my cousin, yeah. What's it to you?

"Two? Yes, my friend." The item was stored out of sight, but conveniently, on a low shelf next to the tobacco counter.

"My girlfriend," the young soda jerk revived the conversation, "is on Hutchins's staff of undergraduate assistants. She gets straight A's. The whole staff is crazy about him."

The druggist brought to light the familiar small, round container, placed it on the counter, and picked up the dollar with practiced hand. "You want a bag?"

"No wonder, I would be too."

"Oh, you would?" her escort bantered.

"He's so young and handsome. He looks like an undergraduate."

"Huh? A bag? No." Anything could trip the mind, tense with

haste, strung to the highest pitch of hazard. He was sure he had betrayed himself—by their pause, by the druggist's brief, incurious survey—and tried to compensate by overdeliberate possession of his
purchase, neat little round of aluminum, with its Grecian helmeted
head stamped on the lid. Stop twitching. Be a Trojan like the crested
hero—will you hurry up, already, mister? Let me get outta here.
Christ. What I am and what they are, and I go to college too.

He had to abide the transaction though, crowd out, nay, bury
their seemliness and decency, their undergraduate, worthy confor-
mity, with makeshift, with frantic mental rubble: my mother gave me
a nickel to buy a pickle. I didn't buy a pickle. I bought some chooing
gum. Listen, listen, the cat is pissen. Where, where? Under the chair.
He had to abide it: ah, hell, abort it instead. Don't go back. Leave his
damned "An Assessment of U.S. Immigration Quotas" on the Yiddish
newspaper. It wasn't any good anyway. The more he listened to what
regular collegians talked about, the more certain he was. Go home.
You sap, you're always getting yourself into these fixes. Oh, Jesus,
jams. That's you, patent it: Stigman's jams—

"Something else?"

"No."

"He looks just like Nicholas Murray Butler," the soda jerk
quipped. To laughter.

"You'd have to have a bad case of astigmatism."

"Twenty-five cents." With scant smile, mossy dollar bill on the al-
abaster ledge of the elaborately filigreed brass cash register, the key
went down and the flag popped up: 25¢. Keeping the dollar in view,
the druggist made change. "That's fifty," he laid a quarter on the
glass. "And fifty is a dollar."

Scoop up the change. What shackles could stop him now? Hell,
they didn't know who he was, nor did the druggist. Ira pocketed the
silver. So the customer was in a hurry, so—but walk, he'd have to walk
out of the store, a dignified six strides—no, less. If he ran out, some
dumb cop'd think he was a holdup guy, a holdupnik, as Mamie
would say. Jesus, was she still asleep? Anh, you're wasting your goddamn time, he censured himself. And now he began to run. Faster.
Stop thinking. Run. Holdup man. Get shot in the ass with two new
condoms in your pocket. New. What else could the druggist sell him?

They couldn't be secondhand. Secondhand condoms—condrums, they called them on 119th Street, the Irish: scum bags. No, no, don't stop. So gasp. Shot in the ass with two new condoms, just bought, five dollars and seventy-five cents in his pocket, on 112th Street, Mamie's block. So what would she think happened to the dollar she gave him? It grew. And Mom? And Pop? And the *mishpokha*, too. Jesus, dead giveaway. Yeah, dead—and giveaway. One kid, one only kid that my father bought for two *zuzim*, *khad godyo*, *khad godyo*.

Panting, he dashed into the flyer. Stop. Stop. Stop. Hold it. That's what you get from smoking. No wind. No, that's all right. At least grab your term paper: you forgot it, see? Say, if Jonas is there—no, he couldn't be home yet. But say he is. Hello, Jonas, you know what? There it is, there it is. Right on *Der Tag* where I left it: right on the washtub. Boy, was I dumb. . . .

His breathlessness of a moment before strangely converted into long, momentous heaving of chest as he climbed the flight of stairs to Mamie's floor, halted before the apartment's dull red lead-painted, metal-sheathed door. Here goes. He reviewed his alibis—like loading a weapon. Wait! If Jonas had come, the door would be locked. For once he was smart. Why wasn't he smart this way always? The door would be locked, and Jonas would be asking Stella why wasn't it locked when he came home? But maybe she had already ducked into bed beside Hannah. She didn't know from nothin'. Blame Ira when he left. But if the door wasn't locked—let's go.

The door wasn't locked, the tongue still back, held by its catch. The hallway was dark—until where lit at the other end by the kitchen light. Who the hell knew: anybody there and who? He was in deep, deep danger now. Boy. Holding the bolt, he quietly raised the tongue . . . into its catch. You're in deep danger now, boy. No, he could still bluff it out with the forgotten term paper. Come in as if looking for it, grab it—he tiptoed past Zaida's bedroom. And ah—still the momentum of the ruse, he snatched up the term paper, stowed it . . . safely . . . in breast pocket, all the while his eyes fixed on Stella seated at the table in green bathrobe, before her an open movie magazine. Her lips were parted, expectant, waiting. He pointed at the bedroom door, behind which Mamie lay; it was exactly, barely ajar as he remembered leaving it. Stella nodded, docile, expectant. Sound of Mamie's breathing filled the kitchen—Ira leaned toward it a moment, listening with sharpened ears, heard the reassuring snore, stertorous, he thought, regular, impervious, rough with weariness. He beckoned, eyes and head. Boy. Stella arose softly, approached, shallow blue-green eyes in trance, and blond and still humid, entered his embrace, to his swift, imperious pawings, and ruthless signals of his will. He retracted the little tin, displayed it a fraction of a second: it would have to explain all, his going, his absence, his errand—and it did, for when he opened it, she tittered.

"Turn around." He armed his piece. "Bend over," he pressed compliant shoulders. "Wow." He couldn't restrain exultation altogether, at least vent that whisper of gratified vision: of orbital womanly spinnaker unfurled. Unfurled from the release of the green toweling of bathrobe wings, cupped, sleek, ballooning vans of fulfillment. The brain scintillated. Hoist. She weighed a wisp, she lost gravity to furor.

"O-o-oh, Ira!"

"Sh!"

"O-o-oh, Ira, o-o-oh, Ira!"

"Shut up!" Ram-pant. Ra-a-m. Ram, ram, rampant Lions of Judah, gold Lions of Judah on sapphire ground guarding the Torah. Ram-ram-ram, *tikyoo, tikyoo*. Sound the shofar. *Tikeeyoo, matryoo.*

"Ooooh, Ira, ooooh, Ira, ooooh!"

To that last lustful gasp. Breathless both, they separated. Green curtain fell on plump, adolescent rump, too soon, even as he took up cudgel for composure, buttoning up with all celerity. "All right?" he asked her as she turned around.

And received her assent in lambent, pale blue-green eyes.

"Boy, that was good," he breathed in the wake of rapture. "You better get in bed. I'm going to sneak out." For the first time he felt a truly tender impulse toward her, toward Stella. He kissed her—on not so sweetly exhaling lips. "G'bye."

She smiled, girlishly, uncertainly appreciative. "Bye-bye."

A last swift glance at the bedroom door reassured him: all unchanged. Mamie's regular burr of breath rasping out of the dark. Safe. Safe all around. Get rid of his "safety" sticking to him, peel it off as soon as outdoors. Stella had already started toward the front

room, and he in the opposite direction to the apartment door at the
end of the hall. On the very point of raising the balls of his feet to tiptoe, when he heard it—he heard it: bedspring noise, bed creak, groan,
and electric-switch button click all at once. And crack of light under
Zaida's door. Jesus Christ! Ira wavered. He'd never beat it out before
the old man opened the door. Tell Zaida he'd dozed off? No! No! Ira
retreated. Tiptoes, tip toe, Jesus, like a ballet dancer, back to kitchen-
light. Pretend to read Yiddish still? Zaida's door opened, and a terri-
fying slab of incandescence toppled sinisterly from the room across
the narrow passage of hall. God Almighty! He bumped into Stella.

"It's Zaida," she whispered at his back.

"I know."

"He's going to the can."

"Sh!" He agonized caution. Should he send her on her way—to
the bedroom adjoining the front room she shared with Hannah,
asleep too? Was that the safest thing to do? With time passing so?
Maybe she'd wake Hannah—oh, Christ!—and Jonas home soon—
oh, Jesus! Was he ever in a jam! The front-room window. Open it.
The fire escape. Open it. But the noise—get back into the kitchen.
Read Yiddish, no matter what—too late. He retreated into the deeper
dark, into the recess of the front room, tugging Stella with him.

Grumbling, the old man emerged—in his long underwear—
shuffling on his felt carpet slippers. With one hand he kept patting
down the crumpled black yarmulke on his head; the other hand slid
along the molding of the wall to guide and steady him: "*Oy, vey, oy,
vey, Raboinish ha loilim.* What joy have I known? At fifteen a bride-
groom, at sixteen a father. Barely twenty-two, and a bankrupt with
four daughters. What joy have I known? Care, always care, since
youth. And pain, pain and sorrow without measure. Old and afflicted
before my time, widowed and grown blind before old age. *Raboinish
ha loilim,* how long until you are pleased to take me?"

He seemed to become aware of the stream of kitchen light ahead
of him, peered anxiously at it a moment—paused, but then entered
the bathroom. A third luminous bridge spanned the hallway when
the bathroom light went on, and filtered by the frosted glass in the
bathroom door, changed to softer texture when he shut the door.

"Jesus, here's my chance. While he's in there." Ira moved forward.

"He's got good ears," Stella whispered. "He can't see, but he can hear—"

"When he flushes the toilet. Maybe this—" Ira stooped to tear at his shoelaces. "I can make it." Shoes in hand, he straightened up. "You go to bed as soon as I beat it."

He advanced as far as the kitchen light, and bent as a sprinter poised for the starting signal, raised himself on tiptoe, waited with straining ears . . . heard lifted toilet seat bat against pipe . . . stream . . . splash . . . now . . . now . . . he crept forward a step. Now! . . . Now! . . . No! Nothing doing . . . the old guy hadn't flushed the toilet. Oh, Jesus H. Christ. Already the bathroom doorknob was turning . . . bathroom door opening. Ira retreated back into the front room. Off clicked bathroom light. It couldn't be! In this place, caught in this trap, in this fix? It couldn't be real. It couldn't be. Not Ira Stigman. He wasn't—back. Back into deeper dark—

"Wait, he'll get in bed," Stella breathed in his ear.

"Yeah." Soundlessly to make it happen.

But instead, the gray beard, yarmulke, and underwear paunch that was Zaida shuffled toward the kitchen, stood expectantly in the light: "Mamie?"

Sunk! If thought could bellow through cranium, the whole house would hear him. He was sunk.

"Sleeping, Mamie?" Zaida asked with drowsy grumpiness. Dread hiatus, while he looked up disapprovingly at the kitchen ceiling light.

Window. Fire escape. Roof. At least they wouldn't know who it was. It would be a robber making his escape! Still he didn't dare move: with the old man so near, he'd hear the window open, cry out. But if he awoke Mamie, then no help for it: dash for the window. And with—Jesus, oh, shoes in hand—it can't be you!

Zaida peered again, frowned: a whole lifetime of trial by ordeal. Give up, get caught, admit, deny, brazen it, or jump down to the street, to a flight, how high? Height lessened by hanging from bottom fire escape, maybe only break a leg, not killed. Or up fire escape, to the roof, better. Or under bed.

"*Noo*, sleep if you're sleeping. Sleep until Jonas comes. *Oy, vey iz mir*." The old man turned away heavily. "A plague on this night. Something went wrong with my sleep."

He shuffled back toward the bedroom light.

"I heard multitudes clamoring and braying in strange tongues to the sky, and yet I understood: see, it is not perfect, they howled: see, it is not perfect. *Noo?* Ha? *Raboinish ha loilim,* if Thy thought fills the universe, why do we suffer? Then how can Thy thought be perfect? An imp crawled out of the shofar and screamed: There must be a flaw? Foolishness. Foolishness. Oh, why does the Messiah delay?"

Yawning noisily, Zaida scratched under his yarmulke, entered his bedroom. The door closed. The light under it quenched.

Two clocks in the front room ticked, minced each other's intervals . . . synchronized . . . diverged . . .

"I'm going," Ira rasped.

"Wait, a little more," Stella implored. "He'll fall asleep. Another minute, and you'll be sure." She tugged at his arm.

"I can't wait. Your father'll be here next. Jesus Christ." He elbowed her hand away. Stupid bitch, he'd had to fuck her tonight. "Come with me. When I go, you go."

The bland face lifted upward in the gloom, susceptible, suppliant: "You want me to come with you?"

"Yes." Hectic with impatience, he could have raved. "He won't hear me." Ira brandished the shoes in his hand. "He'll hear you. Go right up to the door. If he says anything, say it's you."

"What'll I say?"

"Oh, shit. The lock. Any goddamn thing. Somebody you heard. You're making sure!" Nudging her ahead, his chubby patsy, he tiptoed after: on stockinged feet seeking cover under the soft tread of her house slippers—

"Mamie?" came from the other side of Zaida's bedroom door. "Is that you, Mamie?"

Ira gesticulated, jabbed at the lock, mimed, rolled his wrist about frantically.

"I thought I heard somebody turn the lock, Zaida," Stella said, and at Ira's furious nod, "I'm going to make sure."

"Who is it? Is it you, Stella?"

"Yes, Zaida."

"Don't open the door."

"No. I just wanted to see if it's locked."

Ira pushed her ahead. On toenails to the door, his face all crookedly twisting, he eased back the bolt of the lock, eased open the door, nodded fiercely at Stella, crept out. The door swung to, bolt slid back, all in one interval, with his feet trampling into his shoes on the landing. Let her explain it as best she could. He was out. He was free.

Free! Out! Out in the clear! Never mind laces. Down the stairs. Never mind tripping. Hold banister. Down to the ground floor. Foyer, foyer, foyer. Out. Street. Raven sky-wings brooding streetlamps. Roc's eggs. Nutty. Dodge in between parked cars. Dodge. Ha. Get across, before anybody—Jonas comes. Now: on the double, triple, move your hams, move your good old kosher hams. Hear that, Zaida, pow, pow, pow, wow, screwed her, your grandchild *in flagrante copulante, in flagrante copulante*—and oh, boy, was it good. . . . He passed two doorways . . . three doorways . . . four . . . miracle, to get out of there . . . past Puerto Rican grocery: Hernandez.

Mr. Hernandez, mind of yours truly, Johnny Dooley, steps on your nice, dark iron step to tie—oh boy, oh joy—his laces on? Oh boy, oh joy, got away with it! Now to get rid of that—sticker-tape, ticker tape, dicker-tape, pricker tape, frick-her tape, like Joyce: Sinbad the Sailor, and Tinbad all bad—hope it's still—belly pulled in, and with furtive glance over his shoulder, Ira thrust his hand down under pants belt to pinch the condom loose—and froze. Rigid. Smitten motionless with panic. He had the condom all right; he pulled it up, imminent in pallid phallic plane view and faint semen smell. But the notebook, the notebook! Had he left it on the Yiddish newsprint of *Der Tag*? You goddamn boob! Had he? Reckless with alarm, he pitched the condom up in the air toward the curb—no, no, no, he dug his hand into his breast pocket: he had it, he had it! And he had his notebook, too. Boy, what luck! What luck! He had it still! Had it. Had left no incriminating evidence—huh? Could that little guy coming across the street from Lenox Avenue—shrimp of a guy: looked like Jonas. Christ, that condom so rashly flung just now. He'd tossed it in the air: high as a flaunt, taunt, kid's sparkler. Pale as a slug. Wan in the gutter and full of his sparks. Beat it.

Beat it. He headed east, through Monday's early-morning darkness, legs driving, clicking heels in the deserted street in a rush to leave. Got away! Scot-free. Scut free, too, he got. Scut free, scot-free. He-e-e-ya! If that was Jonas? Nah, some other little shrimp.

III

Hurrying, he crowed his wordless exultation aloud, his cock-crow aloud, and headed east, straight toward Park Avenue. He was the luckiest guy alive, luckiest punk alive, luckiest prick alive, luckiest bastard alive, alive-o. Before him, he could see a fire burning under the great gray viaduct of the New York Central Railway on Park Avenue, a fire in a big steel drum. Just as a Pullman with dim windows rumbled by overhead on wheels muffled by the solid trestle, the flames on the ground below spewed upward. Dreaming in the Pullman, they never dreamed a fire was burning in a drum in the push-cart district beneath them, never knew they were rolling over a Jewish pushcart district, never knew he, Ira Stigman, had paused beside the open phone booth at Gabe's Wholesale Produce on the corner to watch them roll by in the night, never knew him, never knew his wild escapade, his frenzied escape, those up there, sleeping peacefully in trains named *Lake George, Fort Collins,* and *Atlanta.* He felt like tarrying a minute with the thought, tarrying to recover norm. The flames lit up the underside of the trestle to lurid parasol of yellow and scarlet, and lit up the cross-braced pillars too, fitfully, so that they almost seemed in motion, legs of a huge, ambling myriapod. It felt so good leaning against the phone booth, just leaning, subsiding, surceasing. *After life's fitful fever he sleeps well.* Was that from *Lear?* No, *Macbeth.* Only he wasn't sleeping, just enjoying escape, blissful fugitive. Boy, that was good. Better than with Minnie that time. Nice and plump and fresh and humid. Beautiful, beautiful back-scuttle. Celestial back-scuttle. Boy, you could get another hard-on thinking about it. If he ever let himself pull off, that was what he would think about. How could anything be so wonderful and so vile, so rotten, so dirty, and so heavenly? Jumpin' Jesus. Figure it out. Oh, easy: it was you.

Near the drum a large truck was parked, and the blaze from the drum played on a sturdy young fellow on the tailgate who shoveled refuse swept into a heap on the floor of the truck to fuel the blaze: broken slats of vegetable crates, fruit wrappers, packaging material, trash. Each shovelful damped the flames momentarily, flames that leaped up again, hurling light as far as the granite wall at 111th Street, where the massive ramp began. Firelight lapped the stoops of tenements and skimmed along the store windows of the closed, scruffy little shops at the base of the tenements that flanked the pushcart district that found shelter beneath the trestle . . . where Mom shopped Sunday mornings—Ira's lip curled—in the good old days.

Brief spell of respite, damaged respite, like everything else in his life. Then passage again: Ira on the sidewalk exchanged cursory inspection with the young fellow on the truck, felt the moment set in his mind as if it were some kind of a cerebral casting. Passing on, he glanced inside the wide-open sliding doors of Gabe's: two men were in there, a hulking one with a metal-clad clipboard, and a stumpy one with a push broom. On one side of them in the weak light, stacks of crated produce lined the wall; on the other, from sliding door to back wall a crowd of tarpaulin-covered pushcarts were jammed in for the night.

Scrape of shovel, crackle of fire, smell of smoke wafted on the crisp night air, greeted the senses, and the tableau inside Gabe's place added a hint of citron: grapefruit, lemons, oranges, ah. As though exorcising the last of inner turmoil. Ah, dispelling vestige of heinous furor—and terror, guilt—the young guy on the tailgate of the truck dumped all the rubbish into the steel drum—and the rubbish turned into flame writhing upward, flame glorifying the squalor that surrounded the place.

"Take it easy, Giorgio." Snapping down the cover of his metal-clad invoice clip, the hulking and deceptively soft-looking man with slightly rolling gait came out of the wide-open sliding doors, followed by the other, the squat, grizzled, Italian-appearing keeper of the place— or night watchman: he glanced at Ira.

"Me? Take it easy? When you git as old as me, it's too late to take it easy."

"Too late? That's when I thought it was just right." The other clamped the clipboard under his arm, brought out a package of cigarettes.

"T'anks. Maybe fer some, but not fer me."

A match flared. The old watchman's grizzled face leaned into the matchlight, craggy and worn. "T'anks," puffing his cigarette, his visage lost its features. "Dat's a Camel, ain't it?"

"Yeah." The other lit up his cigarette. "You can get in a snooze on the job every once in a while, can'tcha?"

"Me? No. Days only is when I can sleep. But not nights, not even when I'm off. Nights, I don't know what the hell it is: bundles keep bustin' open in my head."

"Yeah?" The man with the metal clipboard laughed. "Damaged goods, hah? No Joisey tomaters, here." He uttered a fat, genial laugh.

"Nah," the old watchman growled rejection. "Not fer me. When I lost my Gina, I lost it all."

"I was just kiddin', Giorgio. You know how it is."

Was he dreaming, somnabulating? No, he wasn't dreaming, somnambulating. Here came a guy, wiry, thin as a rail, in crumpled hat, maybe porkpie shape once, in the sere, weathered garb of the tramp, but disheveled, hurrying toward them. Shaken out of his momentary trance, streetwise, Ira sidestepped to the curb, noted the newcomer's bony face to the firelight: his jaws were spattered with blood, his nostrils raw, his nose askew. Jesus, what a pasting someone had given him: a drunk. Rubbing his lips, oblivious of everyone, the other plunged into the open phone booth outside Gabe's. The light clicked on. No, it was real enough: that savage pummeling racket coming from the half-closed booth was real enough. So was the violent shadow thrown on the sidewalk by the feeble dome light of the booth: the figure of a man banging, hammering the coin box.

"Dat's right, beat the shit out of it," the night watchman encouraged. "Wake up de neighborhood. Waddaye, crazy?"

Fresh onset of banging the coin box was the answer.

"Hey, you hear dat rummy, Guido?" the truck driver called to the young fellow on the tailgate of the truck. "He's like a pimp beatin' on his whore, ain't he? Listen to him."

The young fellow leaned sideways on his shovel to get a better view. "Tickle it, dat's right. He's got his finger up her. Hey, bowl it, why don'tcha?" His youthful laugh rang out under the brooding trestle.

A few more bangs, demented, obdurate pounding against the silence, terminated by the old watchman's threat: "You don't git the fuck outta here, I'll take a hunk o' pipe t' ye, ye fuckin' bum!"

With a yank of folding doors, the gleam in the booth blinked out; the other stepped out like a lank, starved animal from his lair into the lapping torchlight of the steel drum. Ira began discreetly moving away, stole another glance over his shoulder as he increased the intervening distance. Obvious, the meaning of the other's importunate crouch, the other's panhandler's glimmering palm extended to the two men. All too obvious his rebuff: the blunt jab of thumb, the jeering injunction: "Scram, rummy." To Ira's consternation, the man suddenly broke away from the others and dashed after him. Ira's impulse was to run. Nuts! Just walk away as fast as he could. It didn't do any good. He was caught up within a dozen strides.

"Listen, bud, I'm flat broke. What d'ye say? A thin dime. I ain't kiddin'. I'm broker'n the Ten Commandments. I been ridin' freights since yesterday morning. All the way from Aroostook, from Maine, ya know. I ain't a rummy. Honest, I was pickin' pertaters, I ain't no rummy. I'm just goddamn hungry. I'm starvin'. I got rolled an' I lost my dough." The battered, bony face pleaded, blood-stippled, unnerving. Beef-red nostrils twitched. Was that a new gap in his front teeth as he spoke? Jesus, to be confronted with this apparition in dire need in the night, face-to-face with dire need, unyielding need on dark, vacant Park Avenue, wide, ugly Park Avenue, between the unlit storefronts, penurious hall lights, stodgy brick walls—and the railroad viaduct planted on its immobile legs. Not even an auto passed, nor were headlights to be seen. Were the others at the corner watching, where flames fluttered from the drum like an Indian warbonnet? What the hell had he stopped for?

"I haven't got any money." Ira tried to repel his accoster with surliness.

"A nickel. Anything. I can walk into a beanery with a nickel. Some of 'em'll give you som'n stale with a cuppa java. Waddaye say, pal?" He lifted forefinger to nostrils, brought the hand away trembling: "The fuckin' railroad bull caught me ridin' in the blinds. Between the Pullman trains. Sonofabitch saw me at 125th Street station. He sapped me silly, knocked the shit outta me. I swear I'm tellin' you the truth."

"I haven't got a nickel."

"Pennies. Please! Maybe I can get a roll. A slice o' bread. I'm like to pass out."

Sucker, Ira assailed himself. But who could deny that pleading, bashed, blood-speckled visage? He felt among the coins in his pocket. Two: a big half dollar and a quarter, big enough too, too big—and a condom tin. Oh, Jesus, why hadn't he asked that druggist to break that quarter? A quarter! That was his total allowance from Mom for a day at CCNY. But he had five bucks, Edith's bounty, poor woman. Boy, the way the mind wavered, flickered: screwed his kid cousin. Escaped by the skin of his teeth—and *with* his notebook. Give alms for Zaida not to guess, give alms the little shrimp wasn't Jonas. Nuts. Superstition. But that was the way the mind spun its web: here was a tramp begging: mendicant redressing some kind of arrant imbalance. "Yeah," Ira's voice was much louder than he intended, strident and bold in hollow gloom: "You better wipe your face." Strange, how hostility seemed harbinger of relenting.

"That's right. I must look like a fuckin' mess." At a loss, as if he had given up hope of further comfort, the other turned his face dully. "An' my ear. See that? The fuckin' bull done that too." He began licking his fingertips, scouring cheeks at random. "That's why I didn't wanna hit up 125th Street. Some cop ketch me panhandlin', he'd get my ass throwed in the slammer just to make a pinch."

"I got a quarter. That's all I got." Ira drew out the coin.

"What de ye mean? Ye givin' it t' me?"

"Not unless you can change it." His own sarcasm riled him, it was so devoid of efficacy. "Here, take it."

"Jesus, yer a prince! A whole two bits! God bless ye! God bless ye!"

"Oh, bullshit."

"I'll be prayin' fer ye, honest to God, I'll pray for ye. You're white.

I mean it. Maybe you're a Jew. But you're a Christian. You're a gent."
He tipped the crumpled hat.

Ira crooked his hand in sign of curt disparagement, curt disen-
gagement. "Go find yourself someplace to eat, will you?" He stepped
to the curb. A Christian, my ass, his thoughts echoed.

"Thanks. God bless ye. I'm gittin' some coffee-an', right away.
Two bits."

"Yeah." Broad shadow of the trestle stirred by curling flame of a
fire a block away: God bless you. Ira crossed to the north corner of
114th Street. Jesus, Mamie should know what he'd gotten out of her
dollar: a well-fucked daughter, right under her mother's snoring
nose, a hell of a scare—what a scare!—a rubber condom pale in the
gutter for some dumb kid to find tomorrow, and blow up into a balloon, another one in his pocket. And all of two bits' worth of blessings from a tramp with a crumpled hat who'd got his lumps. Boy, that
was a bargain, wasn't it? If he could only tell it to somebody: the
delirious contrasts in just one night, one day, wild whoosh, pathos,
bathos. But that was the difference between himself and Larry. Larry
could relate his adventures; they slipped easily through regular chan-
nels. His didn't, his were deformed, fitted no channel, could never
be told.

You got to think, Ira continued morosely on his way uptown: you
got to think before you did, think, think, think. That was the trouble:
you didn't think. Try to think. Oh, think, your ass, he suddenly raged
at himself: he wasn't meant to think. He had stood on a flat, a diving
rock by the Hudson and told himself that. He was meant to feel and
to believe. He was made to suffer and to imagine. He wasn't smart.
Everybody knew that. But when would he begin? To think, to try to
think: the practical things, the prosaic, the consequences, the way
other people did, grown-up people, appraising and calculating. Even
young people. Like those Columbia goodies in the drugstore. Oh,
you had to, you had to. That was the way the world was: what did
Gabe earn in that storehouse he owned, how much rent did he pay,
how much rent did he charge each pushcart, how much did he pay
the watchman, how much profit did he make on a crate of oranges or
tomatoes? That was what should concern him. Not feel and suffer
and imagine: what that old wop would say to himself, after the truck

left him alone in Gabe's warehouse, looking out of the little window in the door at the fire in the steel drum. How he remembered, maybe, his dead wife—who knows, he said he was alone: how maybe she picked up horseshit in the gutter like the other Italian women wearing black on 119th Street, horseshit to put on the geraniums in the wooden window boxes. Maybe he had a coal and ice cellar once, like the wop across the street. Maybe he once whistled "Chimes of Italy" when he jabbed his icepick into an ice cake on the sidewalk on a summer morning. That wasn't what he was supposed to think about. He was a freak.

Up the hill rising to the closed brick comfort station under the trestle at 116th Street. The trolley tracks. The streetlights east and west. Rolls of linoleum standing like mummies wrapped in brown paper in the corner store show window. And downhill again to the muted rumble of a train passing overhead. And where was that bum going, that hobo-panhandler? South? After he got his coffee-an' in some beanery someplace. Put his quarter on the counter—to show he had it—ordered a mug of coffee, got his change, and headed for the washroom to wash off his bloodstains. Headed for the West Side, to the Hudson River where the freight trains ran. He was a kid once too. Did he grab his father's hand when the old man came home from work in the evening? Hey, Dad, what about a nickel? Come on, Dad, give us a jitney. Did that rusty bastard in the porkpie hat do that too . . . once? How could you escape feeling, suffering, imagining; how could you extricate yourself at least to some degree? And yet, he would have to . . . someday. When?

It was late. It was dark. He had risked. Who else had risked like that? Not Larry, in his nice comfortable room in the West 110th Street apartment. But it wouldn't be Larry walking Edith back from the ship next Sunday. It was Ira she trusted, Ira she invited. It was Ira who knew. It wasn't big blond Ivan, the physics whiz, saying to the classmate he was helping in the '28 alcove: Now all we got to do is find the right integral. Not Sol, whose father sold trusses on Delancey Street, not redheaded Sol spouting all that Professor Cohen said in class. Not the Columbia students who knew all about Hutchins. No. Nobody. Only he had risked, crazy-risked. And he was going home now.

And here were the four-corners where he lived, where he lived and grew up, with the New York Central viaduct steel millipede nearby always.

He had risked, and he was going home. With half a buck of Mamie's left in his pocket and a half-full condom tin, and five bucks of Edith's. Was there a *barukha* for that? A prayer? Zaida, old hypochondriac, old boy? Jews had a prayer for everything? Was there a *shekh-eyooni*? A prayer for deliverance for having screwed the ass off Zaida's granddaughter, and not being caught? He had risked. And he had gotten away with it. Who had helped him do that and get away? He had pacified her, and Pasiphaë'd her. Who had helped him do that, Zaida, old boy? Was it the imp that jumped out of the shofar? That was a good one.

He heard his own snicker, short and mirthless. Here was where he lived, for now, 108 East 119th Street.

IV

With maybe an hour to spare, Ira made his way along Sunday-darkened 116th Street toward the Lenox Avenue subway kiosk. No more IRT pass now; he had surrendered it when he had quit the summer job, just after Labor Day. He dropped his jitney in the slot and swung the jarring turnstile ahead of him. He had already determined he would be a chevalier tonight, a chivalrous chevalier, so unlike his behavior with Stella the Monday before, two days after Edith's request. And once again, he had reminded Mom he would be home "way, way late," so that she wouldn't worry.

He stayed on the local to kill time, but still he got to Christopher Street too early. So he sauntered . . . along dull Seventh Avenue with its miscellaneous high and low buildings. The September night air had a touch of chill mixed with the darkness. He looked at the moon-faced clock in the gas station window at the foot of Morton Street: twenty minutes to ten. Slow. Slow. *O lente, lente, currite noctis equi.* Slow down. How could you make a house that was only a little more than a half block away seem as far as a house five blocks away? So if he got there a few minutes early, they wouldn't mind; they'd be secure in knowing he had arrived. He crossed Morton to the south side, walked past Edith's house, and as far as Hudson Street to the west, Sunday-silent, Sunday-dark, darker than Seventh Avenue. Tag-end. It was called a street, but it ran north and south, like the avenue it really was—Hudson Street by name. If that pitchy-black Ninth Avenue El a short distance away didn't cut across the view, you could see the Hudson River. They'd be crossing to the other side soon. Underneath. Adventure, wasn't it? Dark, Sunday-dark, the darkness that inevitably came when everyone was at home at the end of a weekend in the fall. Escort the lady home. But the minute you began to anticipate, you contemplated, and the minute you contemplated, memory floated up out of the ooze in repulsive patches. Better be on your best behavior, he cautioned himself: behave, for once, like a gentleman, and don't forget it. Be like Lewlyn, like Larry. Jesus, wouldn't that be a joke: like Larry. Ira turned back, passed the stoops of the two adjacent unrenovated tenements where the Italians still lived . . . and on to Edith's house, on Morton Street, number 64. He rang the bell. At the speedy buzz in reply, he lunged quickly against the door, barged in—

There she was, outside her apartment, two flights up. She called his name as he climbed the carpeted steps, waiting for him at the banister, under the hem of her dark dress a glimpse of sheer silk calves he couldn't help looking up at.

"Ira, so glad you're early."

Still on the floor below, he replied with a matter-of-fact "Figured maybe I better."

How fondly, fingering jet bead necklace, she greeted him when he climbed up to the apartment floor. She *must* like him, he thought: smiling so affectionately. But why? He hung his head shyly, even virginally, bashfully at least, and entered. Navajo rugs, burlap-covered couch. Mantelpiece. Blue wagon painting. Piano. And next to one of its mahogany legs, prominent, significant, bulgy, hefty leather valise, tautly strapped and buckled—standing ineluctably ready. Lewlyn advanced, tall and manly in his greenish tweeds, to shake hands: his dry, cordial chuckle: "I see you believe in getting to appointments early."

"Yeah, well," Ira answered with uncertain matching good humor. "Later than this, it'd be a hard job to get here. You know what I mean? I don't know when I had an appointment at ten at night."

"No, I agree, it's not a usual hour to call. But this is a question of time and tide, as you know. The Cunard Line determined that."

"We're both very appreciative that you didn't wait any longer. Trains, steamships, always put my mind on edge, even when I know I have plenty of time. Does anyone ever get over it? I wonder." Edith sighed. She shut the door—and brought into view the tapa tacked to it, Marcia's present, Marcia's presence, with the dim flowers on the brown tree bark. An instant was all you had to think about certain things: the tapa on the door, and next to the piano leg, the bulgy leather valise, tautly strapped and buckled. Edith was already picking up her heather coat from the couch, and Lewlyn his ministerial black topcoat from the wicker armchair. And a new perception crowded out the old: they were leaving right away.

"It's getting to the point where it's fashionable to be late," Edith said as she got into the garment Lewlyn held for her in his own courtly way. "You probably haven't learned that bad habit yet," she smiled at Ira. "I'm glad you haven't, especially now. But Ira, you didn't bring anything extra to wear?"

"No. I didn't think I needed to."

"The open river allows for quite a sweep of wind," Lewlyn interjected as he got his own topcoat.

"It *is* late September," Edith added. "I'd love to lend you something of mine." She smiled.

"No, thanks, I got a vest. I'll be all right." Ira couldn't quite adjust to the tension they seemed to be under. There was plenty of time. They weren't hurrying. It wasn't that, but he felt a strain, an unsettling pall, that seemed to suspend time in Edith's living room. He felt they welcomed him more than was his due, the way people might welcome a gamboling child, the way some might stroke a cat, arching cat, as a diversion from their own stress or disquiet, welcoming a shift of the center of preoccupation. Or was the tension just natural: because of the long voyage ahead for Lewlyn—and getting to that ship on time. But they had hours yet to go. He could feel himself take a deep breath against ambient nervousness. Or maybe because they were separating, yes, just as Mom had predicted when he had told her and Minnie, over a breakfast of fresh bulkies and lox, about Edith and Lewlyn's awkward arrangement.

"*Azoy? Oy, vey, oy, vey,*" Mom had sighed gustily when she learned that Lewlyn would be leaving Edith to return to England. "It's a terrible thing to toy with a woman's heart. Poor Edith, my heart tears for her," Mom had commented. "Had I had a revolver once, my betrayer would have paid for it."

"If we go now," Lewlyn, hardly the destroyer of Mom's vision, said, "we won't have to bother calling a cab. We can take the subway at Christopher Street. And probably get to Thirty-fourth before a cab."

"It's nice out," Ira encouraged. "I just walked from the subway."

"And we'll have to go all the way to Seventh Avenue before we can hope to get a cab," Lewlyn said to Edith. "Unless I call one from your apartment. Do you mind the walk, dear?"

"Oh, no, Lewlyn. Let's just walk. It's really just a short walk."

"What about the valise? You want a hand?" Ira offered.

"Not now, thanks. I may take you up on that later. You've probably noticed valises have a way of getting heavier as time goes on." He turned his kind gaze on Edith. "Are we ready?"

"I am. I'll just lock the door and turn out the lights." She got her keys out of her purse.

Scarcely anything more was said. They were on their way: out of the apartment, down the carpeted stairs, out of the house, into the night of the street, into the coolness of the night of the street, into the silence of Morton Street. On whose sidewalk Ira diffidently accompanied two people, because they had asked him to, and because he felt that something unknown waited upon his doing so, something distant and obscure he had to reach. And he had to behave, to walk, to appear, as if he were part of the scheme of things, though he didn't know what it was, but only that *their* lives, *their* customs, *their* deportment, all of which they took for granted, and much he couldn't even name, were ingredients of an evolving possibility.

Around the corner of Seventh Avenue he traveled with them, around the gas station, with the hands of the moon-faced clock in the window pointing almost to half past ten. By now Mom and Pop were get-

ting ready to go to bed. Minnie was at a dance. Her folding cot beside
Mom and Pop's bed would be empty. His bed would be empty, too.
He was here, on a school night, in the Village, putting up a cheerful
front, keeping up with two professors—no, two Ph.D. lovers, college
teachers, all the way American, walking to the Christopher Street
subway kiosk, on the way to a ship, on the way to an ocean liner: a Cunarder, Lewlyn said. He was, he reminded them, from Pennsylvania:
he had once been a Christian seminary student, once a priest, and
was talking about courses in Greek, and how much they still meant to
him. And she was his what? Mistress, a word he had heard Edith
sometimes use: a hetaera from Silver City, New Mexico, where she
said her father never carried a pistol, but dropped to the ground
whenever the shooting started. At Berkeley, in California, she had
pursued her graduate work. No, there were no more hetaeras in
Berkeley—only in the dictionary. And he himself, on the valise side
of Lewlyn, who so strongly carried it, he himself trailed all of Galitzia
behind him, Jews and Jews and Jews, an ocean away that he had actually crossed in Mom's arms: Galitzia and the Lower East Side and
Irish Harlem: Jew-boy, Jew-boy, with *these* fine people. Forget it, forget! And remember it, remember. Why were you here? You swiped a
silver-filigreed fountain pen, and gave it to your best friend, which
was why you were here. You won a scholarship to Cornell, but your
best friend was in New York, which was why you were here. Boy, you
wouldn't dare tell them: you wouldn't dream of telling them about
your fat heifer of a cousin you had fucked only last Monday, while
your pious grandfather silently chanted in his bedroom, earnestly
praying for his death. You wouldn't dare use that *f* word with them.
But still you were here with them. All you dared say was what everybody could see: that the night over Seventh Avenue was beginning to
get chilly, that the subway entrance was only another block away.

Down the subway steps. And weren't trains always perverse that
way, when you weren't in a hurry? The local pounded into the station
just as Lewlyn dropped the nickel into the turnstile to let broadly
smiling Ira onto the platform, and before the train stopped, he himself and valise were at the open door to join them. What a neat connection. The moment of haste gave them all a cause for small,
diverting congratulations:

"Lewlyn's luck," he chuckled.

And in a few minutes, they were at 34th Street, standing up to await the door's opening. They got off, and with playful, appreciative smile, Lewlyn turned over the valise to Ira's keeping—and carrying.

It was heavy. And again Ira was impressed with how sinewy Lewlyn must be, enduring and strong his body under those tweeds, what stamina he must have. How many acres did he say you had to grow and harvest wheat for a college education? Did he say ten? The valise was heavy—in either hand. Ira began lagging behind . . . wouldn't betray how much of a strain the valise was. Ahead of him the two lovers walked—really as lovers now, perhaps because so few people were in evidence. Lewlyn's arm was curved around the back of Edith's waist. As if it were a movement in a dance, she leaned slightly against the arm encircling her back—and yet at the same time, stepped forward with a determined jauntiness, as if—Ira tried to disassociate the observing mind from the tugging arm—as if her sprightliness were genuine, arose without inner coercion or pretense. She was enjoying the occasion. Brave, wasn't she, or behaving according to form. Proud. She was, wasn't she? Ira tried to force his gait a little faster, and then, becoming just a bit out of breath, again allowed himself to lag.

They entered the long, white-tiled tunnel connecting the IRT subway station to the Hudson Tubes terminal. Long, long, white-walled cavern. Laboriously he passed through it, fixed grin on his face. Pale, fateful tiles slowly retreating on either side, on either side unreeling the glossy squares of their faces, yielding to other square faces that prolonged a passage nearly deserted, except for two lovers walking gracefully ahead of him. What did it mean? Did it mean anything? Two lovers about to part, trailed by himself with arms beginning to complain, hauling a burden that was beginning to weigh like a ton.

At last, at last, they reached the change booth and entrance of the stale-drafty platform of the Hudson Tubes.

Again Lewlyn paid their fares, and they entered a waiting and nearly vacant train, and sat down, with Edith between them.

"You've done yeoman service, Ira. Thanks." Lewlyn took charge of the valise. He slid it between his legs. "We've made wonderful time, haven't we?" He leaned forward slightly. "In another five minutes this train will be on its way."

"Is it a long ride?" Ira asked.

"No, it's very short—short and rather unpleasant. You ought to have a veil, Edith, against the dust."

"Have one or take one," she answered, as if to someone straight ahead.

He chuckled. "It hasn't come to that, I hope. I'm honestly at a crossroads, Edith. I don't need to repeat it. You'll excuse us, Ira?"

"Oh, sure, sure." Ira withdrew from audience, sat back.

"And I needn't repeat," Edith said, "that the basic flaw in the whole idea of uncommitted friendship is the assumption that men and women are the same. Are built the same, feel the same—react similarly. They don't."

"We agreed it was a risk we took."

"But not each risking the same thing. Not each taking the same risk."

Ira could hear, but didn't venture to look, didn't care to. Voice alone, Edith's stony posture seen out of the corner of his eye, Lewlyn's reasonable, dry, constrained voice conveyed a gravity understood without a glance, made a glance both impertinent and superfluous. Two, three passengers straggled in. The motorman came through the car bearing the control handle in his gloved hand, glanced at the three as he went by. And no sooner had he gone by than Lewlyn said earnestly: "But nothing has been settled, Edith, nothing has been decided. Whole lifetimes are at stake, your lifetime, mine, yes. Cecilia's too. You realize that, I'm sure. I must be given a chance to consider choices. It would be absolute folly on my part not to."

"Which only goes to prove even further how utterly unfair the whole thing is. I haven't any."

"You're sure?"

And now Ira could feel Edith stiffen beside him. "You don't really mean that, do you?"

"How can I ignore other factors when they exist?"

"Rubbish."

"Believe me, Edith, this can only lead to recrimination."

She was silent, with the resolute silence of a refused reply.

"No, really," Lewlyn urged. "With everything up in the air the way it is."

Ira could see her head turn toward Lewlyn, but whether in con-
ciliation, in reproof, in appraisal, he couldn't tell. "It's a great pity
both of us aren't in the same city," he heard her say. "I think your
protestations would soon be tested. And—" She scratched a small ear.

"And?"

"Forgive me." Her voice became stony. Unmistakable, the rigidity
of her posture, even if unseen. "Forgive me for not going on, dear.
Of what use inflicting wounds? All we're saying would lead to them,
as you pointed out. It's certainly not my intention to, and I won't.
We're on the eve of parting, aren't we?"

"Temporary. I assure you, dear. I'm on the eve of departure, that's
all."

The train doors slid shut. Seconds later, the train jarred into motion and accelerated.

The roar within the closely encompassing tube became deafen-
ing. Fetid subterranean gusts swirled through and inside the car;
they spun scraps of newspaper, spiraled dust. At the far end, the lady
in the blue coat, last person to come in, frowned, tucked her coat
more securely beneath her squalid thighs. Ira swallowed hard. Wow!
Plunging through the mud of a whole river above you. He saw Lewlyn's hand move forward, pat Edith's, saw his lips shape words, only
one of which was audible: "ordeal." She nodded. Did she say, "Quite"?
Everything had other meanings, meanings. Quite. Ordeal. Why
would she want to do it, anyway? She could have said goodbye right
there on Morton Street. Goodbye and good luck. But no. And *he* was
going to see another woman, and make up his mind about her, between her and Edith. So why do you have to go all the way to the ship
with him? Why don't you cross the ocean with him too? Anh, don't
get funny. Or snide. You'll begin to sound like Mom. Yeah. . . . Growing late, that was the trouble: eleven o'clock, half past eleven maybe.
Past his bedtime, and the dust made you blink. But you never were in
love, said Minnie. So what do you know, stupid? Let's see: twelve
o'clock maybe, they would leave the ship. Then all the way back to the
apartment: that would be one o'clock. Then to Harlem: two o'clock.
Whew, he'd be walking in his sleep.

*   *   *

If only, Ira's despairing cry ran loud within himself, he didn't dawdle so, didn't moan, didn't temporize. He had been just a bit too timid, and more than a bit. He was, to say the least, amply and fully disgusted with himself. There was so little time. He had overextended himself, overplayed his hand, or whatever cliché fitted the situation. The situation, the story, needed to be resolved, and quickly. He had been too cavalier about his abilities, his ability to cover ground within the limited time he had allotted himself—though it might have been adequate for someone else, younger, brighter, with greater stamina. The novelistic process—and it was a process, not just a form—could only sustain so much. Beyond that, whatever the tolerances of the exact points were, the process would soon become impacted, like an oversized, overloaded engine. It would stop and stall—the way the old engines of a plane became impacted when encountering a flock of starlings beyond the engine's capacity to digest, and the plane, so low in reverse, would crash, the journey unfulfilled.

The roar did indeed subside. The train slowed down. Surrounding tunnel walls fell back into the wide expanse of station sliding by and coming to rest with the train: Lewlyn stood up, Edith and Ira did likewise, and the other few passengers as well.

"Don't you want me to carry that?" Ira asked.

"No, thanks. My turn." Lewlyn picked up the valise, guided Edith to the train doors, and when they glided open, sustained her across the gap to the platform. The three stepped out into the great deserted chamber of concrete: HOBOKEN.

"It's this way." Lewlyn led them to the stairs.

Fresh air, poured down from above, and growing fresher as they climbed, sharpened when they reached the carbide daylight of the news vendor's stand at street level. "Aren't you chilly?" Edith asked.

"Not much. Oh, I can feel it's a little nippy. Maybe that's why I should be carrying the valise." Ira hitched his shoulders.

"Oh, no, thanks, Ira. It's only a short way. You can see where it is from here."

"That building with the lights?"

"Yes. That's a Cunarder pier. Number ninety-two."

"I can still give you a hand."

"No, thanks. You've done more than your share."

"It would warm me up."

"Oh, dear! I knew I shouldn't let you go without more over you."

"I'm all right. I have my vest."

"We'll be there in a minute."

Over cobblestones into the obscurity of a starry night . . . in the direction of a dim, low, hulking row of buildings: the piers. Before the gaping entrance of one of them, weak, yellow incandescence spilled out on the cobblestones. Beside the pier a moored ship blazed with floodlights crisscrossing in basketweave from boom to mast.

"There it is," said Lewlyn.

"Isn't that funny? I always get twisted around. I would have sworn the Hudson was that way." Ira thumbed over his shoulder.

"That's more nearly the direction of the Ohio. Are you all right on these cobblestones, Edith?"

"Oh, yes."

"They're meant for wagons, not for heels, picturesque in daylight. But out of date."

"I better go over to that side." Ira suited action to word.

"Thank you, Ira."

"Oops! Cobblestones is right."

They trod their way carefully.

"I hope you don't regret coming," Lewlyn said gently.

Ira could sense at once the intolerable latency in her reply, a silent latency that brooked no ameliorating in speech. His presence was both essential and superfluous, diversionary, even more than when Lewlyn made those fragmented exonerations, those token apologies, on the train. They were like two people caught in a personal vortex that affected them and no one else, no matter how close.

"Oh, it's picturesque, it's dramatic. Ocean voyages, departures are—" Edith seemed deliberately to pause, clip her words in odd places. "Notably poetic. I'm glad I came. Am I overjoyed? No . . . I'm glad I came—this once. It was necessary for me to come. I'll never have to do it again. I suppose that might be viewed as a consolation of sorts."

"It wasn't very wise of me to ask, was it? I was hoping it would mean the same thing to both of us, something beautiful and shared."

"How can it be?" Edith replied.

"I realize that now. I thought of it as something shared—or I thought you regarded it that way. Even if not a happy occasion. There are those times. Parting with someone close, say, off to war, as we did with my older brother, Andrew. Fortunately he came back from France. I told you about the poppy seeds that fell out of his uniform. Are you still able to cope with these cobblestones?"

"Oh, I took precautions and wore my lowest-heeled shoes."

"That was wise."

A few steps farther without speaking. Headlights of a car approaching the entrance of the pier, headlights that came to a stop, preempted the yellow light on cobblestones with twin beams. Car doors opened on voices quick to laughter. Edith continued, "I don't like to say this, but the thing that I didn't realize was the extent to which Marcia has molded your character. Changed it—I think for the—" She hesitated. "Weakened it."

"I don't believe so."

"I think that's where you're mistaken. The person you were, the person I had the feeling you were when you took me to see your parents, was originally quite different. I'm sure he would have made an entirely different decision from the one you're making."

"That's where you're mistaken, Edith. I haven't made it."

Edith seemed not to hear. "It's as though you're trying to find someone who will help reassemble you, now that you've lost Marcia."

"Oh, Edith." Lewlyn tried to soften his reply with a touch of humor. "If there's anything in my decision, I mean any single factor that will determine my decision, it's whether—really, listen, Edith—whether I'll be able to sustain your very negative view of life."

"I hear Marcia again."

"Simply because Marcia and I happen to agree doesn't mean it's her view, or her view imposed on me. I came to that consideration on my own—be careful, dear!"

"I'm holding her on the other side," Ira assured.

"That's good. Thanks. . . . Edith, I admit, Marcia said when I mentioned my concern, she said: 'I was wondering when you'd perceive that.'" He seemed to wait for Edith's reply, and when she made none, he went on, "I'm speaking for myself, as an individual, trying to assess as objectively as I can a very difficult situation. You must believe me. And please, Edith, don't decide things in advance. It will just interfere with objectivity, with judgment. There are three lives at stake here, three futures: yours, Cecilia's, and mine."

"And all three futures are being decided by Marcia."

"I don't think that's fair, Edith."

"Really? It may be unpleasant, but it happens to be true."

"I don't think so. I'm sorry."

"Well . . . what matter?" Edith moved her head in the increasing light, from side to side, in a swaying motion weary in its resignation. The headlights in front were turned off: car doors slammed, figures entered the pier bearing luggage. "The regrettable thing is that the very negativism you talk about, my so-called negativism, is only strengthened by your own behavior—at Marcia's behest. I can feel changes taking place in myself as a result of all this."

"Like what, my dear?"

"Unfortunate changes. For one thing, I wonder whether any man is worth trusting."

"But I've been honest. I've been honest all the way, Edith."

"You've been honest in your way."

"Why do you say that?"

"You can't be honest. Not until you've been reassembled."

"Oh, heavens! Please, Edith, you keep harping on that. Reassembled out of what?"

"Out of the priest who's come apart, the very one Marcia created in the first place."

"You don't think I would have arrived at the conclusions I did in any event? Even if she had come back, and continued to be my wife? Even if she had not fallen in love with Robert? Not decided on divorce? I would still have begun to be skeptical of the efficacy of prayer, of religion in general."

"Perhaps. That remains moot, as they say."

"Edith, won't you at least wait till I return?"

"I fear I'll have to."

"And suspend judgment meanwhile?" he coaxed. "You owe me that much."

She laughed for the first time—briefly. "Do I?"

Cobblestones gave way to level plank. The three had come to the entrance of the pier, like that of a huge shed. Lewlyn seemed completely oblivious of his valise. He still had not changed hands. God, the man was strong—or completely occupied. The strings of electric lights overhead strove wanly with the expanse of gloom of the interior—till the cluster of lights at the gangway: there, all was brightness, brightness shining on passengers and well-wishers entering the circle of radiance. Voices. Merriment of new arrivals.

Lewlyn displayed his boarding pass to the uniformed guard. The trio were smilingly waved on. Hanging on to the rail, they climbed the cleated gangway from dock to ship—passing above a lane of murky water to the brightly lit deck. The vessel seemed small for an ocean liner; or was it foreshortened by its illuminated areas? Few passengers were visible, but already the pitch of gaiety peculiar to departure was beginning to come from different directions, as more newcomers boarded the ship. In the group nearest them, a woman in a fur stole smoked a cigarette in a silver cigarette holder, like those of an actress on a stage her eyes glittered in the floodlights. A white-jacketed steward appeared, fizzling club soda on his tray, the White Rock nymph on the bottle clearly visible, recognized from Park & Tilford days. Lewlyn had put his valise down, and he and Edith spoke in low tones to each other, which Ira felt he ought to make all the more private by withdrawing a discreet distance away. He stood near the rail, appreciative of the tangy wind that blew so fresh over the river. But it had an edge too, and made him wish he had just one more garment to cover him, a sweater, a shirt, anything. Maybe Edith had one of Lewlyn's pajama tops.

As he gazed at the lights of Manhattan twisting toward him across the rippling water like a gimlet, he was relieved to hear Edith say, "I don't think we ought to wait."

"I think you're right," Lewlyn concurred.

They embraced—eloquently. Lewlyn's hat was off, his coat open, and nestling close to him, clinging to him with body and with lips, was Edith, her body within the coat, within the encompassing arm that held the hat. It was too embarrassingly beautiful a scene for real life—it was a scene to glimpse—and look away from: a man and woman clasped within a shaft of light.

They parted. And just then a band struck up, and music—a new Cole Porter tune—came wafting from an open door of the nearby saloon.

"Take care of her, won't you? See that she gets home safely." Speaking with voice raised above the music, Lewlyn pressed Ira's hand.

"Oh, sure. Hope you have a good trip."

Feeling himself wavering inwardly, and yet having to maintain an overt show of firmness, Ira took Edith's arm and guided her toward the brightly lit gap in the ship's rails where the uniformed guard, the ship's sentry, was still standing.

She walked rigidly. They passed others coming up the lighted gangway, and she stumbled against them. Ira increased the firmness of his grip. They stepped onto the solid pier again. Ira looked back. Lewlyn was watching them from the rail, from the height of the deck above them. And it seemed to Ira that Lewlyn shook his head, sympathetically, and with a certain humorous camaraderie. Could it be that he was relieved to see someone else assume the burden? The two waved a last goodbye.

V

Ira supported the blindly unheeding Edith out of the pier, past arriving automobiles and taxis, over the indistinct cobblestones, back to the carbide brightness of the newsstand. She seemed utterly disoriented, abandoned, aimless. He dared not relinquish his hold on her arm. What was happening to her? So forsaken of self he had never seen anyone. With one hand on the banister and the other grasping her arm, he helped her descend the stairs to the change booth. She was mute the entire way; it was only when they stopped before the change booth that she spoke.

"Ira, do you have the fare?"

"Oh, sure." He still had a good part of the five she had given him. He changed a quarter. Ira piloted the dazed Edith to the turnstile. Two dimes in the slot. And through. And once again, they had very little time to wait before the train pulled into the station. They had evidently left the ship long before its departure, because this time the arriving train discharged far more passengers than the one that had brought the three there. Almost no one was returning yet, and once the various groups of talkative and vivacious newcomers climbed up the stairs, the platform was left deserted.

Ira led Edith through the train doors. They sat down, alone in the big empty car. What should he say to her? Everything he could think of seemed vain, seemed futile and insipid against the impenetrable silence that immured her. "C'mon, train, let's go," he finally said aloud, and then because her self-absorption increased his uneasiness, he demanded irritably, "I wonder how long these trains take to turn around?"

Immobile and expressionless, she made no answer. Distraught, if ever anybody was, looking with blank, protrusive eyes from floor to window of the train, from window to the row of straw seats opposite, and hopelessly at the advertising placards overhead.

Minutes passed. A man and woman came aboard, sat down across the way. At last, doors slid to—the longed-for thrust set the train into motion. In seconds, the dingy tube enclosed them, the stupefying roar rose to crescendo, partly welcome this time as vindicating abandonment of all efforts to speak. But not for the couple on the other side of the aisle—the young man, Arrow-collar clean-featured, with ruby stickpin in his tie and a thin, segmented Charlie Chaplin walking stick between his knees; the young woman, pretty in her pearl earrings and light taupe coat, beneath which the tassels of her slate-colored skirt showed—they were leaning toward each other. And as if enjoying the exertion of making themselves understood, they were apparently shouting at each other at the top of their voices, though not a word was audible across the aisle. Ira watched them, fascinated—until his eyes began to smart. Hilarity engulfed the pair as the train slowed down, and they shrieked with laughter when the train stopped. Ira looked at Edith—she seemed completely oblivious. The situation was getting to be serious. What should he do?

He steered her through the open train doors, then from the platform out to the general underground area, his eyes raised, searching for the tiled tunnel that connected the Hudson Tubes to the IRT subway.

"I think—" Frowning uncertainly, Ira hunted for a directional sign overhead. "We go—it's this way to the IRT, isn't it? Just a minute, Edith, I'll ask someone."

"No. Please. Ira." She checked him, and bending her head, snapped open her purse. "Please, let's take a taxi." She held out another five-dollar bill. "Take it, won't you?"

"Is that what you want?"

"Yes." Like an automaton, she proferred the bill.

He took it from her. Grim, how grim she made him feel, with all the determination and responsibility of being in charge: he had never hailed a cab in his life. "We gotta go upstairs to the street first. All right?" Again he took her arm, and with his other hand on the banister, helped her mount the stairs.

Out of the subway, they emerged into well-lighted, cool, and sparsely peopled 34th Street. There were cabs in evidence cruising by. So *he* was Larry now, worldly Larry; he was Lewlyn, adult Lewlyn. Resolute and stern, Ira held up his arm, signaled. And at once a checkered yellow cab swerved, tires squealing, to the curb.

"We want to go to 64 Morton Street," Ira instructed the driver. "Hudson Street's your best bet. As soon as you can, go downtown on Hudson."

"I know where it is."

Ira held the door open for Edith to get in, followed her. The meter flag snapped down, and they were on their way.

And then—with stunning suddenness—she wept! Wept, sobbed: a torrent of tears he would never have believed possible: heartbroken, uncontrollable. They threatened to wrack her asunder. These were not Mom's tears, filled with old-world imprecations, or even

Minnie's taunting tears of rage. These were tears of such inexhaustible sorrow. God, what to do, how to calm her, quiet her? What would the driver think? For there was no doubt he could hear, though he gave no sign. Anxiety over her state, solicitude over her woe, his helplessness, all assailed Ira at once—immobilized him, at a loss, the victim of a flood. With an effort, he wrenched himself into action: "Edith, please!" he implored. "For God's sake, try to get hold of yourself. You gotta stop that! Edith!"

Sobs. Broken, stifled cries. A spate of tears swamping the glimmering little square of handkerchief she tried to staunch it with.

"Here. Take this one." Ira yanked his own handkerchief, which Mom had just laundered, out of his pocket. "It's clean. C'mon, calm down, Edith. You hear what I'm saying? That's enough!"

"I'll try. I'll try." For the first time coherent words mingled with her sobs. "Oh, dear! Oh, dear!"

"You'll be a wreck, that's what'll happen."

"I know it. I know it. It doesn't matter."

"Sure it does. What d'ye mean, it doesn't matter? You've got classes tomorrow."

"I can call them off."

"All right, so you'll call 'em off. But there's yourself, you can't go on this way."

"Oh, I'm so sorry, Ira. Putting you through this. Oh, mercy!"

"That's nothing. I don't want you to get sick."

"I've been such a damned ninny. I've been such an unspeakable fool."

"Why? What did you do? I don't know—oh, you dropped it." He stooped to pick up her handkerchief from the floor of the cab. "I don't know everything about this. I mean"—he said vehemently—"you know what I mean. I don't see that you did anything wrong. What did you do that was wrong?"

"I deluded myself. Just deluded myself. Clung to wish fulfillment. I've been such a damned fool. How could I have been such a damned fool? Oh, God! A woman my age just plain sacrificing herself to schoolgirl daydreams!"

"About what? About Lewlyn?"

"Yes. Yes, of course."

"He's coming back, isn't he? You said yourself he was just going to England to make up his mind."

"He's not. His mind is made up. No matter what he says. And even if he comes back empty-handed, who knows what he'll do?"

Perplexity gathered like a turbulence in the mind. "What d'you mean? How d'you know?"

"It's only too clear, Ira. Lord!" A sob shook her. "I know when I've lost. I *knew* when I had lost, but did I do anything about it? No! Can you imagine such a perfect fool?"

"Did he say? Did he tell you it was over? I only heard his telling you not to—gee!" All he could do was lean forward in the bounding vehicle and gesticulate against swiftly changing slash of light and shadow. "What? Like don't give up. He hasn't decided, made up his mind. No?"

"Ira, dear, he'd been planning this trip to England for months. They've been writing back and forth. He's been telling me what she said. And I've been conspiring with him to delude myself all this time." She wept softly into the handkerchief against her face. "Oh, dear. Oh, dear. It's like knowing someone will die, and now you have to face the fact."

He tried to catch a glimpse of the street sign. They must be close to destination. He felt an irresistible urge to scratch under his hat band. "Gee, I didn't know."

"You must think I'm a hopeless idiot to go along with this charade."

"No. I don't."

"You'd have a perfect right to. I have no one to blame but myself."

Wordless. They sat back on the cushioned seats, as the street-lamps passed. Silent, solitary, eerie, all of it: the driver steering his cab, his face in profile as impassive in the intermittent light as if cut out of sheet metal, the dark kind, hot rolled steel it was called, the frying-pan kind—oh, boy, was he nutty. Swirling thought seeking respite. . . . The driver steered his curved way along Hudson Street; the cab throbbed south—only a couple of blocks from that same river where he had once thought of killing himself, where the Cunarder now was moored. Or was it? Had it already cast off? The ship moving south toward the harbor's mouth, Sandy Hook, while they moved south between desolate, unlit tenements . . . they were being driven on an excavated street of a buried city . . . by an expressionless driver who never turned his head, an Egyptian charioteer, through a necropolis with streetlights on the corners. . . . Edith continued to weep softly.

"Listen, Edith," Ira tried to assuage. "You're an English professor. I mean, you know literature. You've come to this situation a hundred times reading about it." He fumbled, opened his hands to the dark. "You know what I mean?"

"You mean I ought to have been better prepared, and I'm not."

"Something like that."

"You're perfectly right. I ought to have been better prepared. Better prepared by every minute I was with him. But you see I'm not. I wasn't. Will I be any better prepared when he returns in a few weeks? He's coming back, as you said. Oh, yes, he has to. With the same needs as before." She shook her head hopelessly while she let it sink in. "Another's need becomes my need. Isn't it ridiculous?"

"Two more blocks," Ira leaned forward to speak to the driver. "The one after this one, Morton Street."

"I know it."

Jesus, did he have that five bucks? Ira felt in his right-hand pocket. Yeah. Hell, he didn't need it anyway. He had a few bucks of his own, really of hers anyway. Did the driver think he was the culprit? Who the hell knew? "Here it is. Sixty-four is the middle of the block."

The driver nodded, rounded the corner.

"Right there."

The cab drew up to the curb. And no sooner did it come to a stop than, unassisted, Edith sprang from car to the sidewalk, and eyes streaming anew, crossed the sidewalk to the house door and disappeared inside.

"What is it, eighty-five cents?" Ira peered at the meter.

"Right."

"Here's a dollar. Sorry . . . you know."

"Okay, pal. T'anks." Curtly spoken as the greenback was pocketed. Up went the meter flag. Ira made for the door. The cab, its engine churning loudly in the empty street, the reeking exhaust visible under the nearby streetlight, squeaked a tire against the curb, rolling away toward the dark bend before Seventh Avenue.

VI

She was stretched out on the gunnysack-covered couch weeping when he entered the floor-lamp-illuminated apartment. She sat up when he came in. And uncertain how to comfort her further, to bring her to quiescence, except by his presence, he dropped into the wicker armchair opposite. His damp handkerchief lay crumpled on top of the chest of drawers—the upper drawer was open, and two or three of her dainty handkerchiefs lay on the couch beside her. "I've made a proper fool of myself," she said. "In all ways. Will you ever forgive me?"

His mind thick with the late hour, he could find little soothing to say: "Oh, sure. Gee. But don't you give him any credit?"

For once she laughed—shortly: "For helping make me one?"

"No, no, I didn't mean that!" Jesus, he'd better wake up. "I mean, you're so sure he'll never change his mind?"

"Oh, no. That would be more of the same wishful thinking I've been guilty of all along, that I've been silly enough to indulge in all along. You can be certain that if there is any hope in that direction—and I know there isn't—Marcia will be here to see that he doesn't change his mind. As I say, even if he wanted to. And I'm sure he doesn't. You're an angel to stand by anyone so stupidly redundant."

Checked, he'd better shut up. What did he have to offer to people older, smarter, more sophisticated? What did he know about their lives? Only something about Edith's life: a little something: her affair with Larry, her affair with Lewlyn. He had seen this evening the beautiful, the dramatic parting on board ship. Lucky he hadn't put his foot in it so far, had gotten by with least betrayal of gaucheness. If she were Stella he'd know what to do. So, say, Stella—what a cinch. Alone, boy. All he had to offer now was a sigh. A forked-tongue sigh: sympathy for her plight—sympathy that melted into contemptible self-satisfaction, because she had lost. A triple-tongued sigh, maybe: that he felt he could take advantage of her plight, as he could have of Minnie, as he easily could of Stella, but now didn't dare. . . . Different world, class, everything else different. A grown-up woman. Same old story. How the hell did Larry have the nerve? Now wait a minute. Don't give up altogether: forlorn, drooping havoc-aftermath, you call it? Small, defeated by perjury: Minnie with a Ph.D., if you made changes—in her, in himself.

She was talking, alternately berating Marcia for the ruin she had wrought in Edith's chances of marrying Lewlyn, and Lewlyn for his weakness in listening to the wife who had cast him off, railing even at Cecilia, her artfully winsome letters—of a spinster ten years Lewlyn's senior, desperate to snare him. And to none of it could Ira make any reply. What could he say? Any more than the mirror her eyes sought from time to time could answer. He could sit soberly and listen with pained attention—or half listen—and often understand only half of what he heard.

"I've had such rotten luck with men," she kept repeating. "Yes, I've had any number who deared me and darlinged me, but they were either impossible, like Shmuel, or Larry, young *and* impossible, or Silver City grown-ups, deadly bores, reminiscing till you could scream. Or Boris—I can't stand him physically, even though I have had to. I think I ought to go jump in a lake."

"Oh, now, Edith. Gee."

"That insufferable Tinklepaugh I married so he could finish his doctoral at Berkeley. Oh, dear. My fat cousin Ralph in New Jersey, auto parts salesman, courting me. Wasserman, committing just plain rape. Only that Mexican boy years ago—of course, there was no possibility there, but he was so gentle and tender. And now the only man with whom a marriage would have worked."

What a strange way of putting it: a marriage would have worked. What had he said to Larry once about his sisters' marriages? He had translated into English the Yiddish expression *gitn shiddekh*. And been reproved for it. What subtle distinctions: a marriage would have worked. "But there are others," he ventured.

"I just don't have that kind of feminine attraction. The sexual appeal of someone like Louise Bogan that men find so arresting."

"Oh, I don't think so." That was the best he could say to her—at this hour of the night. Jesus, at this hour of the night he'd be apt to say anything: if she were someone else, someone Jewish, he'd flare up, rudely, agree with her sarcastically, put an end to her lachrymose self-decrying. But it wouldn't be true. Even grief-darkened as her features were, and limp with fatigue her body, she was still so girlishly attractive. But hell, it would be even more ludicrous if he waxed enthusiastic about her sex appeal: praised her Elizabethan features, her protrusive brown eyes, the bun of hair at the back of her head, her ankles, her tiny feet, her hourglass waist. Christ, look at the clock, clock over the arched mantelpiece. She's suffering, sure, suffering, but it's getting past one-thirty. The very number made his eyelids tacky.

"You know what time it is, Edith? It's nearly two o'clock."

"It is? Is it as late as that?"

"Yeah. I think you should go to bed."

"I won't be able to sleep."

"Oh, sure you will. Two o'clock? Boy, I can hardly keep my own eyes open."

She remained inert, brooding—and distant. "I've imposed on you dreadfully. I'm so dreadfully sorry, Ira."

"I know. But you're tired. All right?" He got to his feet, aware of his own unsteadiness. "Lemme give you a hand."

She pushed herself forward on the couch as he approached, tottered slightly when she arose, held his arm a moment, and let go. "I'll be all right, Ira. Heavens. I don't know how I'll ever repay you."

"You know I—" He brushed away bleariness. "If I wasn't so tired, I'd tell you what I mean: I got a chance to see something that I never could have seen otherwise."

"I think I know what you mean. Scarcely repayment, though. My carrying on—as if I didn't deserve what was coming to me—for deluding myself so."

"No, that wasn't—that was only part of it. There was everything else."

She shook her head. "You're incredible. Someone as young as you to feel that way. Who else would bear with such a fool?" Slow large eyelids covered her eyes. "It's time I put an end to this nonsense. Time I went to bed. You're right."

"Maybe I better stay tonight."

Her eyes opened wide, scanning his face. "Oh, I'll be all right. I promise. I'll go to bed."

"No, I mean I'd like to stay." He diluted his boldness, scrambled motives. "It's so late. Just to lie down on the edge of the bed."

"By all means. Of course you can stay, Ira. I just wish I had another bed."

"It's all right. Just so I can lie down."

"I had no idea. I'll be out of the bathroom in a few minutes. I'll put out a towel for you. I'm sure you'll want a facecloth too?"

"Huh? Yeah, thanks." A facecloth? He had only learned lately what it was.

She got her bathrobe, nightgown, and bedroom slippers out of the closet and disappeared behind the bathroom door. He heard the toilet flush, faucet splash. He sat down to wait.

Boom. Was he ever overwrought, exhausted with excitement? The late hour had begun to toll its knell. Not a word spoken, but silence itself resounding. There it went again. Boom. No, it was thought itself reverberating, a word formed at the throat that was never uttered. Tired. Such rending emotion, shattering of sedate surfaces. But you saw it before, he told himself wearily: in Woodstock. The cat. Her hysteria. Would you marry her? You're Lewlyn. All those dimples, smiles, charms, shapeliness, neat ankles, accomplishments, scholarship, degrees? Would you? Only because the steel frames of his eyeglasses intercepted vision did he realize he was shaking his head. . . . So what was wrong? Wrong-ong-ong-o-ong. What had he tried to figure out once? She was acting in her own tragedy. She was sorrowing for herself, the heroine. Could it be he was right? He was right, yeah, he was right. That's how she was. Sorrowing for herself, the heroine. She had lost the only man, she said, with whom a marriage would have worked. So . . . he had *willed* it. He had *willed* that everyone else would be eliminated. And they were. And there *was* nobody else. . . . You're crazy. . . . But if there was nobody else . . . You're crazy. . . . But if there was nobody else, and that's what you willed, from the deepest inside, see? That's what would happen, and so now that's what he would have to do. If he weren't so goddamn shy, if he weren't so goddamn guilty-shy, he could tell already what would happen, right now, tonight, or this morning, or what the hell time it was: five after two. He was twenty-one years old. How old was she? He had come all the way from Galitzia, and she all the way from New Mexico. *Shixal*, Mom called it, *shixal*, fate, *shixal* with a *shiksa*.

The ivory-colored neckline of her nightgown showing under the scattered brown checks of her bathrobe, she came out of the bathroom, tried to smile: "It's your turn. You'll find a fresh towel on the door hook. I'm sorry about the facecloth. I couldn't find a better one."

Ira gaped at her, and still openmouthed, pushed himself to his feet against the creaking wicker. "What's that on your face?" Between loose braids, a pale, waxy layer covered all her features. "That." He pointed.

"Oh. Cold cream. My skin is so very dry."

"Oh. Cold cream. So when do you wash?"

"Before I put it on."

"Oh. So do you wipe it off afterward?"

"In a few minutes. Doesn't your sister use it?"

"I never saw it on her before. Excuse me. I didn't know." He removed his jacket. "I'll go now." He made for the bathroom.

Jesus, you're dumb, he removed his tie, Jesus Christ, you're dumb, he opened his collar, tucked it under. Larry must have seen it, must have known; his older sister used it. But Minnie never did. Why the hell was it, in Woodstock he never saw it? Hey, maybe he better take the shirt off. Yeah. He stank like a—like a polecat under the armpits. What the hell was a polecat? He removed his glasses. Soap up, yeah. Get that Hudson Tube dirt off your puss, boyoboy. And no shave, either. That's the facecloth? Hey, it ain't a bad idea: a *shmatta* made out of a piece of towel. Soap up heavy for now. Tomorrow, get in that bathtub or shower. And don't forget, button up fly. Dry-dry-dry. Keep on pants and socks, right? Jacket too? Jesus, it's really getting chilly. Stretch out on the edge of the bed. Boy, can't wait. He put on his glasses, retracted his shirt collar. He hoped he looked all right.

Tie in hand, he came out. She was already lying in bed, burlap coverlet exposing dark blankets up to her chin. He would be against the wall. Okay. Chance to get as far from her as possible. "It's half past—is there an alarm on the clock? You want me to set it?"

"I've already set it, thanks. I'll wake before it goes off anyway."

"And the window?"

"Just a crack will do."

"Okay." He lifted the sash up. Then kicked his shoes off. He gauged distance and direction to the wall his side of the bed—don't make any mistakes—and rub against her—he switched off the floor lamp. Darkness . . . in semidarkness he made his way, wriggled up his side of the bed. And for Christ's sake, don't wake up the way you did with Mom. Maybe should have kept jacket on too. He lay quietly supine, shank and right shoulder against the wall.

"Aren't you going to get under the blankets?" Her voice came from the other side.

"No. I'm all right."

"Don't be such a goose, Ira. Get under the blankets. You'll catch cold."

"All right, I'll get under that bedcover." He eased himself under the coverlet, stretched out, again wished he'd kept his jacket on. Wo-o-o. Called a goose, boy. Ships and shoes and sealing-wax. Ardent, sculptured embracing in the ship's floodlights. His hat was off, his coat was open, and she within his arms, nestling. . . . Merrily did we drop below the kirk, below the hill, below the lighthouse top—oh, that's who it was the demon hackie was afterward on the ride home: not Pharaoh's hackie. No. It was the Ancient Mariner piloting his cab through the basalt chasm of Hudson Street: the ice did split with a thunder-fit . . . Oh, boy, the helmsman steered us thro-o-o. . . .

So what is truth? said jesting Pilate. And would not stop for answer, said Francis Bacon. Yeah. Ira paused to scratch an eyebrow. Sometimes as he typed, countenances merged, or persons merged. There were times when he thought it was M he was lying so scrupulously separated from by the width of the bed. Not Edith. Because after a while the separation, that separation, ceased to exist—with Edith. And became the same kind of intimacy he had known with M, and still did, even five years after her death. With Edith, there was understandably not the same kind of treasured intimacy as with M, but real intimacy—over a long period of time, an entire decade. Yeah. Where was all this leading to? Why had he begun by saying,

What is truth? said jesting Pilate. Not because he had been talking about a pilot, and the echo lingered. No. And why the merging of persons, the intrusion of one period on another, of youth retracting on age? Was his own mind beginning to become cloudy, become blurred with senescence? No, he didn't think so. He had been listening to a microtape the other day, the kind of tape, or tape recorder, he used to eavesdrop, and this particular tape had been enclosed in a plastic case on which he had written the word: listen.

Listen. He wrote that, or some other warning sometimes, to keep himself from absentmindedly erasing the tape on behalf of some immediate matter that had come up. And he was fortunate he *did* listen. The tape was worth preserving, preserving in the original. He had had, as Edith remarked about men, rotten luck when it came to duplicating these small tapes (which were relatively expensive) onto the cheaper larger cassettes. What was the cause of the ill luck he didn't know, wasn't expert enough to tell. When he listened to the same tape with earphones—he had a very fine though painfully binding headset, almost vise-tight earphones—he heard all that was audible with great clarity. When he tried transferring the tape via patchcord to another, the results were extremely disappointing: all gravelly, speech drowned in gravelly growling, almost as bad as those ancient days on 119th Street, when the coal that each denizen of the tenement bought to be stored in his own cellar bin roared down in a steel chute from truck to sidewalk manhole through a conduit to the cellar below; and waiting for it to pour out of the conduit stood the Irish navvy with streaked visage and bushel basket. (Homeric, the way men toiled in those days, days not so very long ago.) So Ira had heeded the injunction and listened to the microtape. Ah, what is truth? said jesting Pilate. Or do you simply let the statement, Bacon's epigram, overlap with "All's fair in love and war"? The common, coarse expression was—stable talk, the well-bred would call it—blowing one's nuts. Lewlyn had to blow his nuts (glands, he would term them); Ira had to blow his nuts. What male adult didn't have to? And all's fair in love and war.

Ira then did as he had instructed himself, he listened, eavesdropped on the old tape. The year, the year was about 1979, or perhaps the year before. And the place was where he and M and Lewlyn, having aged over fifty years, were having their lunch; it was—judging from the voices of youngsters that seemed to come from the immediate surroundings—and judging from the context—a small picnic area off the road to Jemez Springs. The road was opposite an abandoned copper mine, which geophysicist son Jess had previously prospected, bringing back a few specimens.

Why did one feel that peculiar bitterness? Was it truly bitterness? Difficult to decide what the feeling was, this feeling of listening, not to a voice of the distant past, but to one evoking the distant past. And not only that, but rectifying impressions one had of that past, correcting, giving form to one's fuzziness, giving it substance, as he said, definition.

Perhaps the demonstration of his woeful mental inadequacy (at least, his lack of social sophistication, "gentle breeding") contributed as much to his sense of bitterness as anything else: that he should have been thrown into a milieu that he only scarcely understood, had so little foundation for understanding, so little familiarity with, and so slow an intelligence to comprehend. The reality, this small sample of it, made even more glaring the contrast between what occurred and what he grasped, between the complexity of the actuality and the mote he grasped. Of necessity his interpretation was—and still remained—simplistic. And realization pari passu with that . . . trailing the awareness of the extent to which his abnormal adolescence, his more than usually stricken adolescence, his distorted, cramped, deformed assessments, his judgment of events and circumstances that even with his limited faculties and slum rearing he might otherwise have perceived—and recalled—to a greater degree than he did. One had to make the best of it, peg the trophies of fancy to a few authentic memories.

Begin anywhere, skip anything. There would still be enough left over, enough obtained to provide some indication of the nature of the protagonists, the workings of their minds, the interaction of their personalities. In fact, it occurred to Ira, given his traditions, his warped growth, upbringing, outlook—and theirs—no other way was open to him than to resort to the impersonal, the fictional as transmuted by time, the "electronic" evidence, not only to adjust his portrayal, his interpretation of other characters, but his own as well, inescapably, out of reach of the scribe's gentle mitigations.

Yow! Didn't those earphones hurt! They must have been manufactured at the very acme of the tight, heavily padded set—before the lighter, more comfortable ones were introduced. They muffled outside noises better than those made to be worn on a rifle range. "We were abstinent until the time of our marriage," Lewlyn's words continued sounding outside the ear-phones. "We were very, very careful." That was a tough one, Ira reflected: put yourself in the man's place. What would you have done? Aye. Not with Stella—that was somehow too easy. No moral problem. Just an old habit. It had been the same with Minnie, if such a situation were possible. Neither of them meant, would have meant for either one, more than the most transient emotional surrender; no, not even that, so well understood it was, even when Minnie had been tenderest toward him—it wasn't possi-ble. Understood, understood. And the same thing was true with Stella. Ah, but what if it had been Dorothy? Dorothy in L.A. years later, the year he had pledged his troth, declared his love for M, his intention to marry her? Supposing Dorothy had come out to L.A. to stay with her father, Bill Loem, when Ira had fled out there with him in order to break his dependence on Edith? A dozen years later in the narrative he had to tell. Fortunately Dorothy was in New York, freckled, unlettered, working-class Dorothy. So not even that would have been fair test; he didn't know what would have been. But he was lucky anyway; he was lucky anyway: six months without a woman. So don't judge, Ira thought. And yet, how unconsciously the man would apply one set of rules to Cecilia, the woman he came to love, and at the earliest, to marry, and another to Edith, whom he was to leave. "We were very, very careful," he said: careful. And the word he had used to describe the degree of their self-imposed reserve, "abstinent," wasn't quite apropos in this context. Oh, this was picayune on your part, niggling, Ira censured himself. But then, he was inescapably the literary guy: "absti-nent" was not the *most* appropriate word he could have used—oh, it would do, it would do—better than "celibate." But the word Lewlyn should have chosen was "continent." They were continent.

Ira awoke once during the little that was left of the night, awoke to see Edith's drawn face in the crumbling dark turned toward him—and she must have seen that he was awake and conscious of her gaze—for the face stamped on the brayed gloom seemed indurate with censure—or scorn—or contempt. He felt himself shrink away placatingly: apologizing for sharing the same bed with her, without proffering the ultimate comfort she craved and needed. How puerile could he be not to be aroused by her proximity, not to turn toward her with a hard-on? That was how he construed her gaze . . . even though he attempted in the short interval between her daunting look and the time he rolled over sheepishly and fell asleep to interpret her severity with a palliating excuse: it was the manifestation of the fierce grudge she held against *all* men because of her resentment of Lewlyn. Still, instinct prompted, albeit fuzzily, that he was kidding himself. She wanted to be laid, needed to be laid as a kind of solace against the overwhelming rejection she had suffered. It had been that which had impelled him to his tentative-bold act of staying with her the night. Instinct in him told him that, but how to muster a hard-on for an adult woman, for a real lady, when libido, except for a single encounter with a black streetwalker, had functioned only with minors, only in a milieu of stealth and guilt? It was easy to persuade himself his instincts were wrong.

As she had predicted, Edith awoke before the alarm went off, and as soon as she stirred, Ira awoke too—slid out of bed, sat at the end, scratched, sneezed, chortled sleepily, and slipped on his jacket against the morning coolness. He waited his turn for the bathroom, tried to wash, put on his tie, and came out as Edith, olive-skinned to the vee in her bathrobe, was turning slices of toast on the slat sides of the toaster over the gas flame, while coffee burbled in the newfangled electric percolator.

"Did you manage to get *any* sleep?" she asked solicitously, none of the rebuke of that relentless glare of a few hours before still lingering. And when he assured her he had, "I don't see how you could. Weren't you cold?"

"Not me, no," he lied. "How about you?"

"I suppose I slept a few hours." She protracted the blink of puffy eyes. "I feel like the wrath of God."

"You look all right," he encouraged.

"Do I? Thanks." She yawned. "You're very nice to say so. I feel like something the cat dragged in."

"Oh, no," he protested. "I don't know how you did it after all you've been through, but you look fine."

Her eyes sought out the wall mirror. "You've been an angel to see me through this, Ira. I never dreamed I could be such a fool."

"Oh, no—can I make some more toast?"

"Make all you want."

He stood up and canted four slices of packaged bread against the sides of the frustum toaster. "You gonna want some more?"

"No, thanks, this is about all I can stomach. I'll just have a little more coffee." She filled her cup, all black, eschewing that healthy dollop of cream that Mom always poured. "I'm sorry I don't have anything else to offer you for breakfast except more marmalade. If I'd know you were going to stay the night I would have had some eggs and bacon on hand."

"That's all right." Ira peeped out of the corner of one eye as he gingerly turned the toast. "Bacon ain't kosher."

"My God!" she exclaimed suddenly. "Your parents! I've forgotten all about them. You have no phone? You couldn't call?"

"No."

"You can still send a telegram."

"I'd scare hell out of 'em. Excuse me. I told Mom I'd be late."

"Late? Heavens! Ira, what will they think?"

He licked his lips as he transferred slices of toast from toaster to plate. "I'm telling you: I told Mom I didn't know when I'd be home. Not to worry, that's all. I've stayed over at Larry's a few nights."

"You're sure they're all right? Do they know where you are?"

"I told them what I was going to do. They must have figured out where I was—besides, I left your phone number. My sister would have called if they were worried."

"Thank heaven you thought of doing that."

"Yeah, if she called, you could have told her I stowed away on board the ship."

"I can't get over how cavalier you are with your family. And yet your face lights up when you speak of your mother. Your love for her is so touching."

"Yeah?" He lowered his head, reached for the coffeepot. "Well, my parents are immigrants, I don't have to tell you. And I'm the only collegian in the whole tribe. So I lead the way in things American. You get it? I'm the authority."

"That's quite different from Larry's family."

"Zackly. There's three more of these slices of toast here. You don't want one?"

"You eat them. I'd love to meet your mother."

"Mom doesn't speak English very well."

"Oh, we'd understand each other, I'm sure."

"Yum." He crunched into a second slice. "What a nice jar they sell this marmalade in. Crosse and Blackwell. You know, as soon as I tell my mother I like something, out she goes and buys it. She spoils the hell—heck out of me."

"And your sister?"

"Oh, no. Nothing like that. Minnie practically has to fend for herself. She's my father's favorite."

Edith looked steadily at Ira, appraising as was her wont, a full second—and then her gaze shifted to the clock on the mantelpiece. "I ought to begin dressing. I have a class at ten. But you don't need to feel you have to hurry."

"No? All right."

Her look, animated now, scarcely belonged to the same face that had stared at him so unforgivingly—when?—just a few hours ago? Rancorous, granulated ivory in the gloom, glaring: you lummox, I need. Can't you see I need? Like Minnie, when she came home from Richmond rejected. So what if he said to her, You know, you stared at me during the night. What did you mean? Yeah, he was a lummox, all right, that he should have to ask her such a dumb question. But what would it have led to? What would a woman say when you asked her that? Evade? Or answer candidly? I suppose I wanted you to hold me. Nah. How could she? But she had lost so much, she had lost so much. "How many classes have you got this morning?"

"Two. One after the other, and an hour and a half each."

"Oh, boy."

"Fortunately it's the same lecture in both. And it's old ground too: women poets in America. Emily Dickinson, Amy Lowell, Teasdale, Flanner, Taggard, Léonie, and of course dear Edna. Not all today. I may introduce them to Marianne Moore." She began undoing her loose braids. "Please finish your breakfast, Ira."

"Thanks. That'll be easy."

"And have some more coffee." She stood up. "I'd love to chat, but I don't dare."

"Oh, wait a minute. You know something? I owe you four dollars. Change from that five. It only came to a—"

"Don't you mention it."

"What?"

"Mention it."

"Aw, gee, why not?"

"I don't want to hear about it. You make me feel ashamed of myself, owing you so much. Please!"

"Boy, I ought to go into business."

"I just don't know what I'd have done without you. You know that very well."

"Yeah?" He could sense the circuitous route of his own discontent at his failure in the face of her need. "You know something? You'd have been better off. Maybe both of us."

Edith stopped on the way to the bathroom. "Why?"

"You wouldn't have gone. See what I mean? I mean if you hadn't had me to go along with you, then you wouldn't have gone."

"I admit my going was sheer folly, and I know I behaved like a romantic idiot afterward. B it why both? Unless you would have spent a better night at home in your own bed. And I imagine you would have."

"No, I could have gone home."

"Then what *do* you mean? Not that I don't appreciate your staying."

"I saw something beautiful, and you had to pay a lot for it. So you hated me."

"Oh, fiddlesticks!"

"Didn't you stare at me during the night?"

"I may have. I may have wondered what the strange man was doing in my bed."

"Oh, was that it? You didn't hate me because I caused it? I didn't help you afterward." He gesticulated.

"Caused what?"

"All you suffered last night."

"Heavens, child! Caused it? You stood by me magnificently. No, because of what *I* cause. You are the strangest lad!" The face above

the checked bathrobe became businesslike. "I've got to run." And as
an afterthought, plucking a dress of bronze lozenges from the closet,
before she entered the bathroom: "The cause is my playing a role,
that's the cause. Trying to extract a very little beauty on false pre-
tenses—from a hopeless situation. That can be very costly emotion-
ally. But I really believe I learned this time." The bathroom door
closed.

Beauty. Beauty. Beauty. They were always talking about it. Ira
munched toast and marmalade. He knew what a beautiful statue was,
or thought he did, music, a poem, a picture, yeah, even like a few
times in the country, in Woodstock, when the dirt road curved out of
sight a certain way, or streams of light came through the mountains
like the swirls of amber seashells. Yeah, and the ship too on the dark
water amid all the lights. And that scene of the two lovers parting,
gee whiz: as if parting forever. That could be beautiful. He understood that. But as soon as he tried to concentrate on why it was beautiful, the thought sailed away, flew off in all directions, like a dandelion
when you puffed on it. He became drowsy. Jesus, he *was* drowsy.
Beauty. Beauty. Beauty. Hell, what was tragedy all about? *Romeo and
Juliet*, which he didn't like: it gushed with amorous sentiment. And
all he had ever known was hardly beauty, but that sordid exaltation of
years past of slipping the little brass nipple of the lock—up! And fast
as you could into Minnie's dingy bedroom. Was that beautiful? Or
Stella sliding down with parted thighs on his hard-on. Or back-scuttling her, hoisting her up while the radio band blared dance music
live from the ballroom of the Commodore Hotel.

As the keyboard played its melody, every sense became an antenna. See?
You're cracked. The only guy who came that close was Joyce. But even he
didn't come anywhere near that close: to beauty of fear, beauty of furtive-
ness, of sordidness. The guy was afraid to venture, afraid of the shock, of
real terror. There was something phony about the way that Bloom agonized at two o'clock in the afternoon, or whenever it was that Blazes Boy-
lan gave Molly the business. His agonizing was bullshit. If it was that tough,
he would have interfered—long before. But hell, if he was a Jew, and he

was, he would have talked about it to her, gone to a medico. Found some other way if they still loved each other. Naah. The guy who was so interested in finding out how far into the marble the statue's nates went was Jimmy Joyce, the timid harp. Not the semi-demi-hemi half-assed Yiddle of his invention—cut it out. He was getting somewhere.

Edith came out of the bathroom, fully attired, groomed, her bronze dress blanching her olive skin by contrast, her delicate lips rouged, and forced into a smile, her face still piqued and strained. She seemed unwilling to speak, beyond essentials. "Would you help me pull the bed up? . . . Don't bother with the dishes." She took a last sip of cold coffee, looked up at the mirror, and ran a tiny fingertip over her large eyelids, made a hopeless moue. No, she didn't want Ira to escort her to the university. Unseemly—the thought crossed his mind—to be seen at such an early hour leaving the house together. No need to. It was a fair morning, although cool; she let him help her into her dark, satiny jacket. And yes, here was Lewlyn's set of keys. Ira could have them: the door had to be locked from the outside.

"You're welcome to stay as long as you please," she said. "And if the phone rings, just ignore it." Her utterly sober face in black cloche hat, she tugged the lapel of his jacket and kissed him. "Please call me in the next few days."

"All right."

She opened the apartment door to leave. How gamely she braced her shoulders back, tightened her lips, lifted her chin, took a fresh grip of her briefcase handle. Boy, that took courage. Without effort he noted her behavior those last seconds: the petite woman resolutely determined to meet the world. She shut the door behind her, and he was suddenly aware of a shamefaced admiration for her. Could he have behaved with such resolve after what she had been through? He was relieved he wasn't called on to prove himself, wasn't put to the test. He would certainly have failed. Even now, all his inclinations called for a nap, right there on the gunnycloth-covered bed. But better get home, he told himself, before Mom started to worry. Get home and have another breakfast—and a real nap. His eyes were like some kind of synchronized device, one eyelid closing as he forced the other open. Wash the few plates and coffee cups on the card table. That would be a decent gesture. He picked up the few breakfast things, took them to the small sink in the kitchenette, rinsed them, soaped and again rinsed them, placed them on the drainer.

Well, there could be no mistaking now: enough time had elapsed to break any connection between her leaving the house and his, if that was what she wanted. She must have crossed Washington Square Park by now. He could just see her advancing with quick step and with fixed, unhappy expression on her face, hurrying toward the offwhite administration building, and now and then having to smile mechanically at a student or colleague. God, what they didn't know.

VII

And suddenly another memory came floating back, memory to the man at the keyboard before the amber monitor: not of the woman in the black cloche hat, whom he had genuinely loved for a time, whose image, wraitnlike, was receding, like Eurydice's, back to an underworld he had once inhabited, but of his wife in Maine, in Montville, M in the Army-Navy surplus-store coveralls Ira had bought her while he worked as a toolmaker for Keystone Camera Co., near Boston. This more enduring image came flooding back, his tall, cheerful, brave wife in her khaki coveralls, leaving the warmth of the house for the frigid outdoors, carrying milk pail in gloved hand (who had to teach herself to milk, for the sake of their two boys, because no stores were nigh in that rural countryside her husband had brought her to). And returning to the warmth of the kitchen again, chilled, nose white and cheeks rose—chilled in her khaki coveralls, with not too much milk in pail, for the cow was nearing the end of her cycle, and needed breeding again, needed a calf, which as it turned out she never could have—for some reason—as the Yankee neighbor knew, who moved away after he sold the animal: a true Yankee trader. He had been married to her for fifty years, fifty years plus four months. He had to say it again, fifty years. Was it not a wondrous thing, the pioneer courage of M's New England tradition, her fortitude, her fidelity?

The five years that had intervened since her death seemed so agonizingly slow, as if time were suspended, not allowed to proceed in a normal sort of way. He could, with the flick of a key, recall her voice, her intonation, the subtlety of her logic. He recalled the time he had become, despite her calming protestations, so very upset, the very evening after they moved into the apartment that housed them during their stint in Mexico, when the superabundance of *cucarachas,* roaches, big enough to throw a saddle over, as the old quip goes, roaches big, brown, and ubiquitous, filled the new household. They epitomized all that was vile, hideous, in childhood spent on the East Side, but even more so, early boyhood and youth spent in Harlem, spent living on 119th Street. So much that had become nasty and hateful to him about those early years of his life seemed closely associated with scurrying roaches, roaches, by the way, not half the size of these, ever lurking in some crevice despite Mom's constant forays against them. He hated them worse than he did bedbugs—or even lice. After nearly ninety years, there still remained in memory the image of a doomed roach spreading his glistening outer shell to bring into play his billion-year-atrophied, gauzy wings in vain attempt to escape the sole of his pursuer's shoe. Ha, the bastard, how could he keep from exulting when he heard the small squish that marked the end of his loathsome career: you bastard, you can't have it both ways: wings and a sheltered life. . . . But those roaches lived in Harlem; and they were mere shavers compared to these whoppers in the land of *alegría.*

After Ira and M got back from the light supper tendered them by Señora Orozco and her veterinarian husband, Dr. Orozco, who had been instrumental in finding them the apartment, Ira began a preliminary, and shortly a hectic, search of the premises. Investigation revealed that one of the primary, if not *the* primary, nesting areas, retreats, snug havens, was an armchair, buff in color, a lighter shade than that of the insects themselves. Lifting the overstuffed cushion that constituted the seat of the chair he exposed, to his horror (M was so much more temperate about it), enough roaches to lug the seat of the chair away—in his overwrought imagination. They had a can of anti-roach spray, and he began wildly spraying them, but hell, why spray the beasts in the living room and fill the place with scented fumes of DDT? He hauled the chair out on the balcony, and he sprayed, and he sprayed, first the chair right side up, then upside down, and the sides. It was a frenzied *matanza,* and never did he enjoy a revolting task more. In the end, they left the chair out on the balcony overnight.

They felt better after they went back into the apartment. He did certainly, and M did too, because he did.

"He prayeth best, who loveth best, and all that sort of blarney," Ira growled as he dropped down on the seat of a plain wooden dining chair. "Thank God, I prayeth worst."

"Oh, no."

"Oh, yes. When did you ever hear me pray? You don't mean my cussin', my profanity? That's the Harlem street where I was dug up."

She settled into a wooden chair opposite him at the table. "No, you're always appealing to the best in you, your conscience, your oracle. I never saw a man struggle with himself so. Isn't that what you do?"

"What's praying about that? . . . Say, you know, hon, that's more or less what Skelsy told me in L A. where I fled from my dependency on Edith in '38. Jerk that I was. I could have moved a half-dozen blocks away in Manhattan and gotten just as lost. But then, as soon as I was broke, I would have—anyway, Skelsy kept telling me, 'You're a new kind of guy to me. You keep asking yourself if a thing is right. I never do. I try to figure out if it'll work.'"

"Who is Skelsy?"

"A very dangerous man, I assure you. He was biding his time under the guise of a bookkeeper working for the state. But every once in a while he had to go on a bash. Why? He had to talk. And I was the recipient of some of his confidences. He had been a rumrunner during Prohibition. An expert marksman with a pistol. I gather he dispatched three competitors on an island who had tried to muscle in on his high-class trade, expensive liquor they bootlegged from Canada in small speedboats. He and his partner, a Swede, but the Swede was found shot, killed, and his speedboat floating around, empty. Oh, I must have told you about him. We lived in the same rooming house in L.A., just after I left Edith's the last time."

"You told me about your landlord who got a bad heart searching for gold."

"Yes, during the Depression. Quinn. Climbing mountains, living on flapjacks after his wife gave him the heave-ho. She told him to come back when he had made some money. Mean to tell me I've never mentioned

Skelsy in all these years? As a matter of fact, it was Skelsy who told Quinn, when we were having a drink, he should have ripped his wife up to the belly, made her suffer."

"How awful. No, this is the first time I ever heard you mention him. Skelsy?"

"Well, for Pete's sake. He didn't believe you could ever make money staying within the law. And—would you believe it? He wanted me for a partner."

"You! A partner in crime? My lambikin."

"Yeah, me. I ain't such a lambikin. He said of course he didn't expect me to hold up under a third degree. You know, that's when the cops grill you, beat hell out of you to make you confess. I couldn't hold up under that. But he was sure I'd never double-cross him. The guy was really very astute. He promised to get me a cute Swedish chick too," Ira teased.

"Flaxen-haired, I'm sure. How could you resist?"

"Scared as hell. What do you mean, resist? I'll never forget the teardrops so cool on my cheek after I rode the freights home to New York—half the way home anyway. To you in your rented bedroom-studio on the ground floor—" Ira chortled. "How could I resist?"

Faint scent of residual DDT. The quiet. Feeling of sojourning in a foreign land, of the Mexican night outdoors.

"But hell, we weren't talking about that. How did I get started on that?"

"Coleridge, don't you remember?"

"Oh, yeah, Coleridge and *cucarachas*. You accused me of always praying. What's praying about appealing to your conscience? That's not praying. Where's the deity?"

"I don't think Coleridge necessarily meant a deity as you and I think about God," M replied. "I just feel he was limited by his time. What he meant was something universal. He couldn't help but make the universal into a deity. God."

"Maybe so, but you're a clergyman's daughter."

"Now don't be snide, love."

"Siccusa me, boss. My amject apologies. Carlyle wrote that when he interviewed or visited Coleridge, the old boy kept intoning an interminable monologue about sumject and omject."

"Seriously, darling—what am I trying to say? What I'm trying to say is that had he had the chance to—to live in our times, be exposed to a modern existentialist view of things, our view, his 'He prayeth best, who loveth best,' and the rest—" She smiled at her involuntary rhyme. "Oh, you know what I mean. That end, the meaning, Coleridge's definition of the object prayed to—all that—would have been quite different."

"You could be right. Yeah . . . I've got no philosophy whatsoever. I don't have to tell you. But I remember reading in one of his commentaries on *The Ancient Mariner*, he does say something to the effect that 'He prayeth best, who loveth best' is an unfortunate obtrusion of morality into the poem. And the reason I remember it is that he uses the word 'obtrusion.' Now I know what 'intrusion' means, 'extrusion.' 'Protrusion,'" Ira raised his voice for emphasis. "But what the Jesus is to obtrude? Do you know?"

She rubbed her eyelid thoughtfully. "No, I don't think so. I'm not sure."

"Does the fumigant make your eyes smart?" Ira asked.

"No, you got the worst of it. The eye just itched."

He watched her a moment longer. And all at once, before she dropped her hand, he realized she had brought into a single focus many of the features of her appearance that made her outwardly what she was, that he conjured up when he thought of her: the aging, distinguished, gentle brown eyes, the hair that in younger days he had seen the Cape Cod sun burnish into a radiant gold—and now streaked lackluster with gray. Her once pretty teeth looked irregular and fragile when she laughed, and her bony pianist's hands hung down lankly from her wrists. She had become angular and gangly herself.

"We brought the *Webster's Collegiate* along," she reminded Ira. "Isn't it in your study? Why don't you look it up?"

"It's more fun to guess. *Ab, ante, con, in, inter, ob, post, prae, pro, sub, super.* There's the *ob.* Takes the ablative."

"Very helpful. And now that it does, what does it mean?"

"It means I go to the head of the class."

"Smarty pants. You're always the vocal one."

"What do I do, *kvetch*? Gripe? Why do you say I vocalize?"

"It means that I hear you, my belovedest, I know what you're thinking."

"You hear me?" Ira pondered.

"Yes. Did you ever try to conceal a state of mind, an emotion, say a disappointment? Mourning a loss? You moan, you groan, you sigh, you go around swearing."

"Ah, now I get it. No. All right. You go to the opposite extreme. It's true. I haven't got your blue-nosed Pilgrim ancestry, but that little girl riding in the train beside her ma, when you were coming back from Oregon to Chicago, the little girl who dropped her dolly out of the open train window, and then sat there quietly, giving no sign of loss. Not a tear. You told me."

"We weren't allowed to cry."

"Allowed to cry, my ass! Who the hell decides that you're allowed to? I would have howled, why not?"

"Well, we did carry repressing feelings too far." Her gentle eyes rested on him tenderly. "Oh, I'm sure we did."

"Yeah, that's probably why I love you," he admitted grudgingly. "But you say I'm always praying. That makes us even."

"No, that's what makes me love you."

"Oh, yeah? Unfortunate moral sentiment."

She laughed.

"Ain't it?"

"In me or Coleridge?"

"In both of you, I guess. It's odd, you know. I recognized it as a kid," Ira recalled, "I mean *The Rime of the Ancient Mariner*. Everything about the poem enchanted me, especially that first time I read it in the ninth grade. But then I could feel a kind of twinge of resentment about that 'He prayeth best, who loveth best.' I used to think, if you'll pardon zee expression: oh, balls."

She laughed, as she always did at his vulgarity.

"So that's what I'm doing. Pop, pop, pop, apah!" he burlesqued. "Pop, pop, pop, apah! The man is always praying, praying, praying, praying praying, braying, braying, baying, baying baying. Boom! Pop, pop, apah. How's that for a chunk of the Fifth?"

"That sounds to me like a chunk of Stigman's Fifth," M replied. "It's approximately in the right key, C minor, and three-quarter time, don't you think?"

"You know, I just got an illumination about Beethoven. His greatest dramas were in his symphonies."

"That's a good observation. There's your friend *ob* again."

"Yeah, right. I'll tell you why he couldn't write an exciting opera: he had such Jovian storms going on inside him, he couldn't adjust, he couldn't empathize with the earthly conflicts of ordinary humans." He paused—

She had stood up. "Just a moment, dear."

"Yeah."

She left the kitchen, returned shortly with her tobacco pouch. "You're a little like that yourself." She sat down.

"Oh, zank you, zank you. To be mentioned in the same breath with sublimity. Boy."

"No, I simply mean," she unzipped the tobacco pouch, "you don't empathize with others very well either."

"I don't?"

"Do you?" She brought out her little pipe.

"No, it's true. I get such Olympian ideas—hey, where you goin' again?"

"To get the alcohol bottle." She picked up the bottle of denatured alcohol from the kitchen shelf, stood searching for something else. "I don't see the pipe cleaners."

"*Mea culpa. Mea maxima culpa.* They're on my desk—let me go get 'em."

"Oh, no, by the time you get out of your chair—" She stepped out of the kitchen door. Gone for thirty seconds, she reentered.

He sat quietly for a minute watching her. "Hey, you know, you do the purtiest job of cleaning a pipe ever the eye did see? Look at that." And as she withdrew the browned end of the pipe cleaner and inserted the other end, freshly soaked in alcohol, "Wish I could do that."

"You can too do that. Of course you can." She swabbed the stubby pipestem. "Anybody can. No, don't pretend."

"Yeah, but method, method, my beloved *frau*. When you do a job, it's done. It doesn't need redoing."

"Actually, this pipe will need it very soon. I should ream out the bowl first. But the stem was beginning to taste bad."

"Reminds me of Larry, the way you smoke a pipe. The char in his pipe closed to a cone downward. The way it should. He smoked the tobacco down to the last shred."

"Don't you?" She bent the pipe cleaner double, dropped it into the large, square glass ashtray on the table. "See how foul the ends have gotten?" She drew out a fresh pipe cleaner.

"Yeah."

"Do you want me to clean yours?"

"Hell, no. Womern, leave that pipe in the ashtray."

"Don't you want to smoke?"

"Not right now. Orozco gave me a postprandial stogie. Anh." Ira lapped his lips in distaste. "I'll tell you: it's not only empathizing. Some guys can imbue an idea with drama. Damned if I can. Damned if Beethoven could. But he could imbue drama with ideas. How the hell is that? Hey, where'd you get the Blue Boar tobacco?"

"Just before we left El Paso. I bought three packages."

"Creeps' sake. Ever providential." He sighed admiringly: She was so impeccably methodical, filling her pipe a few flakes of tobacco at a time. "You're so tidy." He shook his head. "Jaiz. But Mozart could."

"Could what?"

"Do what Beethoven couldn't. Imbue ideas with drama."

"I'm sure I'd rather see *Don Giovanni* than *Fidelio,* given the choice," M commented.

"Well, there you are. I don't even remember what *Fidelio* is about. About a faithful husband, wasn't it—you got the funniest way of striking a book match. Why don't you hold it nearer the head?"

"I'm afraid I'll get burned."

"Nonsense. More apt to the way you do it."

"You do it for me next time."

"Glad to."

She blew out a fragrant stream of tobacco smoke. "Yes, a faithful hubby like mine."

"Who cares about faithful hubbies?"

"I do."

"Oh, you, tenderhearted. You're even a *madre de cucarachas*."

Frowning, M blew out another stream of smoke. "I am not a *madre de cucarachas.*"

"You're not?"

"No, it's very unkind of you to say that."

"Well, I didn't mean anything by it."

"That's the trouble with you. Your mean side comes out when you don't mean it."

"Pretty good."

"No, I'm serious."

"Well, maybe I'm smarting a little bit at being so bested in me own bailiwick. My metus. All right, I take it back. What are you a *madre* of?"

"I'm a *madre* of two sons. And mostly I've been a *madre* of *you.*" Her vehemence indicated something deeper than umbrage at his fatuous remark.

"Me?" He took cover. "What did I do?"

"It's not what *you* did. It's what *I* did." She emphasized both pronouns. "It's what I had to do. I spent all my time taking care of you in your moods, protecting you from your moods, your depressions, despairs. Heavens! Taking care of you, instead of spending the time doing my own work, instead of spending the time composing music."

That he understood. "I guess I have to agree," he said soberly.

"Do you? Are you sure?"

"Yeah, yeah. When it comes to art I understand. So what am I going to do about it?"

"Nothing. Be my beloved hubby. Just like Fidelio."

"That's not enough. Why in hell didn't you, don't you, heave me out of your life?"

"Now, don't be silly. I chose to do it. It's what I wanted to do."

"Yeah? But how can anyone choose something like that?" Ira demanded. "How can anybody want something like that?" It seemed to him he caught a glimpse, an awe-inspiring glimpse, of a truly disciplined, truly resolute mind. Even that glimpse, that inkling, confused him. "I never wanted in that sense, never chose. I'm blind as a thread of water. Moving through dust."

"That's why I have to protect you."

"And you wanted to?"

"Yes. I wouldn't have anything else in the world. Do you realize that my life was already quite settled before I met you? I had made my future secure. I was teaching music at Western College. Elizabeth was teaching in the English department. She and I would find an apartment the year my sabbatical ended. We would live in it together. I would compose music. Quite settled, quite planned. And then you came along and ripped it all to pieces at Yaddo."

"'This is all I have to say to thee.'" Irresistibly Jocasta's last speech in Sophocles' *Oedipus* came to his mind, to the mind of one addicted to utterance. "'This is all I have to say to thee,'" he repeated gloomily, "'and no word more forever.'"

"My honey lamb. You're my honey lamb."

"Yeah. I know. What an impostor."

Fragrance of the tobacco burning in her pipe . . . again the quiet. Feeling of sojourning in a foreign land, of the Mexican night outdoors.

"No, you're not an impostor."

"I'm not?"

"No. You're so involved with yourself that you're surprised when people assert themselves, when they get into *your* world, as I just did, and I'm a little sorry I did."

"No, I had it coming to me. I ought to be reminded more often. Daily. Hourly. Sea nymphs wring his neck."

"Darling, please don't mutter. We were both babes in the wood when we married. We both had a lot of growing up to do. I know I did."

"That's an understatement when applied to me. When we met, you already held down a respectable job. You had been self-supporting for I don't know how many years. Whereas I—Christ, what a blob! Larva! Coddled Junior of a *ménage à trois*. Yech!"

"Darling, you mustn't. You break my heart."

"Boyoboy, if you're not the kindest creature. If it weren't for you, I'd be dead by now. Dead as a haddock."

"My honey lamb, my lambikin. Please!"

"I see what you're doing. Me and my goddamn moods. Taking care of me and my swings, my fits."

"Honey lamb, let's change the subject. Please. Pretty please. For my sake."

"Yeah, for your sake. Oh, boy, what a burden you carry."

"I don't care. As long as you love me."

"Love you? God, women are easy to satisfy. Love you? 'And when I love thee not, chaos is come again.'"

"Now you sound like my honey lamb. That's so beautiful."

"Yeah? It ain't mine. That's why."

She laughed.

"So what were we on before all this?"

"Coleridge."

"Yeah. Okay, tell me, what do you understand by the 'He prayeth best' stuff?"

"The way I interpret it, Coleridge simply meant that all life was mysterious and extraordinary. We may have to destroy some of it to preserve our own life. I forgot to tell you I bought two dozen shrimp on the way home. I'll shell them in the morning before I go to the Diazes'. She's got a gorgeous Steinway."

"Yes?"

"They're in the refrigerator. They were alive once, needless to say."

"*Ach, zo.* I see your point. Alive not too long ago, I trust."

"Oh, yes. I'm always careful about what I feed you." She leaned forward earnestly. "I wish you had my cast-iron stomach."

"I'm glad one of us has it. Then what did you do in the fish market while I sat in the car? Ask the seafood which of them is freshest? Tell them you got a husband with a sensitive gut?"

"No. I ask them what's the latest news in the deep sea."

"Oh, is that it? Using a little feminine guile, were you? You're wonderful. You know? How come about a million other guys didn't snap you up?"

"Oh, I wasn't the conventional pretty girl—like my sister Betty. And I was always falling for the wrong man."

"And you did it again."

"I don't think so."

"It's none of my business why you don't. But thanks anyway."

She laughed lightly. "My funny man."

She continued, a bit wearily, "Life's all unique and the same at the same time. I think that's what Coleridge meant. It's special. Every speck of consciousness is precious. That's what I mean. I think that's what he meant."

"Woof."

"It's the same kind of force. We all share it. Do you think there's any difference between the lives—no, the life of a cockroach and ours? The life force?"

"Well, a much greater degree of awareness."

"No. I'm speaking about the life force."

"That animates us?" He shrugged. "Okay, probably not. So what am I supposed to be? Sorry I killed a bunch of roaches? The hell I am. I wish I'd killed a jillion."

"I didn't say that. I'm speaking about that miraculous speck of consciousness that—that matter turned into."

"Say, how come you're so smart? Musicians are supposed to be dumb. Louise Bogan was always going around denigrating musicians. They were short on brains."

"Verbal skills maybe, but that doesn't mean being dumb. The University of Chicago gave me a Phi Beta Kappa in my junior year. And my history professor asked if he could quote from my paper. So there."

"Yeah."

"I don't think musicians and dancers and painters are any dumber than poets. We think in a different way. So do you, even though you are a writer."

"I wish I'd known you when Bogan told me that, but I was scared of the dame anyway."

"You were?"

"What a bimbo in a clinging peach velvet dress. I think she measured men by their powers of frigulation. She said Dalton—you know, the third in Edith's ménage—she said he came to town like a bunny rabbit. You can imagine what she'd have thought of me."

"You don't come to town like a bunny rabbit."

"Thank you, love. Not since I met you. Say, while we're talking of specks of consciousness, maybe love is the highest thing in the speck. Or the best. How's that?"

"I like the idea."

"You mean the sentiment."

"No, the idea. The thing you were talking about, the idea, the idea filled with sentiment."

"Glory be. You mean it? I did it? Hosanna!"

A moment of silence, silicone silence, Ira and M under the yellow incandescents on the kitchen ceiling, the specks of memory which, until moments ago, lay irretrievably buried, now excavated and so pleasingly retrieved and reconfigured through the passage of time.

A new moment of silence, a solitary moment, as the gloaming light cast shadows over the books he loved so well. The last streaks of twilight had disappeared over the Palisades so long ago, and now, as Helius' horse-drawn chariot raced by on its evening run, the desert sunset illumined the basalt horizon.

A moment of silence. The monitor hummed. Had he only dared look at her then with the passionate homage he now so keenly felt.

GLOSSARY OF YIDDISH AND HEBREW WORDS AND PHRASES

Note: Some spellings reflect Galitzianer pronunciations and may seem unfamiliar to speakers of "standard" Yiddish. Some words are mixtures of Yiddish and English.

a brukh is mir   I'm broken up
a ferd noch   another horse; one more horse
a ganzeh yeet   a whole Jew
a gitn shiddekh   a good match
a gutn yuntiff   a good holiday
ai bist die a hint, mein ziendle   oh, you're a dog, my son
alles veist er   he knows everything
a meeseh mishineh auf dir   a wretched fate to you
a nar und shoyn   a fool already
auf eibig   forever; German **ewig**
auf mir g'sukt   said about me
a yeet mit a boort   a Jew with a beard
aza gitteh kup   such a good head
aza Paskudnyack   such a contemptible, odious person
aza Parsheveh shmutz   such a contemptible louse
aza shver leben   living is so hard
azoy   right; is that so
azoy doff sein   that's the way it has to be
azoy id es shoyn   so it is already
azoy shein und azoy troyrick   so beautiful and so sad

barukha   prayer, blessing
Barukh atah adonoi, elohainu, melekh ha oylum . . . l'hazman hazeh   a ritual prayer, said especially at Passover
betterien   batteries
bist shoyn a groyseh moyt   you're already a big girl
boort   beard
briderl   brother (affectionate diminutive)
brukhis   blessings
bulbas   potatoes
chardash   Hungarian dance performed at weddings
cheder   Hebrew school for boys of pre–Bar Mitzva age; **cheder yingle** schoolkid
chompken   chomp, chew loudly
Christlikher   Christian
davening   praying
der alter   the old man
dreck   dung, trash
drei   turn
dreidel   a top marked with four Hebrew letters, used for a Hanukkah game
Eretz Yisroel   land of Israel
ehrlikher yeet   honest Jew
erev Shabbes   evening of Sabbath
farshtest   understand
ferfallen   lost
fertsfeilet   (German) depressed
folentser   lazy person
freg nisht   don't ask
fress   eat; feeding frenzy
fulkomen   entirely
gesheft   store, business
gevald   havoc; a cry of alarm
gey gesinteheit   go in health
gey gezunt   go in health
gey mir in der erd   go to hell, drop dead; **gey mir in kehver**   go to your tomb
gimel   a Hebrew letter
glatt   strict
gleibst   do you believe
goldeneh medina   golden country; America
Got sei dank   God be thanked
goy   gentile (noun); **goyim**   gentiles; **goyish**   gentile (adj.)
Haaretz   a Hebrew newspaper ("The Land")

hairst vus er sugt   did you hear what he said
Havdalah   prayers recited at the conclusion of the Sabbath
hint   dog
hulladrigas   unseemly women
hullupchehs   stuffed cabbage
ikh farshtey   I understand
jhit   Jew (Russian, derogatory)
Kaddish   Hebrew prayer for the dead
kaput   finished
keekhle   roll, small dry cake
khad godyo   one kid; a phrase in a song sung at Passover
khassid   devoutly Orthodox Jew, Hasid
khlop   to strike a blow, to yammer
khokhma   wisdom, intelligence
kholyerina   cholera, plague
khoomitz   crumbs
khusin   groom
knish   (vulgarism) cunt
koptsn   beggar
kvetch   complain
l'chaim   to life
ligner   liar
loift shoyn   he is running already
lotkehs   pancakes
lucksh   noodle
lusst nisht ausredden a vort   you don't let me get in a single word
lymineh golem   clay monster
lyupka   (Polish) love
makher   boss, big shot
malamut   Hebrew teacher
mazel   luck
meeseh chaiye   ugly animal
mehvin   maven
mein kindt   my child; **mein orrim kindt**   my poor child
mensh   man (indicates maturity, dependability); **menshen**   men;
   mensheleh   little man
met   death
mishpokha   relatives
mishugeneh   crazy; a crazy person
mit gesundheit   with health; do it in good health
mitzva   a good deed or Biblical commandment
moshav   farm; commune
mujik   Russian peasant

nokh a bisseleh, nokh a shisseleh   just a little bit
noo   well
noo, vus den   well, what then
nur breng mir nisht kein benkart   just don't bring me a bastard
nur dem   only the
oona tateh   poor father
oormeh   orphan
orrimen Talyaner   poor Italians
oy, gevald   cry of alarm, concern, or amazement
parveh   Kosher term indicating that the food is compatible with meat and dairy
Paskudnyack   an odious person
pirogen   potato and dough dumplings
pishkeh   a little pisser
plotz   burst
pooritz   smart guy
Raboinish ha loilim   God in Heaven
rebbeh   Hasidic rabbi
rov   rabbi
rusjinkeh   little Russian
sehr gut   very good
Shabbes   the Sabbath
sheineh   beautiful
shekheyooni   blessing said at the beginning of holiday or happy occasion, lit. "that He let us live"
shikker   drinker, drunkard
shiksa   gentile girl, usually a servant
shim   a Hebrew letter
shixal   fate
shlemiel   an ill-fated person, a bungler
shleppers   laborers
shlimazl   someone with continual bad luck, an unfortunate
shmaltz   fat
shmatta   rag
shmertz   pain
shmooze   chat
shmott   convert
shnorring   begging
shoyn   already
shoyn millt alle fon   already will all go
shul   synagogue
schvartze   black
sie hut nisht gevissen   she didn't know

F r o m   B o n d a g e

sis mir git   it's okay with me
s'kimteh dir tockin a shekheyooni, Tateh   indeed, may a blessing be
   given to you, Father
s'pahst nisht   it doesn't fit
tanta   aunt
tateh   father
tockin   indeed
treife   nonkosher
tsitses   habitually goes "Tsk-tsk"
tzaddikim   righteous men, holy men
vehr veist   who knows
vus macht sikh   what's up?
yeet   Jew
yenta   shrewish or gossipy woman
Yiddishkeit   Jewishness; Yiddish life or culture
zaftig   full-figured
ze vun sikch balt geshlugen tsim toit   they almost killed each other
zol gehen mit mazel   may you go with luck
zus verfollt veren   you should rot
zuzim   coins (archaic; occurs in song **khad godyo**)

A B O U T   T H E   A U T H O R

Henry Roth, who died on October 13, 1995, in Albuquerque, New Mexico, at the age of eighty-nine, had one of the most extraordinary careers of any American novelist who lived in the twentieth century.

He was born in the village of Tysmenitz, in the then Austro-Hungarian province of Galitzia, in 1906. Although his parents never agreed on the exact date of his arrival in the United States, it is most likely that he landed at Ellis Island and began his life in New York in 1909. He briefly lived in Brooklyn, and then on the Lower East Side, in the slums where his classic novel *Call It Sleep* is set. In 1914, the family moved to Harlem, first to the Jewish section on 114th Street east of Park Avenue; but because the three rooms there were "in the back" and the isolation reminded his mother of the sleepy hamlet of Veljish where she grew up, she became depressed, and the family moved to non-Jewish 119th Street. Roth lived there until 1927, when, as a junior at City College of New York, he moved in with Eda Lou Walton, a poet and New York University instructor. With Walton's support, he began *Call It Sleep* in about 1930. He completed the novel in the spring of 1934, and it was published in December 1934, to mixed reviews. He contracted for a second novel with the editor Maxwell Perkins, of Scribner's, and the first section of it appeared as a work in progress. But Roth's growing ideological frustration and personal confusion created a profound writer's block, which lasted until 1979, when he began the first drafts of *Mercy of a Rude Stream*.

In 1938, during an unproductive sojourn at the artists' colony Yaddo in Saratoga Springs, New York, Roth met Muriel Parker, a pianist and composer. They fell in love; Roth severed his relationship with Walton, moved out of her apartment on Morton Street, and married Parker in 1939, much to the disapproval of her family. With the onset of the war, Roth became a tool and gauge maker. The couple moved first to Boston with their two young sons, Jeremy and Hugh, and then in 1946 to Maine. There Roth worked as a woodsman, a schoolteacher, a psychiatric attendant in the state mental hospital, a waterfowl farmer, and a Latin and math tutor.

With the paperback reprinting of *Call It Sleep* in 1964, the block slowly began to break. In 1968, after Muriel's retirement from the Maine state school system, the couple moved to Albuquerque, New Mexico. They had become acquainted with the environs during Roth's stay at the D. H. Lawrence ranch outside of Taos, where Roth was writer-in-residence. Muriel began composing music again, mostly for individual instruments, for which she received ample recognition. After Muriel's death in 1990, Roth occupied himself with revising the final volumes of the monumental *Mercy of a Rude Stream*. The first volume was published in 1994 by St. Martin's Press and in paperback by Picador in 1995 under the title *A Star Shines over Mt. Morris Park*, and the second volume, called *A Diving Rock on the Hudson*, appeared from St. Martin's Press in 1995 with the paperback from Picador following a year later. This third volume, *From Bondage*, was constantly being revised by Roth until a few months before his death. When Roth passed away during the holiday festival of Sukkot, he left behind a trove of manuscripts, which will be published in the coming years. He had divided the *Mercy of a Rude Stream* manuscripts into what he called two "batches": the first batch being four manuscripts, *From Bondage* being the third of the cycle, which begin in 1914 with the outbreak of World War I and the Stigman family's move to Harlem. The second "batch" of the *Mercy of a Rude Stream* series is written in a different style and voice, and in manuscript form is divided into five separate "sections" totaling 1,457 manuscript pages. These sections of the epic, in contrast to the first "batch," take place in the 1930s and chronicle the relationship of Ira Stigman and M, the composer whom he would eventually marry.

While still alive, Roth received two honorary doctorates, one from the University of New Mexico and one from the Hebrew Theological Institute in Cincinnati. Posthumously, he was honored in November of 1995 with the Hadassah Harold Ribalow Lifetime Achievement Award and by the Museum of the City of New York in February of 1996.

All Orion/Phoenix titles are available at your local bookshop or from the following address:

Littlehampton Book Services
Cash Sales Department L
14 Eldon Way, Lineside Industrial Estate
Littlehampton
West Sussex BN17 7HE
telephone 01903 721596, *facsimile* 01903 730914

Payment can either be made by credit card (Visa and Mastercard accepted) or by sending a cheque or postal order made payable to *Littlehampton Book Services*.
DO NOT SEND CASH OR CURRENCY.

Please add the following to cover postage and packing

UK and BFPO:
£1.50 for the first book, and 50P for each additional book to a maximum of £3.50

Overseas and Eire:
£2.50 for the first book plus £1.00 for the second book and 50p for each additional book ordered

---

BLOCK CAPITALS PLEASE

name of cardholder ....   *delivery address*
                     ....   *(if different from cardholder)*
address of cardholder ....
....
....
....
        postcode ....   *postcode* ....

☐ I enclose my remittance for £...............................

☐ please debit my Mastercard/Visa (delete as appropriate)

card number ☐☐☐☐☐☐☐☐☐☐☐☐☐☐☐☐

expiry date ☐☐☐☐

signature ....

prices and availability are subject to change without notice